The Chang

E.M. Phillips

To the memory of my father,
Lieutenant Ben Forrow
and fellow officers and crew of
HMS Arawa,
on convoy escort duty in the Mediterranean and North Atlantic
1940 – 1945

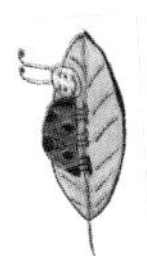

The Changing Day

E.M. Phillips

The final book in a Cornish Trilogy

The Changing Day

Published 2008 by Sagittarius Publications
62 Jacklyns Lane, Alresford, Hampshire SO24 9LH
Tel: 01962 734322

Typeset by John Owen Smith

ISBN 978-0-9555778-3-3

Printed and bound by CPI Antony Rowe, Eastbourne

THE CHANGING DAY

Beauty and love are all my dream;
They change not with the changing day;
Love stays forever like a dream
That flows but never flows away...

Andrew Young

Prologue

October 1939

Audrey Dunne stopped buffing her nails and stared at her daughter. She said, 'Would you mind repeating that; I think I must have misheard you.'

Joanna sighed. 'I *said*, I've applied and been accepted for the WRNS. I report to Greenwich on Monday.'

'You might have warned me, not presented me with a *fait accompli* – and why the hurry?'

'Oh, you know,' Joanna shrugged, 'Hitler. A little thing called a war; doing my bit.'

'And just what use do you imagine a first class honours degree in English Literature will be to the navy?'

'I've no idea.'

Her mother narrowed her eyes and struck home. 'You've always hated the "all girls' together stuff" as you call it. I should think that between school and university you would have had enough of female communal living to last a lifetime.'

Joanna thought about all the parties and dances, all the suppers in a chaps lodgings, the flirting and going to the flicks before being give a leg up over Somerville's wall by a couple of merry undergrads after lock-up. She repressed a smile; she hadn't actually done a lot of the "all girls' together stuff" since leaving school.

'You have a point there,' she said, 'but I daresay I'll survive.'

'What about the offer of that junior lectureship at Edinburgh?'

'I phoned the Dean yesterday. He said he quite understood and wished me well.' She gave her mother an affectionate, slightly exasperated smile. 'Come off it Aud,' she said, Audrey hated being called mummy or mother, too ageing she said, and quite outmoded once a child could blow its own nose, 'you joined the Red Cross almost before poor old Neville had finished announcing we were at war,' she hesitated then said, 'I think Dad would have been cheering me on.'

Audrey answered swiftly. 'I'm sure he would, but as he was an army man why are *you* joining the navy?'

Joanna grinned, 'As an army child don't you I think I need the change?'

'Hmm, I don't feel too happy at my daughter taking herself off to some dockyard full of sex-mad sailors.'

Joanna might have pointed out that quite a few mild – and one not so mild – dalliance with sex mad undergraduates had, she hoped, equipped her to deal with anything the navy might have on offer, but only replied peaceably, 'I daresay I'll survive those as well,' unaware that time would prove her quite so spectacularly wrong.

1

Tollmouth, Hampshire April 1940.

Mark Eden noticed the girl when she first came into the wardroom. Beyond merely pretty she stood out from amongst the crowd of young women packing the room, those in summer dance dresses outnumbering those in uniform. He watched her go from one eager partner to another, without any great show of enthusiasm, until she quite deliberately gave her latest, a gangling young sub lieutenant the slip, and vanished through the blackout-curtained port.

The urge to follow was quite irresistible; murmuring a regretful excuse he offloaded his own dance partner onto the gunnery officer and set out to track down the elusive Wren. Now after a thorough and exhaustive tour of the empty decks he had finally run her to earth.

Watching from the shadow of the bridge as she leaned against the after rail of the ship, he weighed carefully whether to make a quick return to the wardroom and the thirty-something blonde who was a dead certainty for a pleasurable end to the evening, or take a chance on this younger and more attractive alternative. As he hesitated the moon came fully from behind the thin cloud cover, outlining a spectacular form that even the uniform failed to devaluate.

Abandoning all other plans for the evening, he ran a hand through his hair, straightened his tie and moved quietly across the deck.

* * *

Staring down at the black water of the harbour as it moved sluggishly against the ship's stern, Joanna fanned her warm face with her hat and wondered for the umpteenth time why she had allowed herself to be coerced into yet another of these on-board hospitality affairs, where there was always the hazard of being manoeuvred into dark corners and unoccupied cabins by one or more of the Officers and Gentlemen currently aboard.

She recollected with a wry smile Audrey's dire prognostications about the navy, which had turned out to be pretty accurate but easily dealt with. As her long ago plunge into the minefield of sexual gratification had been neither gratifying nor particularly successful she was in no great hurry to repeat the experience with anyone, let alone any randy here-today-gone-tomorrow sailor.

She put on her hat and glanced at her watch. Hell, another half-hour at least before the return ashore but a whole prairie of wild horses wouldn't get her back into the stuffy, noisy wardroom. Hunching her shoulders she leaned both arms on the rail and thought longingly of her own Spartan but peaceful quarters; what wouldn't she give now to be stretched comfortably in one of the old leather chairs, with a nice pink gin for company…

She jumped and gave a faint squeal of alarm as an arm was laid alongside hers on the rail and a voice murmured close to her ear, "'In such a night as this, when the sweet wind did gently kiss the trees…'"

Oh *God,* she thought, it seemed no sooner had she managed to give one of the bastard's the slip then up popped another...and quoting Shakespeare, for heaven's sake? Without turning her head she answered with crushing careless dismissal, 'The Merchant of Venice: Act Four, Scene two; what do you want, a gold star? It must be the hoariest old try-on in the whole of Shakespeare.' Sparing a glance at the arm now leaning beside her own she noted the number of rings on the sleeve and realised she might have been more diplomatic.

'I came to ask you for a dance, not collect a brush-off from teacher,' he answered with mild sarcasm.

Turning, Joanna tabbed him as the lone wolf she had watched stalking a tarty blonde Senior Wren from the Admiral's staff, and reluctantly gave him full marks for attractiveness. But it was on the cards that this particular mature wolf was undoubtedly married and playing away from home. Play on, she thought, but not with *me.*

'I'm afraid I'm not in the mood for dancing,' she answered politely, and turned away to lean again on the rail,

'Don't tell me I have to pull rank to get a dance on my own ship.'

'You haven't had to resort to that so far this evening sir, so why bother now?' she answered rashly and he peered at her with added interest.

'Have you been watching me?'

'Off and on – and I don't get into "come to my cabin" competitions with other Wrens; particularly when like you, they outrank me!'

'For Pete's sake,' he gave an exasperated sigh. 'Look, if you need an introduction before you'll even give me a dance my name is Mark Eden, I'm Number One on this bucket and it's my last night in port for a while. By the time the *Miranda's* first patrol out of Tollmouth is over the war might actually have started and we may never meet again. So now you know who I am and what I am and where I'm at, how about that dance?'

She hedged. 'It's too hot in the wardroom.'

'What's wrong with out here on deck? God knows the music is loud enough; I should think Hitler can hear it in Berchtesgaden.'

She gave in with an exasperated sigh. 'Very well, sir, my feet, but only my feet, are at your disposal!'

This one, thought Mark, would take a little more time and trouble to impress than the Admiral's *numero uno.* Abandoning the hoped for satisfactory end to the evening he sighed and taking this unexpectedly resistant young woman into his arms, moved sedately across the deck to the strains of Artie Shaw.

As one dance followed another Joanna began to relax, thinking she just might have read him wrong. Perhaps he really did only want to dance. When the strains of the last waltz finally sounded from the wardroom, he gave a long slow smile and released her. 'Thank you, I hope you enjoyed that as much as I did.'

She answered obliquely, 'Yes, sir, it was very *restrained.*'

He looked down at her with raised brows. 'You thought I was going to drag you into my cabin and have my way with you didn't you?' he asked mildly.

She flushed. 'I thought nothing of the kind!'

'Ah,' he put both hands on her shoulders. 'Perhaps it might have been wiser if you *had…*'

The sounds of a raucously sung Auld Lang Syne drifted from the deck below as he lifted his mouth from hers, after a kiss that seemed to have gone on for a very long time without being either greedy or demanding; a kiss, which to her embarrassed annoyance she had enjoyed. She felt a slow blush creep from neck to hairline, but managed to ask with cool sarcasm. 'Of course, you *are* married, aren't you?'

'Umm, but only loosely: Mrs Eden took off several years back with a larger bank-balance than I could muster and is at present living it up amid the fleshpots of Singapore.'

'Oh really?' she was disbelieving

'Yes, really, anything else you'd like to know?'

His grey eyes were mocking her. She let her own blue ones travel slowly over his face, before lingering meaningfully on the sprinkling of grey in his smooth dark hair. Old but sexy, she acknowledged, in fact, very sexy and perhaps not *that* old. He shook his head slightly, and gave a sardonic smile. 'I know what you're thinking and yes, I am knocking on quite a bit.'

'How far are you knocking?'

'Try thirty-six, but the grey is premature.'

She didn't attempt to repress her grin. 'Oh, I thought you were *much* older. So how is it that you are only a Number One?'

'Because, you rude child, until the war I was a Vet, and you don't get to be an Admiral straight away if you've spent the last ten years of your life with your arm up a cow's backside.'

She spluttered then laughed out loud. He smiled. 'That's much better. You know, I watched you in there for quite a while; the sight of so many young men trying so hard and getting nowhere had me wondering how far this old man might get.'

Joanna was wary again, conscious that he might be playing a game for which she didn't know the rules. 'No further than the young ones, sir.'

'Quite right; I'm sure you have a rude name for old married men who make passes at young women.' He paused slightly before adding, 'By the way, if you are having dinner with me tomorrow evening I think you should stop calling me Sir,' he held up his hand as she made to speak. 'Don't tell me that tomorrow you'll be washing your hair all evening.'

'How *did* you guess?'

'Experience,' he gave a sudden grin, then added, 'just one thing before you go, darling, do you have a name at all?'

Sudden anger sparked in her eyes. 'Dunne. *Sir,* Third Officer Joanna Felicity Dunne.'

'I suppose your friends call you Jo?'

'Not if they want to stay my friends they don't, nor do they call me darling until I've known them for a lot longer than forty minutes … and,' she added recklessly, 'awful as the food is in my mess you can forget about that dinner. I *never* go out with married men.'

She turned and walked away from him across the deck and down the companionway, joining the crowd now waiting to board the Liberty boat. Risking one backward glance as the boat pulled away she saw his tall broad-shouldered figure outlined against the moonlight, one hand raised in a mocking farewell salute.

* * *

The next morning she made a discreet visit to the plot room to find the *Miranda* was on temporary patrol of the channel and likely to be in and out of port on a regular basis. The thought of another possible meeting with the ship's First Lieutenant made her skin crawl with embarrassment. As she hadn't exactly repelled that kiss and her response to his dinner invitation could have been phrased more politely, she decided that if she were unlucky enough to spot him in the distance she'd make sure that *he* didn't see *her*.

But as the days passed without incident she decided with a certain sense of relief that she had seen the last of the much too smooth Mark Eden. As she had no intention of getting involved with a middle-aged charmer and he wasn't the type to be chasing after a snooty junior Wren, she judged that she could safely put him right out of her mind.

* * *

'I've brought your letters up for you,' Monica dropped two envelopes on Joanna's bed. 'One from your mama, the other delivered by a sweet little blonde Midshipman; now who could be sending *you* a letter by special messenger? I'll take a bet it's from the sex-on-legs from the *Miranda* who followed you out on deck that night of the party.'

'I doubt it.' Joanna turned the letters over. Yes, this one was from her mother, hopefully containing a cheque, but the other...?

She slid a thumb along the flap of the unstamped envelope and drew out a single sheet of paper.

To: Third Officer Joanna Felicity Dunne
From: Lieut. Mark Laurence Eden
It is not easy to track down just one Wren in a naval town, but when you get to know me better you will realise that I am a very persistent man. Although we missed our original date (I did ask you to dinner, didn't I?) may I hope that you will dine with this married man tomorrow night?

In case you should think of standing me up I shall be outside your quarters at 1900 hours precisely with an armed escort.

PS I promise not to pounce.

Joanna sat back, remembering those lively eyes under straight, dark brows, that caressing voice, the warmth of his hands on her back and the practised kiss...

'Wake up dozy!' Monica was impatient. 'It *is* from the old lecher, isn't it? Has he asked you out?'

'Yes, tomorrow – all your fault for dragging me to that party,' she put the note on one side; Monica snatched it up, scanned it swiftly and gave an exasperated sigh.

'Only you could walk out on a real man like that and get a second chance – if you're not up for it maybe I could take your place.'

'Feel free.' Joanna opened the other envelope, took out the hoped for cheque, kissed it, then concentrated on her mother's bold, almost illegible Italianate scrawl.

'Darling,' she read aloud. *'I would have sent you a cheque before now, but I'm so frantically busy I've scarcely time to breathe...I've met up again with an old friend whom I haven't laid eyes on for years. We had such a sweet boy and girl romance when we were young, and now that his wife is refusing to leave the country and be with him in London poor Leo is so lonely – and you know how it is in wartime. Do give me warning when you are coming on leave, darling and I will keep the time clear for you...* Oh, Lord,' Joanna sat back, her jaw sagging. 'She's got another man – after all this time.'

'If you don't stop reading that drivel and tell me about *your* man, I shall do for you with this fruit knife,' and Monica flourished the minute, pearl-handled blade menacingly.

Joanna pushed a hand through her hair. 'Mo, have some sense. He's married.'

Monica gave a snort of laughter. 'At least you know exactly what the married ones are after!'

'Thanks. I'll blame you if I decide to go then get ravished on the doorstep tomorrow night.'

'Lucky old you, I'd say, and I bet it isn't called a doorstep.'

'Oh, Lord, all this jargon – what is it then – a poop deck?'

Monica flopped back on her bed. 'Shouldn't think so, but don't ask *me* what you call the doorstep of a Victorian villa masquerading as a shore bound naval establishment. I don't have a clue.'

Joanna laughed, thinking how nice it was to have someone like Monica with whom she could gossip and let her hair down. Resolutely putting her mother's inconvenient and inconsiderate love life out of her mind she lay back on her bed. Gazing at the ceiling she offered tentatively 'If I *do* decide to go tomorrow night – and I only said *if* – will you lend me your black silk stockings?'

'Ho, Ho!' Monica grinned and raised an eyebrow. 'Madam will kill you if she sees you wearing those with uniform – but you can have them if you give me *all* the sordid details afterward.'

'There won't *be* any sordid details,' Joanna said with conviction, 'but I'd like the stockings, just the same!'

* * *

The next evening as promised he was waiting outside her billet. She walked down the steps, saluting him punctiliously, making a point of it so that he had to reply in kind.

'Spot on time.' He seized her elbow and keeping it in a firm grip walked her towards a waiting taxi. Of course, she thought, he *would* be the sort who could find a taxi in a town where they were rare as hen's teeth...He gave the driver directions to a hotel on the outskirts of Tollmouth then sat back and half-turning toward her let his gaze rove over her figure, his eyes lingering appreciatively on her long shapely legs. 'Well, me Queen, as they say in my part of the world, you're a sight to gladden any man's heart!'

Carefully placing her ankles together she pulled her skirt down over her knees. 'Perhaps after ten days at sea that doesn't take all that much to achieve.'

'How did you know I've been ten days at sea?'

'That's privileged information...and I am not allowed to divulge my sources.'

'Ah, so you've been keeping tabs on me!' He gave a knowing grin and she blushed. Bloody man...but he was rather nice.

There's absolutely nothing to worry about, she argued silently as she stepped into the hotel foyer, *what the hell, no one gets ravished in a hotel restaurant, for heaven's sake.*

'How does a Vet from where-ever-it-is end up as a Number One on an armed merchant cruiser?' she asked later as he leaned across the table to refill her wineglass.

'It's Cornwall, actually: lots of sea, lots of sky and lots of cows and sheep. I chose the Navy I suppose because I can navigate and read a chart. I was brought up on the Dorset Coast and sailed since I was a boy; only a small boat, although I've a rather larger one in Porthryn. Still, it was quite a jump to the *Miranda.*'

'Cornwall is a fair way from home,' she observed.

'Much too far for my mother's peace of mind; she used to send me home-made cakes and tell me to post my socks home for darning right up until I got married!'

'Amazing,' she looked at him over the rim of her glass. 'My mother couldn't bake a cake if her life depended upon it, she never offers to darn *my* socks and I'm a lot younger than you.'

'So you are.' He took the glass from her hand, placing it back on the table before holding out his own hand in invitation. 'But let's not discuss our mothers – or our ages. Let's just dance.'

This time he held her close as they moved smoothly across the floor. Within minutes she was acutely aware of the effect on her of his hard, confident body and wondered uneasily if perhaps he was rather more dangerous than she'd thought. However, as he didn't seem the type to lose control after a few glasses of wine and a spot of dancing cheek-to-cheek, she felt safe enough, at any rate for this evening.

She demurred, but only half-heartedly, when he suggested they should take their time and walk back along the cliff path. Any unease she might have previously felt at accepting his invitation had long since vanished and she didn't particularly want the evening to end. Only when they finally turned into the dingy cul-de-sac that housed her quarters, was she suddenly aware of the lateness of the hour and how loud their footsteps sounded in the dark deserted street. 'I'm late,' she whispered as they stopped before the steps. 'Another five minutes and you'd have had to give me a leg-up through the galley window!'

'Sorry. Will you be in trouble?'

'Don't think so. Madame looks the other way – within reason.'

'Do you really call Miss Hawkins that?'

'Not when she's within earshot; but how do you know her name?'

'Classified Information,' his mouth twitched, 'I'm not allowed to divulge my sources.'

She gave a little huff of laughter, '*Touché*!'

They climbed the steps and stopped outside the front door. There was a small silence; she glanced up at the windows. 'I think its time I said goodnight and thank you for a lovely evening.'

She offered her hand like a nicely brought-up schoolgirl and for a moment he looked baffled, then giving his slow grin took her hand in his. Suddenly heady with the knowledge that for the first time *she* was calling the tune Joanna asked with feigned innocence, 'Well, do I have permission to go in now, or are you hanging around hoping for something more?'

Without a word he took her face between his hands and kissed her long and deep, setting every nerve end jumping and sending an electric charge shooting down through her body to crash somewhere around her knees. Breathless she put her hands against his chest and pushed him away whispering, 'Hey, not so fast, sailor!'

'Sorry.' He stepped back, spreading his hands in apology. He was in shadow and it was too dark to see his face but she could feel him laughing at her. There was a pause before he murmured, 'Your fault. *If* we are to go on meeting, and *if* you don't want to be kissed like that again, then you shouldn't look at me the way you have tonight.'

Flustered and feeling she'd made a fool of herself she straightened her hat. 'What way do I look?'

'Too bloody inviting for comfort!' he hissed and walked smartly down the steps and along the street without a backward glance.

* * *

'I thought you were out for the night.' Monica peered sleepily over her bedclothes. 'Been hauled up before the head prefect for a wigging, have you?' She struggled into a sitting position, yawning and rumpling her hair.

'Fortunately the head pre was in the loo so I missed the where-have-you-been-until-this-hour-Miss Dunne routine.' Joanna heeled off her shoes and carefully rolled down the sheer stockings. 'We went to the Queens over at Longley then walked all the way back.' Still shaken by that kiss she stood and began to unbutton her skirt.

'I lent you my stockings so don't try to wriggle out of telling.' Monica hugged her knees. 'Look me in the eye and tell me he didn't kiss you again.'

'He did that all right, but you can relax – I'm not going to sleep with him.'

'It's not the sleeping that causes the trouble, but the prelude to it. Not that I would know about such things first hand.'

'Huh! You may in civvy-street be the Hon. Monica "tease-them-senseless" Monroe and the delight of the chinless wonder brigade at Knightsbridge Barracks, but here you're just another jealous Wren.'

'True.' Monica slid back under the bedclothes. 'So put out the light and snuggle down on your virginal couch …or should that be bunk?

'A virginal bunk somehow seems a contradiction of terms!' Joanna leaned to switch off the light. 'Mind you, he's quite a kisser.'

'Trollop,' Monica yawned again. 'Tell me about it in the morning…'

Long after Monica slept Joanna still lay awake, reliving the evening: how she had felt when they were dancing, how startled but excited she had been by that kiss. But she'd have to be stupid to imagine that one goodnight kiss would mean very much to *him*.

She thumped her pillow, trying to find a cool spot for her hot cheek. So much for watching her step! Oh *why* did he have to be married? Was bloody Mrs Eden really in Singapore or was that just a line shoot and she was sitting somewhere in the Home Counties with a couple of children and knitting long white socks for hubby?

*　　*　　*

Mark Eden also lay sleepless, staring with unblinking eyes at the bulkhead above his own virginal bunk, regretting he hadn't at least tried to make a pass earlier in the evening and take advantage of the fact that the hotel usually had more than one empty bedroom. Not that she would have been likely to oblige on a first date, although if he was to continue seeing her that was most likely the way things would go. He sighed. His women were usually a darned sight older and a lot less starry-eyed than Joanna Dunne, and really, that was the way he preferred them: it avoided all those tiresome tearful reproaches when the time came to say goodbye.

On the other hand, there would be no harm in meeting her again. The thought of some attractive regular company without any messy involvement did have a certain charm; whiling away the odd hour ashore with such a fresh young companion would be very nice indeed and do no one any harm. He wasn't a complete cad; he could keep his hands off her. He stretched and smiled. Yes. Why not? Third Officer Joanna Felicity Dunne, he thought virtuously, would have nothing to fear from an occasional evening spent in the company of this Jimmy the One.

2

Tollmouth, July 1940

Joanna ticked off another day on her desk calendar and wondered how much longer she could bear her present mind-numbing position of dogsbody to Section Officer June Rose, who quite clearly thought an assistant with an Oxford degree more hindrance than asset. Casting a jaundiced eye over the two clerk ratings bent industriously over their desks, she ruminated that if this was as exciting as life in the Navy was going to get, then she might as well have stayed in Kensington and rolled bandages for the Red Cross.

Restless, she pushed back her chair and walked to the grimy window to gaze through the criss-cross covering of brown sticky tape. Outside the day was grey and gloomy, matching her mood. Tomorrow evening she should have been meeting Mark again, but with the news coming through from France there seemed little chance of that happening.

Their meetings over these last weeks, none longer than a few hours and all spent on the dance floor or in bars and restaurants, had swept away her last vestige of resistance to Mark Eden's charms. Each meeting had been for her a small step into paradise; she just wished she knew what he was thinking and whether he felt the same. But each time they met he behaved exactly as that first evening, except that now when he kissed her goodnight he kept it brief and swift, leaving before there was any possible unwary flaring of passion, at least on his part. Absently she rubbed a finger over the grubby window. What was she doing wrong that kept him at such a frustratingly respectable distance?

'Dunne, where are those charts I asked for earlier? They are supposed to be out and ready for collection.'

She turned around to face an irate June Rose – and which sadistic parent she wondered, had saddled a child with a name like that. Conscious that little Mabel Price, the least confident of the clerks was cowering guiltily behind her typewriter, Joanna fibbed glibly. 'I'm sorry ma'am. They were ready but I must have filed them again by mistake.'

'By *mistake*?' the officer echoed, in a tone reminiscent of an outraged Lady Bracknell.

Joanna's mouth twitched; she said hastily, 'I'll get them out again, ma'am.'

'If you kept this office clear of all your male admirers, Dunne, and spared the time to keep the clerks on their toes, you might manage to do your job properly.'

'Yes, ma'am, I suppose I might.' Joanna pulled out a long drawer and ran an eye over the contents. It really wasn't that poor little kid's fault, she'd probably just been over zealous in filing everything she could lay her hands on before the old bat returned... she gave Mabel a conspiratorial wink and handed her superior the rolled charts. 'Hadn't you better hurry ma'am or you'll miss your meeting.'

'Very possibly, thanks to your inefficiency – you had better pull your socks up Miss Dunne. You're no use to me if you can't keep some kind of order and control in this office.'

'Oh *ma'am,*' Joanna's eyes widened, her expression one of hurt and sorrowful innocence. 'Cow!' she said as the door closed, and immediately resumed her window gazing. Pushing up the sash she leaned out so that she could see the *Miranda* moored on the port side of the harbour. What was Mark doing now she wondered, and had he time to think of her?

* * *

'Are we all ready to go?' Lieutenant Commander Wheeler cocked an inquiring eye at his Number One.

'Yes sir.' Mark broke off his conversation with the Navigation Officer. 'Everyone's back on board, apart from Stewart and Hayes; I sent them ashore to collect extra ammunition for the pom-pom. We're a case short at this morning's count.'

The captain grunted. 'Those blighters from the *Chloe* I expect. Always foraging around for something,' he crossed the bridge, raising his binoculars to make a quick sweep around the harbour. 'There'll be one hell of a lot of craft milling around out there when we do move – anything coming through from shore about that?' As his Number One shook his head, he made another sweep with the glasses. 'God Almighty!' he dropped them on his chest and turned incredulous eyes on Mark. 'There are a couple of rusty old coasters and a 'Saucy Sal' steaming right into the ruddy harbour and about to barge across the Commodore's bows – someone had better chivvy them out of his way PDQ!'

'Sir, an urgent message from HQ,' Midshipman Evans projected himself up onto the bridge, trying unsuccessfully to keep his voice from sliding up the scale with excitement.

'Save the greyhound impersonation for later Mid!' Briefly, the captain scanned the message before handing it to Mark. 'Well, this is it, Number One. I'm going over to HQ. Evans, clear off and chivvy those stores buggers back on board.' He watched the midshipman race down the deck. 'Doesn't that Snotty ever *walk* anywhere?' he demanded, 'he'll break his neck one of these days,'

Mark smiled. 'He's just young and eager, sir.'

The captain turned to leave the bridge. 'He'll feel a lot older and a damned sight less eager by the time we're through with this lot; we all will. Better nail the CPO and run through the boat drill again – and keep 'em at it, Number One. Oh, and tell the galley to lay on a hot meal ASAP, it could be some time before any of us gets another.'

* * *

The Vice-Admiral let his gaze rove slowly over the assembled captains before turning to poke a long forefinger at the wall map of the Normandy coast. 'As you already know, Dunkirk has been heavily bombed and most of the town is on fire. Although the Navy's still taking men off from the harbour mole, thousands more are pouring onto the beaches along the Normandy coast – and they're all relying on us to get to them before Jerry. So those beaches are where *you'll* be heading.' He looked around the crowded room where men stood or sat on chairs and benches or perched on windowsills and radiators. 'You've all seen what's filling the harbour here: everything from pleasure steamers and fishing smacks to rowboats with outboards and a sail. Many of the larger vessels will be manned by some of our regular Navy chaps, but most will have their own skippers at the helm. A hell of a lot of them on the smaller boats will be just weekend sailors and you'll have your work cut out keeping some kind of order, at least on the way over. Once you arrive I'm afraid for the small craft it will be a case of every man for himself and the devil take the hindmost. Just help and protect them all you can.' He looked at his watch. 'I have a meeting now with all the volunteer skippers. Commander Naughton here is O.C. of *your* part of the operation and will fill you in on the details. Good hunting, gentlemen.'

Commander Naughton was short and spare, with a close bristly beard and moustache and the savage air of a rat-catching terrier. He turned to take the navigation charts borne by a senior Wren officer; unrolling the first and hanging it over the Admiral's map he swept a hand along the length of it.

'Up to last night we were using Bray Dunes and Malo-les-Bains, but don't count on that still being possible. What's left of the army could end up spread ten miles or more along the Normandy coastline. There's organisation of a sort at Dunkirk but the beaches where you'll be heading will more than likely be a shambles. Bear in mind that although enemy guns are a fair way off as yet they are moving fast. By the time you arrive you could be under heavy shell fire, and while daylight holds it's a dead certainty that you'll be strafed from the air as well.

'On the way out use your loud hailers to keep the little boats astern of you if possible; that way they have the best chance of making it.' He turned again to hang another chart. 'All ships and attendant craft from Tollmouth will be heading for this particular stretch of the coast; as you can see it is has a fair amount of shallows and sandbanks, so Navy ships must keep well offshore. Send in your boats with the minimum of crew and just ferry the troops back. Time will be of the essence, so use scrambling nets and take everyone on board, not only from your own boats, but from any other small craft until you are full – then get the hell out of it. Dover will be your destination for disembarkation and refuelling so it'll be a while before you make your home port again,' he paused then added quietly, 'It will be a crowded sea over there, gentlemen, with little margin for error.'

There was a general stir and a noticeable rise in the tension already filling the room. While the Captains murmured amongst themselves the Commander turned again to the Wren officer. 'I'll need another assistant, Miss Rose. Tommy Leger says your department is well up to strength, so who can you spare?'

'Well, Commander, there is a new rating – '

'No good: I need someone more senior, who's been here a while and knows her way around – how about that Third of yours with the legs – she looks as though she has a brain between her ears. What's-her-name…'

He snapped his fingers and she stared at him frostily. 'Do you mean Miss Dunne, sir?'

'That's the one: bright as a button – Tommy says you can have a senior rating from his department instead.' He gave a rasping chuckle. 'Got a look fit to kill when I gave your Miss Dunne the eye on the stairs last week, so she'll be likely to keep her mind on her work'

'We are extremely busy Commander and it will be awkward to replace her at such short notice. Also I'm not sure that she will suit you, she seems to attract rather a lot of attention from a number of the *younger* members of the naval staff – and she can be difficult.'

He snapped irritably, 'I don't want to put your department under pressure but you don't need raving intellectuals to do the work, do you? I can take care of the snotties and I guarantee she won't be difficult for long.' He gave his fearsome smile again. 'Sorry to deprive you, but we all have to make sacrifices, don't we?'

*　　*　　*

Joanna greeted the news of her transfer with astonishment and a faint stir of apprehension. The Commander's irascibility and lack of charm were well known throughout the building. 'What? Go right now, ma'am?'

'Immediately, although you may wish yourself back here before many hours have passed. Commander Naughton does not have a reputation for being patient, nor is he likely to allow your many hanger's-on.'

Biting back the observation that she couldn't be held personally responsible for the occasional visit by the odd randy sailor, Joanna, ignoring the directive that respirator bags were for gas masks only and not designed to hold cosmetics or love-letters, stuffed the contents of her desk drawer into hers and made a hasty exit for the cloakroom to examine her make-up and pull a comb through her short curls. *He can't kill you*, she told her reflection, *and anything has to be better than putting up with that old bat breathing down your neck all day.* Checking that her stocking seams were straight and tugging down her jacket, she walked briskly down the stairs to tap on the Commander's door, only quailing slightly at the answering ferocious, 'Come!'

Composing her features into a suitably businesslike expression she entered.

He was sitting with his elbows on his desk, watching the door with steely blue eyes. In the far corner of the room an extremely harassed-looking Second Officer sat at a desk strewn with papers. She looked up briefly at Joanna's entrance and rolled her eyes toward the ceiling.

Joanna braced herself. 'Third Officer Dunne reporting, sir.'

'Took your time, didn't you – suppose you were in the heads puttin' your war paint on. Now listen,' he pointed a bony finger, 'I never repeat anything more than once, and I don't expect anyone to make mistakes. See you are at your desk by o-eight-thirty each morning; don't expect to leave when the clock strikes eighteen-hundred; forget about any hanger's on – I won't have blasted half-baked spotty youths calling themselves naval officers cluttering up the place. I take two sugars in my coffee and I don't want to hear what you have to do in the galley to get it!'

She asked sweetly and with assumed innocence, 'Would that be black or white, sir?'

'Black.'

'Cup or mug, sir?'

He sat back and glared at her. 'You ask if I need it stirred and you'll be back with Section Officer Rose in Charts so fast your feet won't touch the ground. Now get next door and Miss Jones here will be out in a few minutes to show you the ropes.'

'Sir.'

Joanna left. The Commander, she thought, had all the hallmarks of being a mean old bastard, but although the future was looking a little hazardous her new post at least showed definite prospects of being rather more stimulating than Charts.

* * *

Few men aboard the *Miranda* slept as they steamed through the night towards the French coast. Mark and the Chief Petty Officer had put the crew through the drill for launching their boats until every man was heartily sick of the sight and sound of them. Up on the bridge Captain Wheeler stood and swore hoarsely through the loud hailer as his craft was regularly overtaken by grizzled skippers tearing every ounce of speed out of their fishing smacks, while duffel-coated weekenders surged past in gleaming motor launches.

Long before they reached their destination they could hear the relentless pounding of artillery from the shattered town of Dunkirk; see and smell the thick acrid pall of smoke as an offshore wind carried the fumes of burning oil towards them. As the sky lightened German FF6's appeared, raking with machine gun fire the small boats making the long haul through crowded waters towards unfamiliar beaches, while warships, frigates, armed merchantmen and cruisers emptied their own guns into the attackers, creating a hideous non-stop nightmare of noise.

While the *Miranda's* ship's boats nosed in between shallow-draught French fishing smacks, Channel Island ferries, pleasure cruisers and launches crammed with men in dirty, crumpled khaki, dotted here and there with the light blue of the RAF, her crew watched and waited to help the survivors aboard. Time after time their boats set out, returning overloaded and lying low in the water until the ship was filled to capacity.

Under incessant gunfire, bombed and strafed by fighters, little boats and big ships together paid a terrible price, many of the boats and their human cargo blown to pieces before they had a chance to reach the comparative safety of the craft standing in deeper waters.

The *Miranda* was hit on her second trip to the beaches of Normandy. Heavily loaded and turning for home she was caught in the searchlights and holed amidships above the water line, creating carnage amongst the men crowded between decks.

An armed merchantman, she was too small to warrant a surgeon and Mark, pressed into service in a makeshift sick bay, assisted by a stolid mess steward and a green-faced Midshipman Evans, rolled up his shirtsleeves and did the best he could in the appalling conditions below decks. On the edge of exhaustion, shutting his ears to the unrelenting bombardment from the shore and the strafing 'planes, he pushed to the back of his consciousness the knowledge that somewhere out there in that shambles, with the men he wouldn't leave until he was either killed or carried off the beach on a stretcher, was his brother Kit...

* * *

For every second unoccupied with work Joanna waited for news. When a sympathetic Signals officer she knew passed the message that the *Miranda* was hit but safe in Dover with dockies swarming around a great hole in her side. Grateful that it would at least mean a respite before Mark's ship was made ready for sea again she thanked the messenger and got on with her mountain of work.

The Commander, she had quickly discovered, was a slave driver *par excellence*. After enduring each day his caustic tongue, his apparently inexhaustible non-stop energy and appetite for tackling everything at breakneck speed, the unfortunate Miss Jones was frequently close to tears. Although commiserating with her unhappy senior Joanna had a strong suspicion that the Commander's bark was a good deal worse than his bite. She rather enjoyed her own occasional run-ins with him, and at this time of worry and nervous tension was grateful for the hours of unceasing work heaped upon her shoulders while she waited for the *Miranda* to come into her home port again.

* * *

Arriving for work on the seventh day she found the Commander had been at his desk most of the night and he greeted her early morning arrival wearily. 'Seems we shall be getting our share of ships coming in here to unload now and they'll be a lot of Froggie troops comin' in – word's out that we have to get all of *them* off the beaches as well as ours!' He sounded aggrieved at such temerity on the part of the French. 'Jones says you speak the lingo … that right?'

'Yes sir.'

He scowled. 'That lot upstairs think anyone who can *parlez vous* might be useful down there. Personally I wouldn't trust you not to be more interested in finding that chap you're always looking for.' The fierce eyes challenged her. 'Go on, before I change my mind, but don't think you're going to skive around for the duration. You can go now, then be back here by fourteen hundred – and stick to that schedule until you're no longer needed.' He eyed her up and down. 'And get some trousers and jerseys out of stores. This department can't afford to pay for your blasted stockings and dry-cleaning bills!'

* * *

His mug of coffee arrested half way to his mouth, a grimy unshaven Captain Wheeler peered toward the shore through bloodshot eyes. 'Am I losing my marbles, Number One or are there a load of jetties along those beaches that aren't on our charts?'

It was first light and an eerie silence hung overall. They were approaching their furthest point yet along the coast. Shrouded as they were in heavy mist it was difficult to distinguish sea from shore.

Mark raised his glasses. Along the beaches as far as the eye could see long, thin black lines stretched out into the water. He rubbed his eyes then re-focused the glasses. 'Not jetties, sir, men. All standing in line right up to their armpits in the water, like they're queuing for the NAFFI,' his glasses raked the beach. 'Christ, what's it going to be like when the planes arrive? They won't have a chance in hell; it'll be like a fairground shooting gallery.'

Midshipman Evans took his turn with the boat crews as the Stukas dived and the mortars found the range of the shallows where the men queued, some upright and holding wounded comrades; others, weary beyond thought, sagging exhausted under the weight of their sodden clothing, apparently oblivious of the bodies that floated around them and nudged against their legs and chests.

Their cutter came alongside and Mark looked down onto the filthy but still alert face of their midshipman; just eighteen, God Almighty, at his age I was still in school, he thought, hauling the latest batch of rescued men the final few feet up the nets and onto the crowded decks. 'Down below and take an hour's rest,' he ordered the crew, '– and you Mid.' He squeezed the boy's shoulder. 'Well done lad ... Cox'n, come with me, you too Lofty; the Captain wants us to take one more trip then finish off.'

'Reckon we can lift a few more, Mr Eden.' Cox'n Baines grinned, teeth white in his blackened face, 'Cor, what wouldn't I give for a pint o' bitter right now!'

As they again approached the lines of troops, chest deep in water as they had been for hours, all night perhaps, a towering figure at the head of the nearest column gave a mighty shout, waving energetically and calling with powerful lungs.

'Mark, you old bastard, about bloody time you showed! How many flaming cows d'you think you're going to find in this paddling pool? Come over here and get my blokes off...I've a present for you!' And he gestured at the sagging figure he was supporting with one strong arm.

Mark put his mouth close to the Cox'n's ear, yelling above a sudden shattering onslaught from the guns, 'Mr Baines – that's a man who could find you a pint of bitter in the Sahara desert! Get him and the rest of that shower aboard.'

*   *   *

With part of her fo'c'sle shot away and two guns temporarily out of action, the *Miranda* limped back to Dover. Below decks Captain Josh Milton wolfed bully beef out of a tin and watched over the man whose head he'd held clear of the water all through the long night.

'Thought someone I knew would eventually turn up!' Josh paused and waved his jack knife in greeting as Mark descended the ladder again to pick his way between the blanketed figures on the lower deck. 'Didn't expect you though, you jammy bugger – you haven't even got your feet wet!'

Mark knelt beside his brother's unconscious form. 'He's taken one hell of a whack on the head.'

'He's tough, he'll be OK. He was on the arse-end of a stretcher and got caught in shell-blast. But like you said, he's only got a spot of concussion, a busted shoulder and ribs and in danger of dying of exposure ...nothing much, really!'

'Thanks for taking care of him, Josh. He's the only baby brother I have.'

He shrugged and grinned. 'Couldn't leave the Padre behind, could I, else who would pray for my soul?' He looked furtive and lowered his voice. 'I say, Mark, before he wakes up again and starts ear wigging: you wouldn't have a surplus woman you might spare for me when we get into port? There's nothing like fear to make a bloke permanently randy and I haven't had a bunk-up since Pontivy!'

'Forget it. We're headed for Dover and I wouldn't know about any spare women there; anyway, the state you're in you wouldn't even get as far as the bedroom door, never mind the bed.'

'You think not?'

'I know not; get your head down while you can, you big ox.'

'OK. You're the boss around here, 'though why I'm taking orders from a bloody brother horse-doctor beats me!' He gave a huge yawn, the lids closed over his weary eyes and he slept, snoring disgracefully all the way back to port.

Shortly before they entered harbour Mark went below again. Wedging himself alongside the slumbering Josh he squatted beside his brother, who opened weary pain-filled eyes.

'Hi, good to see you awake, mate. How is it?'

'Not so bad, but it will put me in the bin for a while. Then home I suppose.' Kit turned his head fretfully from side to side. 'I shall miss getting back with the blokes…not that there are many of us left, apart from old Josh here and a couple of his tank crew…'

He was feverish and white with pain. Mark gripped his hand. 'Hang on, Kit, we're almost back.'

He forced a smile, passing his tongue over dry lips. 'Any messages, Mark – shall I give Ellen a great big slobbering kiss from you?'

His brother grinned. 'One day that woman will lay you out flat, and if she took it into her head to leave the whole house would collapse…mother would never forgive you!'

Kit croaked, 'She won't go…she's been threatening it ever since we were kids. Anyway, I can run faster than her now, or could before this. Any other messages you want delivered?'

'Give my love to mother, of course.'

'What about Pa?'

Mark frowned. 'You can tell him I'm still alive if he's interested, which I doubt.'

Fretfully Kit rolled his head. 'You should call a truce now. You know it's up to you.'

Mark's mouth hardened. 'I won't crawl to the old sod, for you or anyone else. Sorry, but there it is. Now shut up and rest.'

Kit's eyelids drooped, masking his pain. 'After you get shot of all of us do you have to go back again?'

'Yeah, until we have everyone off the beaches or the old tub gives up, whichever happens first.'

'Come down to the house before I finish my sick-leave.'

'I will, Kito, providing *he* isn't there, so none of your devious plans for reconciliation.' Mark stood up, shaking his head decisively. 'They won't work. It would only upset mother and you know I won't have that.'

He climbed again to the bridge, leaning on the voice pipes, watching as every turn of the ships screw brought them closer to the faint outline of the white cliffs. As always, in any snatched moment of relaxation, he thought about Joanna and was filled with the feelings and desires that he had fought so hard against these past days; a hopeless battle, which he had lost somewhere around *Miranda's* third trip to the beaches.

What the hell conceit had made him imagine he could go on seeing her and be content to leave her each time with no more than a goodnight kiss? She'd got under his skin in a way he'd vowed he would never allow another woman to do, but just where he went from here, he'd no idea. Joanna Dunne was not the kind of woman he was used to dealing with and certainly not the type to be lured into any casual affair. In any case, that wasn't an option. His morals may be dubious but he drew the line at the outright seduction of a girl thirteen years his junior.

He groaned aloud and rested his head on the cold wet rail. He had never felt like this before about any woman. Joanna was so young, and so very warm under that cool, capable exterior. Since the debacle of his marriage, when he had stayed in Porthryn and Vivienne returned to her Bond Street Salon, he'd determined that anything more than the most casual of relationships was finished for good.

But Joanna had changed all that, just by looking at him with those extraordinary eyes and lifting her face for his kiss. He had no idea what she might feel for him; knew if he had any shred of decency left he shouldn't want her to feel as he did. Of course she may not be as unspoiled as she appeared, but leaving that aside, she was still much too young and vulnerable for him

3

Tollmouth, June 1940

After the safe delivery at Dover of the troops that included Kit and Josh, the Miranda had refuelled and returned to the Normandy coast that same night. Now, with Dover at saturation point and filled with mostly French troops, she was steaming at last towards her home harbour after seven days of hell. Mark took off his cap to push weary hands through his hair. If the Captain's reckoning was right and their luck held, the next trip across the channel would be their last. Would he have time to see Joanna he wondered, before they made that final crossing ... his train of thought was interrupted as Evans clattered up the companionway.

'Mr Eden, sir, Captain says we've orders to refuel in the morning ... and he says would you care to go ashore until twenty-two-hundred, then relieve him until first light?'

'You may tell the Captain that I shall be happy to oblige,' all Mark's weariness vanished. 'What about you, Mid, any girls waiting for you out there?'

'Not tonight, sir, but I bet I know which one's waiting for you. Would you like me to take a message? Cheers my day that does...lovely legs, sir!'

'That'll just about do, Mr Evans.' Hiding a smile he turned to go below, adding over his shoulder, 'if you can just rustle up some hot water for a shave I might overlook the impertinence.'

'Thank you, sir – and sir, I've got some Cologne my sister gave me. You can have a splash of that if you need it.' Evans face was apparently devoid of guile.

Mark growled, 'When I want to smell like a Parisian tart, Mid, I'll let you know! Now move, before I clip your ear, you precocious brat!'

He left the ship and had begun threading his way across the crowded quayside; heading for Naval HQ and hopefully, Joanna, when near at hand he heard the unmistakable voice asking in clearly articulated French, '*Comment vous sentez-vous, Caporal*?'

Hunting around with his tired eyes he couldn't at first see her amongst the figures packing the dockside. A ragged line stretched before the mobile WVS canteen; to the right of that and running along one side of the quay and with ambulances standing by lay two ranks of stretchers, with Navy nurses and VADs passing briskly between them. The returning troops moved slowly, like figures in a dream, crowded, knocking against each other, apologising hoarsely.

'Sorry Mate, me effin' legs is like rubber...'

'Got a spare fag?'

'Seen anything of Tom? He was with me in the water then I lost the old bugger...'

'Ah wouldn'a mind being that lucky wee Froggie on the stretcher there … ah wish that piece o' lovely was lightin' *my* fag!'

Mark swung around at this, seeing her immediately: straightening up from where she crouched to place a cigarette into the mouth of a wounded man. As he watched she turned to the orderly by her side with a crisp, 'George, this is Corporal Jean Batiste Ronde. The doctor wants him on your next run – and don't take that cigarette away in the ambulance, will you?'

'No, miss.' The orderly was obviously used to her shorthand. Mark could see him thinking *another poor sod isn't going to make it,* 'you can leave him to me…I'll see he's all right.'

The man on the stretcher raised a heavily bandaged hand. *'Adieu, merci beaucoup, Mademoiselle – avez-vous le bon ange.'*

She stood up, pushing a hand through her short curls and smiling down at him. '*Au revoir; bonne chance, Jean Batiste.*'

She was wearing a pair of Navy bell-bottoms and an over-large jersey, her hair needed washing, her eyes were weary and one cheek was smudged with dirt, but to Mark's hungry eyes she looked like a million dollars on a silver salver. In a few long strides he was at her side, seeing with a quickening of the pulse her startled flush of recognition before she smiled, saying, 'Well, what a thing, sir!'

Bugger the audience he thought, and caught her in his arms.

A raucous cheer went up from a dozen throats; there were shouts of 'Oi! Oi! – watch it, miss – the Navy's 'ere' and a barrage of catcalls sounded from the stretchers.

He didn't hear them; he could have been alone in a desert with this woman for all he noticed, or cared, just the sight and the sound and the feel of her all that was left in the universe. With pounding heart he loosed his arms, but with her hands about his neck she held him to her, pulling his mouth down onto hers and he was lost again, drowning in the sweetness of her.

After a long, dizzying minute he raised his head. Breathless he asked, 'How soon can you get away? The Old Man doesn't need me back until twenty two hundred and I've a thirst like a desert camel!'

In a quiet corner of the bar she looked at him over the top of her glass. 'You are different,' she said.

'I am? How?'

'I don't know, just different. Is it as awful as they say out there?'

'Um, not too good.'

'Earlier, on the quay you made a mistake didn't you?' The deep blue eyes were intent on his. 'When you kissed me...that was different. That was real.'

He looked away, steeling himself to keep the distance between them.

'I knew when the *Miranda* was hit and went into dock.' She turned the glass in her hands. 'I was so frightened for you.'

'Tell you something...' he reached across the table, took the glass; setting it down he caught both her hands between his own. 'I was frightened for me, too!'

'Do you have to go back?'

'Yes, on tomorrow's evening tide, hopefully for the last time. When it's all over we'll have leave but I probably shan't get much more than a few days as we'll be laid up for repairs – here, I hope, or Pompey. I'll need to be back on board while all that's going on.'

'Mark,' she smoothed her fingers over the roughened skin of his hands. 'I don't know how to say this because I'm never quite sure what you're thinking.' She paused, her smile uncertain. 'Look, I should have taken leave a month ago, but I wangled to hang on until we had more than just a few hours to spend together.' She looked up into his face, at the grey eyes grown suddenly still and watchful and her mouth turned downward. 'You're not going to make this easy for me, are you?'

'No, because I'm pretty sure you're about to say something you shouldn't.'

'Scruples,' she said slowly, 'are not for times and situations such as these.' She smiled a little crookedly. 'All at once I find myself rather shy and out of my depth. Please make it easier for me by saying you know a little place somewhere, as I'm sure you do.'

'I do, several, but I'm not taking *you* to any of them!'

She lowered her eyes for a moment, hoping she wasn't going to blush. 'I'm not exactly inexperienced you know. I have done it before – and if you're thinking about the difference in our ages, forget it.'

He raised her hand, turning it to kiss the palm. 'I don't think I can do that.'

She said dryly, 'Try, it can't be all that difficult!'

'Maybe, but I still won't take you anywhere.'

'Then let me take you. Monica's brother knows a place – '

'No.' He shook his head firmly. 'I won't leave you with regrets.'

She answered swiftly. 'This is no time for regrets...'

'You say I've changed, but what may I ask happened to the cool, collected, rather haughty Joanna Felicity Dunne I met three months ago – you know; the one who wouldn't even dance with me until I pulled rank?'

She let her eyes travel slowly over his face, before saying softly, 'You happened to her sir; you happened.'

* * *

The final trip was nearly the last the old ship made, but battered, leaking and barely making five knots the *Miranda* came safely into her home port.

Not all of her crew saw Tollmouth welcoming them back on a sun-drenched morning: not Cox'n Baines who'd been at sea twenty years, nor 'Guns' who was fresh out of King Alfred's and had joined ship just two weeks before, young Paddy Flynn, temporarily moved from steward to sick berth attendant, Petty Officer Peter Marriot, Stoker Jock MacNabb…and Midshipman Parry Evans.

Mark Eden sat in his cabin long after the stretchers had left the decks with their still burdens, and mourned the bright-eyed boy who would never again race to carry a message ashore for his Jimmy-the-One.

* * *

As he came through the gates Joanna was waiting for him, standing by a borrowed car, giving her uncertain smile before he bent to kiss her with dry lips.

'I suppose this means that you still want my body,' he sighed and shook his head as throwing his bag onto the back seat he slid in beside her.

She fingered the stubble on his chin. 'Not until you've had a bath and shaved that I don't!'

At this he gave a wry smile and lying back against the seat closed his eyes. 'Wake me when we get there, darling…' he murmured and was almost instantly asleep, only occasionally half-waking on the journey to Winchester. Leaving the city Joanna drove a short distance through narrow lanes; stopping at last before an old whitewashed Inn that stood alone in woodland above a bend on the Itchen River.

The setting sun gilded the tree tops and a pair of swans glided slowly back and forth in the clear water, while on the far bank two small boys gathered up their nets and jam jars of tiddlers, preparatory to the journey back home. It was all very peaceful and far from the sights and sounds of war. Silencing the engine Joanna sat for a few minutes watching Mark's sleeping face, grey beneath the dark stubble, the skin tight, two vertical lines etched between the brows. As though sensing her gaze he stirred, opening his eyes, and she leaned across to gently kiss his mouth, murmuring, 'Wake up sailor, we've reached harbour at last!'

They were too late for dinner, but an understanding barman made them sandwiches, which they ate washed down with lukewarm beer, sitting close together in the deserted snug, each busy with their own thoughts. Mark, although desperate to have Joanna in his arms, was troubled by a conscience he hadn't until recently known he possessed, while Joanna, although equally eager to *be* in his arms was beginning to have second thoughts. Suppose he realised the assurance of her sexual experience was based on nothing more than that one brief and not very successful coupling on a far off Oxford night, with a boy who had proved as awkward and unskilled as herself? The man she was now proposing to go to bed with was no hesitant, clumsy student, but a very real, very grown-up man, used she was quite sure, to far more sophisticated and skilled bedfellows than herself.

The meal over, they climbed the creaking oak staircase to their room under the eaves. Relieved when Mark left her to bathe and shave his sprouting beard, Joanna curled up on the cushioned window seat of their room and watched the full moon riding high in the sky, wondering again what he was really thinking about her engineering of this time together; sensing reluctance still in his guarded acceptance of her arrangements.

'I'm not free and light years too old for you,' he'd said on their arrival as he took their cases from the car. 'I do want you desperately, my darling. But don't you see it's all *wrong;* the wrong time, the wrong place –'

She had interrupted him, shaking her head, saying stubbornly, 'But the right people and that's *all* that matters.' And he had given way. Now here they were, completely alone at last and she had absolutely no idea of what to expect of him, or how she would manage the next few hours. When the door opened she turned, shivering and rubbing her hands over her cold arms; trying to read the message in those tired eyes.

With a towel wound about his waist and hair still wet from the shower he crossed the room and dropping onto the wide canopied bed sprawled face down. 'Give me a minute!' he murmured thickly and burying his head in the pillow was in seconds deep in exhausted sleep.

'Well, I'll be damned!' Relieved of her immediate anxiety she gave a nervous giggle. Undressing quickly she slipped the silk nightdress borrowed from Monica over her head, then eased carefully into bed beside him, pulling the sheet over them both. He groaned and rolled over onto his back and for an hour she lay, watching his face, calmed and softened in repose, the frown lines between his brows smoothed and fainter now, until she too drifted into sleep, her head against his shoulder and one arm flung across his chest.

* * *

In the pale light of early morning he awoke and drew her sleepy body closer against his with a whispered, 'Is it really you?'

'Umm…' She wound her arms about his neck; the slip of satin against his skin brought him wide awake and he began to trail his fingers down her neck and over her body. She opened her eyes and he watched them darken with a mixed question and invitation that had his blood racing. 'Too many clothes!' he murmured and she sat, letting him draw the nightdress over her head, then in sudden confusion clasped her hands across her breast.

'Oh, Joanna Felicity Dunne,' with a tender inward chuckle he laid her back on the pillows, 'what a terrible little fibber you've turned out to be,' he murmured, 'you are about as experienced as a postulant nun…'

Later, when at last they lay quiet again, he leaned to kiss her mouth. 'You lied to me a little, didn't you darling?' he asked, smoothing the damp hair back from her forehead and smiling down on her face still flushed with the aftermath of passion. 'Just how often *have* you made love before?'

'Ah!' She turned her head away. 'Only once – and it was nothing like *that*!'

He smiled. 'You are a bad girl, Joanna Felicity to tell me such a fib, but you were quite wonderful and I think, no, I *know* that I love you.'

'Not as much as I love you; that would be impossible.'

'Ah, but there are so many parts of *you* to love,' he began to count on her fingers. 'I love your beautiful body; I love the skin and the flesh, the bone and the very soul of you, and I want to go on loving you for the rest of my life.'

She traced her finger across his lips. 'Is that all?'

'You want more?' Pulling her towards him he fastened his mouth on hers. 'Well I never,' he murmured after a very long kiss, 'would you believe it? Here we go again!'

With his sleeping head cradled against her breast Joanna watched the sun creep through the casement windows and wondered just what she had been so worried about.

* * *

They drifted through the days and nights. Sleeping and eating; walking on sunlit mornings through the peaceful green water meadows; at evening treading the narrow winding streets of the city, ending in a crowded pub with tiny bars and Scotch under the counter for anyone in uniform. Returning late to their quiet room, to satisfy again and again the craving that now haunted and consumed them both, they were lost in a world far from war, and the separation and heartbreak that parting again must inevitably bring.

Joanna, discovering in herself a passion and appetite for love she had never imagined possible, found in Mark's arms such ecstasy and fulfilment that she wondered how it would be to return again to a sterile, comfortless bed; one that held no warmly exciting and excited body to turn to in the deep reaches of the night.

It was painful to pack again after just three short days and return to a town now gearing itself grimly for a conflict grown suddenly immediate and menacing.

'I'll get a message to you if I can leave ship at any time.' Mark turned to her as she stopped the car in a quiet side street beside the docks. 'We shall be laid up here for a few more days before we move along into another berth for *Miranda*'s repairs and wait to take on new personnel.'

With a pang, he thought of young Evans then resolutely blotted the image from his mind. 'I imagine it will be straight on to convoy duties after that, so God knows when we shall again have any real time together.'

She put her arms about him. 'Just come back. Whenever, or however doesn't matter. I shall be here.'

He kissed her once more before breaking away with a breathless,

'God keep you!'

She smiled, 'You always say that.'

'I mean it.' He kissed her again then stepping from the car bent to salute her. 'Take care, Joanna Dunne.'

She watched him walk away; blinking back sudden tears she re-started the engine and drove the car back to the garage, dreading the return to quarters and her narrow, lonely bed.

* * *

Three weeks later she stood at her window, watching the *Miranda* and her sister ship the *Chloe* leave port to make their rendezvous with the main convoy. As the Commander came through from his office she moved quickly away from the window and back to her desk.

'Miss Jones said to remind you that you have a meeting with Vice-Admiral Stewart at noon, sir. The papers are in your brief-case on the filing cabinet.'

Alec Naughton looked at her tightly controlled face and hurumphed noisily. 'I've got used to you, Miss Dunne.' His voice was gruff, 'but your SO is asking when she can have you back.'

Joanna's heart sank, but she kept her voice steady.

'I'm ready whenever you say, sir.'

He cleared his throat again. 'Of course, you could stay, I suppose. I'm in need of a good right hand; one who isn't scared half to death or takes umbrage every time I shout, like Miss Jones who has requested a transfer ASAP!'

Startled, she looked up.

'I'd like that very much, sir, but I'm not senior enough.'

'You want to try putting in for that other ring on your sleeve then, don't you?' he made it sound like a threat. 'When did you join the Service?'

'November, 'thirty-nine, sir,' she added dryly, 'It seemed a good idea at the time.'

'Then you'll soon have served long enough to be entitled to it…with my recommendation.'

'Thank you, Commander; I should like very much to stay with you.' She looked up innocently. 'But may I remind you that you are going to be late for your meeting?'

'Then don't stand around nattering and wasting my time,' he snarled, 'and where've you hidden my bloody brief case?'

She smiled as he swept out, banging the glass partition door and sending a couple of files balanced on a shelf crashing to the floor.

She'd certainly be earning that extra piece of braid if and when she got it! But even without it, if she stayed and made herself indispensable, there would be no return ever to that old cow in Charts. Now she would be able legitimately to watch the plot and follow the progress of all the convoys leaving from Tollmouth. In future she would know exactly where the *Miranda* was at sea, and everything that happened to her before she made port again, although whether that knowledge would prove to be a good or bad thing only time would tell.

4

Singapore, July 1940

'Dougie darling … it's from Mark … he wants a divorce – imagine, after all this time!' Vivienne turned from the dressing table, dangling the letter between disdainful fingers. 'Well, really. The rotter wouldn't play when I wanted it years ago.'

Douglas Payne shrugged himself into the white evening jacket held ready by a silent Malay servant. 'I dare say he's found himself a bit of fluff who won't give in without a ring on her finger. I don't see why the blighter wants to stir things up now – and I'm not being dragged through the muck after all this time just so's he can make an honest woman of his latest tottie!' He dismissed the servant with an impatient wave. 'Did you know he'd been romping with Arthur Chiltern's missus while she was in Weymouth?' he demanded. 'Damned man; let him whistle for his divorce. I should think he's got enough possible co-respondents scattered about the South of England for you to divorce *him* and leave me out of it.'

'You don't know Mark. His women aren't likely to tell on him and he can be as stubborn as a mule.'

'What you ever saw in the man is a mystery to me,' he grumbled, 'dull as ditch water...mucking around with a load of animals in that God-forsaken place.'

'Well, he was rather sweet; and so good-looking and sexy.' She sighed. 'But yes, you're right; dull, out of bed anyway; but he had potential.'

'Hah!'

'But he did!' She returned crossly, annoyed at this expression of disbelief. 'Daddy thought the world of him and was ready to set him up with the perfect practice in Knightsbridge. But would he? No!' She picked up a buffer and began to polish her nails with swift, impatient strokes, 'Said he'd no intention of wasting his life in ministering to a load of farting Pekinese and constipated flat cats.'

'Flat cats? Why should they be flat?' The slightly protuberant blue eyes were puzzled. Vivienne allowed her own lids to flutter momentarily heavenward.

'Cats who live in flats, Dougie darling.'

'Oh, I *see;* ha, ha, quite funny!'

She studied him dispassionately, noting the swelling paunch, the tight cummerbund. That pink spot on top of his head was marginally larger than six months ago and he really wasn't all that bright out of the boardroom. Still, life in Singapore was very attractive and Dougie a steadfast lover, who happily pandered to her every whim and fancy.

She had a sudden vision of Mark as he had been eight years ago, when they'd first met at Millie Brampton's party. Like a Greek god and they'd had their clothes off almost before the introductions were finished. A pity the excitement and passion had faded so quickly. His attraction for her had been purely that of the sexual animal, but once he had whisked her off to Cornwall and she was reduced to the role of wife to a rural vet she'd soon tired of marriage. A couple of years at Porthryn had seen the limit of her endurance...he smelled of animals and disinfectant. Too disgusting!

And his *friends*! She wrinkled her nose at the memory. God, but they'd been boring, apart from that sexual athlete Josh Milton over at Penmarrion. If she hadn't been a little afraid of her husband's intimidating eyes that missed nothing, Josh might very well have succeeded in getting her into his bed.

It would all have been so different if only Mark had taken up Daddy's offer, but he'd been stubborn as always, refusing even to give it a try.

She turned again to the mirror, studying herself carefully: the splendid violet eyes, lovely cheekbones and flawless skin, the fine lines hidden under careful make-up: she flicked back her dark shoulder-length hair and lifted her chin. She sighed. Nudging thirty-two was no joke in this climate; she would have to see that divine little Indian doctor tomorrow and get some more of his special lotion.

Engrossed in her narcissistic musings, she absently crumpled her husband's letter and let it fall to the floor, where the servant would find and burn it next morning with the rest of the rubbish.

* * *

The Mediterranean, July 1940

My darling Joanna,

I've had no answer from Vivienne yet, Mark wrote, *but that doesn't surprise me. I'm leaving it all to Arthur Hallam my solicitor now. It will happen, sweetheart, but is bound to be a slow business and at some time in the future we shall have to beware the King's Proctor and be very careful_about our meetings. I'm not having your name dragged through some dreary court.*

I miss you so, and ache for your sweet body and all the wonderful, exciting things it does to mine, but I think you probably know the effect you have on me without being told.

Your letters...three together – arrived yesterday. Really, darling they brought a blush to my cheek, so that even our new midshipman noticed and asked if I needed a glass of water. I never knew Wren slang could be so informative; what a bad girl you are...

* * *

Joanna lived for such letters. The days dragged and the weeks passed without the *Miranda* putting into her homeport. The air raids, sporadic at first along the Hampshire coast increased; at first in daylight then later through the hours of darkness as well and sleep became impossible as the roar of guns rivalled the scream and explosion of falling bombs. Joanna worried ceaselessly about her mother in London, stubbornly driving her Red Cross ambulance through the raids that cut a nightly swathe of fire and destruction across the capital.

Their working quarters on the dockside suffered extensive incendiary damage and Headquarters were moved well beyond the port to a heavily sandbagged semi-basement in what had been a girls' school. Here everyone began a troglodyte existence, where the only sight of daylight and relief from the smell of brick dust and wet sand was found in the brief dash between raids for a snatched scratch meal, followed by a few hours of attempted sleep whilst the walls of their quarters shook around them.

'We must have done something awful to deserve this!' complained Monica after one particularly devastating night when they'd managed no more than an hour's sleep apiece, and that spent huddled into the basement shelter, ' but for the life of me I can't figure out what.'

'Next week when our forty-eight is due we'll both go up to mother's place.' promised Joanna, 'There are marvellous posh shelters in the basement of Gordon Mansions – with a *bar*, would you believe? – so we should be able to get a decent night's sleep, even if we have to spend all our pay getting pissed to achieve it.'

'And we can have coffee at Peter Jones and tea at Fortnum's!' Monica clasped her hands in prayer. 'Oh, Lord love us,' she exclaimed fervently, 'but I'd rather die trying on hats in Harvey Nicks than depart this world under a bomb with Tollmouth written on it.

That would be too sordid for words!'

* * *

Audrey Dunne welcomed them both with an abstracted kiss and instructions on fixing the blackout frames, before departing to drive her ambulance.

'So noisy out there, darlings and terribly bad for the hearing!' she complained as she carefully damped and shaped plugs of cotton wool to fit into her ears. 'Now if you want to eat later just go along to Jerome's. He's moved the restaurant down into his cellar so one can eat in peace. If you hear me come in late don't bother to get up and don't worry,' she looked at her daughter's raised eyebrow, 'Leo will be gone long before *you* are awake.'

Joanna put her feet up on the cream leather couch and rolled her eyes at Monica. 'Who is he, Aud,' she asked, 'some big-wig in the War Office, with a paunch and a Colonel Blimp moustache?'

'No, darling ... and do take your feet off that couch. He's quite a famous surgeon now, but I knew him years ago when he was still a struggling junior hospital doctor, with a stingy allowance from his father but enough charm to get him almost anything he wanted.'

'Including you?'

'Not at that time!' She looked faintly scandalised. 'I was only sixteen; in my day nice girls didn't do that sort of thing.' She sighed. 'I was crazy about him but he fell for someone else and married terribly young. After I met your father we lost touch until very recently. I suppose a little of the old magic and certainly a lot of the old charm is still there; but he can't afford a scandal so we are very discreet. I'm not even going to tell you his name because you'd know it at once...he's operated on Royalty, you know!'

'Wow!' Joanna opened her eyes wide. 'What's his speciality, Proctology?'

'Don't be coarse.' Audrey paused in the act of putting on her cap to give her an appraising and suddenly shrewd look. 'You used not to be quite so outspoken, nor so interested in your mother's private life.'

'Yes, well.' Joanna grinned. 'I'm a big girl now and allowed to be nosy about your sordid goings-on.'

'You *are* getting coarse; I think we should have a little talk before you go back to that dreadful place.'

'Now you're for it!' Observed Monica solemnly as the flat door closed behind her hostess. 'Wait until she worms out of you all about your shenanigans with your Number One! I can hardly wait.'

Giggling, they put up the blackout and after rummaging in the all the likely places and drawing blanks, eventually found Audrey's supply of black market gin hidden in the ornamental coal scuttle. An hour later, just as the sirens began to wail they sprinted along the Cromwell Road, to sit in Jerome's basement and eat steak smothered in mustard sauce, with *pommes frites* that melted in the mouth. Then replete and far from sober returned in the midst of an extremely noisome air raid to the welcoming safety of the shelter beneath Gordon Mansions.

* * *

'Where is Lady Monica this morning?'

Audrey floated into breakfast on a tide of Chyphre perfume, her hair tied up in a blue chiffon scarf and wearing a silk negligee that would have had Joan Crawford chewing the carpet. She looked, thought Joanne admiringly, quite incredible for a fifty-something woman who had been driving an ambulance half the night and doubtless spending the rest of it doing God only knew what else with darling Leo.

'She's no lady just an honourable. She had breakfast early and went out with one of her guardsmen cousins. We're meeting for lunch at one.' Joanna leafed disparagingly through a pile of pre-war fashion magazines. 'God – these look as though they came out of the ark – don't we have papers delivered any more, Audrey?'

'Goodness, no, I haven't time to read them.' She gave her daughter a deprecatory glance. 'Do send for the porter and get that uniform pressed darling, it looks as though you've slept in it.'

'I did. You must have noticed, even if you *were* busy with darling Leo, that there was one hell of a raid last night. We slept in the shelter and I have not yet got to the stage where I'll take my clothes off in front of fifty or so complete strangers; not the sort who live in South Kensington, anyway.'

Her mother bit into a triangle of Melba toast. She asked, 'Who is he Joanna?'

Joanna narrowed her eyes. 'Who is who?'

'*Whom;* the man, with *whom* you are sleeping,' Audrey selected another piece of toast. 'Please don't look at me as though you are about to use some alarming piece of Naval vulgarity in denial. I know you much too well.'

'Why do you want to know?' Joanna hedged, 'you've never bothered about anyone before.'

'Oh!' she waved her hand airily, 'I doubt that you've ever slept with any of your young men, apart from that scruffy little undergraduate with the beard – and I assume you only went to bed with *him* to see what it was like. But this one, whoever he is, seems to have had quite an effect on you.'

'Well...' Joanna began, and her mother raised pained brows.

'Must you begin your sentences like that?'

'Yes, well ... Oh hell, why do you always get me rattled, Aud?' She was exasperated. 'Look, I've no intention of going into any more intimate details of him than you have of your old boy friend. He's a Navy Lieutenant on an escort ship. We had one perfectly splendid long weekend leave together and a few odd nights since. I love him madly and he loves me. But he's knocking on a bit and married and his wife's bunked it to Singapore with a rich silk exporter and doesn't seem too keen on rushing to give him a divorce. Will that do for now?'

'My dear, with so many obstacles in the way of a walk down the aisle, I do hope that you, he, or both, are taking all possible precautions.'

Joanna began to laugh.

'Oh, Audrey, you really are the limit; of course we're being careful. I thought you were going to go all old-fashioned and snooty on me!'

'I suppose I should.' She sighed then looked up, giving a sudden enchanting smile. 'Oh, be happy, darling. And what does age matter? The ten years difference between your father and me didn't. The time we had together was wonderful, and I should still have spent it with him even if he'd been drawing his pension and was a bigamist to boot.'

Joanna was moved but not foolish enough to show it. She grinned and raised her eyebrows. 'Well, mine's a bit more than that, but what about your Leo? he sounds a real old *roue*'

'Oh darling, he's very sweet and an absolute love, but when that sort of man has a wife and family he will always put them first, which is absolutely right.' She sighed again. 'However, when he is in London all week and she is in the country, well, all these air raids do rather get the adrenaline running, don't they?'

Joanna nodded. '*C'est la Guerre*!' Say no more, mother dear. I quite understand.'

*　　*　　*

'Not in a million years,' said Monica, 'could I have that sort of conversation with *my* mother. You are lucky.'

'Aren't I, though; and good luck to her with darling Leo whoever he may be; Audrey has had quite a few boy friends over the years without, unlike your mother, inflicting any of them on me as a stepfather, and this Leo is the first to get as far as the bedroom, I can tell you that. She's no home-breaker so he's nothing to fear on that front. All the same, if he ever makes her really unhappy, I'll have his bloody hide.'

'You *have* changed.' Her friend regarded her thoughtfully. 'Actually you know, in the beginning when we were at Greenwich, I thought you were really quite a stuck-up, toffee-nosed bitch.'

'I probably was, but coming from a fully-fledged, paid-up debutante from Cheltenham Ladies College I take that as a compliment!'

* * *

The last train to Tollmouth appeared to be in no hurry to arrive at its destination. Leaving an hour and a half late and to the wail of sirens it then stopped and started half-a-dozen times before finally being diverted into a siding, there to stay for the remaining hours of darkness. As bombs and incendiaries rained down Joanna and Monica cowered on the gritty floor of their carriage playing poker with a couple of Canadian sailors, all four trying not to show how terrified they were.

Weary and strained, with no time even for a quick tidy and change of shirt Joanna, in a vain attempt to reach her desk before the Commander, might just have made it if she had not had the misfortune to collide on the staircase with a shore-bound Rear Admiral, who spent fifteen precious minutes telling her she was a disgrace to the Service, being improperly dressed with a grubby collar and one button undone. Eventually dismissing her with the bellowed order to '*Walk*, blast it woman, and not tear around like a blue-arsed fly!' he stomped off, leaving Joanna wilting and hanging onto the banister.

'And just what the hell time do you call this?' snarled the Commander as she hurtled through the office door and bolted behind her desk. 'I've been scouring the place for you – I can't find those reports for this morning's meetings in your bloody awful filing system!'

'Sorry, sir, I was delayed by Admiral Barclay.'

'What did he want – to know the way to his office?' his eyes snapped. 'If you must chat up every damned old fool in the building, do it in your own time, not the Navy's – and when you've found those reports do something about your face and your blasted uniform; you look like the wrath of God!' He left, slamming the door behind him.

Shaking with fury and close to tears she swore with unaccustomed profanity and vigour, 'Sodding bloody Navy...bastard bloody men!' She hitched her behind onto the corner of her desk, complaining aloud to an empty room. 'None of the buggers ask 'Why?' do they – just go straight for the jugular; bastards, all of them!'

She yelped in fright and leaped to her feet as the Commander flung the door open again to glare at her across the room.

'You officially have your promotion as from now. Not that you deserve it after this morning's showing!'

She stuck her chin in the air, daring to inject rather more than a faint hint of sarcasm into her reply. 'Thank *you,* sir!'

He stared at her for a moment then lowered his head like a bull about to charge. 'Miss Dunne, just what is the matter with you this morning?'

'Nothing sir. Absolutely nothing.'

'Then get that damned insubordinate expression off your face.'

Exasperation overtook discretion and drawing herself up to her full five foot eight and a half she glared over his shoulder at a poster informing her to Keep Mum and Remember That Walls Have Ears. Ho, do they, she thought, well listen to this, old cock...

She took a deep breath. 'Sir, I have been travelling all night because Jerry was bombing the train lines to hell. On arriving at HQ I was held up and torn off a strip...several strips in fact, by Admiral Barclay for being both improperly dressed and in a hurry. Now you've just told me I don't deserve the somewhat delayed promotion for which *you* put me forward. So yes, I am just the tiniest bit cross, *Sir.*'

'Anything else, Miss Dunne?' he queried, dangerously mild, 'before I send you back to your old post.'

Oh, God, she thought dismally. I've just insulted the most bloody-minded old so-and-so in the building and cut my own blasted throat! Suddenly deflated she looked down at the floor. 'No sir.'

'Are you quite sure about that?'

'Yes sir – and I do apologise.'

'So you damned well should.' He swung towards the door snarling, 'Better read the memo on your desk and do something about it before you clear off back to Charts.'

She looked down, focusing through a blur of angry tears on the slip of paper on the blotter.

Memo to: Third Officer J.F. Dunne

From: Lieut. D.L. Eden, First Lieutenant H.M.S. Miranda

Ship docked 0.600 hrs this morning. Desperate sailor will rendezvous at Trafalgar House at 19.00 hrs pip emma, for re-fuelling and close inspection of favourite female personnel.

He halted at the door and turned. 'You have my permission to clean up and go to breakfast,' he said gruffly, 'and tell that damned impertinent Number One of yours when you see him, *not* to send his snotty delivering such deplorably suggestive love notes in the Navy's time to my newly appointed Second Officer. Because you were late I opened all the mail, including that one. I'm not a bloody cretin but even one of those could read between the lines. Understood?'

'Aye aye, sir.'

'And get that other ring on your sleeve.'

'Aye aye, sir.' She tried hard to keep a straight face but her mouth wouldn't co-operate.

He held her gaze for a moment, then as he turned to go growled over his shoulder, 'Don't touch the kippers, they're totally bloody inedible!'

5

Tollmouth, August 1940

'Where can we go?' Breathless, she pulled back from Mark's embrace. 'Oh, Lord, but I wish I could take another forty-eight, but I've been at home all weekend and I dare not risk being late back tonight.'

'It's all right. I'll see you delivered back safe and sound. I have four days and I've booked in at the George just along the coast. Far enough away from prying eyes and hopefully, the attention of the Luftwaffe; quickly, we have to find a taxi or I may ravish you right here on the pavement!'

Displaying a rare sensitivity not often found in taxi drivers, the cabbie closed the glass partition and averted his gaze from the couple on his back seat. Keeping his eyes on the road and his mouth shut he drove them out of the town to their destination in the quiet little fishing village along the coast; rewarded for his discretion by a generous tip and the request to return at ten thirty sharp for the journey back to Tollmouth.

They went through the civilised performance of eating dinner. Tasting nothing, all the while touching hands and making love with their eyes. The meal over they walked past the dragoness at reception, Mark daring her with a look to comment on their climb together up the creaking wooden stairs to his small room, well away from the restaurant and dance floor below.

He turned the key in the lock then took her in his arms. 'I can't tell you how I've longed for this; how much I've wanted and needed you.'

His voice shook and his hands trembled as he slid them down the length of her body, pulling her hard against him, helpless against the sweeping tide of desire.

After the weeks apart it was this overwhelming this urgent this impossible to wait.

'Slow down!' Her own voice was unsteady; she reached up and began to unlace his tie.

'I can't!' He moved her backwards towards the bed. 'It's been too long. I want you now.'

He lifted her onto the covers and then knelt above her, tugging impatiently at her tie and shirt buttons. She pushed her hands against his chest. 'Why are you holding me off?' he demanded, his eyes suddenly stormy.

'I'm not. I just don't want any of the old Navy-style "wham, bang, thank you ma'am"!' With an expression of innocent inquisitiveness she began slowly to unbutton his jacket. 'Now simmer down and just let me get *your* clothes off, sir, then you can do the same for me. When we've done all that we'll compare notes and see which of us is most ready, shall we?'

* * *

'I love you.'

'Don't sound so surprised!' She stroked tender fingers over his hair and neck as he lay, his legs still twinned about hers, his dark head half-turned into the pillow.

'You know the old one about the earth moving?' The words were muffled.

'Of course,' there was laughter in her voice, 'did it for you?'

'Umm...I've just realised I never knew what it meant before. Look out of that window, will you and I'll bet you'll see California. I swear we've spent the last ten minutes on top of the San Andreas Fault!'

'Was that where we were?' She laid her head against his, mocking him gently. 'Well if you stay just where you are, in the one hour and thirty six minutes left to us I should think you could possibly, no definitely, climb back up again and this time stay there rather longer than ten minutes before the next 'quake, don't you?'

* * *

'I've been watching the plot,' she said later, 'you lost a lot of ships.' She shivered, tightening her arms about him. 'Every time the signal came through that you were under attack I died a little.'

'Fortunately, darling, you won't need to do so again before Thursday night. I've booked this room until then. Is there any chance of you having an overnight pass?'

'Oh, God, don't! I'm amazed that after today I'm not permanently confined to quarters for the duration – and I have to do some sewing before tomorrow morning.'

She told him about her misfortunes with the Admiral and the

Commander. The promotion she almost lost.

He laughed and kissed her rueful mouth.

'My poor darling; congratulations on the promotion but you were lucky not to have landed right in it.'

'I know, but don't look so smug. He said that you were damned impertinent, and to stop sending your snotty with suggestive love notes in the Navy's time.'

'The cheeky old bugger!'

'Oh, he shouts a lot, but he's really a sweet old thing.'

'But I'm a lot sweeter.'

'Umm, so you are; prettier too, but isn't it time we started to get dressed before that sour-faced old bat in reception thinks you're taking too long over showing me your etchings?'

He began to browse his lips over her throat, murmuring, 'To hell with the sour-faced old bat, I haven't finished showing you the half of them yet!'

* * *

'I'm going home for a couple of days,' he said, as they were driven back, the dying wail of the All Clear sounding across the town: it wouldn't last but was a welcome sound. 'I'm not deserting you, just going down to see my mother, and Kit before he's posted again. I'll also collect my car. It'll be a lot more convenient to have it here if I manage any more of these flying visits.'

'What about your father? Or haven't you one of those?' she looked at him curiously. 'You never mention him.'

He said shortly, 'Oh, I have one all right, but I only visit when he's out of the way.'

'That sounds a bit odd; not very filial and all that.'

'We don't get on.'

She turned to look at him, surprised at his tone. In the dimness of the cab his expression was closed and unreadable. 'I'm sorry. I didn't mean to pry.'

'It doesn't matter.'

She frowned, 'Then why so secret?'

'No secret: I can't stand him and he feels the same way about me.'

'Why?'

'That, darling, is actually none of your business.'

'That's damned uncivil of you.' She felt her temper rising, 'in fact, it's bloody rude!'

He turned on her the sort of look he might have given an unruly child. 'Shall we just leave it there?'

His continued calm dismissal was infuriating. She thought angrily, I don't like you when you do this to me; aloud she said: 'That's just the sort of stupid put-down I'd get from my old college tutor when she couldn't justify her objection to something I said or did.'

'Well if she was as old as me she probably found your thrusting young inquisitiveness, not to mention your bloody mindedness, highly irritating.'

'That's unfair,' she snapped, 'I didn't think you'd bring up the age thing; and I'm twenty three now, not twelve.'

He didn't answer, but sat back, folding his arms, the ghost of a sigh escaping him, his expression unrelentingly grim.

She felt as though an abyss had opened beneath her feet. What on earth had his father done to him that her innocent question could wipe out all the tenderness and passion and the laughter of the evening and turn him into this stranger? She stole a glance at his profile, unsure whether the uncompromising expression masked hurt or anger.

'Are we having a row?' Her voice shook a little.

Staring with apparent interest at the back of the driver's head he answered distantly, 'I don't think so; it takes two to do that and I certainly have no intention of taking this conversation further.'

She moved into the far corner of the seat, sticking her chin in the air in the gesture he was beginning to know so well; there was a long silence before she said very clearly, 'You're bit of a bastard, aren't you, *sir*?'

Oh, God, he thought, but this is one infuriating woman! 'Come here.' He crooked a finger, and when she had somewhat warily and stiffly closed the gap again, took her into his arms. '"When you call me that, *smile*!"' he drawled.

She relaxed against him and began to laugh.

'You can just stop that,' he growled, 'it isn't everyone who gets away with calling me a bastard and lives to tell the tale!' His mouth twitched. 'How you have the nerve to shift the blame for starting all this nonsense onto me, I'll never know.'

'Ain't that just like a man,' she said, and pulled his mouth down onto hers.

* * *

'Are you thinking of gettin' out, Sir – Miss?' Their cabby gave an apologetic cough, 'only if one of you wants to get back to the 'otel tonight...'

Joanna hastily buttoned her jacket and straightened her tie before leaning forward to give him a conspiratorial smile. 'I hope we can find you again when we need a taxi. I never knew a man who kept his eyes on the road as well as you!'

She ran up the steps of her billet, turning back at the top to blow a kiss before slipping through the door.

Mark met the cabby's eyes in the rear-view mirror; the cabby grinned. 'Nice to be young, innit sir?'

Mark retrieved his cap from the floor; smacking it against his leg to remove the dust he said, 'I imagine it's marvellous,' he leaned back and closed his eyes, 'bloody *marvellous*...I just wish that I was!'

*   *   *

Dorset, August 1940

'Not bad sailing weather for this time of year.' Mark took the dinghy around St Albans Head and set course for home. 'Better get back, though, there's a sea mist coming in.'

'I wonder how much longer we'll be able to sail along the coast like this.' Kit lay back in the stern, the tiller under his good arm, squinting up at the barbed wire along the cliff tops.

'I'm surprised they still let us, but I suppose everyone's given up on the idea that Adolph's going to invade us now.' Mark looked back at him over his shoulder, 'Where might you be going next? Any ideas?'

'Haven't a clue.' Kit rooted under his Guernsey for the pipe and tobacco pouch in his shirt pocket. 'I have to go before another medical board when I get back, but the old Doc doesn't think I'll get passed this time for overseas service. My shoulder hasn't healed all that well yet.'

'That should give you a decent spell with the girl friend.'

Kit looked up over the flame of his match. 'Haven't got one.'

'Oh? I thought you and Alexis Thingummy were...?

He shook his head. 'Had to finish it, she was after my body and I couldn't let her have it!'

'Couldn't you, you know, take the old dog collar off?'

'Afraid she wanted off more than my collar. No Mark, unlike you, I have to set my limits; can't go jumping in and out of bed now. The Bishop wouldn't like it.'

'The Bishop isn't likely to get it,' returned Mark, 'but, Kito, that's one hell of a way to have to live.'

He grinned. 'There are ways of spending one's leisure time other than in bed. You should try some of them.'

When he didn't answer, Kit stirred him with his foot. 'Come on, tell me!'

'What?'

'Why you've been wearing that disgusting, dopey, pleased expression ever since you arrived yesterday. Bertie Morley's lady still missing him is she, and looking for a replacement now he's in Egypt?'

Annoyed, Mark felt himself blush. For pity's sake, he thought, I should have got past doing that by now! He cleared his throat.

'No, but if you get a chance will you go and see someone for me?'

'Depends. Who? What? Where?'

'A girl, a very special girl; I want to bring her down to see Ma when I get the chance, but the *Miranda* will be off again soon and it could be a long time before I have another leave. If you're likely to be around for a while I'd just feel happier if you could see her from time to time. Not that I don't trust *her;* it's the other blokes I don't trust!' He gave a wry smile. 'When you meet her you'll know why.'

'A *girl* – a bit out of your league Mark,' Kit eyed him carefully, 'and what do you mean by 'very special'?'

'I mean that I am completely and utterly in love with someone more than twelve years my junior. I'm not asking you to approve, just to look out for her.'

'I neither approve nor disapprove. Not today anyway. See? No dog collar!'

'Look, I made a mess of things with Vivienne.' Mark held up his hands at his brother's derisive snort. 'I know; you don't have to say it. You warned me; everyone warned me...'

'Yeah, you really made a mess of that one, didn't you? I suppose you've already got this one into bed. Let's hope you aren't making another costly mistake.'

'I didn't seduce her, if that's what you mean,' Mark was angry. 'In fact I tried damned hard not to go as far as that.'

'Just did the old mature charmer bit: a little light flirting, an amusing kiss or two. You forget; I've watched you doing it for years.'

Mark winced. 'That's a bit below the belt.'

'So are most of your affairs.'

'I don't have affairs, just brief encounters, or I did have before Joanna.' He stared at his brother, antagonism stirring in his eyes. 'Don't judge me Kit. I do enough of that for myself. I'm not proud of my record but I'm damned if I'll be a hypocrite and say I'm sorry for the way I've lived my life so far. We can't all be saints.'

'If that's a cheap jibe at me, you couldn't be more wrong. Wearing my collar back to front doesn't make me immune you know. My randy past frequently beckons.'

'Sorry. I'm sorry. I don't even know why I'm telling you all this, except that I need to make you understand how important Joanna is to me. I'm going ahead with divorcing Vivienne and when that's all cleared up we will marry. Joanna loves me in spite of all I've been and actually wants to spend the rest of her life with me.'

'Told her all about you and father, have you?'

His brother scowled. 'No I have not. I won't have her dragged into that.'

'She doesn't know all you've been then, does she?' Kit made an impatient gesture. 'For God's sake, Mark; at least be honest with yourself.'

'I've told you, just leave it alone. I want to start clean with Joanna, but that doesn't include having my nose rubbed on father's toe caps – again.'

He stooped suddenly to fiddle with a perfectly tied shoelace, his voice sounding flat and tired. 'I'm not asking for you or anyone else to approve of my private life. Just, while I'm away, whether for a few weeks or months, or for good, look after her for me, Kit, please. Look after her.'

'So it's really happened to you at last, has it?' For a long moment Kit looked at his bent head, before saying gently, 'Welcome back into the real world; painful, isn't it?'

Mark grinned wryly.

'Very!'

* * *

'Take care, darling,' Mary Eden kissed her eldest son, holding his face between her hands for a moment before letting him go. 'Come back as soon as you can.' She smiled. 'And next time bring her with you!'

He raised his eyebrows. 'Kit's been blabbing, has he?'

'No, darling, your eyes have been giving you away ever since you arrived.'

'I'll bring her some time, I promise,' he kissed her again then turned to grasp his brother's hand. 'Write me. Let me know what's happening...to everyone'

'I will,' Kit grinned. 'Keep your eyes skinned for those U-boats.'

He stood with his mother at the door as together they watched the

Riley out of sight down the driveway.

'I won't worry.' she smiled brightly, clutching the handkerchief in her pocket, determined not to weep. 'He'll be all right, I just feel he will.'

'He may possibly manage to dodge all the submarines,' Kit answered laconically, putting an arm about her shoulders, 'but he'll be damned lucky to survive if father ever catches up with him again. The blighter's just pinched all his petrol coupons!'

* * *

Mark knocked on the door marked 'Section Officer J.F. Dunne, Operations' and poked his head cautiously around the edge. Joanna sat alone at her desk, looking up with a quick frown until she saw who it was, then stood and came towards him smiling.

He stayed at the door, just for the pleasure of watching her walk across the room toward him. He said, 'If anyone comes, I'm here to look at the plot and find out who's been doing what and how and to whom, while I've been away!'

'That won't wash with my boss should he find you in here, the Plot Room is at the other end of the building.' She pulled him into the room. Closing the door and leaning back against it, she put her arms about his neck, lifting her face for his kiss.

He obliged enthusiastically before asking, 'Do you always look at people that way when they interrupt your work?'

'Quite often, because some only come to look at my legs.'

'Tell me who and I'll – '

Footsteps sounded in the corridor. Quickly she motioned him away from the door and snatched a folder from the filing cabinet.

'I'll take you through to show you the plot in a moment, sir.' She said in clear, business-like tones then as the door opened added smoothly, 'Good afternoon, Commander, did you want to take the papers for the Admiral now, sir?'

'I might as well if they're ready, but of course they are, or you wouldn't be standing around doing nothing, would you?' He took the folder then looked at Mark, who had straightened to attention, 'What are you doing in this office, Lieutenant?'

'I'm just back from leave, sir. Thought I'd see the plot and check up on a few things.'

'Well you're in the wrong place for that, aren't you?'

'Er, yes, sorry, sir.'

'What's your ship?'

Mark hesitated. 'The *Miranda*, sir.'

The commander stared at him for a moment, and then transferred his gaze to Joanna, whose own eyes looked guilelessly back. He jerked his head toward Mark. 'Don't tell me, his name's Eden. Couldn't he have sent a memo as usual?'

'I think his Midshipman is busy on board, sir.'

'Hmm.' He tucked the folder under his arm. 'I shan't be back before you're off duty, Miss Dunne. Make sure you wind things up here before you hand over.'

'Yes sir.'

He made to leave then turned at the door to stab a bony finger at Mark.

'I want her back here at o-eight-thirty hours tomorrow, wide-awake and fit for work. Understood?'

'Aye, aye, sir.'

As the door closed Mark sagged against the cabinet, eyes shut, one hand mopping his forehead the other clutching dramatically at his heart.

'What are you sweating for?' she asked. 'I told you: he's just an old sweetie.'

* * *

'Time to go again,' Mark shook her gently, hating to disturb her sleep; but the hands of his watch were at six-thirty and she mustn't be late.

She groaned softly and turned in his arms. 'Tell me the war is over and I don't have to get up until Christmas!'

'The war is over and you don't have to get up until Christmas,' he repeated dutifully.

She smiled, still keeping her eyes closed, 'Liar.'

'I'll run you a bath.'

'If you are supposed to be heading for the bathroom,' she murmured a few minutes later, 'why are you still doing what you are in this bed?'

He raised his head. 'Just keeping your thermostat ticking over, darling; it's cold out there.'

Firmly, she pushed him away and he rolled groaning and shivering to the floor, missing the minuscule rug and landing with his feet on the cold linoleum.

Still only half-awake, he headed for the door, growling and grumbling, 'If we're to come here often I'll buy them a ruddy carpet.'

'Mark.'

He halted. 'Yes?'

She sat up and threw him his dressing gown. 'For God's sake put that on in case you meet some old biddy in the corridor who has never seen anything like it before!' grinning, she watched him go then stretching and yawning reached for her own robe.

Another day another separation; how long this time, she wondered and how did they both still manage to laugh when every parting brought such pain. She closed her eyes as the hot tears gathered. *This is always the worst part, when the awful knot comes in the stomach and the pain starts deep inside, to nag and tear at the heart and guts until that moment when I can hear his voice again, feel his arms about me, and his body lying with mine...*

She left the warm bed and the imprint of his head on the pillow. Gathering sponge, towel and clothes into her arms and forcing her mind to focus on the day ahead, she left the room without a backward glance.

Work was the only panacea for this pain. When she stepped through the door of Naval Headquarters she would cease to be the Joanna Dunne who had lain in her lover's arms throughout the night, becoming, by some supreme act of will, the Miss Dunne who was efficiently reliable, always in control of her emotions and ready to deal with any situation that might arise.

She would watch Mark do the same: putting on with his uniform the air of authority, that imperturbable rocklike calm; leaving behind the younger, loving, not always so calm Mark, and replacing him with the *Miranda*'s older and sterner Number One. Each time they parted now was like a little death. She would only truly live again when, and if, he came back to her. But there was no time now for tears. They were a luxury she could only allow herself after he had gone.

Lifting her chin she went to meet the day.

6

Tollmouth, December 1940

'I wonder if you can help me; I'm looking for a Second Officer Dunne.'

Monica turned from closing the door of her quarters and looked down at the man who stood on the pavement below. Hell's teeth, she thought irreverently, I didn't know chaplains came in that sort of package – and wasn't there something familiar about that lean, dark face and the appraising grey eyes?

Smiling her devastating debutante smile, she descended the steps in a way that would have sent any C.P.O. at Greenwich into a screaming fit. On closer inspection she saw the eyes were rather more blue than grey and they crinkled now in the most engaging fashion. Trust Joanna, she mused without rancour, first the best-looking Looty in Tollmouth and now a dishy vicar…' she smiled again. 'I'm afraid you are out of luck, sir. She is on duty until eighteen-hundred.'

'I think we should drop the formality,' he touched his collar. 'I'm really only masquerading as an officer, you know.'

'Oh good, I'm terribly bad at all that sort of thing; that's why they hide me in the Dead Files section. But I'm sorry about Joanna. I hope you haven't made a long journey for no good reason.'

The eyes crinkled again. 'That rather depends on whether or not *you* are on duty right now.'

She gave a slow smile. 'Would you by any chance be Mark Eden's brother?'

'How did you guess?'

'It wasn't too difficult. You are quite a lot like him to look at and I recognised the approach.'

He gave a snort of laughter. 'I thought I might take Mark's lady to some reasonable eating-place for lunch, but as she is unavailable I suppose you wouldn't…?' He looked at her enquiringly.

'Oh, but I would. I've caught the dog watch today and have no duties whatsoever until that magic hour. This way, Padre, first right, second left and it's chips with everything!'

Ten minutes later they were seated in Sam's Caff, drinking strong tea and awaiting their gourmet meal of sausage, peas and chips.

'I come to Sam's,' she confided, 'because if my mother saw me here she would have a blue fit, which is by way of being a bonus!'

'That sounds like serious mother-trouble.'

'Oh, I suppose she's not too bad; but she and daddy divorced and I now have a step-papa who looks like a fat Charles de Gaul and is a Lord *and* a Brigadier. My ma is now *seriously* regal.' She looked with mock solemnity at his widening grin. 'And don't laugh; I suspect she even goes to bed in a tiara.'

'What about your father?'

'In Hong Kong, with some floozy, no doubt; he's only a Sir so *she* won't be getting a tiara. We haven't met for years but he sends me very nice cheques for my birthdays and Christmas.'

Kit put his hand over hers. 'Problem parents – a lot of us have them.'

'Do you?'

'No, but my brother does; one parent, anyway.'

She looked into his eyes, a sudden spark of mischief in her own. 'You are still holding my hand,' she whispered, 'and Sam is trying to put our food on the table!'

He blushed and withdrew his hand so quickly that he almost upset her water glass. She gazed at him in delight.

'Gosh, I don't think I've seen a chap blush like that since I kissed a boy called Aubrey Hamilton-Webb at my tenth birthday party! You're not really a bit like Mark, are you?'

*   *   *

'Urgent message for you, ma'am,' the perky little rating dropped an envelope onto Joanna's desk and exited with a sketchy unnecessary salute and a giggle. Joanna looked after her resentfully, feeling half inclined to call her back and tick her off, then shrugged and let it ride. I'm being a miserable cow since Mark went back, she thought. Wondering what unpleasant request might be lurking within the envelope she sighed and picked up her paperknife.

Joanna,

You have a date for tonight, so powder your nose before you leave. Christopher Eden, who is apparently known to his buddies as Kit, will be loitering with intent to take you to dinner. Just remember I saw him first. One Eden is quite sufficient for you to be going on with.

I took him to Sam's for lunch and he didn't bat an eyelid, but I'm sure he would like something more civilised tonight.

Have a nice time...Hon. Mon.'

Now what on earth, wondered Joanna, can Kit Eden possibly want with me?

* * *

She was taken off guard by his resemblance to Mark, feeling her heart give an involuntary thump as he turned at her footsteps, removing his cap with a gesture that immediately made the meeting informal.

'My brother told me to look out for the most beautiful piece of commissioned tottie in Tollmouth and as you are the first down those steps this evening to fit that description...' He spread his hands with almost an actor's grace, 'I need no longer "call upon my soul within the house"'

She gave a somewhat frosty smile. 'Do all the Eden men quote Shakespeare on greeting strange women?'

'I say, did he really?' he laughed, 'the old dog; not from Twelfth Night, I hope, that's my prerogative.'

'No.'

'Let me guess.' His eyes sparkled. 'Could it have been "On such a night as this…"'

'It could and was.'

Dear Lord, he thought, first the delectable Monica, now this; is the whole of the Tollmouth Naval HQ full of stunning women? He let his gaze linger on her face for a few moments then laughed a little awkwardly as she raised inquiring brows.

'Oh, yes – you must be wondering why I'm here. I was ...' involuntarily his eyes slid down her body, 'in the neighbourhood.'

'Which of course is no distance at all as the crow flies from Dorset and you just thought: as I'll be passing Tollmouth I'll go and see Mark's girl.'

'Yes, well, no!' he gave a defeated grin. 'All right, he asked me to come.'

She didn't know whether to be pleased or irritated; was Mark perhaps checking up on her? And this brother of his was a most unlikely looking parson. She hadn't missed his swift removal of at least one layer of her clothing. She gave him an oblique look. 'Oh did he? I can't think why.'

She began to walk down the street, and he fell into step beside her. 'Don't take it out on me. I was only following orders – he's bigger and older than I am. Look,' he stopped and caught at her arm, 'If I buy you dinner, will you call a truce?'

He saw her mouth curve into a smile.

'I think I can manage that.'

'Where shall we go then?'

'The Swan is a good bet. It will probably be horsemeat,' she said gravely, 'but they cook it well.

*   *   *

He sat back from giving their order, looking into those navy blue eyes, thinking again: What a stunner … and that voice!

When she had come down the steps towards him he'd been visited by what was referred to at Theological College as an Impure Thought. Then she smiled and he was visited again, this time by a whole battalion of the damned things. Floundering a little he explained, 'Mark only asked me to come and be sociable, and as I'm in camp at Hayling, which is actually only about five miles as the crow flies, it seemed rather a good idea.'

She remembered the look he'd given her and suppressed a sudden giggle. 'How on earth did *you* manage to become a chaplain, or shouldn't I ask?'

He answered her solemnly. 'Remember how parents used to send the dim-witted sons into the Army or the Church? As Mark got most of the brains and I was already a Cathedral chorister the choice was obvious – until now, when I seem to have managed both!'

'Somehow I can't see you as a conventional vicar taking tea with the Mothers' Union.'

'Neither can I, in fact, I might like to stay in the army, even without a war.'

'Perhaps you should – I hate to think how much trouble you might cause in any Young Wives Club.'

He put himself out to be an engaging companion and Joanna relaxed and began to enjoy his company. She was curious about his encounter with Monica and steered the conversation round to their meeting earlier that day. His eyes took on a thoughtful and definitely predatory expression at the mention of Monica's name.

'Will she be free tomorrow d'you know?'

'She'll be off duty from noon tomorrow until the same time on Monday, and I happen to know she never goes home unless she's *very* broke.'

'Great, I'm here until Sunday. Mind you,' he grinned, 'not every girl is keen to be seen out with a dog collar but I shall take the plunge. A pity none of my lot are likely to see us together, my stock would go up considerably in the mess.'

'Oh, I shouldn't think you need that.'

He looked up at this, delivered as it was in the driest of tones and caught a very shrewd look in those blue eyes.

'Tell me,' she propped her chin on one hand, 'Do all the Eden males put up this smoke screen to hide their real selves? At first sight Mark comes across as a total cad and you play the fool; as Mark can actually be rather a moral stuffed shirt on occasions I'd take a bet that you are also a bit of a fraud!'

'Well deduced, Miss Dunne.' He mimed applause. 'Now tell me which different persona should I take as the real Joanna – the haughty young woman I first met, Monica's friend, or Mark's "special girl"?

'Ah, there you have it – I don't even know that myself,' she laughed. 'I should have known better than to cross swords with you; Mark did warn me.'

'I shall have to have a word with him about that when next we meet.'

'I can't even make a guess at how long that might be,' she looked down, her laughter fading. 'On really bad days I get the horrors and imagine he won't make it back. If that happened, I just don't know how I could go on without him.'

'I heard that almost every day from the wives and girlfriend's of the men before we went to France.' He was suddenly serious. 'There is no easy answer. You just go on living, even if it's only half a life, and believe that sometime, somehow, you will go on again as two.'

'That's a philosophy that I can't yet subscribe to.'

He shook his head, smiling. 'It isn't a philosophy. It's a faith.'

'In that case,' she gave a wry smile, 'I can only say I wish I had it!'

'You probably have, but if not I shall do my duty by Mark, if not God, and keep an eye on you: a task I shall carry out with the greatest possible pleasure.' he assured her and was rewarded by a very satisfactory blush.

7

Dorset, Christmas 1940

'This is the first really "Home" Christmas I've had for years.' Monica put her face up to the lightly falling snow and Kit tightened his hold on her hand. Even through their gloved palms he felt the warmth begin to spread and wondered if she felt it too. It was strange he mused silently, that after an adult lifetime spent pursuing entirely the wrong women, he and Mark each seemed at last to have found the right one.

Although they had met only a half dozen times Monica felt she had known Kit for a great deal longer than four months. At first she'd hesitated when he telephoned and invited her to spend Christmas with his family. She was inexperienced beneath her veneer of sophistication and worried about spending her leave in his company, only accepting when he assured her that it would be open house to at least three or four other assorted service men and women.

On arrival at Stonehams, an old Regency house on the Dorset coast, she'd been instantly put at ease by her welcome. Mary and Lionel Eden were practised hosts, drawing their guests: two Australian airmen, a French army nurse and herself, seamlessly into the festive warmth and welcome of the old house. She'd found an immediate rapport with Kit's mother, although reserving judgement on his father. Primed by Kit not to mention Mark or even Joanna to him; 'Family problems.' Kit had briefly explained, 'if you talk about Joanna you're bound to mention Mark, and it would be *de trop* to even breathe *his* name because pa may explode.' After this Monica had expected someone large and rather intimidating and possibly as ferocious and difficult as Commander Naughton, but the stocky, white-haired Lionel Eden was quietly courteous and had a humorous glint in the depths of his keen blue eyes that quickly reassured her.

With everyone else electing to play cards after the Christmas dinner, she willingly accepted Kit's invitation to a walk around the village before daylight ended, feeling a stir of anticipation when he took her hand.

'We should go back … you'll be frozen,' he said as they returned from their walk, but she shook her head.

'Not yet ... I'd like to see around the garden first; it must be beautiful in summer.'

They walked on across the wide lawns and through a walled kitchen garden, where a stone archway led to a wooden gazebo set in a small shrubbery.

'This looks a bit Hansel and Gretel!' she exclaimed, peering through the latticed windows, then pointed to a gap in the high hedge. 'Where does that lead?'

'To the cliffs, here...' he guided her through, their breath taken by the wind as they stepped from the sheltered garden onto the headland. Below them the sea foamed along the base of the cliffs and high above a few gulls wheeled, crying forlornly in the cold winter air.

Monica shivered and pulled up her coat collar. 'I'm not awfully good at heights.' She blinked snow from her lashes and turned, bright hair framing a face whipped pink by the wind. For a second Kit hesitated, then took her in his arms and did what he'd been thinking about doing for the past four months.

'Well!' She leaned back, looking up into his face with shining eyes. 'Do you think we could do that again?'

He obliged, but aware of an unexpected inexperience in her response to that first kiss, held her loosely as warmth began to spread rapidly from his arms to rather more interesting parts of his anatomy. Taking his mouth from hers he brushed the melting flakes from her face with his gloved hand, 'We'll go into the summerhouse. There's no fire but it's dry and out of the wind.'

She widened her eyes in mischievous inquiry as he led her back through the gap in the hedge. 'Are you to be trusted?'

'Like the Archbishop of Canterbury!' He opened the blade of his penknife, snicking open the lock with an expert twist. She watched him, smiling. 'You've done that before!'

He grinned back over his shoulder. 'I used to come down here to smoke. Pa always blew my head off if I did it in the house.'

He drew her inside and closing the door behind them with his foot, sank down with her into a cushioned cane chair and again sought her mouth, excitement racing through him this time at her ready response.

'Oh-h-h, who taught you to kiss like that?' he asked huskily, his voice full of laughter.

'Just you, I must be a quick learner!'

'What about all your Guardsmen; those gents Joanna so rudely calls the chinless wonder brigade?'

'Ah, *them,*' she giggled. 'Actually, two of them are my cousins; as for any of the others, most of them have no idea what to do with you if you don't play the game their way; I had to slap one of them rather hard once when he jumped me on the back seat of a taxi!'

He said solemnly, 'I promise I will never jump you on the back seat of a taxi.'

'That's a relief. However…' she sat back a little and gave him a gently enquiring look, 'is what you are doing now all part of a chaplain's brief?'

'Possibly not,' he slid his hand through the top of her coat that he'd just unbuttoned, 'but it feels pretty OK to me.'

Willingly she surrendered to what gradually became a mutual exploration: a gentle, undemanding lovemaking, with a promise of passions still to be aroused.

'Umm…' She laid her head against his shoulder. 'This is lovely.' After a few moments she raised her head and cupping both hands about his face asked 'Do you want to sleep with me?'

'Did you expect that I would?'

'I thought you *might* – I mean, everyone seems to feel its OK now because of the war,' for a moment she caught her lower lip between her teeth. 'Actually, I haven't with anyone before but if you wanted I would with you.'

'Good God,' Kit was startled. 'You mustn't go around propositioning men like that!' He put her from him and stood. 'I think we should go back to the house – now.'

'Can we come here again?' she asked as he re-locked the door.

Taking her hand as they turned to retrace their steps across the thin white coverlet of snow he answered, 'Yes, but only while it is still cold enough and uncomfortable enough to save me from jumping you in the back of a summerhouse!'

*   *   *

Mary Eden and her husband stood side by side at the window and watched their return.

At last, thought Mary, first Mark now Kit; with luck she need not have that particular worry about either of them in the future. If only Mark could bring his girl home and share his good fortune with his father.

At last, thought Lionel Eden. Let's hope he won't bugger up his life and mine like his obstinate, bloody-minded brother!

*   *   *

‘Lovely girl, I only hope she can keep him in order,’ he commented as they prepared for bed that night. ‘Where did he meet her, do you know?’

‘In Tollmouth, I believe. She is in the Wrens.’

‘Tollmouth?’ He looked up absently. ‘What on earth was he doing there?’

She began to brush her hair with long, measured strokes. ‘Visiting someone else, I think.’

She watched his reflection in the mirror as he went through the familiar nightly ritual: emptying his pockets into the china dish on the tallboy; dropping his collar studs into the round leather box; hanging his jacket over the chair. She was conscious again of how little they really talked; how over the years it had become more and more difficult to speak about Mark. It was so long since his name had been mentioned, except in anger. Lionel didn’t seem even to be aware his eldest son was stationed in Tollmouth, apparently indifferent as to where he was, or what he might be doing.

She gave an unintentional sigh and he asked, ‘Is something wrong?’

She hesitated for a moment. ‘I was thinking about Mark and wondering where he was.’

He was suddenly brusque, turning his back on her, as she knew he would. ‘You’re free to think of him all you wish so long as you don’t expect me to do the same.’

Stung into retaliation she snapped, ‘He pulled Kit out of the water at Dunkirk; doesn’t even that make an impression on you?’

She willed him to look at her but he kept his back turned, answering her curtly. ‘The only way he’ll make any impression on me is if he comes back to apologise and make some kind of reparation for all the trouble and unhappiness that he’s caused this family.’

She continued to brush her hair; her lips set in an angry line as she told herself for the hundredth time that Lionel was impossible; quite impossible.

* * *

Later as he lay in his own bed feigning sleep, Lionel could feel her anger stretched taut across the space between them like a discordant, vibrating wire.

Confound it, why did she have to remind him yet again. He tried closing his mind against the images crowding his inward eye, but still they came…

A little boy's arms around his neck...*I love you, daddy.* Hoisting the single sail on the skiff, face red from the effort and straining every muscle: *It's all right, daddy...I can manage.* Offering an injured bird: *I think its wing is broken dad, can you show me how to set it?* Then on the school steps, hands in the pockets of his first long trousers*: I say, pa...could you manage an extra half-guinea? I don't think I'll get through to Christmas...*

All the way to the later battles and that last meeting: the bitter words, the thing done that could seemingly never be undone.

He turned on his side, snapping his mind shut, but the name still hung accusingly in the air between them: *Mark.*

Damn the boy.

The Mediterranean, January 1941

'Here they come again. Steady, hold it ... hold it ...'

Peters watched the Italian dive-bombers shoot out of the sun, three abreast and begin the long nerve-wracking scream toward the convoy. He whistled tunelessly between his teeth, his peacetime occupation as actor with a provincial touring repertory company suddenly more inviting than ever. 'OK, *now* – rapid fire!'

The guns stuttered and the planes kept coming.

'Missed ... Missed ... *Missed!*' He peered at the plumes of water shooting up alongside and well clear of the ship. 'Well, their aim was lousy that time, but so was ours. Come *on*, you buggers – concentrate! I've a couple of popsies waiting for me in Alex and a wife and an old mother at home.'

''Aven't we all,' muttered the pom-pom gunner, waggling his fingers in his ears as the guns blazed across the rear of the convoy. 'at least, by the time I'm through on this ruddy thing, I shan't be able to hear me mother-in-law moaning!'

The voice of their Number One roared through the loud hailer, 'Cut out all the bloody chat down there...Guns, your lot couldn't hit a frigging pig in a passage; for Christ's sake get it together...'

'Aye aye, sir.'

Mark put down the hailer and raised his binoculars to scan the ships to the rear of the *Miranda.* At that instant there was a shattering roar as a tanker exploded and in seconds became a flaming pyre. Oh, God, his mouth dried. There must be at least one sub in amongst them and there would be others following...

Screaming in a sharp dive over the ships came the backup to the first three Stukas; he counted them aloud, 'Six, eight...no, nine.' He swore loudly, dropping the glasses on his chest and snatching up the hailer, 'Enemy attacking aft! Get those fucking guns *around* you dozy bastards!'

He'd have to rouse the old man, gyppy belly or no gyppy belly. He blew down the voice pipe, 'Captain!'

'What?'

'Stukas, sir: nine attacking aft and we've lost the *Manchester* – my guess is we've probably another Sub or two creeping up our rear...just thought you'd like to know.'

'What am I supposed to do – fart at them? All right, Number One. I'm on my way.'

Mark closed the pipe and began to sing softly to himself as the 'planes banked again and began their dive. '*The dogs all had a party, they came from near and far...*' A plume of water shot up on their starboard side; he raised his voice above the scream of the next bomb, 'a*nd some dogs came by aeroplane and some by motor car...*'

The Captain hauled himself groggily up the bridge ladder bellowing, ''Strewth, Number One, can't you think of something better to do than sing your filthy rugby ditties when you're about to meet your maker?'

* * *

Tollmouth, February 1941

'You are good to come and rescue me from the doldrums, especially when you'd rather be with Monica.' Joanna hugged Kit's arm as they paced along the sea front, greatcoat collars turned up against the wind, their breath condensing in the cold air. Beneath their feet the most recent heavy snowfall was beginning to crisp as dusk gathered about them.

'Any idea when Mark will be back?'

'No. Sometimes I just want to sit down and weep; give up; go into a decline.' She smiled, but her eyes were bright with unshed tears and he put his gloved hand over hers, giving a comforting squeeze.

'Now then, no snivelling or you'll get a red nose and I shall not take you slumming in the pub tonight.'

'I'll get a red nose anyway if we don't get out of this wind. Let's go to Sam's for one of his dire cups of tea and something to eat. I'm starving.'

They scrunched their way back through the darkening streets, grumbling at the cold. It was, Kit informed her, one of the worst winters on record.

'It would be, wouldn't it?' she commented, ' when there's hardly any coal to be had, you could end up in the Tower for switching on an electric fire and a nice steaming hot bath with water up to the neck would probably get you beheaded.'

Kit tried hard not to think about Joanna in a steaming hot bath, or any bath, come to that. It was only lust he felt for her, he told himself firmly, it was Monica he loved. But unless he put an end to these occasional meetings, the feelings Mark's woman inevitably aroused in him might sooner or later come between him and Monica. He couldn't bear to have that happen, but he had promised his brother to keep an eye on Joanna; he couldn't go back on his word.

Raising his face to the biting wind he stepped out more briskly. 'At least, Mark is keeping warm. I bet if I'd been in the Navy I'd have found myself escorting convoys to Iceland or Russia.' He shuddered, 'Imagine being at sea somewhere umpteen degrees colder than this.'

When they were settled and able to shed their thick coats in the gloriously over-heated fug of Sam's café, Joanna sighed with relief and pulling off her hat pushed her fingers through her hair. 'After the war, when I'm back in civvy-street, I swear I'll never wear another hat.'

'A pity...I can just picture you in something chic and elegant.'

'Purchased no doubt, from The House of Vivienne – stupid bloody mincing tart...' she made a face. 'Sorry, Kit, it just sort of slipped out. Sometimes I dream I'm chasing her down Bond Street with a machete.'

'Dear me, what a bloodthirsty little thing you are. I shall be very careful not to upset *you* at all in the future.'

'Yes, well, just the thought of her gets me going.' She propped her chin on both hands and stared moodily at the tablecloth. 'Arthur Hallam says she's promised to sign the divorce papers when she gets back from Jakarta, where I gather she is having a perfectly lovely holiday, but I don't know; she's said that so many times. I just have a bad feeling about her...Oh, thanks, Sam,' she smiled as the steaming plates were placed before them. 'I'm going to put you in for a medal for so often keeping me from the internal scouring of our wardroom grub.'

Kit looked alarmed. 'You are not, I hope, going to discuss the state of the Tollmouth naval personnel's bowels – Monica is positively obsessed by that subject!'

'So would you be if you had to eat the food.' She cut into a pale sausage with relish. 'I really only eat here and at Audrey's.'

'Yes, you look it,' he eyed her with concern, 'You are much too thin – '

‘Save the lecture, there’s a dear,’ she interrupted him, ‘what I want to know is when you and Monica are going to get married – or something. She’s like a cat on hot bricks with frustration.’

‘“Or something” is not an option where she and I are concerned and I hesitate, in view of the likelihood of my being posted at any moment, to risk leaving yet another widow on this earth. The frustration, I can assure you, is not all on her side; I do love her and it isn’t easy.’

She eyed him speculatively. ‘Before Monica did you ever…I mean, have you…’

‘Been to bed with other women?’ he supplied. ‘Of course I have, your sharp eyes could hardly have missed the absence of a halo. However, that’s not how I want it to be with Monica. On the other hand I just don’t think at this stage of the war that marriage would be fair.’

‘Well, I think that’s just plain cowardly of you. If Mark and I could have got married we would have, and if he’d been killed a week later I should still have been grateful for that week.’ Brooding, she gazed at her plate. ‘As it is, we haven’t even managed a week wallowing in sin, never mind being married. I just don’t see how you can bear to love someone for ages and not make love, and I can’t see why you’re putting Monica through the same thing as Mark put me.’ She contorted her lovely face into a scowl. ‘There’s something wrong with you Eden men, which is odd given the connotations of the name.’

‘*You* had problems with *Mark*?’ He looked startled, ‘You mean he didn’t make the running?’

‘Far from it; although he kissed me the first time we met I practically had to drag him into bed – and that a considerable time later … I say, you aren’t shocked, are you?’

‘No, darling ... I hear much worse things than that professionally.’

She asked curiously. ‘Do they come to you and confess?’

‘Yes, sometimes.’

‘What a thing… I can’t imagine…’ She went rather pink. ‘I should hate to tell you *my* innermost thoughts.’

‘And I should probably hate to hear them, although if you are desperate I *could* force myself.’

‘Nothing could be less likely.’

‘Well, that’s a relief.’ Kit applied himself assiduously to his meal. This was just the sort of conversation that set his mind jumping along all sorts of forbidden channels. He looked up eventually and found her watching him with an unnerving, knowing look in her eyes.

'It's all right, Christopher Eden,' her mouth twitched, 'as your brother said the first time he asked me out, I won't pounce!'

He gave a wry smile. 'I'm sorry … is it that obvious?'

'Just a tad; I saw it the day we met when you did the old stripper act with your eyes.'

'Oh, that – just habit, I'm afraid, but I do love Monica.'

'I know. That's why you're going to take her and not me out tonight – and every other night you're around Tollmouth.'

He said sadly, 'I shall miss you.'

'And I you; it's nobody's fault, Kit, certainly not yours. I don't think it's mine either, although I'm missing Mark so desperately that I'm probably giving out all the wrong signals.'

'It isn't that, darling, rather that what you do to a man, you do as naturally as breathing.'

She leaned over and put her hand over his. 'Whatever the reason, I'm sorry. I'd *never* risk coming between you and Monica: but Kit, if you won't just go to bed with her don't leave it too long before you ask her to marry you; don't ever have to be sorry for leaving it too late.'

'I can see you'll bully me until I do. I shouldn't care to be some poor little rating who got on the wrong side of *you*.' He smiled. 'Thank you, Joanna – for everything. I shall continue to keep a strictly brotherly eye out for you, and pray for you every day as usual.'

'Will you really? I mean, pray for me?'

'Of course.'

'*Every* day?'

'Every single day; twice in fact, morning and evening, regular as clockwork.'

She turned this over in her mind for a few moments. 'Thank you, I like that.' She picked up her teacup, looking at him over the rim with eyes suddenly sparking with mischief. 'I suppose you pray for Vivienne, too?'

'But of course.' One eye drooped in a slow wink. 'But I don't do so for quite as long, or enjoy it anything like so much!'

* * *

Monica held out her left hand for inspection, and Joanna looked suitably surprised at the diamond and sapphire ring that flashed and sparkled; even in the light from her forty-watt lamp.

'So that's why you went to Dorset again this week – congratulations Monica.' She hugged her warmly. 'When's the happy day?'

'Some time at the end of summer; Kit's just has his posting … to Scotland of all places, so there isn't much point in rushing, and his mother would quite like the time to organise things properly.'

'I thought your parents were supposed to do all that.'

Monica shuddered.

'No thank you; that would mean St. James' Spanish Place and all the trappings. I simply couldn't bear it. Ma and step-papa will have to like it or lump it.' She giggled suddenly. 'As it is Ma's spitting nails because Kit's just an army chaplain, but she's quite bucked about Eden *père*!'

'Why? Is he a belted Earl or something?'

She stared. 'No … but he's a Sir. Didn't you know?'

Joanna gave a dismissive shrug.

'The only time I asked Mark about his father, we ended up having a bit of an up-and-downer about it. Rather, I had the up-and-downer and Mark just sat being terribly calm and superior. I could have brained him.'

'I can't think what the problem is.' Monica was puzzled. 'Lionel is a lovely, sweet man. He has such a twinkle in his eyes and never seems to get grumpy or lose his temper. He reminds me of Mark, only less large and alarming.' She added vaguely, 'perhaps vets and doctors are like that.'

'Oh, a doctor, is he? Well, I know nothing about him and I'm not sure I'd want to. He may seem very sweet to you, but he's certainly done something pretty horrible to Mark in the past, or he wouldn't be so uptight – he refuses to see or even talk about him.'

'How weird,' Monica gave a puzzled frown. 'Mind, I did think it a bit odd when Kit said not to mention you two while his father was around.'

Joanna yawned. 'There must be some ghastly skeleton in the family closet and Mark's discovered it; perhaps the Doc's a secret abortionist!' They laughed loudly together then shushed each other exaggeratedly as a bang on the wall from the next room told them someone was trying to sleep.

Monica snatched up her sponge-bag and dressing gown. 'I'm off for my bath before the old dragon comes to see what all the racket's about.'

'Nighty-night,' Joanna stretched out on her bed. Clasping her hands together across her chest she said dreamily. 'I hope I have the same wonderful dream I had last night – the one where bloody Vivienne is being sat upon by a very large elephant and I'm jumping on top to add to the weight…'

8

The Mediterranean, April 1941

Mark ran a finger down the beaded glass then took a long pull at the well-iced beer. Alexandria, he thought, was a pleasant enough place to spend a week or so while the next convoy assembled.

He was on the veranda of the first floor hotel bar with Harry Templeton, their Navigating officer and the urbane Mike Peters, whose job it was to keep the gun crews on their toes. This he accomplished by haranguing them in his precise and elegant actor's voice to, "For God's sake, chaps, forget the tea break and get the fuckin' tabs up *before* the show, not ten minutes into the first act!" which caused a great deal of mirth all round but had resulted in an increasingly efficient showing when they came under fire.

Now he stretched out his long legs on the cane lounger, contemplating with satisfaction the effect of his tanned knees against the shorts of his white tropical kit. 'Let's make the most of all this sun-drenched leisure, gentlemen, before we pay for it by running through Bomb Alley again a few days hence.'

Mark leaned on the balcony rail, nursing his drink and watching the street below. 'I'm for a few lengths of the pool before going back on board. This soft life between our descents into hell plays the very devil with my guts.'

Peters grinned and lit a cigarette. 'It's not the soft life, old son but the lack of women that's causing your trouble. You really shouldn't sit around in a place teeming with willing ladies and behave as if you were in training for a monastery. The lovely Joanna must have something very special to keep *you* celibate all this time…and our newly married friend here is just as bad.'

Templeton was defensive. 'I didn't get married to start running around with other women.'

'How nice; you and Mark can sit here having little chats about sexual fidelity whilst the rest of us enjoy ourselves.' Templeton lit a cigarette with long, nicotine-stained fingers, waving the match out with an elegant hand. 'I hope you'll think that waiting for a home coming orgy was worthwhile if we get bombed to buggery again next trip. I feel relatively safe with my boys behind all that steel plate, but you…' he drew a whistling breath through his teeth, 'you – up on that bridge; well, the term "sitting ducks" rather comes to mind. I really don't think that if I were in your position I should be saving myself for better things!' He stood up, hitching his immaculate shorts around his elegant form. 'See you later, gentleman; I have a date for my siesta.'

Templeton looked resentfully after Peters' retreating form. 'He's a bastard.'

'No.' Mark dropped into the vacated chair. 'He's as shit-scared as the rest of us, all that stuff is just whistling in the dark. If an afternoon spent trawling through the local talent helps him to forget for a while, good luck to him.'

He was glad when his companion eventually wandered off to play cards with a couple of junior officers from the *Chloe*. Slipping away to the hotel pool he spent twenty minutes pushing his strong body through the water before hauling out to shower and dress before a return to his duties aboard.

Once back in the peace of his own cabin with the gently whirring fan cooling his head, he took up pen and paper to write to Joanna.

There was no need for him to go through the elaborate subterfuge employed by some to say where they were without breaching security. She knew all that; knew when they were being attacked, and by what. Read their "Am Engaging the Enemy" signals as they hunted a U-Boat, or left the convoy to see off a threat from the surface, or to pick up survivors. Was aware of the time when only halfway to their destination they had lost so many merchant ships and their precious cargoes that it seemed almost pointless to continue.

And because she knew all these things he just wrote simply of his love and his longing and of the time they would be together.

If I am home when summer comes again we will go to Porthryn, to walk the cliffs, swim and make love beneath the stars. If allowed we shall take a sail as far as St Michaels Mount, picnic in some small deserted cove then return to the cottage on the cliff and explore again the wonders we have yet only begun to discover in each other...

I love and adore you, and miss you and need you, every minute of every day and all through the long and lonely nights. Please don't 'die a little' when you read those signals...I always think of you when they are sent: watching the plot, your love reaching out to me and enfolding me as your arms and sweet body have enfolded me so often in the past.

Now I must leave and make my rounds of the ship, where even there you will walk beside me. Because everywhere I go, and in everything I do, you are always with me.

Good night, and God keep you, Joanna Felicity Dunne

Your ever devoted

Jimmy the One.

*   *   *

London, May 1941

'You are looking terribly thin, darling' Audrey looked at her with concern. 'Are you eating properly?'

'Of course not … is anyone? Don't go on about it, most of us are involuntary slimmers, what with overwork and anxiety about our chaps.'

'Jerome is still cooking steak, but I'm sure it is horse.'

Joanna laughed. 'I bet that doesn't stop you eating it.'

'Quite right; I need all my strength for the evenings.'

'And Leo – is he coming here tonight, because if so I can fold my tent as well as the next Arab.'

'Yes, he is, but only for the evening. He won't be staying so you don't need to go.'

'That's OK then,' Joanna said facetiously, 'I should hate to feel I was playing gooseberry all evening.'

'Not at all, he never stays more than once or twice a week now. These days we often just go out to dinner or to a film. It's a good arrangement; it keeps us from taking things too far. You see,' she said frankly, 'I value my independence and Leo still loves his wife. Even right from the beginning when it was all shiny and new we made a pact and kept to it; he never talked about his home and family matters, I never spoke about you and your concerns. I'm not the home-wreaking type and it isn't the passion of a lifetime, just comforting...and warm.' She smiled. 'Neither of us are exactly spring chickens you know; we are both a bit long in the tooth for any madly passionate liaison to last for ever.'

'It seems you've managed to have the best of both worlds,' Joanna said lightly, but she had seen her mother and Leo together several times now, and watched the way they looked at each other. Sixteen or sixty, she thought, there was still a lot of passion there. She wondered if the wife Leo still loved felt the same way about him, and just how understanding she would be if she found out about her husband's cosy little affair.

*   *   *

He came in the early evening, looking tired to death, his face pale beneath the thick thatch of white hair. He said, 'Hello, Jo, so lovely to see you again,' and kissed her cheek. He was the only person who used the diminutive of her name but he'd done so from their first accidental meeting months before and somehow she hadn't minded.

'Anything exciting today?' she asked, handing him a drink, 'Any Dukes needing their appendix – or should that be appendixes – out?'

'No Dukes – and as a general rule the plural is 'dices', child, not that it really matters; I don't do innards. Bones are my business and wounded warriors my top priority now.' He smiled. 'This must be my only drink tonight. I'm driving home later *after* I have taken you both to dinner. Gwyn-Jones is back from holiday and has kindly offered to do my list tomorrow and Monday, so I think I may sleep for the whole four days.' He rubbed at a long scar on his temple, a habit when he was tired. 'I wish you'd do the same, Audrey. You'll end up a mental and physical wreck if you keep on running that wretched canteen night after night. Now that the raids have died down, you could at least take a rest for a few weeks.'

'Oh, but darling … somebody must do these things.'

'Jo,' he appealed, 'will you tell her I'm right; maybe she'll listen to you.'

'That's highly unlikely. She never has so far.' Joanna dropped a kiss on his head as she passed behind his chair, 'and you're wrong, Leo, she would go screaming mad and be the most impossible old hag if she had to sit here knitting and twiddling her thumbs.'

'But there are easier things to do, and I worry so…'

'You worry about everyone except yourself.' Audrey went to fetch their coats, returning to chivvy him out of his chair. 'Come along now; we must eat soon if you're to get away in good time, so let's see if Jerome has managed to nab another last-past-the-post at Aintree!'

'I thought perhaps Monica would be with you this week-end,' Audrey snuggled into her thick tartan car rug. It was almost midnight and they were sitting close to the one bar allowed on the flat's electric fire.

'She's gone down to Kit's parents for the weekend,' Joanna explained. 'While he's still in Scotland they like her to spend time there. It must be lonely for them after having him popping home so frequently during his convalescence.'

'And your chap? Have you heard lately?'

'Umm, bloody Vivienne's now having a [illegible] getting him to be the guilty party…says the boyfriend is digging in his heels at the thought of having to pay his whack. Dismal old bitch, she really has got a nerve; she had the cheek to write that in any case they'll be over here for a few weeks early next year and it can all wait until then.'

'Never mind darling, she can't dodge it forever. I remember I used to buy quite a few outfits from her years ago when she first opened that place in Bond Street – she was a bit of a tart even then. Had I known at the time the trouble she was going to cause you I should most certainly have gone elsewhere for my gowns!'

Joanna gave a derisive snort. 'Now that *would* have shown her wouldn't it?'

Tollmouth, June 1941

He's coming home! After all these months he is coming at last!

Joanna stood in her office, silently hugging the knowledge to her, knowing she looked pale and drained; always the outward sign of the inner turmoil that the thought of his homecoming brought.

But outside the sun was shining. The *Miranda* and her crew had survived eight months of convoys and now there would in ten short days be time for Mark and her to be together again, to re-discover each other and pick up the threads of their loving.

The door banged open.

'Don't tell me you're going off sick?'

She smiled a little shakily at the Commander. 'No, sir, but I hope I can take some leave shortly.'

His mouth twitched faintly at the corners. 'Nobody ever looked that ill for me. I suppose you'll want the full ten days owing you?'

'Please, sir.'

'Well stop looking like a sick monkey now and get down to some work. Better start training up that scruffy tow-headed Third of yours who sits around doin' nothing all day.'

'Aye, aye, sir,' she kept a straight face with difficulty. Jean Finch was a model of neatness and efficiency and well able to stand in for her during her absence.

'And remind her I like my coffee with two sugars.'

'Yes, sir.'

He cleared his throat with a threatening growl. 'Can't you stop looking so confoundedly happy as well as sick? There's nothing in regulations that says you're allowed to look happy on duty, not when you're in my section, anyway,' and he wheeled out, slamming the door as usual.

Joanna grinned, the old so-and-so. She must have a good talk with

Jean Finch and try to convince her that he didn't really bite. Well, not very hard, anyway.

*   *   *

She watched Mark threading his way towards her across the crowded bar, then smiled and stood up as he reached the table.

'Congratulations, Lieutenant-Commander.'

He grinned. 'Congratulations to you, too; I haven't seen you since you became quite so high and mighty! '

'Ha, I may run my own section now, but for my sins I'm still accountable to the big bad wolf!'

He pulled his brows together. 'Remember I'm still one jump ahead of you so just a little more respect in future, Miss Dunne!'

'Is that on both sides of the bedroom door?' She sat down, pushing a glass towards him. 'Stop pulling rank on *me* Mark Eden – you can't imagine what I had to do to get you a gin that size!'

He sat opposite, his eyes devouring her face, not yet even putting out his hands to take hers; already counting off the minutes until they could be alone together. Hating this first meeting in a public place but knowing it was easier for both of them after so long apart. There must be time to look, to order their thoughts, to just savour each other's presence.

Joanna propped her chin on one hand, letting her eyes take in every line on his face as she had at their first meeting. Catching her breath in sudden shock that the peppering of grey at his temples had now become twin sweeps, startlingly silver against the deep brown of his skin, with lines deepened around eyes grown more still and sombre than before. As though reading her thoughts he stretched out a hand to cover hers, saying softly, 'It's all right. I'm still me.'

'I know, I know – give me a minute…'

He caressed the back of her hand with his thumb. 'Beneath that make-up, which is a great deal heavier than regulation, you are pale as death. Are you sure you're all right to travel? It's a long way.'

'I'm fine … now.' She covered his hand with hers. 'Waiting for you, when I know you are on your way home always does the most awful things to my insides.'

'I remember.' He looked down into his glass. 'Darling, I can't even find the right words to say to you when there are other people around. I think we have to just drink up and start driving straight away to Porthryn…'

'If you think it safer I'll sit in the back.' She said lightly, knowing with a sense of relief that like her, he felt almost as strange and unsure as they both had been on the way to their very first night in the hotel on the Itchen River.

*   *   *

It was at least thirty minutes into the drive before she felt him begin to relax. When eventually a tentative hand was laid on her knee she turned to him with a smile. 'If we stop at the very next lay-by we may be able to manage that welcome home kiss without either of us actually exploding!'

A few minutes later he swung into a space under a line of spreading oaks, silencing the engine and reaching for her, demonstrating as of old his gift for getting her jacket buttons undone and flipping her shirt from her waist-band in one continuous smooth action. As his hands began to rove around under her shirt, she pulled back to ask teasingly:

'Should you be doing this in broad daylight, on the King's highway and with all that shiny new braid on your sleeve?'

'Definitely, I read it somewhere in Navy Regulations.' He placed one hand firmly at the back of her head as his mouth found hers whilst the other hand continued to rove, a state of affairs only brought to a halt when a convoy of army lorries began rumbling past. He released her quickly and moved to shield her from the road as whoops and whistles and a rousing chorus of '*Do not trust him, gentle maiden*' sounded from the transports. 'Darling,' he murmured, 'your tie is under your left ear...how ever did that happen?'

She straightened it, tucked in her shirt and buttoned her jacket, regarding him solemnly. '*How* far is it to Porthryn?'

'About another four hours driving but if we keep stopping to do this it could take until midnight, so if you think you can behave yourself I think we should drive on.'

'I shall be perfectly all right so long as you keep your hands on the wheel.'

Laughing, he swung the car away from the trees and putting his foot down soon overtook the army transport, grinning and waving as they ran the gauntlet of cheers and catcalls from the troops hanging over the tailgates. Joanna's complexion pinked at some of the more ribald comments and he glanced at her in amusement.

'See what happens when you can't keep your hands to yourself? Quite shocked them, you did, poor young chaps!'

'Just shut up will you Eden, and drive.' She sat back contentedly, loving the sight and feel of him beside her, happy beyond words that the tired, watchful look had gone from his eyes.

Ten whole days ahead, to be out of uniform, push the war on one side and just love and live for each other. This, she thought, must be the happiest time in her whole life.

And Mark, glancing frequently at the lovely clear profile beside him, knew that no homecoming in all his thirty-eight years had been as joyful and as full of promise as this.

Porthryn, Cornwall, June 1941

'I'll leave you now.' Jim Kelsey, Mark's partner picked up his tweed hat, all stuck about with fishing flies, his leathery old face creased into a mischievous smile. 'I've moved back to my old quarters over the surgery, Mark, so you can keep your own house for a while. I've told Mrs Bodley you'd be getting your own breakfasts and not to appear before noon.'

'Thanks Jim, for holding the fort – and for looking after Oscar.' Mark rubbed the ears of the chocolate Labrador that had been glued to his side since their arrival. 'I'd like to come down into Porthcurnow in a day or two and have a sniff around out of surgery hours.'

'You do that.' He climbed into his battered old Morris, a beaming smile for Joanna. '*Au revoir*, my dear...enjoy your leave.' He drove away down the dirt road in a cloud of dust.

Joanna watched until he disappeared. 'Exactly what I intend to do...' She gazed thoughtfully at the adoring Oscar, observing, 'If it's peace and quiet we are needing for the next hour or two...or three,' she observed, 'perhaps it would be a good idea to take *him* for a walk first, then give him a whopping great meal to be getting on with or he'll be expecting to make it a threesome!'

The late afternoon sun was filtering through the curtains as Joanna propped herself on one elbow to peer down at Mark lying supine with eyes closed and a smile on his face. 'Do you think you might manage that *every* time in future?' she asked,

He pulled her down and began lazily to caress her naked back while the sweat cooled on his body. 'I reckon – if you're prepared to wait another eight months, *and* if you promise to walk around again first without your skirt but still wearing stockings and your shirt and tie – God, that is *so* sexy!'

'Ho, you liked that did you?'

'Loved it – it was better than one of "Gun's" blue movies.'

She laughed and tweaked the hairs on his chest. 'Let's just rest for a little now then we could share a bath before taking Oscar for a moonlit walk…there will be moonlight, I hope?'

'I'll arrange it, darling – So we rest, bathe, walk Oscar, and then?'

'Then we eat that delicious cold meal your Mrs Bodley left us, and drink the entire bottle of Chablis which I saw cooling in a bucket in the larder.'

'And then?'

'What a strange question...then of course there is *this* again.'

*   *   *

As he came down the stairs she looked up from setting plates and cutlery on the kitchen table. In fawn cavalry twill slacks and an open-necked check shirt she saw for the first time how he might fit into the life of this place.

'Well, blow me,' she said vulgarly. 'It gives a girl a bit of a shock to see you out of uniform for the first time!'

He raised questioning brows. 'Darling, one can't get more out of uniform than stark naked and that can hardly be a surprise to you by now.'

'You know perfectly well what I mean.'

'Umm, as for you...' he held her at arm's length to turn her around, 'are those bottom-hugging trousers and that shirt *quite* respectable?'

'Do you think I should do up some more buttons?'

He traced a finger down the hollow between her breasts. 'By no means, just leave well alone!' Whistling to Oscar he took her hand in his, 'Come Cressida, the moon shines bright...'

They walked along the pathway that wound along the edge of the soaring cliffs, Oscar weaving back and forth, his tail waving aloft. Far below them the waves broke in a line of white foam against the beach. 'Can you climb down there?' she asked, shivering a little at the distance.

He laughed. 'No, you little Londoner, that's why it's the perfect place to swim and sunbathe. All this part of the headland and the cove belongs to the cottage and through my garden is the only way onto it. But it's too steep to reach the cove from here, for that we must go by sea. My boat is moored about another quarter of a mile on in Porthryn proper...step lively now, and I'll show you.'

*   *   *

'It's lovely.' She stood looking down at the slim green and white ketch. Attached by its ropes to a buoy, it rode gently in the calm water of the small harbour, polished brass lamps shining either side of the cabin doors. She read the name aloud. '*Camelot* … you really are an old romantic, aren't you?'

'Less of the old … now, what do you think of Porthryn?'

She turned to gaze up at the lines of grey stone cottages tumbling down towards the harbour wall; in the moonlight the place looked like the pictures of smuggler's villages found in children's books. Half a dozen rowing boats were pulled up on the shingle above the high water mark and to the left of the harbour loomed a large square stone building from which came the sound of voices and laughter.

He said 'That's our one-room local, The Wreckers; that's what they used to do for a living around here…wrecking. There are some more cottages in the fold of the hill just above.' He gestured to the looming headland. 'Before the lighthouse was built around the point, the villagers would light marker beacons up there and lure the ships onto the rocks.'

'How jolly; I hope they've given up all that sort of thing now.'

He laughed. 'You never know with Cornishmen. There's a fair amount of beach-combing still goes on beyond here on the big sweep of bay towards Tregenik, but I'm sure that's purely opportunism. Tomorrow we'll sail and I'll show you my cove and the little cave where even from the water one cannot be seen.'

* * *

Crete had been invaded, London laid waste from Whitechapel to the West End, and the German Army was advancing across Russia, but in the cottage above the cove and in the blue waters around Porthryn, the war was pushed aside. One lazy day followed another and every night seemed made for love.

The invisible Mrs Bodley came and went, leaving in her wake a clean house and delicious meals. They sailed and swam, played darts and drank in The Wreckers; Mark, warmly welcomed home by neighbours and friends suffered a sore head each evening until his ward room, pink-gin-accustomed system was re-educated into the drinking of rough cider. Several times they drove to Porthcurnow and poked around the surgery, Joanne earning the gratitude of both James and Mark by untangling the mess that was their accounts and setting the books straight.

James rubbed his hands over the order restored to his desk. '

Better nip over some time to Poltreven and sort out old Josh Milton's books – his locum is no accountant – if you think ours are a mess, you should see his!'

Mark shook his head firmly. 'Not bloody likely, no woman of mine goes within a mile of Milton's place – he might just be home on leave. He may have saved my brother's life and he's a first class vet, but he can get a woman into bed quicker than it takes the average man to even think about it!'

'Fancy,' remarked Joanna, not quite under her breath, 'from what I've heard that seems to be endemic amongst veterinary surgeons.'

'Ah, some of us reform,' he answered straight-faced, 'but not Josh Milton. Any man who can be snatched out of the sea at Dunkirk then ask me on the way back if I've a spare woman he can have for the night is not someone to whom one would expose one's nearest and dearest, however grateful one might be.'

Unwilling to cast a shadow over their happiness, it was not until almost the end of their leave that they spoke one evening of the return to war.

'This is absolute heaven.' Joanna turned to lean back against the rough wall and gaze at the low, stone built cottage, its windows glinting in the light of the setting sun. 'I shall always remember these days as the happiest of my life.'

'There will be many more such times, even if we must wait for them.'

'What are you going to do next, Mark?' She queried, dreading his answer. 'You won't be staying with the *Miranda* now, I know that.'

'I've transferred to MTBs. I get my first command when I go back.'

She turned aghast to stare at him.

'Oh, darling, *why*?'

'Because it was offered; because I'd had my fill of sitting in convoy waiting to have my arse shot off; because MTBs are fast and exciting; can hit back. Because – oh, a dozen reasons: and I knew you'd look like that, which is why I haven't told you before.'

'But Mark – a bloody Dog Boat; you total *nit*!'

She was horrified. The MTBs were notoriously dangerous; wooden hulled, petrol driven, they were potential death traps. One direct hit and they could go up like a petrol soaked bonfire on Guy Fawkes' Night.

He grinned, a trifle crookedly. 'Now, now, show some respect if you please!'

'To hell with that; now you'll be running around so damned fast I shall never know where you are.'

'And just as well; but really, darling, one can at least fight and very effectively, and there are all kinds of things – '

'Yes, I know; cloak and dagger stuff on raids, tearing through convoys pooping off your torpedoes and playing chase-me-Charlie with flaming German E Boats aren't you,' she demanded with heavy irony, 'a trifle *old* for that Boys' Own Paper stuff?'

He was immediately on the defensive. 'Pete Hamilton is older than me and he's managed all right.'

'Pete Hamilton,' she pointed out scornfully, 'is a regular, seasoned Naval Officer, not a frigging Cornish vet.'

At this he burst out laughing, pulling her into his arms to smother her face with kisses and making clucking noises like a fussy hen until half-laughing, half-crying she had to give in.

'Oh, damned well go and play with your bloody rowboat if you must. Just don't come whining to me when some short sighted passing fish kicks a hole in it.'

'Darling, I'm likely to be running up and down the channel for quite a while so I can *swim* back home should anything go wrong. Now come on. Stop giving me a hard time and being difficult or I shall refuse to ravish you all night.'

'Never mind about tonight – it's what you'll be doing in the channel on all those other nights that worries me.'

She held him very tightly to her, keeping her face hidden against his chest, and he kissed the top of her head, holding her close, conscious of the tremors running through her. 'Sweetheart, all we can do is just live for the here and now. Although I know you'll not be able to keep quite such an eagle eye on my comings and goings in the future that may be no bad thing,' he shook his head sadly, 'for oh, my love – you are much, much too thin and I think that watching *Miranda*'s every move has done your system no good at all.'

'Just leave my system out of it,' the muffled voice was shaky. 'If you don't fancy going to bed with a skeleton why not just come right out and say so?'

He began to laugh again. 'God, but I do love you, you aggravating female,' he slid his hands down the length of her, coaxing and caressing until she put her arms about his neck, pulling his head down to hers, murmuring: 'You did say *all* night?'

'I did? Surely not!'

She moved closer, tightening her arms. 'Oh, yes you did.'

'I exaggerate, of course. But how is it,' he asked, as they turned toward the cottage, 'that you are showing an increasing ability to get your own way with me – it's never happened to me before.'

'Not even with Vivienne?'

He scowled, 'Especially not with Vivienne.'

She said serenely, 'Then that is obviously something which is vastly overdue!'

9

Things were going so well; they were so happy that she had put off for as long as possible even the mention of Kit and Monica's approaching wedding, but now it was their last day at the cottage. They would leave early tomorrow and she could no longer dodge tackling him. 'Have you heard from Kit recently?' she asked, striving to sound casual and at ease.

They were anchored just off the cove; Mark perched sideways untangling a mackerel line while she lay back in the stern of the *Camelot* pretending to read a book.

He continued to sit with his back towards her, hunched over the line, elbows on his knees as he replied absently, 'Umm, just before I left the Med. Why?'

'You know that he and Monica are marrying in less than three weeks?'

He turned, brows pulled together. 'Yes.'

'I just wondered if you'd be able to get leave for the wedding.'

In a second his face was stripped of expression. Oh, Mark, she thought despairingly, please don't do this to me again.

'I should think it most unlikely.' Abruptly he turned back to face the water.

'But if as you say, you're going to be close to home for a few weeks ... Mark, this really is a bit much. He's your only brother; surely you'll at least make the effort.'

'He will not be surprised by my absence. He knows the reasons.'

'But *I* have been invited by Monica and I *don't* know; how do you think it will make me feel to go without you?'

He rounded on her. 'I don't want you there, with or without me.' His voice was taut with anger, 'and there is nothing you need to know. Either you trust me and accept that I have my reasons, or you go right ahead and do exactly as you wish regardless.'

'And if I do?'

'I'd rather not answer that right now. '

'Mark, please try to see it from my point of view.' She felt the threatening tears begin to gather, but angrily shrugged the weakness aside. 'Monica is my friend and so is Kit. He was wonderful to me when you were away. He came to see me, helped me so much. I can't imagine how anything you may have against your father can make you behave so badly. For God's sake tell me, what did he do to you?'

He didn't move; just sat staring at her. When finally he spoke, his voice was tired and defeated.

'Better to ask,' he said, 'what I did to *him*.'

'I don't want to talk about it. I don't want to see the indictment in your eyes that I still see in my mother's and Kit's, however hard they try to disguise it.' His own eyes were cold and hard. 'But I suppose you have to know before you go and join the enemy.'

'That's not fair. You're pre-judging me.'

'Oh, you'll be the same; too honest, too straightforward, too black and white.' Impatiently he dropped the line into the bucket at his feet, making a mess again of the hooks and spinners. 'I'm not blaming you for wrecking our leave. Being you, you had to ask.'

'If it's going to be wrecked it will be you doing the wrecking,' she was stung into anger, 'and if you don't bloody well *look* at me properly I swear I'll go straight over the side and swim back.'

He almost smiled, then turning right around rested his forearms on his knees, 'Still the same old persistent Joanna…' Clasping his hands before him and fixing her with weary grey eyes he said, 'All right, you won't be satisfied until you know it all, will you? Just don't forget that you asked for it.'

'You have to realise,' he began, 'that my father was, and no doubt still is, a very powerful determined man. He made up his mind from the day I was born that I should follow in his footsteps. Go to the same school, the same University and the same medical school, no question about it, and I was the obedient little boy who did as I was told and accepted the path I was pushed along. It was only when Kito started to grow up that I began to understand just how much I was being pressured.'

'Kit once told me your father hardly even noticed *him*,' she ventured.

'Damn' right! Baby brother had it easy. He arrived eight years after me – I was the heir and Kit the spare so my mother could give free reign to her affections without being accused of spoiling him; he wasn't sent away to school at eight to be homesick and bullied and beaten, he chose to go when he was eleven and won a place at a Cathedral choir school.' He paused to say vehemently, 'No son of mine will ever be sent away from his home when he's little more than a baby.'

'I couldn't agree more, but go on…'

'Although I began to resent that all the pressure was still on me I went along with it, I had to, by then it was ingrained. I even did my first year in medical school before I allowed myself to face up to the fact that I couldn't go through with it.' He gave a wry, reminiscent grin. 'So far as doctoring was concerned I'd only ever been interested if it was to do with animals. If any kid in the neighbourhood found an injured creature of any kind, he'd know where to bring it. *"Is Mark in? I've got something for him!"* my poor mother spent half her time in the vacations finding boxes and cages for my menagerie. In the early days Father encouraged me, I think he was pleased when I asked him how to set a bird's wing or a rabbit's leg because he saw it as a step on the road to the Royal College of Surgeons. Anyway, the upshot of it was that I came home half-way through my second year and told him I'd quit medicine but had passed the entrance exams and gained a place at the veterinary school in Glasgow.'

Joanna almost reached out her hand to take his, but restrained the impulse and let him continue uninterrupted.

'My father doesn't lose his temper in any normal way (nor do you, she thought, but kept silent) but by God, he can just blister you with a look and a few well-chosen words. He didn't want to hear any more rubbish about veterinary school; I was to stop playing games – go down on my knees if necessary to the Dean and apologise – and get back on my course. I called him – well, never mind what I called him – then walked out and went straight up to Glasgow where, as he cut off my allowance and refused to pay my fees, I worked every night and through every vacation to pay my way. Food and clothing were very far down on my list of necessities; I lived in the most disgusting, bug-ridden room in a filthy tenement and existed mainly, if memory serves me right, on lard sandwiches and the occasional bun. If it hadn't been for mother sending me regular fivers behind my father's back, to buy the necessary books and arranging with my Godfather to meet half my fees, I couldn't possibly have survived.'

He looked down at his clasped hands for a moment, then up to stare over her shoulder.

'I didn't forgive him for that and didn't go home when he was there for the next five years. But as soon as I passed my finals I thought I'd go down to Stonehams and rub his nose in it. Say: 'There you are, you old bastard, I've done it in spite of you!' But it was all a bit of an anti-climax. When I got home everyone was away for the weekend and only old Ellen there to let me in, so I thought I'd leave him a note; which was when I found the money…'

He paused, closing his eyes, seeing himself as he had been then:

thin wrists sticking out of the too-short jacket sleeves, worn flannel trousers, feet in socks full of lumpy inexpert darns in down-at-heel shoes. Going through the silent house to his father's study, opening the desk drawer to find pencil and paper to leave a triumphant note, and beneath the paper the roll of crisp white ten-pound notes in the elastic band.

'He'd been having a lot of work done on the house over the past few months and was going to pay in cash. I didn't know that, or care. I just thought: 'You owe me for years of hunger and humiliation, for never having money for clothes, or to take out a girl or have a decent meal.' So I put the money in my pocket, tore of a bit of paper off his pad, wrote a very rude note to say what I'd done then went straight up to Oxford to stay with Kit, who'd just started at Keeble and was having himself a whale of a time.'

'Is that what it's all about?' she was incredulous. 'Hell's teeth, Mark, I'd have probably done the same thing myself!'

'No my darling, that is not what it's all about. It gets much worse.' His face, which had begun almost to relax, tightened again and he shook his head. 'This is a disaster in two acts, and the first one isn't yet finished.

'By the time my parents returned, the study had been cleaned. My insulting message may have been blown to the floor in a draught and been sucked up by the vacuum cleaner, or simply cleared away as rubbish. I don't know, but the upshot was that when father went to pay his account a few days later there was no money, no note, and the only people in the house had been me, old Masie, who'd been cleaning there since the year dot, and the irreproachable Ellen. When I got a message calling me home immediately I wasn't over-worried, although I knew I was in for a rocket about the money I was feeling cocky and belligerent enough to face him out. My God, Joanna,' his face blanched at the memory, 'I'd rather run another Malta Convoy than ever go through again what I did that day. He not only tore me apart verbally, calling me a liar and refusing to believe I'd left a note, but he clouted me ... *clouted me*! I was nearly twenty-seven, for God's sake, but by then I was so bloody demoralised and ashamed that I just stood there and took it. Then he told me to go and get a job, save until I could pay back what I had stolen – *stolen*, mind you, and kicked me out again.'

'How much money was it?'

This time she did take his hand, but he only pressed it briefly before withdrawing it from her clasp. He smiled grimly. 'It was three hundred pounds, a lot of money in nineteen thirty-one. I'd already spent over half of it on paying my debts, getting some decent clothes and living it up with Kit and his pals. But I was lucky. My professor at Glasgow got me the job of assistant to Jim here in Cornwall. I couldn't afford a car and I think I was possibly the only Vet in the county who visited his patients on a bicycle! I scrimped and saved for almost two years to get the rest of that money together. Any little pleasures or social life of any kind was out of the question until I finally had all three hundred quid in my hand.

'When Kit rang out of the blue to say he'd got me an invite to a party he was going to in London, I was off like a shot. I thought I'd have a bloody good evening then go down to Dorset the next day, drag Kit with me as a buffer, say I was sorry and give the old sod his money back.'

He paused for so long, that Joanna became impatient and prodded him with her foot. 'Hey, come back to me; I need to hear part two. What happened next?'

'What happened next,' he repeated, 'was that I met Vivienne.'

There was another long pause. He sat looking down at his hands in a bemused fashion, then sighed and closed his eyes briefly before continuing.

'You have, if doesn't strain your credulity too far, to accept that I was a relatively inexperienced, *almost* virginal twenty-nine-year-old, really kicking up my heels for the first time in my life. All I'd ever had in the way of sex was a rather grubby affair at Oxford with a biology student from Somerville. On the other hand Vivienne was a very experienced and spoilt daddy's darling, who was used to getting everything she wanted, and at that stage of her life she wanted me. Frankly, I didn't stand a chance. She bowled me over like a lamped rabbit and before I knew it we were on the couch in the master of the house's dressing room, stark naked and doing things unheard of outside the Karma Sutra. It was a revelation and I took to it all like a duck to water!'

At this Joanna failed to repress a howl of laughter and he gave a half smile, rubbing a hand across his face before continuing.

'I neither knew nor cared where Kit might be; twenty-four hours and a massive hang-over later Vivienne and I had spent all three-hundred quid, one-fifty of which had gone on a diamond and emerald engagement ring. I couldn't *not* go home: I'd told them I was coming and I honestly thought that Pa might understand that I'd met the most wonderful girl in the world and was going to be married, and that I'd save up the money again ... Christ, but I was naive!' he paused a moment to shake his head, adding sheepishly, 'I suppose it might have been better if I hadn't stopped off in the village first to get a spot of Dutch courage.'

'Oh, Lord, you never arrived there pissed, did you?'

'As a newt in a brewery!' he admitted. 'Needless to say he went for me again; telling me in searing terms that I was a drunken swine, tearing my new and at that stage tender romance apart. Calling Vivienne, quite rightly, as it turned out, a number of names I doubt even you have heard, despite your two years affiliation to the Senior Service. It really was the straw that broke the camel's back. I lost it completely and I went for *him*. I'm not proud of it, I still feel sick when I remember, but I knocked him out cold and he went down with a hell of a crash and split his head open on the fender.'

He paused, looking down at his hands again. 'I suppose I was lucky to get away with it. He wasn't a young man and I might have killed him.' He bent to take the line from the bucket and began picking at the tangled mess again. 'To my eternal shame I did a bunk that night; I've never seen him since and I understand he refuses even to mention my name.'

She said cautiously, 'Yes, well that does explain quite a lot.'

He gave a derisive snort. 'So now that you've heard all the sordid details it shouldn't be difficult for you to see why I shall not be at Kit's wedding. If you really can't keep away I suggest you keep very quiet about knowing me at all, or if you must admit to it, make sure my father believes our affair is over.'

She said tightly, 'I didn't know we were having an *affair*. I thought that we loved each other.'

She saw his brows contract and his mouth set in a straight line, but he kept his head half-turned and made no reply. She persisted. 'Did I make a mistake, then?'

Avoiding her question he returned to the attack. 'He branded me a liar and a thief and bullied and humiliated me. Actually, you would probably like him. Find him charming. Kit does, Monica apparently does, my mother, I think, loves him very much, so he has all the guns on his side.'

'Did you ever pay back the money?'

'Yes eventually, but not until after Vivienne had high-tailed it back to Bond Street and her London crowd. A little less than two years was all she managed here and she kept me poor all that time, that's why I never divorced her when I should have – I couldn't afford the luxury. The only reason I managed to pay my father back and buy into the partnership here was because I inherited a fair sum from my Godfather, when he died suddenly a few years ago.'

‘So if you paid your debt all that keeps the whole thing going is that you won’t go back to apologise? A pretty bloody silly state of affairs during a world war, I must say.’

‘Black and white,’ his mouth twisted at her sarcasm. ‘I told you so!’

‘Smart arse,’ she sat back, watching him with steady, thoughtful eyes; after a minute or two she said, ‘Let me hear you say that again.’

‘Say what?’

‘“Affair,” I want to see if it hurts as much as it did the first time.’

He winced visibly. ‘Jesus, you don’t pull any punches, do you?’

‘Say it, damn you.’

‘I can’t.’

‘You didn’t have any difficulty before.’

‘That was in the heat of the moment.’

She sighed. The tit-for-tat could go on all night and there was little point in rubbing salt into his wounds. He was too angry and embarrassed to be conciliatory. She had forced him into this; she must make the peace.

For a long time they both sat in silence. He was still fiddling with the line then sensing her eyes on him glanced up quickly then looked away again. At that moment she longed to put her arms about him and say it didn’t matter and that everything was all right: but it *did* matter and it wasn’t all right. Would never be all right until he did what he should have done years before. Eventually she leaned back on her hands, staring at his bowed head with narrowed eyes.

‘So … you’ve always been a bit of a bastard then have you – Sir!’

Startled, he turned. She watched the struggle in his face; saw the smile break at the back of his eyes, the lines around them deepen and knew then that the long haul back had begun. It wouldn’t be easy, but it was a start. But some time, somehow the whole mess would have to be sorted out or she would be condemned to spend the rest of her life dodging his family, which could prove to be more than a little taxing Joanna thought, after her best friend was married to her lover’s brother…

Mark took the old blue canvas yachtsman’s cap from his head and hung it with great deliberation on a handy cleat, ‘When you call me that…’

‘*Smile*!’ she finished.

He held out his arms and as she went into them knew a fleeting moment’s regret that she would not be at Monica and Kit’s wedding, but thought, with a new-found philosophy, that it was a small sacrifice to make for love, and that amongst so many she would surely be scarcely missed.

* * *

Joanna was uneasily aware that things still were not right by the time they returned from leave. Mark was solicitous and over correct and both of them trod carefully around the subject of the wedding while making no further reference to his confession. It didn't appear that anything had changed other than that she now knew why he was estranged from his family. She could accept the reasons for this and forgive the weakness and downright stupidity that had caused it, but it was not quite so easy to forget that he had been so sure that she would turn against him.

* * *

She made the excuse, which was quite a valid one that she was unable to take leave again so soon to attend the wedding. Monica was disappointed but accepted the reason without question, although Kit gave her a look compounded of understanding and compassion when she told him as they sat together on the headland at Tollmouth.

'He's told you about him and pa hasn't he?' he asked, filling his pipe then shielding the match against the breeze. She nodded and gave a sigh. 'Well, I suppose that's a step in the right direction.' Kit flicked the spent match into the litter bin. 'I never thought he would. He shuts me up pretty damned quick if I ever try to talk about it.'

Joanna shrugged. 'He's not in love with *you* and perhaps you are not as persistent as *me*, but I'm glad you know why I'm not coming. I can't tell you how sorry I am to miss your wedding.'

'You'll never change him, you know,' he warned. 'Like father he's very strong and very stubborn: I doubt that either will ever forgive the other. It would take something of a quite monumentally cataclysmic happening to achieve that.'

'Well I'm not into the business of changing people – I'm quite happy to leave that thankless task to the clergy.'

'Ouch,' he grimaced. 'I hope you don't try that sort of *riposte* on Mark – I'm sure that would be considered insubordination in your hidebound Service.'

'Only if I were on board his ship.'

'I guess then you'd have to call him Sir?'

'No, I only ever do that in bed,' she answered then blushed. 'Sorry … forgot your collar again,' she said then giggled in a way that even now made his heart shift just a little. He scowled ferociously and stood up, pulling her to her feet.

'I'm not sitting here any longer with you or I'll have no reputation left. I must go.' He bent to kiss her cheek. 'We'll send you a piece of cake. God keep you.'

'Mark always says that.'

He smiled. 'Then God keep him too.'

She watched him walk away across the greensward then turned again to stare across the channel as it glittered, deceptively peaceful and harmless in the afternoon sunlight. 'Amen to that,' she said.

10

Tollmouth, October 1941

'We'll be off again soon,' Mark brought their drinks from the bar and settled beside her on the bench.

It was early. The comparative peace before the influx of the shore parties from the ships began meant they had the bar almost to themselves, only a few elderly regulars sat in a far corner playing cribbage.

'At least we've had a good run for our money.' Joanna fiddled with her glass, gave a careful smile and willed her hands to stop shaking, 'How soon?'

'A few days, I've booked into the George for a couple of nights from tomorrow. Can you make it both evenings – even overnight?'

'I'll try. I expect so.' He squeezed her hand.

'I'll leave you the car keys and I've plenty of petrol coupons. My boson's missus sold his car last week and he's passed me his ration.' He grinned. 'So if you get the chance and you want to go down to Porthryn for a few hours of peace and quiet, just go. Jim won't mind.'

'I might be glad of the company, although I must get up to see Audrey again on my next pass.' She sat, turning his hand over in hers. 'I wish you didn't have this habit of leaving me just as winter is on its way; I know where you are going and I think your bed may be even colder than mine.'

'I won't ask where – you'll only tell me its privileged information!'

She said gloomily, 'Perhaps it's just as well we're not married; I think I'd be asking for the license money back.'

He smiled faintly and drummed his fingers on the tabletop. 'Kit's on the move as well.'

'Monica said. She's being very good about it.'

'He's lucky to have a Navy wife. I wish I had.'

'Is Vivienne still coming home next year?'

'So she assures me.'

She kept his hand in hers. 'I want to make love; now.'

'Me too darling, but I have to be back on board in an hour and you may not have noticed, but this place is a bit public.'

She laughed. 'Well, I suppose I must wait until tomorrow night.' She stood up. 'Come on, if you've only an hour we'd better walk off our frustrations and not sit here twitching at each other.'

'I shall miss that narrow strip of water,' he said as they paced across the greensward, the cold wind whipping their cheeks. 'And I shall miss coming home to you so regularly...about time we started getting a discount at The George, I reckon, don't you?'

'Some hope. I'm surprised the dragon-lady doesn't charge extra for turning a blind eye when you blatantly sign in as Mr and Mrs She knows perfectly well we are nothing of the kind.'

'Just anticipating…we'll get old Kito to do his stuff when I'm free if those stuffy old bishops will let him. It would be nice to keep it in the family.'

'What family?' She stopped, turning to face him, holding his arms, her eyes pleading. 'Mark, before you go won't you try to see your father again?'

'I can't, even for you.' He shook his head. 'I'm sorry,' A telltale pulse throbbed at his temple, a sure sign of stress. 'I regret what happened; I always will. Although he was never a soft touch as a father he rarely laid a finger on me until that day; we had some good times and he was great company. He'd never say it, but I think he was proud of me before all the trouble blew up.'

She sighed. 'I sometimes wonder *what* men use to keep their ears apart; whatever it is, it's not a brain that's for sure. God alone knows where they keep that.' She looked at him severely. 'And please don't tell me. You have a very coarse look in your eye!'

He made the effort and smiled. 'I've some very coarse thoughts in my mind! Come along; let's go and sit in the car and I'll tell you what they are.'

*   *   *

East Anglia, December 1941

Mark put down his pen and pushed the letter he was writing aside; lighting his pipe he strolled outside the hut. An MTB was just coming alongside and he watched it berth, hoping he wouldn't have to turn his exhausted crew out again that evening. It had been a close shave the previous night; he supposed they'd been lucky to get away with one casualty. Only poor old Browne hadn't made it back. He was glad he'd paid him well for those petrol coupons.

What was Joanna doing now he wondered; he closed his eyes briefly, bringing her near, smelling her perfume, touching the warm skin, pushing his hands through the curly hair...what a fool he'd been not to have cleared up the business with his father before he left. She was right, it was bloody farcical, but how *could* he face it after all these years? Suppose the old devil just froze him out and turned his back? What a complete idiot he'd look then.

Here I am, he thought wryly, wearing this uniform, responsible for my craft and the men in her. Taking decisions every day that may mean life or death for all of us and I still can't bring myself to go and say I'm sorry to the old man. Better do something constructive and get back to my office, finish that letter... *Dear Mrs Browne, I am so terribly sorry...*

He had a horrible feeling that there would be a few more of those to send before this tour was over.

* * *

Singapore, December 1941

'They've bombed Pearl Harbour!' Douglas Payne bellowed the news from where he sat hunched over the radio.

Vivienne switched off her hair dryer.

'What was that?'

'I said: they've bombed Pearl Harbour!'

'Who has darling ... surely not our boys in blue?'

'No, the Japs,' he stood in the doorway, a worried frown puckering his brow. 'You know what that means don't you?'

She picked up a comb and turned back to her mirror. 'I wish you wouldn't ask me questions you're just about to answer yourself.'

'It means America will be in the war now ... can't help herself.'

She began combing through her hair. 'Well, if they come in we shall all soon be back to normal, thank God.'

'I hope you're right.' He stood chewing his moustache. 'Think I'll toddle down to the club and see which way the wind's blowing; got a lot on until we go to the UK in March.'

'Do that, Dougie darling, and whilst you are out get Hanif to send up some more gin, will you? The Bradley-Clarke's are coming tonight and you know what an old soak *he* is once he gets going!'

* * *

The Brigadier perched on the corner of the Chaplain's table. 'I don't like the look of it, Padre. Hong Kong fell to those bastards last night. You'd think they would have let us get Christmas over!'

It was the end of the morning service and Kit turned from folding his stole to give him a questioning look.

'How long before they're here?'

'Not long, I imagine, but they'll have a fight on their hands. Half the Far East Fleet is across Singapore harbour and every gun ready and waiting. Still, I'd like to see a few more of the civilian Brits getting out from under our feet. The Indian business chaps have got more sense; plenty of them are on the move.' He eyed him keenly, 'you could go, you know. You're not obliged to stay and fight.'

'Perhaps not by the army, but I shall stay and fight if necessary.'

'That may be a wiser choice than risking the 'planes and subs.'

'I've a sister-in-law living on the Heights.' Kit pulled his surplice over his head and began unbuttoning his cassock. 'Perhaps I should go and see her again; check if she and her "friend" are packing up; if not I'll try to persuade them they should leave.'

The Brigadier grinned. 'You don't sound keen, Padre.'

'I'm not, sir, but needs must if the devil drives.'

'Bit short in the brotherly love department, eh? I'm surprised at you. See you in the mess later?'

'If I live Brigadier, a large whisky waiting on the bar would be in order!'

* * *

Vivienne was frankly incredulous at Kit's blunt suggestion that she and Dougie should leave at once. She lounged back in the cane chair in her cool, expensively furnished house, eyeing him over her pre-lunch cocktail. 'Don't be silly, Kit. Dougie has his business to think about. We can't possibly leave until March.'

'It's more than likely the Japs will be here before then.'

Vivienne's eyes widened. 'Goodness, you don't imagine the Army, or the Navy will let them get this far, do you?'

'Somehow I doubt anyone will be able to stop them. Don't you read the papers or listen to the BBC?'

'No, it upsets me. I don't want to talk about it.' She swung an elegantly shod foot, looking at him from beneath her lashes. 'I'd rather hear what big brother's latest piece is like. At a guess I'd say thirty, divorced and anxious to get him to the altar before he does his usual bunk!'

'No.' Kit couldn't help a malicious smile. 'Young, quite lovely, unmarried and couldn't care less about getting him to the altar.'

'Young *and* unmarried?' she widened her eyes again. 'Well, well, that's not a bit like the Mark I've been hearing about these past few years.'

'I rather think that Mark has ceased to exist. Joanna is...different, and rather special.'

'I don't believe it!' she shot a sly sideways glance at his overly non-committal expression then gave a knowing chuckle. 'You fancy her yourself, don't you?'

He flushed; bloody woman. 'I'm married, Vivienne.'

She gave a crow of laughter, 'As if that ever stopped any man.'

'Well it stops me.' He picked up his cap. 'If I can't persuade you to leave, there is little point in my bothering you further.'

'Don't be such a stuffed shirt, Kit, just because I scored a bulls-eye.' She stood and followed him to the door. 'I can't wait to get home in March and see this paragon.'

'I doubt you'll do that unless you're determined to drag them through the courts.' He stood at the open door, looking at her with hostile eyes. 'You've kept him dangling long enough, Vivienne. Be generous and let him have his divorce, after all you did the walking out.'

'We'll see.' She arched her brows. 'In the meantime you just watch your step. We can't have a scandal in the Eden family. I can just see the headlines in the News of the World: *Naughty Vicar Caught in Love Triangle* – Lionel would have a *fit*...oh I *say*... I never thought I'd hear a parson call any woman that. You *are* a bad boy!'

Kit stormed down the hill, flung himself into the nearest church, crashed to his knees and banged his head on the pew in front of him; twice.

'Father, forgive me…' he clutched his throbbing head, 'but, dear Lord, even *You* have to admit that woman is an absolute *cow*!'

* * *

Tollmouth, Christmas 1941

Joanna sat watching Monica pack the last of her belongings then cast a disparaging glance at her friend's civilian clothes. 'Did you *have* to get pregnant quite so quickly?' she demanded, 'Couldn't the pair of you have found the time to be careful?'

'We thought we had.' Monica paused to give an unrepentant grin. 'Let's face it … it's all for the best. I've never really been top Wren material, have I?'

'Seems a bloody drastic way of getting out of the Navy. You sure you can bear to live at Preston Thingummy? Especially with old doom and gloom housekeeper Ellen around. From what I hear she's totally batty.'

'Well, there is that.' She turned and sat on her case. 'Quick, do this up for me before I topple off … Ta.' She snapped the locks and stood up. 'Mary is having the old coach house flat tarted up for Kit and me: that way we shan't be in one another's pockets but can still be company for each other now that Kit is overseas and Lionel away so much.'

'Rather you than me.' Joanna prowled to the window then turned with a shudder as a sudden gust of wind flung sleet against the panes. 'God, but I hate this weather; Christmas in Tollmouth and not a snowflake in sight. Do you think Kit has your letter yet telling him what a clever boy he's been?'

'Hope so. At least he's staying put in Singapore for now so it isn't as if his mail has to chase him around like some of the poor blighters ... there!' she fastened the strap around the last bag. 'All finished. The taxi will be here in a minute. Give Audrey my love when you go up next week, won't you?'

'Of course,' Joanna picked up the heaviest case, preparatory to carrying it downstairs. 'Bye the way when do we get the rest of your wedding pictures? Mother keeps on about them every time I see her. All we've seen so far is you and Kit leering over the cake!'

'Well,' Monica followed lugging a canvass valise, 'you know how it is; Uncle Piers wanted to do them but what with paper shortages and not much in the way of leave right now he's only been producing them in dribs and drabs. But you shall be next, I promise. They are worth having just for my Mama's hat. Thank the Lord it's so large you can barely see the expression on her face!'

Joanna watched the taxi pull away and gave a last wave before turning back into quarters, unutterably depressed and alone. She was beginning to feel she'd rather had Tollmouth. How she longed to be in Porthryn again with Mark, free to walk the path along the headland, the wide sea at their feet and the endless sky above them. Suddenly nostalgic for the lovely Cornish woods and meadows she repressed a sigh, how long, she wondered, must she wait in this grim and dreary place before he returned; how long before they could journey once again to the cottage on the cliff and close the door against the world?

11

London, January 1942

Audrey said, 'I thought you were bringing the wedding photographs this time.'

Joanna chased a mushroom around her breakfast plate, but didn't look up.

'Sorry Audrey, I forgot.'

'Really!' her mother was put out. 'Just make sure you remember on your next leave.'

'I'll do my best.'

But I shall not be showing you Monica and Kit standing before the church. Joanna kept her head down. *On one side her mother in that awful hat with the Lord and Brigadier in full fig, cap covered in scrambled egg and a chest full of medals glinting in the sun.*

On the other Kit's mother standing beside her husband, the eminent Orthopaedic surgeon Sir Lionel Eden, the latter looking kindly and benevolent, if a little tired. As I have seen him look so often, sitting comfortably on the couch in this flat.

Leo, your darling Leo; Mark's father and your occasional lover, the man of whom I was so fond, and whom Mark still faces across a seemingly unbridgeable chasm of anger and guilt.

*   *   *

She had told no one about the awful shock of those photographs. Never breathed a word to Monica, never gave a hint to her mother who, as the weeks passed forgot about them as the news from the Far East worsened; Malaya was overrun, Singapore fell and Vivienne, Douglas and Kit all disappeared without trace.

If on the very few occasions when she went home Joanna saw Leo's dark blue Lagonda parked outside the mansions, she would take herself off to the cinema or a concert, staying away until she knew he would have left.

'He does so miss seeing you, darling.' Her mother complained. 'Surely you could manage to be here some time when he is visiting?'

And Joanna would trot out the excuses: A friend from Oxford in town. A dinner date with one of the girls she trained with. A film she didn't want to miss.

How she would cope when Mark returned and whether she would ever find the nerve to tell him the truth was something she pushed far into the back of her mind, refusing to think that far ahead. In any case, even if she did dredge up sufficient courage, what could she say?

'Oh, by the way, I thought you'd like to know your father and my mother have been at it like knives together for the past couple of years...'

Or:

'How are you about making love with the daughter of the woman your father is having his leg over on a fairly regular basis?'

Impossible, she would just have to keep it to herself.

Had Kit been there, she would have told him and he would have helped her to do what was right; what would be best for everyone. On her own, without him to act as intermediary she could see no way to say anything without hurting her mother and causing even more trouble for the Eden family. The long standing feud between Mark and his father apart it appeared to have been a reasonably happy family before the news had come that Kit was missing.

* * *

Until advancing pregnancy made travelling too difficult and uncomfortable Monica came several times to Tollmouth. On these occasions Joanna resolutely put all unwelcome thoughts out of her mind to give her friend all the love and support she could, each time humbled anew by Monica's steely courage and shining faith that Kit was alive and would be coming back to her.

'Mind you,' she confided to Joanna on one of these visits as they sat in Sam's Cafe wolfing Spam and chips. 'Vivienne could hardly have put the lid on everything for you and Mark more effectively could she – disappearing like that? I often wonder if she and Kit and Dougie have all ended up in the same place. If they have Kit will have an awful job being full of Christian charity towards her!' She broke off to giggle in the old, happy way. 'Did I tell you he wrote that he called her a heartless, mischief-making bitch when he went to call?'

'Umm … but that's nothing to what I call her in my nastier moments.' Joanna scowled, 'why couldn't the silly cow have got out? I suppose Kit had to stay but she didn't; oh, *God*!' she closed her eyes. 'I'm sorry, Monica, that was disgustingly selfish and thoughtless of me.'

'It's all right.' Monica put a hand over hers. 'I just know he's alive, so I can look forward to having his baby and to both of us waiting until he comes home.'

After she'd seen her friend off at the station, Joanna walked slowly back to quarters, wondering how she might feel if she were carrying Mark's child. Not that there was much chance of that, she had wryly to acknowledge, there would be a long and stony road for herself and Mark to travel before he would allow such a thing to become reality.

* * *

Dorset, June 1942

In May a brief, hastily scribbled letter arrived from Douglas Payne, smuggled out from Changi Jail to Hanif Jawala, and forwarded to the Edens after the merchant's escape by fishing boat and steamer, on a roundabout and harrowing journey to America.

A relieved, almost jubilant Monica telephoned Joanna to say that Kit had been together with Dougie for a short time in Changi before being moved with several hundred other POW's to a camp near to the Burma/Thailand border, while Vivienne was apparently safe amongst those women and children interned in Singapore, so that it was with a lightening of her spirits that Joanna drove to Dorset on a bright spring day when Monica's baby was a few weeks old.

Leo she knew was safely in his London operating theatre but still she was full of trepidation as she drove the Riley through the gates of Mark's home. Would he approve or disapprove of her visit if he found out she had been to his home? Probably the latter she thought, but she was only seeing her own best friend and meeting his new niece on his behalf. Surely even Mark could not object to that. However, the thought that she must come face to face with his mother made her stomach churn. She had no idea what he might have said about her or what sort of welcome she would receive. She thought nervously that even if Mary Eden were a lot less bright than she sounded she would surely have guessed that Mark and she were lovers, and there were few mothers would approve of that.

The drive up to the house appeared endless, but after some hundred yards a bend in the avenue of beeches revealed Stonehams in all its glory.

She stopped the car, her lips shaping a soundless whistle at the sight of the mellow Georgian house standing amid a profusion of trees, flower beds and shrubs, before it an immaculate grassed oval around which swept a wide gravelled drive. Fading into the distance was what appeared to be at least an acre of well-mown lawn dotted with more trees and flowering shrubs.

She felt a sudden unreasonable resentment against Mark for not mentioning the little matter of this impressive ancestral pile. It was not surprising that Monica, used as she was to moving in such circles, would accept it without comment, but Mark might have at least given some clues as to his background.

Putting the car into gear again she drove on. All this, she thought apprehensively was going a bit too far.

Monica heard the car and flung open the door, running down the steps to enfold her in a hug. 'Oh, marvellous timing; Mary has gone to do the church flowers so we have an hour or so to ourselves ... Come on,' she towed her inside, 'come up and see the sprog … she's asleep, so we can natter in peace!'

Church flowers? For God's sake! Joanna entered a large square hall, smelling of potpourri and furniture polish. She turned around to view it better, thinking that Audrey's flat would practically fit into this space alone. Barely repressing a sarcastic snort she followed Monica up the wide, curving staircase.

The small person sleeping peacefully in the nursery, her profile showing unmistakably her mother's tip-tilted nose, was duly admired, Joanna fascinated by the tiny perfect hands and fluff of golden hair.

'Daddy actually came all the way down from Fort William to see me in the nursing home and positively drooled over her!' Monica's eyes sparkled. 'I felt really proud of him in his uniform; I'd forgotten how good-looking he is. He was just the same as ever: you'd never know he'd had such a terrible time getting back from Hong Kong. Thank God the doxie cleared off as soon as they hit Dover.'

'Did he arrive in his kilt?'

'No, ducky … nice tartan trews: very dashing.'

'She should grow up to be a real beauty with all that handsome Highland blood in her veins, even if yours *has* been diluted by Chelsea and Cheltenham.' Joanna peered more closely at the sleeping baby. 'Eyes blue or grey?' she asked.

'Blue but going grey,' Monica laughed, 'Eden eyes without a doubt, nobody could possibly suspect the milkman.' She paused to sweep her hair back in the old familiar way. 'Oh, bully, isn't it marvellous to have some time together again? Now lets dig the Tollmouth dirt … I do sometimes miss it all.'

'I wasn't expecting all this…' Joanna gestured around at the elegant drawing room as they sat drinking their coffee, brought in by the shuffling, doleful Ellen, 'I thought you had your own place.'

'I have, but during the day I bring Laura over. It keeps Mary from brooding too much over Kit.'

'Have you heard any more about where he is?'

Monica shook her head. 'No, the Japs aren't as efficient – or perhaps not as mindful of the Geneva Convention as the Germans...' She tailed off, adding. 'I wish I could write. It's so terribly far away.'

'He'll be all right.' Joanna squeezed her hand. 'Nobody gets Kit down, you know that.'

'Well, I'm trying not to think about what may be happening, just fixing my mind on when he'll be coming home. Today we're going to be normal and enjoy ourselves. So come on, tell me all about the gang I left behind.'

* * *

As Mary Eden returned to the house she heard the two young voices deep in conversation and laughter. So, she thought grimly, Joanna Dunne had arrived.

The initial pleasure and satisfaction she had felt when her son had at last seemed likely to marry again had soon faded with the realisation that the woman in Mark's life was little more than a girl. Mark had made no attempt to lie about their relationship and it was obvious she had been living openly with him in Porthryn.

Straightening her shoulders Mary Eden opened the drawing room door, her gaze going directly to the young woman who stood at her entrance and held out a hand in greeting as Monica introduced her.

'How do you do, Lady Eden.' her voice was clear and confident, with a little husky break in it that Mary decided probably drove most men wild.

She forced a tight smile and took the proffered hand. 'I understand that you are…' she hesitated deliberately, 'Mark's girl!'

'I believe I am.' The reply was as coolly polite as the question and Mary Eden's pre-conceived notions about Joanna Dunne received an unpleasant jolt. She gave her a longer and more searching look, aware that this was no simple child whom she might, as she had hoped and imagined, deflect from continuing the unsuitable liaison with her son. This young woman would not easily be vanquished in a battle of wills.

The baby woke and as Monica left the room Mary seized her

opportunity; inviting her unwelcome guest to walk in the garden where, swiftly abandoning her previous polite small talk, she began a none-too subtle questioning of Joanna's plans for the future. She was not by nature unkind but found it almost impossible to be fair and impartial. Apart from the immorality of it all, she thought despairingly, this girl was so many years her son's junior. Although she appeared mature and confident, how could she possibly cope with the complex and difficult Mark?

Joanna answered her questions honestly, without attempting to dodge the delicate, but none-the-less determined probing. 'We can hardly make any long term plans,' she acknowledged finally, thinking that was the understatement of all time. 'In fact now that Vivienne is interned I can't see we can make any plans at all until the war is over.'

'Such a tiresome, headstrong girl,' Mary stooped to pull up a weed. 'We assume she is still alive, but who knows? I wouldn't have thought she was a natural survivor. Much too selfish and fond of all the good things that money could buy.'

Joanna frowned, 'Kit wrote that he'd been to see her last Christmas. I can't believe she and her chap didn't have the sense to get out. They both must have seen it coming.'

The older woman said distantly. 'Yes. I suppose you feel that has made life rather difficult for you – and Mark too. Of course, *I* have no idea of any plans he may have. I see so little of him these days.'

Suddenly impatient with all the veiled hostility Joanna stopped and faced her. 'Look,' she began reasonably, 'I'm sure that you would like to see an end to our relationship, but I can't finish it – neither of us can. I'm sorry if you find that hard to accept, but that's the way it is.'

Mary answered coldly, 'It used to be called living in sin,' then at Joanna's sudden ironic smile qualified the bald statement with a caustic, 'it still is, although I am aware that *some* might think that applied to the realities of wartime romance it is rather a old fashioned view. However, old fashioned or otherwise, the sentiment stands.'

Silently Joanna counted to ten determined not to be drawn into futile dispute with this inflexible woman, who was undoubtedly from a background and upbringing that looked upon sex before marriage as a crime only slightly less heinous than murder. As such, she was unlikely ever to be in sympathy with anyone who chose to 'seize the day' and live life to the full before time itself ran out. She began walking again, her head up a faint flush staining her cheeks.

'I'm not making any excuses. We love each other very much and there is too little time to waste a moment of it.'

Lady Eden pursed her lips. 'How does your mother feel about all this? Has she met Mark?'

'No, not yet, but she knows about us.' Joanna was straight faced. 'Unlike you, she probably lives in fear that I'll change my mind and land back on her hands!'

'Perhaps like me she prefers the quiet life.'

'Perhaps.'

Her opponent's eyes narrowed. 'Kit once described you to me as a good friend but a disturbing one…' her nostrils flared slightly. 'I'm not quite sure what he meant by that, or how you might have disturbed him.'

Joanna said cryptically and with deliberate provocation, 'We have had our moments!'

For a second Mary Eden's step faltered. These modern young women, with their uniforms and lipstick and lack of morals! Surely she didn't mean… She tried unsuccessfully to repress a shudder. Thank heavens Kit was safely married to Monica, and Mark old enough and hopefully responsible enough not to fatally compromise himself with this girl. She shuddered again. It seemed Mark's women were destined to be a thorn in her side: first Vivienne, now Joanna Dunne, each thumbing their noses at convention in their own particular way.

It was quite disgraceful. Why on earth couldn't he have settled down with a dear girl like Monica?

She took Joanna's hand as she left with no more warmth than at their meeting. 'I know your reasons for not visiting whilst my husband is here and I respect your loyalty to Mark. However, you must feel free to visit Stonehams again whenever you wish. Monica, I'm sure will always be pleased to see you.'

Whew! Joanna walked to the Riley metaphorically mopping her brow. Sliding behind the wheel she thought over the little parting speech and shook her head decisively. No, Lady Eden, you do *not* know my real reason for avoiding your husband, she thought with mordant humour, and hell might freeze over before I'd ever tell you. In fact, I'm highly unlikely ever to clap eyes on you again if I can possibly help it!

She drove off, watching the two women in her rear view mirror; Monica, radiant with her baby in her arms the woman beside her stiff and unrelentingly hostile.

Reaching the bend in the drive Joanna put her hand out of the window to return Monica's farewell wave. One visit to the ancestral pile was quite enough. Mark had been right to keep her apart from his family; in future she would stay well clear of Stonehams, his father – and Lady Mary Eden.

12

Tollmouth/Porthryn, August 1942

Mark climbed from the taxi and fumbled awkwardly for his change. It still hurt to turn his head but at least he was alive, unlike those poor bloody Germans in Holland.

Although they had ultimately been successful in taking off the three SOE agents sheltered by the Dutch underground, there'd been an ambush near the beach. Inevitably, when the three men had a running fight to the MTB, Mark's crew were involved in something rather more unpleasant than their usual smooth and efficient operation of loading and swift, uncomplicated departure. But the boat's Vickers guns had made short work of the opposition and they had got away swiftly with no fatalities on their side and only a handful of wounded.

The two weeks in hospital in Norwich had been quite welcome, despite the painful furrow that now ran from his collarbone to his left earlobe. However, he thought philosophically, had it not been for the freak accident of that bullet first glancing off the MTB's bridge rail before reaching him, he wouldn't now be making himself comfortable against the wall at Naval H.Q. and awaiting his lover's appearance.

Just for once, Joanna didn't know where he'd been for the past couple of weeks, or that he was back in Tollmouth. It would be a novelty to take her by surprise!

He stood to one side, out of her line of sight, watching her come down the steps as she had on their first date. Different steps, longer and wider but still taken with the familiar smooth stride.

He stepped forward.

'Good evening, ma'am!'

'Bloody *hell*!' said Second Officer Dunne, and slid down the last two steps to sprawl inelegantly on the pavement.

She clutched her glass of brandy and drank deeply, 'Don't you ever, *ever* do that to me again!'

He was contrite. 'I thought it would be better than having you feel like death waiting for me to arrive.'

She glowered. 'You owe me a pair of stockings.'

'Yes, darling,' he kept his arm about her and signalled with his eyes to the barman for another drink. When it came, she eyed it mistrustfully.

'You don't have to get me drunk to have your way with me!'

'No, but it might help.' He grinned. 'I'm not exactly my usual active self. A few more of those and you may not notice my shortcomings.'

She studied the angry scar showing above his collar. 'I hope that doesn't go too far downward...'

'No, darling, but it does restrict my more vigorous movements.'

'How would you know? Or did you find some tart in Norwich on whom to bounce around and test out your athletic abilities?'

'Not a chance, they were all booked. Look, I really am sorry,' he kissed the back of her neck and she closed her eyes.

'Just keep going and in time you may be forgiven.'

'Would it be too soon to start the forgiving at the George tonight?'

'I thought you'd never ask,' she said.

'Mark…I have to tell you something.'

He groaned and rolled over; fumbling for the bedside light he looked at his watch. 'Joanna! It's four o'clock in the bloody morning.' He glared at her accusingly, 'you woke me up.'

'It won't keep…Mark, I've been to Stonehams. I went to visit Monica and the baby. I met your mother.'

'Is that all?' He lay back, closing his eyes. 'I know. She wrote me.'

'Oh,' she was deflated. She hesitated then confessed. 'It was hairy. She was like an iceberg and I wasn't as diplomatic as I should have been.'

'Uh, huh, I guessed as much from reading between the lines of her letter. I could have told you what she'd be like if you walked in on her after all this time without a wedding ring on your finger. A great stickler for the conventions is my ma!'

'Why on earth did you have to let her know we were sleeping together?'

He grinned. 'The poor dear was getting herself tied in knots trying to find out. I got fed up with all the ladylike fishing around and put her out of her misery.'

'Well, thanks for warning me…'

'You didn't ask and I didn't think you'd walk straight into the lion's den.'

‘I didn’t expect her to get the knives out, did I? Anyway I only went to see Monica. You’re not angry I went without telling you first, are you?’

He turned his head on the pillow to look at her. ‘Should I be?’

I don’t know. Well, yes, perhaps. I thought you might.’

‘But you went just the same.’ He scowled. ‘Totally undisciplined; I wonder old Naughton hasn’t slung you out months ago.’

‘I only misbehave with *you*! It’s a lovely house; you should have warned me about that, too.’

‘There are some things a man doesn’t want his friends to know.’

‘Will you ever want to live there?’

‘No. You and I will stay in Cornwall. In the fullness of time Kito and Monica and their undoubtedly numerous offspring can have it. Vicars always have too much time on their hands; that’s how come they built all those ruddy great rectories to hold all their kids.’

‘I’m glad you don’t want us to live there; I’d be expecting your mother to leap out on me every time I opened a cupboard. But you must go and see the baby as soon as we go back. You will, won’t you? You’ll have plenty of time to visit.’

‘I’ll go…I promise.’

She was silent for a moment, then, ‘Once, when you were away, just for a few minutes, I got to wondering how it would be to have your baby.’

His hand moved over her smooth, flat belly. ‘Not yet, darling, don’t go broody on me.’

‘Oh, it didn’t last.’ She leaned over to kiss him, ‘but I do hope this war ends soon and we can get married. We shouldn’t leave it too long.’ She touched the sweep of silver at his temples. ‘You won’t want howling babies around when you’re in your dotage, will you?’

‘We shan’t have howling babies,’ he rebuked, ‘ours will just coo.’

‘I do love you, Mark Eden.’

‘So I should hope, otherwise I would feel duty bound to stop you getting to where you are about to right now!’

She looked down on him innocently. ‘I thought it would take the strain off your arm. Sir.’

‘It’s not my arm I’m worried about – ahh!’ he gasped then began to laugh. ‘When did I give permission for you to do *that*, Miss Dunne?’

* * *

Joanna was prepared for a battle, but to her surprise her request for seven days leave whilst Mark was still on sick leave was achieved without the usual accompaniment of growls and grumbles.

'Which was flaming gracious of the old man seeing I've taken nothing in all these months but one forty-eight to see Audrey.' she commented, as they left Tollmouth, heading again for Porthryn.

'Now that you've met my mother, we must take time for me to meet yours.' His eyes were on the road, but he didn't miss the involuntary tensing of her arm against his. 'We can perhaps leave a day or two early and visit her before you're due back.'

She had been dreading this. How could she possibly introduce him to Audrey? The minute she heard his name the cat would be out of the bag with a vengeance – and it would be only a matter of minutes before Mark figured out the connection between Darling Leo and his father; then he would go right through the roof! Nor, she though gloomily, would her mother be pleased by her silence over these past months. Between the pair of them she would be like the meat in a poorly constructed sandwich.

'There's no great hurry.' She answered, after a pause that was a fraction too long. 'She's a busy woman. Too busy just lately, I think. She didn't seem quite her usual self the last time I was at home.'

'I'm sure we can find a mutually convenient time.' He gave her a sideways glance, commenting dryly, 'Why my wanting to meet your mother should put that look on your face, I can't imagine.'

'What look?' she snapped.

'Don't start that; I'm on sick leave and shouldn't be upset!'

'Well, I don't want to talk, or think, about anything but us for the next seven days, so I'd rather you didn't mention going back, my mother, or what sort of look I have on my face.'

'No darling.'

'Nor be smug and superior.'

'No darling.'

She smiled and laid her head against his shoulder. 'Keep quiet and just drive, will you, Eden.'

He touched his cap obediently.

'Yes ma'am.'

She stretched luxuriously in the big bed then turned on her side, watching with sleepy eyes the breeze-blown curtains. A bar of sunlight fell across the polished floor, lighting the colours in the thick rug. She stretched again and smiled, thinking of the night just passed. She could hear Mark moving about in the room below and talking to Oscar. There was the rattle of the dog's dish then shortly after a tantalising smell of frying bacon wafted up the stairs.

James Kelsey had turned up the previous evening with the bacon and a half dozen eggs; payment he told them, for the safe delivery of a back-to-front calf. Her tummy rumbled; slipping out of bed she reached for her dressing gown, such a mouth-watering smell couldn't be ignored.

'*Two* eggs each! Should we?' She came behind him to wrap her arms about his waist. 'What a terrible shock to the system.'

'We'll risk it.' He grinned, neatly laying eggs onto plates already laden with bacon and tomatoes. 'I want to see your skinny ribs acquiring a little more cover during the next few days.' He gestured with the slice. 'Toast is over there.'

She made a face. 'Thank you kindly, but I've no secret desire to waddle around like Jelly-Roll Symons in Ops.'

'That might be going a touch too far.' He put down the pan and kissed the top of her head. 'Umm…you smell lovely.'

'So do you … of *Parfum de Porc frit*!'

He laughed. 'Flattery will get you nowhere, my girl. Sit, eat.' he ordered.

'Are you going to be this masterful all the time?'

'Yes. I quite fancy having *all* my own way this leave; after all I am on the sick list.'

'Good, because I'm tired of knowing it all, coping with it all and ninety-eight per cent of the time, being right!' she tried to keep her tone light, but her voice shook a little. 'Oh, Mark, it's so good to let it all go for a while.'

'It doesn't get any easier, does it?'

'No, and I don't get any better at living only half a life without you.'

He looked at her with compassion. 'I'm always there, you know, just behind your shoulder.'

'Umm, that's why nobody gets to kiss me goodnight anymore – and it isn't behind my shoulder that I want you!'

He grinned. 'I can't recollect you complaining about that last night. However, I hope you don't make a habit of teasing young men with the promise of kisses you don't give.'

'No darling, I only tease old ones.' She raised her coffee cup, looking at him over the rim. His heart turned and he was flooded again with such tenderness, such a depth of love. How unbearable it would be to leave her again. It had been worth the taut nerves, the searing pain of the bullet to come back to her; to sit in this familiar room like two normal people having breakfast together before they walked again the narrow paths along the Cornish cliffs.

'Mark,' she gave her gentle, charitable smile, 'why do you suddenly have rather damp-looking eyes?'

'Rubbish!' he busied himself with his breakfast. 'Stop nattering and get on with it. I haven't been slaving over a hot stove so that you could let those eggs congeal on your plate.'

Her smile deepened. 'Did I tell you I love you?'

'Not for at least an hour.'

She reached for the toast.

'I must be slipping.'

They walked until even Oscar was glad to sit panting beside them in the shade of a wind-sculpted tree as they lay side by side, gazing up through the branches at the puffs of high white cloud in the heavenly blue of the sky.

He took her hand. 'Let's talk about after the war.'

'Oh, yes…which bit first?'

'Being on our honeymoon and sailing *Camelot* to France and all the way around the coast of Spain to Italy.'

'Lovely … and?'

'Sharing a bed *every* night.'

'Heaven! Then?'

'Every Sunday doing this: walking Oscar and lying on the grass listening to the sea...and sailing.'

'What about the winter?'

'Oh, then,' He turned his head to smile at her, 'then we shall get up late and light a huge fire. One of us will go for the papers and we shall sit and read and listen to the radio and snooze together on the couch after Sunday lunch – until some idiot cow falls in a ditch and I have to go and help pull it out!'

She leaned to kiss him. Oscar gave a warning rumble and stepped between them to lay full length, head on paws, grumbling quietly. Mark laughed and fondled the silky ears and told him he was no longer the only one and must learn to share. But Joanna knew Oscar was special to him; had been his only companion on his rounds and in the long, lonely evenings, so she allowed the old dog his little victory of coming between them.

Lulled by the hiss of waves breaking gently on the shore and the myriad chirruping, rustlings and whispers of a Cornish summer, they dozed in the shade of the tree until roused by Oscar raising his head to utter a low warning growl.

Joanna slowly opened sleepy eyes to find a short-nosed, rugged, lived-in sort of face hovering above her. Beneath thick curling brown hair a pair of lazy tawny-brown eyes moved slowly from her face down to her toes and back again, an all too familiar light of lechery in their depths.

The wide mouth split into a grin and one large foot nudged Mark in the ribs. 'Hi, Eden! Mrs Bodley of the disparaging sniff said you had come this way and I wasn't going straight home again without getting a dekko at the lady.'

Mark opened his eyes and squinted upward. He groaned. 'Oh, Lord, who opened your cage, you big ape – and what the hell are you doing home? I thought you were still in North Africa.' He sat up and turned to Joanna, warning, 'Better get off your back and quickly, my girl … the Beast of Penmarrion is here!'

As they all walked back together to Porthryn, Joanna decided that Josh Milton certainly lived up to his reputation, so far as appearances went anyway. Within minutes the bold eyes had expertly stripped, assessed and approved her. Mark, she noticed, treated him with good-humoured tolerance and of course he had every reason. Here in the flesh ... and at some six foot three of well-built manhood there was a lot of that, was the man who had saved Kit's life.

He stayed and shared their meal. Chatting amiably, eyeing, when he got the chance her legs and generally behaving as did most of the visiting males at Tollmouth HQ. She thought crossly that when this war was over she'd spend the remainder of her life in baggy corduroy slacks and vast jerseys. *That* would soon put paid to characters like Josh Milton stripping her with a look.

But he was good and amusing company, finally taking his leave as the day began to fade with the observation that he was for an early but hopefully not lonely bed. 'Must make the most of my leave,' he winked at Joanna. 'Not a lot of tottie in the desert, you know!'

Mark watched him drive away then turned to her, smiling and shaking his head. 'Sorry, darling, he'll still be doing that at ninety. Damned good job he lives twenty miles off!'

'It doesn't matter. He's quite fun in his way.' She held out her hand. 'Let's give Oscar a last treat tonight and go and say goodnight to the moon.'

They stood on the cliff edge watching the three-quarter moon laying its pathway of silver across the dark water. How many more times would they do this she wondered, leaning back against him, his arms clasped about her waist? How sure they had all been almost three years ago that this war would soon be over. Now here they were, still in the thick of it and with no end yet in sight. Soon this all too brief idyll would be ended: he would be gone from her again and she would fret and worry and walk her room when sleep would not come.

'I can feel your brain buzzing...' He kissed the crown of her head. 'There must be a great deal of thought going on in there tonight!'

'You know far too much about me, Mark Eden.'

He slid his hands up to cover her breasts and bending his head brought his lips close to her ear murmuring, *'"For she and I were long acquainted and I knew all her ways..."'*

She mocked him gently, 'Such a romantic!'

He turned her in his arms, 'But I still think "and so to bed" quite the best quotation I know!'

'That was old Sam Pepys and *he* wasn't very romantic!'

'Who cares?' he countered, 'it's the thought that counts!'

13

London, August 1942

Audrey Dunne examined her face more closely in the dressing table mirror before reaching for her box of rouge to add a little more colouring to her cheeks. Putting her fingers to her temples she tested the pain. It was not too bad tonight so one tablet should see her through the evening.

Going into the kitchen she filled a glass with water and drank thirstily, then returned to her bedroom carrying the re-filled glass. She shook a tablet from the box by her bed then stood weighing it in her hand for a moment. Better put them away well out of Leo's sight…the doorbell rang and swallowing the tablet quickly she pushed the box into the bathroom cabinet before going to welcome her visitor.

'Audrey.' Leo kissed her cheek, then held her hands and stepped back, looking at her with an expert eye. He said accusingly 'You've not been sleeping well again.'

'What sort of greeting is that?' She laughed and led him into the sitting room. 'Sit down and let me see to the drinks.'

He sank into a chair, taking the glass she offered with a smile. 'Seen anything of Jo lately?'

'No. She's on leave somewhere with her chap. I dare say I'll get a postcard some time.'

'I've missed seeing her all these months.' He looked at her keenly. 'Not been avoiding me, has she?'

'I shouldn't think so. She's just so strung-up and edgy these days. She can't stay put for more than an hour at the time.' Audrey sat down, swirling the liquid around in the glass, realising for a panicky moment that her hand was unsteady and Leo had such sharp eyes…she put the glass down carefully and clasped her hands together in her lap. 'Where to tonight?' she asked brightly, 'Jerome's place or somewhere different?'

'I thought Vereswami's would be nice, so long as we don't look too hard at what is under the chapatti!'

'Fine,' she kept the smile. *Damn, a car journey: would it jolt the pain that waited, silent and ready to spring like a hungry tiger? Still, he was driving down to Dorset tonight so she wouldn't be late back.*

She picked up her cape. 'Let's go,' she said.

She enjoyed the meal. Amazing, she thought how one's life goes on, no matter what. Eating, drinking, sleeping ... she smiled across the table at him. Darling Leo, how sweet he was and what a staunch and reliable friend, but oh, dear, he was looking old. How long did they allow a surgeon to go on working at such a pace, even in wartime? Someone, sometime, would have to say 'enough.'

'If you go on staring at me like that I shall think I'm dribbling or something equally disgusting,' his voice cut across her thoughts and she started.

'Was I staring? How awful,' she smiled. 'No, I was thinking how very nice you are.'

He gave her the kind of direct, appraising look she had begun to dread. He said abruptly, 'You can scarcely keep your eyes open; I'm taking you home.'

'Perhaps I could do with an early night.'

He drove swiftly, weaving smoothly through the evening traffic, turning his head occasionally to glance at her pale profile. When they reached the flat her took her arm and steered her to a seat on the couch. 'Stay there. I'll make some coffee.'

'Not coffee,' she said quickly and he looked at her enquiringly. 'It ... it doesn't seem to agree with me lately. Just a glass of water will be fine.'

He went into the kitchen. She heard the water running then as his footsteps faded along the corridor to the bathroom she leaned back, closing her eyes in an effort to keep the nausea and pain at bay. When she opened them again he was standing before her, in one hand the glass of water in the other her box of tablets.

'I thought you might need an aspirin...' He held up the box. 'Audrey, how long have you been taking these?'

She lifted her shoulders then gave a rueful smile, 'Too long.'

'Oh, my darling,' he sat beside her and took her in his arms, then as she buried her face in his neck and clung to him, the telephone began to ring.

* * *

In the cottage on the cliff Joanna hugged the 'phone, stifling her sigh of relief that despite Mark's insistence on meeting her mother a disaster had been averted, at least temporarily. Replacing the receiver she explained with casual ease, 'She says sorry, but she won't be there as she'll be spending the week-end with a friend in Epping.'

Mark shrugged. 'Shame; it would have been nice to meet her at last.'

'Umm,' Joanna was puzzled. 'Odd, though, I didn't even know she *had* a friend in Epping. Anyway, that gives us another night here – and I know how we can spend *that*.'

*   *   *

Leo watched Audrey put down the 'phone. 'That wasn't the most convincing lie I've ever heard! Do you think she believed you?'

She gestured helplessly. 'Who knows with Joanna, I think so. It was the only excuse I could think of on the spur of the moment. She didn't seem suspicious; in fact she sounded almost relieved.'

'Strange that she should ring this evening – and at that moment,' Leo held her hands and looked at her with sad compassionate eyes. 'You must tell her, Audrey.'

'Not yet Leo, give me a little more time. I really couldn't cope with meeting her man right now, let alone baring my soul.'

'When would you have levelled with *me*?'

'Probably not before you had guessed for yourself...Darling, don't look at me like that. I've *enjoyed* my life, especially these past few years with you, which is more than many can say, although I might have enjoyed the years in between more if Archie had lived a little longer.' She smiled and reached to take his hand. 'You have been so good to me. I'm glad of the time we have had, and that we've managed our little affair without hurting your wife.'

He gave a wry smile, 'Not such a little affair, given the way I still lust after you!'

'And I lust for you – but you must go home now. I shall be all right.'

When he left she turned out the light then pulled back the curtain to watch him go, waving and sketching a kiss as he ducked into the car. Letting the curtain fall she returned to the couch and spreading her wool shawl over her tired body sank down onto the soft cushions. Too much effort to go through the rigmarole of getting to bed, she thought wearily, tonight she would just stay here and indulge herself in a few memories.

Because when one was reaching the end of the line, memories were really all that one had left.

*   *   *

Mary Eden heard the car stop and put down her book with a sigh of mingled relief and exasperation. Lionel was so late that she'd begun to get seriously worried.

He crossed the room to kiss her cheek. 'Sorry I'm late Mary. You really shouldn't wait up for me.'

'I need to know that the one man left around here is safely home.'

There was an edge to her voice and he gave her a swift frowning glance. She put up a hand to push back her hair. 'Don't scowl like that. At your age you can't afford any more lines.'

He moved toward the drink cabinet. 'I need one of these…and you?'

'Yes, a very small one.'

'You know, one of the nicest thing about you is that you so seldom say, 'Isn't it rather too late to have a drink?'' He smiled briefly adding: 'Even if it is.'

'I might if you took to doing it too often.'

He didn't answer at once, but stood with his back to the empty grate. She watched the familiar bullish look settling on his features that meant he was preparing to meet some problem head on. She had smelt the faint trace of perfume on him, always the same scent. Surely after all this time he wasn't going to tell her?

Please don't say it…it's cowardly of me, but in spite of everything I think I do still love you and I don't want to know. I can manage if I don't know…

'I've had a shock tonight.' He looked down into his glass, 'An old friend…' He paused and raised his eyes; seeing the tense watchful look in hers, the way her hands gripped her glass, his heart sank. He said abruptly, 'I think you should know where I have been tonight.'

'Really, Lionel, I'd rather you didn't tell me.' She stood quickly. 'Whatever it is it will have to wait until morning. It's late and I want to get to bed.' She made to leave the room but he stopped her with a hand laid on her arm.

'I'm sorry, but you *have* to listen.' Taking her hand he drew her down onto the couch. 'I discovered tonight that a very dear friend is dying,' he said without preamble, 'I want to feel that I can be some help in the time she has left, but I can't spend all the time I shall need with her unless I tell you why she is so important to me.'

'Lionel, I said I don't want to know!' She drew away from him.

He sighed, rubbing the long scar on his temple. 'Just for once, will you take off your comfortable and convenient blinkers and see that I, that we both, have a problem.'

She gestured angrily, 'Very well, if you insist.'

He was silent for a few moments. All the way on the drive from London he had been rehearsing what he would say, but now the moment had arrived it was proving extraordinarily difficult to find the right words. Although he'd never mentioned Audrey, since their affair had begun he'd always had a nagging awareness that Mary suspected there was another woman, but with typical avoidance of the unpleasant had refused to put her suspicions into words.

There were many more things beside his infidelity that should have been talked over and discussed he thought grimly, the painful business of Mark for a start. But for some years now their marriage had been nothing but a sham, so that it had become impossible to speak freely and honestly about anything beyond the banal everyday happenings of work and home…

Bitterly, he voiced his thoughts aloud. 'The trouble is that we don't really talk; at least not about anything that matters.'

'*You* do not talk. Given the opportunity I should be more than willing.'

'Well I'm going to talk now…'

Seating himself on the couch and leaning forward, elbows on his knees, quietly and as dispassionately as he could he told her of the friendship that had begun over forty years before, between a girl just out of the schoolroom and a young struggling medical student. How after a short, very innocent romance they had parted and eventually gone their separate ways, meeting again by chance one night when she drove her Red Cross Ambulance into the forecourt of his hospital.

'…When we were both off duty we met to talk. It was enormous fun to exchange news of all that had happened in the years between and chat about old friends. I drove her back late that night, we had a few drinks, then there was the father and mother of a raid and somehow we ended up in bed. It was bloody marvellous and we both enjoyed it.' He shrugged at her sudden outraged intake of breath. 'I'm not trying to excuse myself; it was just one of those things that happen. Neither of us expected it to develop into anything deeper; it was quite a while before we became regular lovers.'

'And that is supposed to make it all right, is it?'

'No; but it doesn't make it all wrong, either.' He stood and began to pace about the room. 'War does some funny things you know. Working day after day in that madhouse of a city; then spending sleepless nights hoping it wasn't your turn to be blown to glory had us both randy as hell. Perhaps we were too old and frightened to be doing the jobs we were doing; maybe going to bed became so important because we were both in need of comfort as much as sex.' He shrugged and spread his hands. 'We enjoyed each other; we still do.'

'I wish you wouldn't go on with this.' Two angry spots burned on her cheeks. 'I don't want all the sordid details.'

'Sordid?' he paused to muse over the word. 'I don't think I ever thought of it as that. Even at sixty-plus a man needs to feel he can still take a woman and have her enjoy the taking. If that's sordid then I must misunderstand the meaning of the word.'

'I suppose you made all the usual excuses…including that your wife didn't understand you. The trouble with you, Lionel, is that this wife always has understood you, too damned well!'

He grinned at the sudden spirited charge, hearing a distant echo of the passionate young woman he had married so many years ago and loved so much.

'No, it wasn't at all like that. We never discussed either our families or our future; I knew she had been widowed early in her marriage and had a daughter. She knew I was married and had two sons. She was fiercely protective of my reputation; never even used my name: only the pet one she had for me when we were young. She accepted that I could never be entirely free of you and my life here and we both knew that someday what we had must end. But we had grown very close; too close to part, although at one time we did make a rather half-hearted effort to try.' He looked directly into her eyes. 'You knew that there was someone else, didn't you? How and when did you guess?'

She gave a dismissive shrug, unwilling to show her hurt. 'I think I've probably known since the beginning. She uses Chyphre perfume and you sometimes smell of it: you do now.'

'The oldest mistake in the book,' he shook his head. 'I wish you'd said. As time went on I just couldn't bring myself to tell you and I was stupid enough to think I hadn't given myself away...Mary, I *am* sorry.'

'For what – for making love to another woman, or having to admit it?'

'For neither of those things; only for hurting you.'

'Of course, an Eden admitting to being in the wrong, to dividing a marriage – that would never do, would it?'

He retorted with sudden bitterness, 'It might not have happened at all if you hadn't decided years ago that it was time to exchange one bed for two – with six feet of carpet between them. Even when he still loves, a man eventually loses the desire to cross *that* divide.'

She clenched her hands in her lap. She did not easily lose her temper but now she could feel it begin to simmer and bubble, although her whole body felt icy cold. Now she wanted to hurt him as he had hurt her: when she spoke her voice sounded remote and chilling, even to her ears.

'That was minuscule compared to the divide you forced between Mark and this family!'

Abruptly, he turned his back, going to the fireplace to lean an arm against the wide mantle, watching her reflection in the mirror. 'What the hell has that to do with my going to bed with another woman in lieu of you?' He spun around suddenly, his voice raised in anger. 'You are my *wife*, for God's sake, and I don't turn my back on my responsibilities. Even when I was no longer welcome in your bed I didn't go looking for a substitute. My meeting with someone else was entirely fortuitous and she gave me what you no longer could, or would: comfort, warmth and the courage to meet and work through every bloody wretched terrifying day.'

Turning again to lean against the mantle shelf he burst out. 'Christ, Mary, I'm old, I'm tired, and I have to have something or *someone* to make me find it all still worthwhile. Don't do this to me. Don't throw Mark in my face. Despite everything he's said and done I still think of and worry about him – '

'Forgive me if I find that difficult to believe. You branded him a thief and a liar and turned him out of his home…' her voice shook. 'You deprived me of my son and made this house into an empty shell.'

He said quietly. 'He is my son too, you know, and I also have had to live in this empty shell with a cold and unforgiving wife.'

She was silenced and sat unmoving, staring down at her tightly clasped hands. For a long time she struggled, anger and wounded pride battling against an unwilling acknowledgement of her son's guilt and her own part in bringing about this dreadful, painful situation. Eventually she broke the silence.

'How can we talk together now – about Mark or anything else when we are strangers to each other – and you are so difficult?'

'I know … I know.'

She raised her head to meet his eyes. 'We were both much too young to have married when we did. You were arrogant and ambitious and I was too immature to deal with you. I allowed you always to dominate and have your own way.' She paused, then added vehemently, 'when Mark went to war I hated you for denying him his home and me for all those years: I thought that if he were to die I would never want to look at you again and would hate you to the end of my days.'

'You should have fought me, not shut me out. I would have admired you for fighting.'

'Look what happened when Mark did that! I didn't have the courage – or the will, to fight you openly…' she paused before adding with brutal honesty, 'I think by then I didn't care.'

He gave a cynical turned down smile. 'Well then it looks as though we've pretty well messed it up, doesn't it? If I read you right I'm a lousy father, an adulterous overbearing bastard of a husband and you're a wronged wife. So where do we go from here? Do you move or do I?'

'I'm not sure that I want to go anywhere.'

'Then I guess after all this I should be the one to move out.' He looked contemplatively into his glass. 'You are probably entitled to expect that at over sixty a man is old enough to behave himself!'

'Is any man ever old enough to do that?' Her hand shook and she held out her own glass. 'Would you pour me another of these? Dutch courage is a wonderful thing!'

'You've never needed that before.'

'Well I need it now.' She sat up, her shoulders very straight. 'Do you want to talk about this reasonably or do you want a fight?'

For a few moments he busied himself with the drinks, returning to place her glass in her hand. 'I think we can manage without the fight.' He gave a wry lift of the shoulders. 'If you think we should take the discussion further tonight perhaps you'd like to start.'

She took a deep breath. 'I don't want to leave – and I don't want you to leave me. Quite simply the upheaval would be worse than trying to carry on in some semblance of normality. If I did as I feel like doing right now and burst into tears you'd be forgiven for seeing that as blackmail and a way to keep you here…' He made to move towards her but she shook her head. 'No, don't. I've never been a weeping woman and I won't start now…' she fought for control. 'Tell me about your – friend…you must love her to care so much.'

She didn't say 'More than you love me' but the unspoken words hung in the air and he thought carefully before answering.

'Yes, I do, but not in the way I loved – still love – you. I'd be a hypocrite if I said I was sorry it happened as it did, but now very soon it will be over, for good.' He stood, nursing his glass, looking down on her with steady eyes. 'For the short time she has left I should like to visit her when I am in town – to keep an eye on how the disease is progressing, then see she is moved to a good nursing home when the time comes and be with her at the end. If I am asking too much to do that and still live here, then you have every right to say so.'

'Isn't it a little late to talk of rights?' She sighed and leaned her head back against the cushions. 'Of course you must do what you think will be for the best. Does she have children? Do they know?'

'A daughter; she hasn't yet told her – and won't until later.'

'Where is the daughter?'

'She's a Wren and stationed somewhere in Hampshire.'

For a moment she had a fleeting vision of Mark's girl and wondered whether to take advantage of this sudden lowering of Lionel's defences and tell him about that unsuitable young woman, then decided that too many secrets aired at once might prove counter-productive. Besides, that problem could wait, for now there must be no more evasions between Lionel and her, no more nurturing of anger and frustration. Now she would have to talk honestly about her feelings and needs and hope that in time he would do the same. In refusing to face the shadowy knowledge that there was someone else, she had almost lost him: she would not make that mistake again. She said, 'I'm too tired to think straight now; perhaps in the morning, when we are both feeling wide-awake we can sit down and work out what's to be done.'

Lionel's head was too full of Audrey, and the trauma of the weeks ahead of them to allow him to sleep. Although it was a relief to have brought matters to a head with Mary, he thought it unlikely that the barrier that had grown between would ever quite be demolished, but he would do his best to salvage all that had been, and still might be, good in his marriage.

To have discovered in his later years the warmth and joy that he'd known with Audrey was more than he had ever expected, or deserved. He still wanted her, still longed to lie with her in his arms and knew that her death would leave a dreadful gaping wound that may never be healed.

On the edge of sleep Mary wondered how long it would take them to establish a new, more honest relationship. Would he change at all – be less controlling, more open with his thoughts? Would she ever be able to forgive his infidelity, or think of it without anger and a sense of betrayal?

He had said he had loved her, but did he still love her enough to stay for good, and would he ever forget his late, last love, or ever think about her without pain…she drifted off to sleep.

Lionel, once sure she slept left his own bed and stepping quietly through the silent house went down to the drawing room. Taking the whisky decanter and a glass from the table he carried them to his study and sitting at his desk drank steadily in an effort to dull the pain and sadness of this sombre day.

He remembered how it had been years ago; when he and Audrey were young. A whole summer they had had together; a summer of parties and dances and moonlit walks, before fate and her father stepped in and put a stop to the burgeoning adolescent romance. How would it have been, he wondered, if she had not been sent to a finishing school in Switzerland, and he had not gone to a party the following Christmas and met Mary? Would he and Audrey have married, had a good life together, raised children, loved and cared for each other as they now did?

He thought about Joanna, who had found a very special place in his heart and hoped she would be happy with her chap, whoever he was. The war, this bloody war made everything so hard for lovers, young and old…he sighed and tipped the last of the whisky into his glass. He hadn't been this plastered since his student days, he thought blearily and raised his glass in a silent toast: to Audrey, and Joanna and all lovers, whoever and wherever they may be.

14

Tollmouth, September 1942

'I'll book in at the George, then drive down to Stonehams on Monday and stay overnight.' Mark took her case from the car boot, grimacing slightly at the tug on his wound. 'Although God knows what I'll do with myself for the next two weeks until I'm due back. When can I see you next?'

'I'll ring at lunch time and let you know what old Naughton's been storing up for me.' She looked around quickly, then as no one else was in sight, kissed him swiftly on the mouth, before turning to run up the steps of her quarters.

He slid back into his seat and fired the engine, reflecting that she was the only woman he had ever known who was capable of parting in such a way: quickly, no fuss and with never a backward glance. He drove on, heading for the George.

After the week at Porthryn the idea of going back to spending their evenings or nights together in the hotel was singularly unattractive and on a sudden whim he swung the car into the town, parked behind the Central Hotel then crossed the road to the Wallis Estate Agency.

'You want a furnished cottage along the coast – just for two weeks?' The agent gave a broad grin. 'I've a half dozen you can choose from; you'd be surprised at how few people have shown themselves keen to stay facing old Adolf across that little strip of water!'

* * *

'Ha, Miss Dunne, you've managed to drag yourself back on duty I see!'

'Yes, sir,' Joanna stood to return the Commander's glower with a straight face then threw a sympathetic grin at Jean Finch, who was rigid with apprehension. When he continued to stand in the doorway, she gave him ten seconds before she looked up with an inquiring, 'Sir?'

'Get through that lot ASAP will you? Then my office.'

'Yes sir.'

'*God,* but I'm glad you're back, ma'am!' Finch let out a pent-up breath of relief as the door slammed. 'How do you stand him all the time?'

'Quite often with some difficulty,' Joanna picked up a folder, suddenly business-like. 'Now give me a quick run down on what you think is and isn't urgent in all this.'

Yes, and you can be a bit of a tartar when you start as well! Finch hastened to do as she was asked; this was no place in which to take one's time over anything...

Automatically Joanna ran through the papers in the file, discussing them with the younger girl, part of her brain busy with speculation as to why the Commander might want her in such a hurry. When they'd finished she put the papers aside and risked a quick visit to view the plot, out of habit scanning the wall to see what was going on with the convoys.

'Where's the *Miranda*?' she asked the Wren PO, after a swift glance. 'I thought they were due in about now.'

'Went down last week, ma'am; Thursday, I think.' She looked with concern at Joanna's white face, 'did you have someone on it, ma'am?'

'No,' she recovered herself quickly, 'but I knew some of her crew well.'

'I don't think there were many survivors. She took two torpedoes in quick succession; they blew her apart and she went down almost immediately.'

Joanna went back to her office feeling shaken and sad, thinking she must tell Mark tonight.

Oh, this bloody, *bloody* war…

'Sit down.' Commander Naughten motioned her to a chair and studied her for a few moments in silence. Lord! What wouldn't he give to be young again, though that chap of hers was no spring chicken; going grey as a badger and had to be pushing forty... Still, there was a hell of a difference between forty and fifty-eight….

'Sir.'

It was a gentle reminder that he'd been looking long enough, and he brought himself to heel with an overloud *hurumph*!

'We're on the move … thought I'd give you plenty of warning, but no mention of it outside this room.'

'No sir.'

'Don't know if you have any hang-ups about the Yanks, but if you do you'll be no use where we're headed.' He darted a shrewd look at her face. 'At least, I know you can keep the buggers in their place ... can't have any larking around on this job!'

'Which is?' she ventured.

'Hush-hush ... Falmouth – American and Dutch liaison; some of their Naval top brass ...probably expect it to be one big party. It all sounds like the frigging Diplomatic Corps, but I dare say we shall manage.'

'When do we go, sir?'

She held her breath. Please, not until Mark has gone back. 'Beginning of August; we have three weeks.' She let out her breath slowly as he continued, 'I trust you to pick yourself a Third and a leading Wren clerk to take who have more than the average brain power and can keep their mouths shut?'

'Yes, sir.'

'Run this lot without falling flat on your face, Miss Dunne and if this war last another year or so I'll see you made up to First Officer even if I have to shoot someone to achieve it.' He shuffled papers around on his desk. 'Now, I shall need you at a meeting at twenty-one-thirty hours tomorrow so better cancel any plans you may have made – and remember: not a word outside about this.'

'No sir.' She turned to leave but he halted her at the door.

'Just for the record I shall be N.O.I.C. of this outfit.'

She looked around swiftly and caught the tail end of his sharp smile. 'Congratulations, sir, I shall bask in the reflected glory.' she said composedly and turned the door handle.

'Damned cheek,' he glowered at her retreating back. 'Ruddy women in the Navy … none of you know your place!'

*　　*　　*

'You mean I have to spend tomorrow evening on my tod?' Mark scowled.

'Now then,' she admonished. 'It's not my fault.'

'Of course it's your fault, looking as you do – I bet it isn't a meeting at all. The lecherous old sod just wants to get you alone when everyone's gone in order to chase you around his desk.'

'Everyone never goes – and a fat chance of being chased anywhere with nosy little ratings scurrying about at all hours.'

He leered alarmingly. 'I've found the perfect place for me to chase you, darling – want to come and see?'

'Umm, ra*ther*.'

'Can you stay the night?'

'Of course I can't. You appear to have forgotten that we only returned from Cornwall yesterday.' She looked at him severely. 'I need to be in quarters by twenty three-thirty latest tonight. I've lost a lot of beauty sleep over this past leave.'

He laughed, taking his arm from around her shoulders and starting the car. 'It doesn't show!'

Once away from the town he drove fast for a few miles, slowing down eventually to bump down a pot-holed track. Turning in between a pair of opened wooden gates onto a rectangle of gravel he stopped before a small clapboard bungalow. A rickety wooden veranda ran around this edifice, the paint was peeling and the door had a knocker that wouldn't have looked out of place on Baron Hardup's castle. Joanna gave a gurgle of laughter. 'What is this...an off-shoot of the House of Usher?'

'Certainly not; this is our love-nest for the next two weeks – and the bed *is* aired!' He looked smug. 'Mrs next-down-the-lane did the honours and cleaned up.'

'You can always find someone to do your dirty work for you, can't you, Eden?'

'Not all of it, darling,' he opened the front door. 'Our evening meal, the smell of which you can even now feel tickling your olfactory nerves, is all my own work...'

'You know, I think I might keep you. Audrey never did teach me to cook, which wasn't surprising as she seldom made a meal herself. She said her Swiss finishing school put her off cooking for life!'

'I had noticed that you've seldom ventured more than an imperfectly boiled egg. Did *you* not learn such things at school?'

'I used to get frightful migraines every time Domestic Science came around,' she looked at him with wide, innocent eyes, 'they were so bad that I had to lie down while Matron patted my head with eau-de-Cologne and fed me sweet tea.'

'Did she, indeed?' his own expression was cynical. 'Well as I'm nothing like as gullible as Matron I shall send you on a cookery course the moment that you are out of that uniform.'

'Oh?' She paused. 'That might be difficult, because I was thinking of getting out of it in about ten minutes, Sir!'

Later as they sat over the remains of supper she told him about the *Miranda*, holding his hand across the table, tears starting to her eyes.

'Sometimes I can hardly bear it; all the people we've known who no longer exist: the Captain and all the others on the *Miranda*; poor old Baines and little Evans at Dunkirk…and dear Kit in some ghastly camp at what should be one of the most wonderful times of his life.'

She wept then, fishing for her handkerchief, mopping her face one-handed as he kept tight hold of the other. 'He once told me that he prayed for everyone. Morning and night, he said, regular as clockwork. I think of that often, and wonder if he still does. I wish I could for him, but it's a bit like cooking…nobody ever showed me how!'

'I'll do it for you; I'm quite good at it.' He leaned to kiss her wet cheeks and stroke a gentle hand over her hair.

'Thanks.' she sniffed hard. 'Good job I didn't marry a Vicar. I'd have been a total disaster and got him de-bagged or unfrocked, or whatever it is they do.'

He got up then to come around the table, sitting down and lifting her onto his lap, cradling her in his arms.

'Oh, Joanna Felicity Dunne,' his voice was suddenly husky and unsteady. 'You have no idea what you do to me when you cry. I wish I could stop the war for you. I'd even stop the world for you if I could.'

15

Malaya, November 1942

Kit looked up from wrapping torn strips of cloth around Duncan's suppurating wound as the first working party as returned; emaciated, stumbling and exhausted, the stronger supporting those too weak to walk alone.

'We're almost through, all but the last odds and sods,' Arnie Travis collapsed onto the veranda, automatically scratching at his legs, raw from endless months of trying to ease the itch of mosquito bites. 'It's better than laying that bleedin' road but Gawd help the poor bastards *that* camp's meant for – the swamp starts no more'n fifty yards from the palisade.' He took off the remnants of his Aussie bush hat to swat at the flies that immediately gathered around him.

Kit examined Arnie's legs. 'I'll try and get some clean water tonight or at least the rice water before they tip it out, and soak some of that muck off.'

'Any luck with the quinine?' Major Buckley eased himself down beside them. 'My blokes are going down like ninepins ... have another go at rat-face tomorrow, will you Padre?'

'I'll try.' He examined with interest the incipient ulcers on his own legs. 'D'you suppose we shall end up with these for life?'

'I bloody hope not; just about ruin my chances on Bondi Beach!' Arnie rolled off the veranda. 'I'm going to get me head down before the waiter arrives with the tucker,' and he ambled off, spitting accurately at a very small lizard on a bamboo pole; the lizard promptly fell off and played dead.

Buckley watched the Australian out of sight. 'Weird chap; if that lizard had been bigger he would have had it in his tin and cooked it, you know!' he sounded outraged, in a well-bred sort of way.

Kit laughed. 'So would I. Wait until you've been here a few more months, and you'll do the same.'

He was finding Buckley something of a trial. The Major and some twenty of his sappers were the remnants of a Special Services recognisance group that had taken to the hills and carried on a kind of guerrilla warfare for months before finally being ambushed and captured. They had arrived at the camp complete with boots, socks, caps and uniforms more or less in one piece, plus mess-tins and spoons. Most of these accoutrements disappeared within days, swiftly spirited away by the old hands to be bartered for food and tobacco with the Thai villagers. Buckley, sure that the guards must be responsible, had raged and fumed and demanded to see the camp commandant, only the assurance from Kit that he would get a good beating and kicking should he be so unwise as to confront that gentleman had calmed him down.

* * *

Later that evening, gnawing hunger only temporarily assuaged with the one scoop of rice which was their twice-daily ration, Kit lay on his bamboo cot, the sounds and smells of a hundred men around him and thought himself back to Dorset and Stonehams, Monica, and baby he had never seen.

His early captivity had been plagued by riotously erotic images of having endless sex with Monica, but as time passed he'd found that if he let his mind just float he could leave the present to walk and talk with his wife without always imagining himself in bed with her; even at times sail with Mark, or have a quiet and gently carnal peek at Joanna's legs; hear his mother's laugh and watch his father pouring his end of the day drink. Doc Matthews had said they were hallucinations brought on by their diet, or lack of it, but Kit couldn't argue the point since with him since the Doc had dropped like a stone a month back within days of contracting cerebral malaria.

Whatever the cause, thought Kit, cerebral sex was one way of getting to sleep.

He returned to consciousness to the sound of young Lachie muttering his Hail Mary's into his hands. Rolling off his cot Kit knelt on the hard-packed earth to say his own evening prayers, afraid to dwell on the unlikely possibility of them ever being answered. His last conscious thought before sleep was that tomorrow he must plead again with the camp commandant for the medical supplies Kit knew were plentiful but deliberately kept from the prisoners.

* * *

'Yoshida San,' he put his fingertips together and bowed politely. 'All of us have dysentery and many are sick with malaria and can do no work. If we could have some quinine and perhaps a little meat and vegetables with the rice we would be fitter and work harder.'

'You get food... rice is good. Japanese soldiers fight on rice belly.'

The commandant stayed on the second step of his quarters. He must, or he would be lower than this tall Englishman. When he came out to inspect his ranks of filthy scarecrows at the morning and evening *serits,* Corporal Ikushima was ready to rush forward with a wooden box for him to stand on.

Kit kept his eyes lowered. With Captain Yoshida it was always better to keep the eyes lowered. 'We have had nothing for their illnesses since we came, Yoshida San. Soon everyone will be either too sick to work – or dead.'

'Quinine come, all medicines come soon ... tomorrow perhaps. Now men work and forget sickness.' He turned and walked back into his office. Kit bowed again and returned to the bamboo posts and straw roof that was their infirmary. Sixty or so anxious faces were raised to his but when he shook his head, all but young Duncan sank back again into weary resignation.

'Noo luck with the ould bastard, Padre?'

Kit shook his head again and smiled at the boy whose knee, shattered by a guard's club, refused to mend. He'd been the piper to his Highland regiment and still wore his ragged kilt. A chosen few had celebrated his nineteenth birthday the week before with a thimbleful apiece of saki, stolen from the Commandant's store by the resourceful Arnie.

Kit sat beside him now, taking out a worn and grubby pack of cards. Time moved slowly for Duncan and a game of cards helped pass the painful hours.

'Think oor bloke's come to get us oot soon, Padre?'

He looked up into the eyes that still had hope in their bright blue depths.

'Bound to sometime, old son...' He fanned the cards out on the bed. 'Let me see...how much it is you owe me now?'

'Four hundred and six pounds, five shillings an' sixpence' was the prompt reply, 'an' I'd give it ye right now if some bleeder hadna pinched m'pay-book!'

* * *

'Wimmin, Padre – about four 'undred and gawd knows how many little 'uns.' Arnie's eyes were out on stalks. 'Blimey, if only the Nips had got us building that camp an' 'alf mile closer I reckon I'd 'a' been in with a chance, 'cause there's a few spring chickens in among the old hens!'

'Fancy.' Kit was gently sarcastic. 'How fortunate you weren't at Service this morning or you would have missed them…'

'I can't manage that, Padre … mind you, if you could really turn the water into wine I might think about it!' He leaned over Duncan, diving into his shirt to produce a small piece of fruit. 'Here you are, mate ... swapped a length of wire I found when we was finishing off the latrines!'

'Just what *was* your trade before the army?' inquired Kit, and Arnie gave a fearsome wink.

'Never you mind Reverend! But I did most of it at night and no one never saw me!'

'Where you get?'

Bow-legged, bull-necked Corporal Kano stood over them; reaching forward swiftly he snatched the fruit from Duncan's hand.

'Off the bleedin' Christmas tree, you squint-eyed, fuck-faced little bastard!'

Kano's English was minimal and his IQ even less, but no one could mistake the insult of Arnie's contemptuous reply. Without a change of expression Kano swung the heavy club he carried and Arnie crashed down, blood pouring from his head. Kit started forward in protest then collapsed in agony as the end of the club was driven into his abdomen.

Grinning and munching on the fruit, Kano turned and strutted away on his bandy legs. Arnie held both hands to his split and bleeding scalp and gazed sorrowfully at Kit, who laid clasping his stomach and retching into the dust.

'For Christ's sake, Padre, will yer stop trying to muscle into heaven ahead of the rest of us?'

But Kit didn't hear him. His pain-filled eyes were on Duncan who, seemingly oblivious of the two battered and bleeding bodies on the ground, lay with tears of impotent rage running down his boy's face, his lower lip trembling like a child, crying: 'He took it! He took it, and it was *mine*!'

Oh, dear God, Kit thought in sudden despair, where the hell are You and what are You doing that You haven't the time to see what's happening here?

London, November 1942

'Audrey, my dear it's time to tell her.'

She held Leo's hand, summoning a smile.

'I know, I should have when she was here last month but I didn't manage it ... I'm a coward, Leo. I just couldn't find the words.'

She lay back, smoothing the soft blue counterpane with her free hand, the ghost of a mischievous smile touching her lips, 'so nice to die in luxury!'

Her speech was slow and slurred. He bent to kiss her forehead.

'You've done so well, my darling...Is it all right for me to tell her now?'

'Please.'

'I'll drive down tomorrow and ring from somewhere in Falmouth; that way she won't have to wait around for hours wondering why...'

Falmouth, November 1942

Nell Collins stuck her head around the wardroom door, 'Telephone for you, Dunne,' she grinned, 'sounds like one of those old fruity-voiced charmers, you lucky girl!'

Joanna left her book on her chair and went to the small hallway outside the wardroom, thinking it was probably that persistent Executive Officer from the US Destroyer who'd already rung twice that week, in which case he would be unlucky. She picked up the 'phone with a cool: 'Hello. Second Officer Dunne,' then almost dropped the receiver when she heard Leo's voice.

'Jo? I have to speak with you. Can you get away for an hour or two?'

She opened her mouth, but no words came. *Shit*! Had he found out about Mark and her? She put a hand on the wall to steady herself.

'Jo … Joanna: are you there?'

'Yes. What is it, Leo? Where are you?'

'In Falmouth ... I'd rather not talk on the 'phone.' His voice was clipped, noncommittal, 'will you meet me in the Kings…say in about half an hour? In the bar.'

'Yes, of course.' She rumpled her hair distractedly. 'Leo, what are you doing here?'

'I'll tell you when we meet. Half an hour, then: all right?'

'Yes. Yes, of course…'

She replaced the receiver and leaned back against the wall, aware that Jean Finch had stopped on her way into the wardroom and was viewing her with concern.

'Is everything all right? You look as though something's dropped on you from a great height.'

'Not yet it hasn't, but I have a horrible suspicion it's about to … Oh, *God*!' She clapped both hands to her forehead. 'Finch, be a dear and get me a large whisky. I don't want to go back in there with all that chatter or I may just throw up!'

'Shall I get you a chair, ma'am?'

'No. I'll be OK.' She waited for Finch to bring the whisky then gulped it, her teeth chattering against the glass. Fishing in her pocket for change she asked, 'If you could just call me a cab for about twenty minutes...outside quarters? I'm going to put on some make-up. Lot's of make-up.'

Finch's eyes were huge. 'Will you be back tonight?'

She gave a half-hysterical giggle. 'Yes. He's way past sixty if he's a day! Look, just 'phone the station rank, will you? Ask for Andy ... and tell him it's urgent.'

In her room she narrowed her eyes at her reflection, then washed and towelled her wet face vigorously muttering aloud, 'Time for something a little heavier than regulations...God, woman, do you have to look like a sick cow – he can't eat you!' She gave an agonised groan. *Kit, where in hell are you? Right now I need you more than ever.*

She made up carefully, changed her collar, gave her shoes a quick polish, finished off her drink then went down to sign herself out.

Andy was waiting, reaching to open the door when she appeared. Running down the steps and buttoning her greatcoat she ducked into the cab. 'The Kings Hotel, Andy; sorry it's a short journey but I doubt my legs will carry me there.'

'Trouble, is it?'

'With a capital 'T' I imagine.'

'Nothing happened to the boy friend, I hope?'

'No, it's me in the firing line this time.' She sat forward on the seat as he swung away from the curb. 'Thanks for coming, Andy.'

With Mark's car left garaged in Tollmouth, Andy and his ancient taxi had been a godsend. Now he drove carefully on the wet roads, drawing up before the hotel as the town clock struck eight. She passed him the fare and a generous tip. 'I may, or may not need you later. I'll call from here if I do. Thanks, Andy.'

'Anytime, miss. You be careful now. Nighty-night!' He grinned and drove off, leaving her hesitating on the pavement. Gathering her courage in both hands she marched up the steps, through the revolving door and into the foyer. When she walked into the bar it was with her head up and looking a confidence she didn't feel.

He was sitting at the far end in one of the small plush-curtained booths that afforded some privacy from the main tables, and stood as she came towards him.

For over a year now she'd been dodging him, but, Oh, dear, she thought weakly, all the old affection rising up at the sight of this man who had treated Mark so harshly, darling Leo, I hope I'm not going to have to fight with you.

He kissed her cheek and then as she sat down pushed a glass toward her.

'Drink up ... you look chilled. I'm sorry to drag you out.'

'It's all right.' She eyed the drink doubtfully. 'I've just had a large one of these, Leo. I drink that and you may have to carry me back to quarters singing!'

He didn't smile. She gave him a straight look.

'You haven't come just to drink and chat. If you've something unpleasant to say, I'd rather you said it and not beat about the bush.'

He hesitated, then asked, 'Joanna, when were you last home?'

'About a month ago; I had a forty-eight ... look, where's all this leading?'

'How did your mother seem when you were there?'

She frowned. This wasn't what she'd been expecting. She would be really angry if he'd been talking to Audrey about Mark behind her back.

'All right, I think.' She answered him shortly. 'Rather tired. She didn't want to go out much, but then Audrey hates the cold weather.'

'Yes.' He frowned and was silent a moment, then almost absently took her hand. 'Joanna, this is not a good place for what I have to say. I had planned we should walk but the rain put paid to that.'

'Leo,' her hand tensed in his, 'if you're going to be angry with me, will you *please* get it over with.'

He looked startled and released her hand. 'Angry? Why should I be angry?'

'You tell me.'

'Let's start again.' He rubbed his temple and Joanna, conscious for the first time of how he'd acquired that scar, averted her eyes.

He took her hand again. 'There's no easy way to tell you this, Joanna. Quite simply, your mother is seriously – terminally- ill. She has been for months and now I must tell you because she has very little time left.'

Stupefied, she raised incredulous eyes. '*Audrey*? You've come to talk about Audrey? I thought…' she looked at him in mounting terror as his words sank in. 'Leo, she *can't* be. Not Audrey.'

'She has a brain tumour and there is no cure.'

Joanna sat still quite unable to properly grasp what she was hearing. She looked down at her hands and was surprised to see them begin to shake. With a tremendous effort of will she stopped the trembling and sat rigid and still.

Alarmed at her control Leo moved to sit beside her, putting an arm about her and holding her gently. 'Hey, let go…just let go.'

'I don't think I can,' she gave a long, shuddering sigh, 'all that time: driving that ruddy ambulance through the blitz … and then *this*. Leo, are you quite, quite sure?'

He nodded, 'Quite sure.'

'And there's absolutely nothing can be done?'

'Nothing at all; it is a particularly aggressive tumour. All we can do is to make it as easy as possible for her.'

'Is she in a lot of pain?'

'She has been, but not now.' He gave a tight, sad smile. 'Morphine is seeing to that, and she is in the best possible place. I took her yesterday to a private clinic at the back of Russell Square and close to my hospital. I can visit her morning and evening and I shall be on call during the day. I'll remain in London while she still needs me.'

'How long before...?'

'Two weeks, perhaps a little more … or less, it's difficult to say. It has been a long battle.'

She said accusingly, 'She should have told me when I was home. Or you should.'

'Jo, dear, she just couldn't, and she wouldn't let me. She was like any other mother trying to save her child pain. Can you understand that?'

'Yes.' She rested her head against him, falling silent again before turning at last to ask: 'Isn't it going to be terribly difficult for you – to be in town all the time.'

He said abruptly, 'My wife knows about your mother. We talked it through some weeks ago, when I first knew about Audrey's illness. We reached a compromise.'

Joanna wondered how it had been for Leo to have to face that inflexible woman with the truth. She squeezed his hand. 'That must have been very difficult for you. Thank you for being so brave for Audrey's sake. In your place I don't think I would have been.'

'Oh, *you* wouldn't have made such a mess of things to begin with.' He gazed at her with rueful affection. 'I imagine that your chap will be the only one in your life. I've just had what some would call the misfortune, but I prefer to think of as the very good fortune, to love two women, but in very different ways.' He sat back. 'But now we must be practical. I'm staying here tonight. Can you leave with me tomorrow morning?'

'I'd like to see anyone try to stop me!' She was silent, supporting her head on her hand, trying to get her thoughts in order. 'I'll go straight back this evening, and arrange to take...' She looked up at him, the full enormity of what had happened bringing close the tears that still wouldn't fall. 'Leo. How long do I need?'

'I think you should ask for three or four days now. She will not want you to be there for too long. Jo dear, it won't be easy; very soon she won't really know, or care, *who* is with her. I think it would be more than she could bear for you to be there at the end.'

He wrapped his arms about her as the dam broke and the tears came at last. 'Courage,' he urged, stroking her head as she buried her face in his shoulder. 'Remember I'm here. You don't have to go through this alone.'

All the times I have had to break this sort of news, say these words...

He took out his handkerchief and began to dry her tears, 'We see this through together you and I; that way we'll manage to keep each other from falling apart, and make it more bearable for *her*.'

16

East Anglia, December 1942

I took four days compassionate leave. Joanna wrote to Mark. Darling it was dreadful, she was so thin and tired and just waiting to die. Now that she can never meet you, never see how dear you are to me, I am so desolate and sad for not taking you to see her when I should...

Mark stopped reading and passed a hand over his face. Never had he felt the distance between them so deeply. She needed him so much and here he was with the width of the country between them, standing by a cold sea wall ... with an effort he focused his eyes again on the letter.

It took only a few days. I was glad for her, but feel as if someone has sneaked up and cut off a limb...odd, because we were never really a very close mother and daughter, but I loved her, liked her as a person, and I think – hope – that's how she felt about me. Despite her illness, those last few days we had together were good and I guess we made up for some of the absences. I've had tremendous help and care from Leo ... Tell you more about him when next you come on leave...

Now more than ever you are with me, waking and sleeping, through all the days and nights. Over and over I tell myself that all I have to do is keep going until I can once more hear your voice and feel your arms about me. When the church bells rang for El Alamein I just longed for the day when they will ring again for the end of this war and the beginning of our life together. Like Cleopatra, I have immortal longings in me...when did I not I hear you ask...

Take care of you, and come back to me –

'Captain...'

He spun around, glaring at his startled Midshipman, snarling: 'Don't bloody creep up on me like that; what the hell d'you want?'

'Sir,' Simon Webb was flustered and lost his usual aplomb, 'I ... I didn't creep...I called out twice, from the steps.'

'Well, what is it?'

'Lieutenant Stone's gone sick, sir.' God, the boy thought, the old bastard was looking at him as though he'd like to murder him. 'The Doc thinks its appendicitis and he thought you ought to know right away in case we're out tonight.'

For a moment or two the cold grey eyes continued their hostile stare before resuming a more human and reassuring expression.

'Thank you Mid.'

Poor little sod, Mark thought. Eighteen, looking about twelve and straight out of Dartmouth, but that hadn't stopped him getting up the skirt of one of the local girls. When he needed a secretary what did they send him, he queried morosely? A hormone-ridden schoolboy who wanted to prove he could have a girl in every port, that's what.

'Right,' he stood up, pushing Joanna's letter into his pocket. 'In future, my son, remember not to come up close behind a man like that. If I'd been our CPO I'd probably have knifed you – as a purely reflex action, you understand?'

'Yes sir.'

Webb wasn't sure whether this advice was serious or a leg-pull. The men who had been with the Flotilla Captain from the beginning called him the Dread Mark, albeit behind his back, but Webb himself stuck warily to a rigid formality, both in and out of his presence, particularly after the tongue lashing he'd received when that girl's father had come storming onto the base. But he caught his quizzical look now and decided it had been a joke about the likelihood of being knifed.

The old man could be a terror, but occasionally he was really quite human.

Mark replied to Joanna's letter that evening, sitting in his shore office with nothing to disturb him but the occasional sounds of laughter from the nearby quarters. When he'd finished he sat for a long time, swinging gently from side to side in his swivel chair, aching with desire for her and feeling on this particular evening that he would surely go mad with the need to lie again in her arms. The hell of it was that the more time they spent together the worse were the months apart.

Abruptly, he stood up and left the building, almost catching the Marine sentry napping, irritably acknowledging the delayed salute and giving him a sharp reprimand before crossing the square to put his letter in the mailbox.

I'm a miserable old bugger, he acknowledged as he returned. I frighten wet behind the ears eighteen-year olds and bollock weary sentries; I should be ashamed of myself. Re-entering the building he returned the sentry's salute with one worthy of a visiting Admiral, which made him feel better for at least ten minutes and caused the marine to wonder if the Old Man was going off his chump at last.

Falmouth, Christmas 1942

Joanna leafed absently through a magazine, thinking that it seemed to be her lot in life to sit around in bars waiting for an Eden to appear.

The place was deserted, all sensible people being at home with their families; even the lethargic barmaid had disappeared. However, when one's only home was a naval quarter and one no longer had a family, a bar was as good a place as any to be at lunch-time on Christmas Eve.

Now she was missing Mark desperately and longing to be in Tollmouth in case he should come home. The Kensington flat was still there. No one wanted to buy a London residence, however desirable, during a war. She was grateful for the use of a place in town, but without Audrey it was as yet too painful to stay there for any length of time. However, one thing was clear in her mind. Before today was over, she must level with Leo about Mark and herself. The deception had gone on long enough.

'Somehow I never had you down as a girl likely to be reading 'How to knit a tea-cosy in one easy lesson!' '

Leo leaned over to kiss her cheek then dropped into the seat opposite.

She managed a smile, casting aside the magazine. 'Found it on the chair – and I was deeply engrossed in 'How to make an apple charlotte' in what appears to be a half dozen very difficult ones!'

He looked around the bar and grimaced with distaste.

'What a gloomy hole. I've booked Christmas lunch at the Kings. They assure me it will be real turkey.'

'You should be at home, Leo, instead of driving all this way to see me. Not that I don't appreciate it very much but you won't get back until late evening and that's one hell of a drive at night.'

'I couldn't leave you all alone on Christmas Eve; and I've been thinking: why don't you come back to Stonehams with me and spend your leave there?'

'I can't!'

He looked startled at her sudden obvious panic.

'Why not? Mary's always invited several Service people at Christmas. Our daughter-in-law Monica would be so pleased to have another young woman to talk with and there are two RAF types already arrived, so you'd have plenty of company and it would do you good. After all, it's not as though my wife knows who you are.'

She took a deep breath.

'Have you never mentioned Audrey's name to her?'

He frowned. 'No. I never mentioned her by name, any more than Audrey talked about you, at least, not until I'd met you, and never about your private life. That was our agreement.'

'That's what I thought.' She took another deep breath. 'Leo, I have something to tell you. I've been trying to pluck up courage ever since you first rang me weeks ago, then every time I see you I flunk it...' she faltered momentarily, 'but now I can't bear it any longer.'

'My dear child,' he took both of her hands in his. 'Whatever it is, it can't be that bad.'

'Don't you believe it,' she met his eyes, hers level and unflinching. 'Here goes… I've already met your wife. I went to Stonehams a few weeks after Laura was born; Monica and I have been friends since we signed up on the same day and trained together at Greenwich. When I went to Stonehams I knew perfectly well who you were – the photographs of you at Kit's wedding rather blew your cover.'

'Hang on…'

He looked confused. No wonder, thought Joanna, her heart thumping, but not half as confused as he's going to be in the next few minutes…

He sat back and she could almost hear his mind working. The silence began to stretch to an uncomfortable length. Finally, he shook his head.

'Why on earth didn't you *say*?' There was a dawning look of accusation in his eyes. 'You were dodging me for months, weren't you? Why, Jo? It doesn't make sense. Why should it matter that you knew my name, for God's sake? You know it now and I'd have told you at anytime if you'd asked. It was only that your mother always insisted on that little subterfuge for my sake. I still don't see why you won't come with me for Christmas. As a friend of Monica's it would be the most natural thing in the world.'

'Leo, just listen to me … there's more.' She was painfully reminded of her quarrel with Mark, and how his confession had gone from bad to worse. 'For a start I couldn't possibly face your wife again … we didn't, er, exactly hit it off and now that you've told her about you and mother...'

She hesitated, feeling panic beginning to grip her once more. There wasn't any way to cushion what she had to say. She closed her eyes and took the fence head-on.

'Leo – oh hell, look; your son Mark and I have been lovers for over two years. He doesn't know I know you, he never met Audrey but he knows all about her friend Leo because I told him –'

'WHAT!'

At his full-throated roar Joanna winced and the barmaid materialised as though by magic through the bead curtain behind the bar to glare suspiciously at Lionel.

'Please, Leo, let me finish … your wife knows about Mark and me, so do Kit and Monica. The only reason *you* don't is because everybody pussy-foot's around you, avoiding even breathing our names. You turn up with me on tow for Christmas and it'll be explanation time with a vengeance!'

There was a charged silence. His lined, craggy face was heavy with either anger or disbelief; quite which she wasn't sure. She closed her eyes again and kept them closed because quite suddenly the room was behaving in the most peculiar fashion, see-sawing madly one moment, then spinning the next, and from somewhere a long way off someone seemed to be ringing a bloody great door-bell...then a very firm hand was pushing her head down onto her knees, an authoritative voice calling for brandy and a minute later a glass held to her chattering teeth. Spluttering as the spirit found its mark she hauled herself back from what felt like a long spiralling fall off Beachy Head.

She opened her eyes cautiously, met Lionel's flinty gaze and closed them again quickly. He growled 'Don't you *dare* faint on me again young lady; I've a great deal more to say to you yet!'

His voice and face were grim but the fingers on her pulse and the hand on her forehead were reassuringly gentle.

'Sorry Leo.' Her own voice sounded tinny and far away; she shook her head, trying to clear it.

'Are you all right to walk?' She nodded, and he ordered peremptorily, 'Right. Finish that brandy and then out to the car.'

She said 'Yes, Leo,' and obediently tipped her glass, shuddering as the brandy seared her throat. Keeping a firm grip on her arm he steered her through the door and down the steps.

The cold air hit her like a blow, magically clearing her head of any lingering dizziness and she sank back thankfully into the comfort of the car as he settled himself in the driving seat and fired the engine.

'Where are we going?' she ventured, as he drove swiftly through the outskirts of the town.

'Somewhere a lot less disgusting than that boozer. For God's sake, Jo, the places you know!'

He was terse and uncommunicative on the drive. She sighed faintly. Oh, well, you could only die once.

He turned the car off the road after a mile or so and stopped on the grassy headland. 'Now,' he left the heater running. 'Let me hear it all.

Begin at the beginning and try not to miss anything out. I'm too old to have to keep back-tracking!'

'I'll try, but please don't shout at me again. I find it difficult enough to deal with the snotty remarks Mark can hand out from time to time, but at least he doesn't howl at me like a bloody banshee.'

He put up a hand to cover a smile. 'Get on with it then.'

'Well, we met at a party on board the *Miranda* early in the war…'

She took it slowly, trying to get everything in the right order finishing, '…we've only ever really quarrelled twice and both times were about you. In the beginning he wouldn't talk to me about you; just said you hated his guts as much as he hated yours and because I loved him so much I assumed you were some rotten old sod who made his life hell.'

'Is that why you started dodging me?'

'No, that was later, after I pushed him into a corner over Kit and Monica's wedding so that he had to tell me all about the money, and Vivienne and … and what he did to you. Then, when Monica sent the photographs and I realised *you* were the rotten old sod, I didn't know what to do. Mark was away and I couldn't tell anyone without breaking his confidence, although I might have told Kit, but he'd already been posted overseas. I felt awful about not seeing you again because I'd been so fond of you. I think that for me you were the substitute father I once thought I didn't need.' She laid her head against the dashboard, close to tears.

He was moved then to take her hand and say gently: 'You could have told me; I would have understood.'

'I didn't know that did I? You were the big bad wolf,' she raised her head and gave an uncertain smile. 'I couldn't anyway: not behind Mark's back. Now it's all such a horrible mess. I'm going to have to tell him when he comes on leave next and I feel so awful about never taking him to see mother. She would have liked him and been so pleased, but I couldn't do that without letting the cat out of the bag … and he can be such a stuffed shirt sometimes. How the hell could I, *can* I explain about you two? I'm damned if I can think of a delicate way to tell the man I'm sleeping with that his father was doing the same with my mother.'

There was another long silence. He sighed before answering.

'Well, it's quite a mess and I have to accept the lion's share of the blame, but for the life of me, I can't see an easy way out of any of it.'

'Join the club!' She stared moodily out across the sea. 'He *did* leave a note about the money, you know. You shouldn't have called him a liar.' When he didn't answer she added crossly: '*I'd* have taken it if I'd spent six years living on jam sandwiches and with my arse hanging out of my trousers because of you.'

'Oh you would, would you?'

'Yes. I bloody would!'

This time he didn't hide his smile; suddenly overwhelmed with affection for this young woman who was prepared to tackle him on Mark's behalf. 'You are absolutely right. I should have believed him about the money because whatever else he may have been, he wasn't a liar. And I should most definitely not have laid my hand on him all those years ago. I was just so angry with him to think he was throwing away a promising career.'

'He's a very good vet!' She defended quickly.

'I'm sure he is,' he was dryly amused, 'and I now wish him nothing but the best in the life he chose for himself.'

'He thinks you'll never forgive him and that you hate him.'

'I suppose he does, but then he's never given me the chance to tell him otherwise, has he?'

She began to smile. 'Kit said he got his pig-headedness from you.'

'Kit always was too observant for comfort.' He gave her a long look. 'So, you really love that obstinate, tiresome, son of mine, do you?'

'I do, very much.'

'Then between us we shall eventually have to work something out.' He leaned forward to start the car, 'but first, turkey and all the trimmings at the Kings!'

She gave a last wave as the Lagonda reached the corner just as the church clock struck six; watching the car out of sight before turning to climb the steps to her door.

Well, nothing much had changed except that she felt part of the load had been lifted from her shoulders. If, when Mark returned, she chose the time and the place with care she felt that now she would be able to lay the whole mess before him and hope that he wouldn't be too angry, or see her long silence over her friendship with his father as treacherous.

The clock chimes faded away. A few more hours to Christmas Day ... She hugged her arms to her, looking up at the clear night sky, asking silently*: Mark, Kit, where are you now ... and are you thinking of me as I am of you?*

17

Malaya, January 1943

10.1.43 wrote Kit. Laboriously, because his stub of pencil, hoarded and used sparingly for almost a year, was slipping in his sweaty hands and the wooden cross porous and uneven. He added the name Duncan Cameron: just one more memorial to another dead soldier. He shivered, feeling himself again in the early grip of malaria.

'He put up one helluva fight!' Arnie had come from behind to stand by his side. 'A good kid, but he was never goin' to make it, was he?'

'No. But dying by inches of starvation and disease is no way to go when you're only nineteen. There are easier deaths.'

'Well, however you go, when you're dead you're dead, mate. Nobody lives for ever.'

'I thought we'd recently celebrated the birthday of one who did just that.'

Arnie smacked him on the shoulder. 'You're a good mate, Padre, but you can count *me* out of believing in miracles. I'm too busy just trying to stay alive. Look out…' he spat on the dirt floor. 'Here comes that bastard Kano...'

'Captain Yoshida want you.' The guard halted before them, legs astride, swinging his club, pointing at Kit. 'You go now quick.'

He walked on shaky legs to the Captain's bungalow, expecting at every step of the way to feel the blow to the kidneys or the back of the knees that Kano was so fond of delivering. Arriving at the foot of the bungalow steps he stood bare-headed, swaying slightly with the fever until he could see the shining boots appear on the steps above him. He bowed low and waited.

'Today you go to woman's camp,' Yoshida rose and fell on his toes. 'Many sick and not working; all must be fit for work.'

'Yoshida San, I am a priest, not a doctor. We *have* no doctor.'

'You take care of men in this camp. You take care of women too.'

'I shall need some medicines.'

'Medicines come soon: perhaps tomorrow. You make women better for work.'

The boots disappeared and Kit bowed again, watching the

corporal out of the corner of his eye. As he turned to go the club swung, catching him across the lower back but he was ready; rolling with the blow and dropping to the ground, covering his head with his arms against the expected assault from Kano's boots. Instead there was a volley of screams from Captain Yoshida who crashed back through the bungalow door to set about the corporal with his hands, slapping and punching and cursing the guard. Standing silently, with hands hanging by his side Kano made no effort to defend himself against the blows that rained down upon his shaven head.

With no idea why the enigmatic and normally impassive Yoshido should be defending him, but grateful for the reprieve Kit regained his feet and walked unsteadily to his hut. Once there he sat shaking and wondering how, with no medicines or treatment to offer, what on earth he was supposed to do in a camp full of sick women and children. He wasn't made any happier to find that Kano was to be his guard and guide to the camp, but the corporal walked without his club and in silence, his face bruised and lips split, one eye bloodshot and half-closed.

The place was swarming with flies and mosquitoes, but remarkably clean and tidy. Wash-lines of twisted string and wire were loaded with mostly ragged garments of varying sizes, from a child's small shirt to a voluminous flowered silk dress. As Kit crossed the compound curious faces were turned his way, the groups of women and children squatting over improvised cooking stoves interested, but wary of the bearded, unkempt figure in ragged khaki and his battered, sullen escort.

The camp Commandant was unusually tall for a Jap and very different from Captain Yoshido. Speaking quietly and in fluent English he explained that he had requested medicines and had hopes that some would be released to his camp from the stores accumulated from Red Cross supplies.

'You will find your patients in the long hut at the end of that path there.' He gestured towards the far end of the camp. Kit bowed his thanks, and still trailed by Kano walked slowly across the compound.

A tall dark-haired woman wearing a native sarong with the *soignée* air of a pre-war mannequin stepped from the long hut and came towards them. Casting a withering glance at the corporal she addressed herself to Kit, demanding imperiously.

'Are you the doctor? About time. I hope you've brought quinine and vitamins. Over a third of the women are off their feet and these stupid guards don't seem to understand. They expect us to stay alive on bugger all but lousy Nip rice and be grateful as though this fucking place is the Ritz!' She paused for breath, favouring Kano with another disparaging look, before adding: 'All I can say is, God help the Japanese women if this shower of performing baboons are anything to go by!'

Kit took off his stained and crumpled cap, a spark of pardonably malicious laughter lighting his eyes.

'Hello, Vivienne – fancy meeting you here!'

Her eyes widened, she took a step forward then gave a little cry and caught at his arm. 'Kit?' Tears sprang to her eyes and she gripped his arm tight with bony fingers, her face suddenly shocked and concerned as she took in his shivering, emaciated form. 'It *is* you…but you are ill … why on earth did you come? I asked for a doctor, and they send you!' She brushed impatiently at her tears then lifted her shoulders in a despairing gesture. 'Oh, Kit,' there was a catch in her voice, 'have you any news of Dougie?'

'When I left him in Changi he was busy running some racket to smuggle letters out and said he'd get one to my father. He had this chap on the outside – Hanif someone; Dougie said he was your wine merchant.'

'Hanif Jalawa?' She was incredulous. 'What good would he have been?'

'He had some scheme to get away...one of his dozens of relatives was 'fixing' it.' He took her hands as the tears began to spill again down her cheeks. 'Dougie reckoned he would make it. So you see they probably will have had something to keep hope alive for you and me.'

'You'd better come in before your legs give way. You look almost as ill as some of my patients!' Wiping the tears away with the back of her hand she turned to glare at Kano, 'I think we can do without the organ grinder's monkey, thank you.' Pointing to the veranda steps she ordered, 'Sit there!'

Kano sat.

She led Kit into the hut where dozens of women and children lay on bamboo cots; dragging a stool across to the doorway she commanded him, 'Now *you* sit down!'

'Yes ma'am.'

She grinned suddenly. 'I've never been so pleased to see anyone in my life.'

'Even after my last farewell?'

'Yes even after that!'

Gratefully, he lowered himself onto the stool. ' Now tell me what's been happening to you and how you came to be here, then we'll have a go at your commandant and see if we can twist his arm to get some medicines for your patients. Because, believe it or not, I am the doctor around here, even if I haven't seen a vitamin pill since leaving Singapore!'

They had been in at least half-a-dozen camps, she told him, their longest stay anywhere no more than three months before they were marched on again, always further away from civilisation to end up permanently, it seemed, in this last specially constructed compound.

'We are lucky, really, those who've survived so far. Originally we were about five hundred, but lost so many of the old and the very young on the marches.' She played with the thick plait of hair. No longer a shining black river cascading to her shoulders, it was dull now and streaked with grey. 'Captain Anchi who is in charge was a University professor in America before the war and is a sick man – we think he has TB he coughs so much. The army don't rate him very highly, which is why he's in charge of a bunch of women.' She gave a sly, sideways grin. 'Actually, under different circumstances I might quite fancy him.'

'No old horse, now, Vivienne,' he warned, 'and you'd be wasting your time trying to shock *me.*'

'OK, Rev.' She gave his arm a squeeze, 'I promise, no old horse whatsoever.'

* * *

Falmouth, March 1943

My dearest, always most beloved and still my own Number One,

I've arranged some leave for next month...thought I would go to South Ken and pack up the last of Audrey's clothes (a job I've been shirking), air the flat then try to snatch a few days at Porthryn. James says he will roll out the red carpet and kill the fatted calf ... metaphorically speaking, I hope!

In the unlikely event that you may come home soon your car is languishing at the back of the SO's mess at NHQ Tollmouth. CPO Hawkins in engineering stores has the key. Leo is fetching me then driving to the flat so that I can train straight down to Cornwall when we've finished there. Darling, I shall miss you so when I climb into our beautiful big bed, but perhaps beneath the nice clean sheets and pillowcases there will linger a little something of the scent of you. I hope so ... then I shall be able to close my eyes and pretend you are there beside me.

11.45 p.m. and I am burning the midnight oil. Guess who interrupted my letter writing? I won't keep you in suspense ... it was your friend and mine, Josh Milton, sporting a Major's crowns and an MC ribbon and offering me dinner; what a thing! He was looking terribly pleased with himself...almost as though he'd turned Rommel back single-handed. It was a very nice dinner but I made sure he didn't get a chance to play footsie. He did look rather dismayed when all he got at the door was a peck on the cheek and my thanks. That'll teach him to come sniffing around when a girl is already spoken for, I bet I shan't see him again in a hurry!

Time you were back in Tollmouth again, my love. At least we are in the same country. Poor little Jean Finch's husband is in Gibraltar. She hasn't seen him for two years, and she looks such a baby. I don't think I'd have been very good wife material at twenty, but I should be ripe, if not over-ripe by the time you manage to make an honest woman of me. Not that it seems to matter much now... How could I love and want and need you any more than I do?

I think of you constantly, love you to distraction, and will wait for you, if necessary, to the end of time.

Goodnight, goodnight…

Always, Joanna'

* * *

Portsmouth, April 1943

Mark stepped from the car, glad to stretch his cramped legs. The train journey from Norfolk had been long and uncomfortable and he was grateful a car had been waiting for him at the station.

With luck, he thought, he would catch part of Joanna's leave. His pulse quickened at the thought that she may even now be waking alone in their bed, remembering the inevitable result of them being together and waking from sleep at first light. How she would turn in his arms and say: "Hello, you!" with that lovely little catch in her voice…

He realised his young FANY driver was holding open the car door and saluting. Hauling himself back firmly from his daydreams he returned the salute then climbed the steps of Naval HQ to keep his appointment with Rear Admiral Cunningham.

* *

'Had enough of Norfolk yet?'

‘I hadn’t really thought about it, sir – too busy.’

Mark was non-committal, knowing by now all the signs. A big move was in the air for him. His old boss hadn’t brought him all the way back from East Anglia just to admire the view.

The Rear Admiral lit his pipe and puffed contentedly for a few seconds before continuing. ‘Got a brand new type MTB coming off the stocks; it’s a beautiful job. Twenty-one inch torpedo tubes, a couple of depth charges and bristling with Vickers machine-guns. We need a captain to command a flotilla of them operating from the Kent coast. I know you’ve been running the show up in Norfolk since Campbell bought it and it’s time the promotion was put on a permanent footing. I’ve persuaded the powers that be to put you in charge. It’s all yours when ready.’

Mark was torn between delight and dismay. The promotion was more than he could have hoped for but the move would bring him very little nearer to Joanna. Still, it had to be better than operating off Norway, or being posted back to the Med. He met the gaze of the famous Cunningham eyes: one brown, one blue, both razor-sharp and asked hopefully, ‘Do I get to hang on to a few of my own boat lieutenants, sir?’

‘Hang onto the whole boiling lot if you want, you’ll be glad of experienced hands. You know how sticky things are getting in the North Sea and all along the Channel. The Germans are arming everything they can get their hands on now and moving supplies in their damned converted landing barges, which are hell to spot, even in daylight.

‘How soon before the new boats are ready, sir?’

‘They’re due delivery within the month, but going by your record I imagine you’ll want to go down to your new base soon to start on all the paper-work and get your crews assembled. Take your pick of what’s already on offer to make up your full compliment of officers and crew for each boat. As you might imagine, by now we’re scrapping the bottom of the barrel and some of the extra hands you’ll need will be pretty raw, so you’ll have your work cut out bringing them up to scratch.’

He paused to hand him a well-filled box file. ‘You report to Commodore Reggie Hyde at Sheering. Better take your leave as from now. You can be spared for ten days to get your own affairs sorted before you sign for the new craft and run your sea trials; all right?’

‘Yes sir.’

Through a cloud of blue smoke the Rear Admiral gave him a tight smile.

‘Sorry to disrupt your domestic arrangements, Eden, but war is war, you know.’

‘Only too well sir.’

‘Lovely girl…’ he gave a wolfish grin at the involuntary flicker of the Lieutenant Commander’s eyes. ‘Freddie Naughton’s an old shipmate of mine; we were boys at Osborne together; he thinks the world of her.’

‘So do I sir.’

‘Well, you’ll just have to continue keeping the postman busy, won’t you? Now I suggest you cast off and give the lady the good news.’

*   *   *

‘Sorry sir,’ the voice on the switchboard was polite but firm. ‘Second Officer Dunne is at present on leave.’

‘I know.’ Mark shifted irritably in the ’phone kiosk. He was curt and impatient; a call to Jim had told him she hadn’t yet arrived at Porthryn. ‘I should like her first contact address.’

‘I’m afraid I’m not allowed to give you that information.’

He growled belligerently.

‘For your records miss, my name is Lieutenant Commander Eden and I have not come all the way from East Anglia to have *you* give me a hard time. Now just give me that address – unless you’d rather I came down and asked Commander Naughton in person...’

‘Sorry sir, its 23 Gordon Mansions, Cromwell Road, South Kensington.’

‘Thank you – and you are...?’

‘Leading Wren Murray sir, and I’m ever so sorry.’

He smoothed the irritation out of his voice. ‘No, Miss Murray, *I’m* sorry. That was very rude of me.’ His good humour restored he put the receiver down and left the kiosk whistling. Just time to grab some lunch, get his car and make straight for London and Joanna.

His blood tingled. He felt ten, no, perhaps that was exaggerating a little, but at least five years, slip from his mind and body; particularly his body.

She hadn’t yet been to Cornwall, so they could drive down as soon as she was finished at the flat and still have several days and nights together before either had to return to duty – and the visit to South Kensington would also give him a chance to meet and thank the Leo who was being so helpful.

*   *   *

When the doorbell rang Joanna was half way to the kitchen. Seeing the peaked cap and blur of uniform behind the frosted-glass door panel she called over her shoulder, 'I'll get it Leo; it's the chap from the Sally Army. Could you bring the big box out?' and crossing the hallway opened the door wide with a welcoming smile.

Finding Mark's arms about her, the deep warmth of his voice in greeting and his mouth on hers she was too swept with the excitement and immediate joy of his presence to register that his arrival couldn't have been less opportune. She clung to him breathlessly until the sudden loosening of the arms which strained her against him, and his voice, no longer warm but sounding both harsh and bewildered, demanded: ' What the hell are *you* doing here?'

From behind her Leo's rather shaken but urbane reply of: 'A reasonable enough question, I'd say!' jolted her out of delight into panic as the full enormity of the situation hit her and she flung her head up with a loud, anguished, 'Oh *shit*!'.

Of all the nightmare scenarios she might have imagined, this had to be the worst.

At that precise moment like actors in a well-rehearsed farce, the expected Salvation Army Captain and his bonneted lady helper appeared behind Mark at the open door.

It was Leo who took charge of the situation.

Passing the box he carried to the Captain, and sweeping several paper carrier bags of clothes from where they stood on the hall table, he escorted the bemused pair down to their waiting van; leaving Joanna and Mark standing motionless in the hallway, facing each other across a gulf of anger and misunderstanding as wide as the Grand Canyon itself.

Mark found his voice first. 'What the *fuck* is going on … and what exactly is my bloody father doing here?'

'There is an explanation!' She held her hands out before her and backed away from him, controlling a terrible urge to burst into nervous, overwrought and possibly uncontrollable giggles. The situation was both dangerous and farcical, at any moment now Leo would re-appear and then the balloon really would go up.

'Then let's bloody hear it, *now.*' his face was thunderous.

'Just calm down before Leo gets back – '

'*WHAT?*'

Too late she realised her mistake. If she had found Lionel's shout unnerving when she had first mentioned Mark's name, it was nothing to the effect that his son's roar of fury now had on her.

'Don't do that!' she yelled back, panic lending her sudden strength. 'I'm not one of your bloody ratings up on Captain's defaulters, so don't bawl at me as if I were!'

'You called him Leo!' he brought his voice down to a terrifying, menacing calm. 'Do I understand that my father is the same Leo who was having an affair with your *mother*? God Almighty! Just how long have I been kept in the dark? And how *dare* you be on any kind of terms with a man who treated me like shit, tried to wreck my career and cheated on my mother?'

'I didn't know myself who he really was until after Kit's wedding–'

'Jesus Christ, woman, that was two *years* ago!'

'So it was two years; anyway – Leo and Audrey – it wasn't *like* that then and I didn't get a chance to explain. You were so awful that first time I made you tell me about him that I wasn't going to go for another lot. Then it just got more and more difficult.' She fell back another pace at his furious expression. 'Don't look at me like that, Mark Eden … you've only yourself to blame!'

'I'll look at you any damned way I please, but right now I don't choose to either look at, or talk to you any further.' He was coldly, bitingly sarcastic. 'If the pair of you can manage to cook up a half-way believable explanation between you, do write and let me know; perhaps I shall find it as amusing as you undoubtedly have to have been hand-in-glove with each other behind my back for all this time.'

'But I didn't *know* who he was when you first told me about him – and *he* didn't know about *us* until after Audrey died!'

'Oh, please, spare me any more fucking lies…' he turned and kicked the door wide open. 'Just think yourself lucky that I don't even want to touch you right now.'

'Mark, *wait*; you have to let me explain – '

But he had gone, racing down the stairs and wrenching himself with an appalling obscenity past the ascending Lionel. Hitting the front door open with his shoulder and leaving it swinging on a broken catch he stormed out into the street.

Joanna flew to the sitting room window and struggled with the sash, pushing up the window just as the Riley left the front of the building with a screech of tyres and a blare of the horn from a passing bus.

'He's gone!' she covered her face with her hands, weeping uncontrollably. 'He's gone, and this time he won't be coming back ever again!'

*　　*　　*

'What will you do now?'

The evening traffic flowed homeward along the Cromwell Road, from the theatres and cinemas, making for Richmond and Surbiton and all points west, the dimmed blue slits of the headlights looking ghostly in the dusk.

Joanna sat on the leather couch, clutching her coffee cup, calm now but looking suddenly very young and frightened and unsure. She shrugged and her mouth drooped.

'"*I might go on: naught else remained to do.*"' For a moment she battled against further tears, 'I don't know. He won't want to see me but I *must* explain how all this happened. I think I'll just take my courage in both hands and go down to Cornwall in the hope that he may have bolted home.' She gave her wry, crooked smile. 'We were so happy there. If he'll listen to me anywhere, it will be at Porthryn.'

'I don't like the idea of you being alone.'

'I shall be all right now, Leo.' She smiled again, 'I can still call you that, can't I?'

'You may call me anything you like, providing it is not on the lines of Mark's parting shot; that made the Soldier's Farewell sound like a blessing!'

'The Eden men, or at least two of them, don't actually seem to be able to stay in reasonable control when someone gets up their respective noses, do they?'

He shook his head. 'The meeting, Jo...it was a shock. I haven't set eyes on him for almost ten years. He's quite a man isn't he? Not very pliable, damned unreasonable in fact,' his expression was suddenly embarrassed. 'He's rather more like me than I was aware.'

She said with some bitterness, 'Then God help me if the things he told me about *you* really are true.'

'I'm afraid they probably were; but I haven't just turned into a monster, Jo.'

'I know; I'm sorry. I didn't mean that – but how are we ever going to get out of this mess?'

He sat beside her and took her hand in his. '*You* must try to see Mark and make him listen to you, and *I* must tell Mary just how long I have known you and kept that knowledge from her. There can be no more skirting around the truth between any of us now'

'What will you tell her?'

'That you and I are very well acquainted, that Mark's girl is

Audrey's daughter. That should be enough to set the ball rolling.'

She squeezed his hand and gave him a pale smile. 'Rather you than me, then. When you do, please tell her that I'm so very sorry and that I regret not making the effort to understand her feelings about Mark and me.'

He gave a wicked grin. 'She might find it difficult to accuse either you or me of being economical with the truth. After all she didn't tell me about *your* visit and the nice little fencing match the pair of you had, did she?'

'No. Stupid, aren't we, the whole lot of us.' She stood up and kissed his cheek. 'Thank you, for staying and helping but you must go home now. Tomorrow I'll travel down to Porthryn and try to beard the lion in his den.'

At the door he held her hand for a moment. 'Tonight, you remind me of your mother.' He bent to kiss her. 'Goodnight. Good hunting and God keep you...' he touched her cheek in understanding at the sudden brilliance of tears in her eyes, 'he still says that, does he?' he asked.

'He always *did*.' she said. Closing the door softly she stood leaning her head against it, listening to his retreating footsteps and gathering her courage for the coming day.

18

Falmouth, May 1943

Monica...

It's all too ghastly. I waited and waited at Porthryn until the last day of my leave, but he didn't come and I've no idea where he is ... this isn't Tollmouth where I knew pretty well everybody's whereabouts. All I know is that he hasn't gone back to his old base. He could be absolutely anywhere by now. What a flaming mess I've made of things.

I wish I could come again to Stonehams and see you and Laura but I can't possibly face your ma-in-law again, especially since she knows about Audrey, although it would be lovely to clear off somewhere with you and just talk.

I think so much about Kit; what a help and comfort he would be and how much you must miss him. Oh, when will this bloody war be over so that we all can be together again ... but then we shan't, shall we? Mark won't be with us all any more ... and to think I imagined that some day I could bring him and his father back together again ... such conceit on my part.

Must go now before I get completely maudlin so give a big hug and a kiss to Laura from me...

Love, Joanna.

* * *

Stonehams, June 1943

Joanna...

Mark is still in England somewhere but I've no idea where. Mary may know but if she does she isn't letting on. I know Mark has 'phoned her a couple of times but won't visit. Just as well I suppose, as Lionel is absolutely furious with him for treating you so badly. I feel so cross ... aren't men the absolute limit?

Thought I ought to go to Cheyne Walk and show Laura to mother and the lord but only stayed for one night, as step-papa was rude about daddy. I wasn't having that as he is fighting in North Africa and the lord just sitting on his backside in the War Office, the fat old fart.

No news yet of Kit. Oh, but I wish we were nearer to each other. I sometimes think I wouldn't even mind being back in our first grotty quarters in Tollmouth ... remember Madam and her eagle eye? But then I look at Laura and think how lucky I am. But I do miss you so much.

Mary doesn't go so far as to send you her best wishes but seems to be mellowing. Lionel sends his love and will be down to see you next month. He says too that you should 'for God's sake find a decent pub to meet in this time!'

Monica.

* * *

Porthryn, October 1943

Joanna put down her case and kissed Jim's leathery cheek 'At least one welcoming smile,' she gave a small shrug. 'I can see by your face that he hasn't he been down at all since I was here last.'

He shook his head.

'No. I told you when you came in May that he'd rung in a very bad temper to say he was in Tollmouth for a few days. Then I got another call... let me see... must have been about the middle of June. I told him then that you'd been here on leave and he said "How nice," and that he hoped you were able to sleep at night. Since then I've just had the odd 'phone call to inquire about the practice and ask if I was still managing or ready to give in and get a locum, the cheeky devil!' He gave her a shrewd look. 'You two have fallen out in a big way, haven't you?'

'Yes. He was hopping mad about something he found out was going on behind his back – no need to look like that, Jim, it wasn't another man.'

She smiled, and he would have forgiven her even if it had been; holding up his hand he said, 'I don't need any details. He's the perfect calm, unflappable gentleman until he blows, when it's everyone take cover until the storm dies down.'

'He used not to be like that,' she said sadly.

'He's *always* been like that,' he contradicted, 'but I grant you he hides it beautifully ... most of the time!'

Although she knew that there was little chance she would ever see Mark again, still she was glad she'd come to Porthryn. Jim was a comfort and it was wonderful to walk the hills and woods with an eager Oscar, drink with Jim at the Wreckers some evenings and just generally unwind. But she couldn't bear to sleep in the bed she'd shared with Mark, curling each night instead on the old couch in the sitting room, refusing to let Jim give up his own bed for her.

She hadn't written, although several times she'd tried; but she had no address and she shrank from the thought of asking Mary Eden to pass on any letter she may write. She had been a coward, deceiving and lying to him and now was reaping the bitter harvest she'd sown. So the letter remained unwritten. She stayed in his house and walked his dog and dreamed hopeless dreams that he would come home whilst she was there.

When in Falmouth, the work absorbed her completely. The continuing secrecy of the job meant that she mixed with few outside her own small circle, even her leisure time tended to revolve around the same crowd of people.

Constantly surrounded as she was by men of all ages and varying attractions, as first weeks, then months slipped by and there was no word from Mark, the temptation offered by some became hard to resist. In reality she wanted no arms but Mark's around her, no lovemaking other than his. But with the passing of time the loss of love and the physical consummation of that love had her floundering in a non-man's-land of repressed emotions.

Walking with Oscar along the cliffs above Porthryn on her first morning, she rounded a headland to come face to face with the amiable but undoubtedly dangerous-to-women Josh Milton.

'Hey there,' his rugged features broke into a dazzling smile, 'if it isn't the sexy Miss Dunne.'

The boisterous light-hearted greeting sparked her into sudden anger. 'If I had to choose the person I'd least want to meet, it would be you!'

'Wow! Old Mark left you in a chastity belt and taken the key?' he queried gleefully then recoiled in mock-horror at her fierce glare. 'Oops! Sorry.'

She swiped viciously with her stick at a clump of nettles. 'Just bugger off Major and find a horse's backside to talk to!'

'How frightfully coarse; and I thought you such a lady.'

'Yes, well ... you get up my nose.'

'I can think of better places...' She rounded on him, her hand tightening around the stick and he leaped back in alarm. 'Pax, pax, nothing personal, just habit, I assure you.'

'Oh, just *go away*, will you?'

He saw the shine of tears and was immediately contrite, 'Ah, look, I'm really sorry – just boosting my own morale y'know. My ice-maidenly old mate Caro, whom I've been hoping to melt during this leave, has already gone back to her ruddy place of work, wherever that may be. When James said you were here without Mark I thought perhaps you'd had a tiff and you might want someone to smooth your ruffled feathers.'

'Huh. You have absolutely no chance.'

'I'm right about the tiff though, aren't I? But you don't strike me as the kind of girl to fall apart over a mere spat. Come on, you can tell your Uncle Josh; I'm really a very nice bloke when I stop being randy.'

In spite of her misery, she had to smile. 'How do I know you've stopped?'

'Because I'd have made a much faster pass by now if I hadn't,' he grinned and took her arm. 'Come on. I've got the car up on the road and I'll take you for a nice long leisurely run into Tregenick for a drink in the Mermaid. I might even buy you one of old Henry Trevellyan's pictures of jolly fisher folk – and I promise not to pounce!'

She gave a wry smile. 'That was Mark's line.'

'My, then he did actually change for the better.'

Josh was a surprisingly good listener and after a while she found herself telling him some of her troubles. He listened sympathetically, without offering any trite or meaningless expressions of condolence, only saying when she had finished: 'Well, me queen, all I can say is that the man needs his head sorted and if he were here right now I'd volunteer for the job.'

'He does have reasons which I can't tell you about because that's family trouble…'

'Well, I've guessed something of that. When a man only goes home to mummy and daddy once in a blue moon there's bound to be some kind of skeleton in the closet. I suppose it's all to do with Vivienne.' He gave her a sideways glance. 'Did you ever meet that lady?'

'I was hardly likely to cross the ocean to shake her hand, was I? No, our falling out was about something a lot worse than Vivienne.'

'She was quite a girl – all wrong for Mark, of course. Pity she took off so soon, though. I thought I was in with a chance there.'

She looked at him in disbelief. 'You really are a rat. I thought Mark was your friend. If you'd been around at the right time you'd even have had a go at getting into Joan of Arc's knickers wouldn't you?'

'Oh, I don't think hers, ducky – didn't she wear all that frightful chain-mail stuff? I'd need a tin opener for *them*!' He grinned, dropping the camp. 'No, the sexy Vivienne couldn't help it. She gave the come-on all right and not just to me. Poor cow, I wonder where she is now.'

'Like Kit, just somewhere in Malaya. The Eden's had a letter, ages ago from Dougie. Didn't you know?'

'I'm not really *au fait* with all that family's goings on – have another drink and do tell me everything about Singapore Lil and her fella!'

In the few days left of her leave he turned up each evening as she walked Oscar. She enjoyed his company, although she was cautious, very much aware of his undeniable physical attraction. But he kept his word … and his distance. Only on her last day as she walked with him to the gate after an evening of talk and shared laughter at the cottage, did he show a return to the old Josh. Leaning back against the wall he pulled her suddenly into his arms with a light: 'Something to remember me by!' and kissed her mouth with a swift expertise which took her breath away.

For a brief heady moment she let herself respond, caught suddenly in a vortex of desire, feeling her control slipping in the sudden fierce heat of her body; knowing that at that moment she wanted Josh Milton every bit as much as he very obviously wanted her.

'Joanna. Oh, Jo...' He pulled her into a closer embrace and began to kiss her face and neck, tweaking a button undone and moving a hand to cup and stroke her breast.

'*No*!' Shaking, she pulled away from him. 'Bloody hell Josh, stop, will you? I'm sorry, really I am – I'm not going to pretend I don't want to, but I just *can't*; not with anyone, not yet.'

'OK … it's OK!' He reached out to brush the back of his hand across her cheek, 'my fault, I didn't mean to honestly, but just for a moment I felt you were ... well … that you were...'

'I very nearly was!'

'Thank God. I thought I'd lost my touch and got it wrong!'

He watched, fascinated, as the dimple at the side of that enchanting and inviting mouth appeared briefly. He put out his hand to lay a finger on her lips.

'When that smile gets as far as these...' he moved the finger to touch her eyes, 'then I shall know it's safe to try again.'

'I'm glad you warned me.'

'Damn. Next time I'll make sure I catch you unawares.'

She shook her head. 'I don't think so. Goodbye, Major Milton.'

He gave a cheerful, unrepentant grin.

'Fuck-all to goodbye Second Officer Dunne – *Au revoir* sounds one hell of a lot better! '

'That has to be the first time *he's* ever said goodnight to a woman that quickly.' Jim observed, leaving the window and retuning to his armchair as she stepped back into the cottage,

'You voyeuristic old man.' she dropped a kiss on his sparse grey hair. 'You shall have a good pair of night-vision binoculars for Christmas. I'll see if I can wrangle some for you out of stores!'

Dunwold, Suffolk, February 1944.

'More wine, Lieutenant Commander?'

Mark shook his head, putting his hand over his glass. 'No thank you ... must keep a clear head.'

The blue-eyed blonde shrugged, smiled, and moved on.

He looked about him restlessly. Once he had been relaxed and at home in such surroundings, now all they did was remind him of Joanna and the night they met. Twice already this evening his mouth had dried and his heart thumped when he'd glimpsed in the crowd a trim back in Wren uniform, and thought for a wild moment that by some miracle she was here in this room.

Richard Stone, his First Lieutenant appeared at his elbow. 'Jolly good party, sir.'

'Hmm,' Mark looked at his cheerful face. 'Dick, am I a bit of an awkward bastard these days?'

'Certainly not, sir, although you can be rather, as our transatlantic pals say, 'ornery' at times!'

Mark grinned. 'Ever the diplomat,' he said. Richard gestured with his glass at a vivacious girl in a low cut dress.

'Nice bit of lovely over there – think I'll chance my arm.'

'You do that, so long as you're fit and wide awake tomorrow morning. Remember you're in charge for a couple of days while I'm along to a pow-wow in Portsmouth and a quick trip to Dorset.'

'Aye, aye, sir, only browsing, you might say!'

He drifted away and Mark resumed his survey of the room, all the old arguments starting in his head.

If she gave a damn she could have written or 'phoned.

How could she, you fool, when she doesn't know where you are? And it was you who went off at the deep end and refused to listen to her.

All right, but she did the deceiving; she went behind my back and ganged-up with the old man. It's up to her and she hasn't even tried.

You don't know that, and least he was there when she needed him, not playing cops and robbers like you.

Not fair. I couldn't help that.

'Day dreaming, Mr Eden?'

The blonde with the blue eyes was back. She laid a hand on his sleeve and smiled. He thought: pretty woman and waited for the expected sexual reflex to kick in, but there wasn't as much as a twinge. A prickle of sweat crawled across his scalp. My God ... he was jolted out of his lethargy. Use it or lose it ... he forced a smile, waving his half-full glass vaguely. 'I'm afraid I'm not very good at all this.'

'That's not how I remember you.'

He looked at her more closely. She smiled again. 'Have you forgotten a party on board the *Miranda* in Tollmouth? Not long before Dunkirk?'

Recognition dawned. *The night I met Joanna.* He kicked that thought aside. 'Of course...' he groped for the name. 'Uh, Hazel, isn't it? I remember you now.'

'I remember *you* all right; you disappeared suddenly just as I was beginning to enjoy myself. I had to make do with a certain Commander Jenner instead.'

'I hope he turned out to be satisfactory.'

'You could say that; I married him!' She inclined her head towards an older officer weighted down with gold braid. 'That's my Tommy – a Commodore now and looking forward to retirement! Shall we go outside for a breath of fresh air?'

She smiled and took his arm, pressing it against the swell of her breast. Mark's heart began a measured thump. The alarm bells were ringing, but what the hell, it wasn't as if this was unfamiliar ground. He'd come full circle ... back to the bored wife looking for a little extra-marital fun and games.

He returned the pressure of her arm. 'Just the night for a stroll,' he said.

In the shadows under a willow he took her in his arms, the first woman other than Joanna he had touched since that far-off night on board *Miranda*, and bent his head to her hungry mouth.

'Four years was a long time to wait for that!' she murmured and he kissed her again, very thoroughly, savouring it slowly. Moving his hands down he pulled her hard against him. No, he hadn't lost it; quite definitely he had not.

Her smile deepened and she eased a finger between the buttons at the top of his shirt, circling it over his bare skin. 'We can stay here for at least half-an-hour, no one will notice.'

He said, 'No one at all!' and sliding the straps of her gown from her shoulders bent his head to her breast.

You're a bit of a bastard, aren't you, sir?

Clear as a bell Joanna's voice sounded in his head. He swore softly under his breath, desire instantly obliterated as though he'd been doused with cold water. Disengaging himself from the Commodore's lady he averted his eyes from her surprised gaze. 'Sorry.' With unsteady hands he replaced the straps of her gown on her shoulders. 'On reflection I don't think I should play out of my league.'

She shrugged.

'Some you win, some you lose. Pity, just as I was beginning to feel really hungry. The *hors d'oeuvre* was nice … shame about the main course!' She raised an eyebrow. 'We might as well go back and dance, or is that also out of your league?'

'By no means.' he straightened his tie. 'I think that's entirely within the bounds of good naval practice – especially with Senior Officer's wives.'

She raised her brows again and leaned to wipe lipstick from his mouth with an ungentle thumb.

'Let's just keep it in the singular, shall we Captain?'

'Very hot in there, wasn't it, sir? I noticed you go out for a breather.' Richard Stone commented innocently as they strolled back together towards the flotilla base.

'Mind your own business, Number One.'

'Yes sir,' he kept a straight face. 'Nice stern though.'

'Not bad,' Mark conceded, 'pretty good upper deck, too.'

'Very well stacked but I wouldn't like to tangle with her old man; too much scrambled egg on the cap.'

'You're unlikely to be in any danger,' Mark assured him blandly, 'and for the record, neither am I.'

'I'm very glad to hear that, sir.'

Mark listed slightly to port and Richard caught at his arm to steady him. So much for keeping a clear head, thought Mark. He was uncomfortably aware that he'd had far too much to drink and that young Dicky thought the old man needed looking after. He disengaged his companion's hand from his arm. 'Ever thought of being a nanny, Number One?' he asked.

'Can't say I have, sir; I'm straight back to being a country solicitor after this lot.'

'Quite right; you'd make a lousy nanny … too much of a fusspot.'

'I'm sure that's true, sir.'

The Captain continued his dignified if slightly unsteady progress toward his lonely bed, his companion much relieved when they finally reached their destination.

'Goodnight, Dicky, I think Master Mark can manage without nanny now!'

'Aye aye, sir.'

The young man watched his captain disappear into his cabin before turning with a sigh into his own.

Poor old sod; wonder what happened between him and his Joanna? He ruminated. Now there was a cracker for you – and a lot classier than old Tommy Jenner's wife. He shook his head, no the old man was well out of it where *she* was concerned. Playing around with the Commodore's wife, well, that would be asking for trouble, wouldn't it?

The meeting in Portsmouth was to do with the Second Front in Europe. Nice to be in on it at last, Mark thought rather sourly, aware, although she'd never spoken of it that Joanna had been in that line of business for some considerable time. Still smarting from the way his mind had played tricks and caused him to make of a fool of himself with the only too willing Hazel Jenner, he made an unsuccessful effort to banish all thoughts of Joanna from his mind.

It was pointless having any regrets about last night. Nor was a room heaving with MTB Flotilla Commanders the place in which to start having thoughts of any kind about that damned, deceitful, two-faced utterly lovely and desperately missed Joanna Felicity Dunne.

19

Dorset, February 1944

For about the tenth time in an hour Mark looked up from his book to catch that same contemplative look in his mother's eye. Finally he decided he'd had enough and shut his book with a bang.

'Would you mind telling me why you keep looking at me as though I've grown two heads?'

She knitted placidly. 'I can't help wondering why you came at all as all you've done since you arrived is pretend to read that book.'

He frowned. 'I'm beginning to wonder why as well. I must say there's a damned odd air about this place today.'

'If there is, it came in with you.'

'Mother, if you've got it in for me about something I'd like to know.'

She put the knitting down, and turned to face him. 'For months you have refused to say where you are stationed and made no effort to keep in touch, never mind about actually taking the trouble to visit. I may not be the top of your list but you might at least have spared time to see Monica. Anything that makes life easier for her and takes her mind off her troubles is welcome, but you couldn't even time that right, could you?'

'Well I'm here now – and I can't be blamed because *she's* in Scotland with her father.'

'Just as well with you in your present mood!' For a moment his mother was silent before adding with faint sarcasm, 'even your 'special girl' Joanna Dunne writes to her regularly, although she is too far away – or too embarrassed to visit her here.'

He stood up abruptly, walking over to the window, hunching his shoulders.

'I have no idea why Joanna should be "too embarrassed" to visit Monica and I'd rather you left her out of the conversation – we are no longer together.'

'I know that.'

'How do you know?' He rounded on her. 'Just who has been discussing my private life in this house?'

'Don't fire up at me like that, Mark. Especially whilst you are in “this house”.’

His eyes glinted with anger. ‘I don’t happen to think it’s anybody’s business but my own.’

‘No? But then you are not the only one concerned, are you?’

He was beginning to feel trapped. Confident that his father would have said nothing about his own affair with Audrey Dunne, or the debacle in London, this duty visit had been to salve his own conscience for the past months of neglect. Since the parting with Joanna he had been unable to bring himself to do more than make the occasional brief ‘phone call. Now what was he supposed to do or say? How could he possibly explain his long absence without going into the whole wretched business of his father, his mistress and the mistress’s daughter? It sounded, he thought with a sudden flash of mordant humour, like the title for some dubious Continental film.

He supposed he might plead that the commissioning and sea trials of his new craft and the organisation and manning of his flotilla had kept him too busy to do more, but that hardly explained his apparent callous indifference to his family.

‘I’m sorry that I’ve stayed away so long, but things happened.’ He chose his words with care. ‘Joanna and I – well, its old news now but it was all very difficult at the time – still is. I suppose she wrote Monica, and she told you.’

‘No, not exactly; your father did.’

His knees folded and he dropped into a chair. ‘I beg your pardon?’

She looked at him with affectionate exasperation.

‘Come and walk in the garden,’ she said, ‘and I’ll try to explain. I always seem to think better in the garden!’

He listened to her in a tense and unwilling silence, pacing beside her across the cold, frost-rimmed grass. There were times, she thought, looking with exasperation at his set face, that I wish you still small enough to be sorted out with a good hard smack!

‘So you see,’ she finished eventually, ‘your father and I were both to blame for what happened, just as you and Joanna are, although I think it a flaw in you that caused much of the misunderstanding. If you had been less secretive and an easier person to talk to she’d have been able to tell you about things as they happened.’

She squeezed his arm affectionately, trying to show she was on his side, however wrong he might have been. ‘I am sure she is a most honest and candid person by nature and deception is not one of her faults. She stood up to me with dignity when I was making my disapproval of her pretty clear.' She was silent and thoughtful for a few moments then gave a twitch of her shoulders, adding ruefully, 'All in all, I think perhaps the most honest and straightforward person in all this mess was Audrey Dunne. She appeared to have had more integrity and courage than the rest of us put together. I often wish now that I could have met her and told her so.'

'How can you say that and be so calm about father going behind your back that way – having another woman? It's despicable!' He was angry, not wanting to concede reason for what he stubbornly chose to see only as his father's gross betrayal of an innocent woman.

'Oh, Mark *really*. Since when was marital fidelity any part of your life?'

'That's different!'

'It always is,' she returned dryly, 'when it is oneself committing the adultery. Of course I was angry and wanted your father to bear all the blame, but I've had plenty of time since to think about the whole sorry mess and realise I was just as guilty as he in creating it. I was the one who shut him out and as good as locked the bedroom door.' She paused to give him a long, level look. 'How long did it take *you* to want another woman when you could no longer have Joanna?'

His face flamed and he was silent, struggling to come to terms with this new mother who talked so freely about her feelings and questioned his own sexual integrity. Finding the experience of being unable to come up with any kind of defence both unique and uncomfortable, he fell back on what he felt was firmer ground.

'You can't deny that Joanna was two-faced and damned unprincipled. She came here and met you knowing about father. She spent a whole leave with me and said not a word, even making sure I couldn't meet her mother by prevaricating and delaying until the very end of our leave. For God's sake, mother; you didn't even *like* the girl, so why start defending her now and trying to shove the whole thing on my shoulders.'

'I'm not, but don't you dare try to wriggle out of it as though your hands are clean. She was devastated by the way you behaved over Kit's wedding when you were so spiteful and unreasonable. She had to tell someone and poured it all out to Lionel when she finally told him that you were lovers – and believe me, that must have taken some courage.'

He fell silent under her anger and she gave an exasperated sigh. 'Do you really think any woman would want to risk *that* sort of reaction again from you? None of us ever care to let ourselves think we have made a mistake in loving a man.' Detaching her arm from his with a dismissive gesture she turned to go back to the house. 'Now I am cold, and tired, and just plain fed-up with you. I suggest you stay out here and do a little thinking for a change. You are your father all over again and I hope to heaven it doesn't take you as long as it took him to grow-up and stop wanting everyone to dance to his tune!'

He watched her march away from him across the lawn, leaving him with the distinct impression that he, Captain Mark Eden, DSC, in his forty-first year and Commander of a Flotilla, had just received a severe metaphorical slap on the legs from his mother.

Thrusting his cold hands into his pockets, he walked on until he reached the gap made in the far hedge by himself and Kit as boys. Pushing through onto the short turf of the headland he stood looking down at the cold grey sea, trying to order his thoughts and feelings on this most extraordinary and disturbing day.

Tilting his face to the leaden unresponsive heavens he demanded aloud, 'How the *fuck* did I ever get into this bloody awful mess?'

For an hour he paced and fumed, like Jacob wrestling with the angel, then resolute at last turned and made his way back to the house through the gathering dusk.

Returning to the sitting room and finding it empty he prowled through the house like a wary cat, finally running his mother to earth in her bedroom. Putting his head around the door he asked, 'Are we still on speaking terms? When I couldn't find you I thought you'd left home!'

She watched him in the mirror cross the room to stand behind her where she sat at her dressing table, her chin propped in her hands. She said, 'I needed to be quiet and not have Ellen fussing around me – and don't think the idea of leaving hasn't occurred to me from time to time.'

He put both hands on her shoulders. 'I'm sorry, Mother; really very sorry.'

'It isn't to me you should be saying that.'

'Oh, yes it is. I shouldn't have needed you to tell me I've been a total pig-headed fool. As if Joanna hadn't been through enough I had to charge in and make it all a hundred times worse.' His gaze met hers in the mirror. 'I have to try to speak to her as soon as possible, though whether she'll listen after all this time I've no idea. Knowing the way she can dig in her heels, I'd say probably not.'

'And what about your father; isn't it time all that nonsense was finished and done with?'

His mouth went down at the corners. 'I don't know about that, Ma. My last farewell to him wasn't exactly designed to make him jump with joy!'

'That isn't all you've done to compound the original offence, is it?'

'Isn't it? I can't think of anything…Oh, Lord!' Understanding suddenly dawned. He clapped a hand to his forehead. 'I pinched all his petrol coupons, didn't I? I'd completely forgotten!'

'You may have, but he hasn't. He still explodes about it at regular intervals.'

'In that case I think I'll put off seeing him for a little longer.'

'Coward! When will you try to meet with Joanna?'

'My next break; I've to return to duty first thing tomorrow.'

'I think you should write now.'

He made a wry face. 'No, Ma,' he shook his head. 'I don't want to write. I'd rather face it out. If she'll have me back we'll come to see you. If not...' he turned away, 'if not, then I'll just have to live with the second ghastly mess I've made of my life, won't I?'

Falmouth, February 1944

'You wanted me, sir?' Joanna looked enquiringly at the Commander, thinking privately that he was being a flaming nuisance as she'd just been going off duty after a particularly hard day.

'Yes. Stop hovering and sit down.'

He leaned back in his chair, allowing himself a good hard look at the dark smudges under her eyes, the hollows beneath the cheekbones and the general fragile air she had about her, while she looked back enquiringly waiting for him to break the silence.

'You've worked with me now for well over three years.' He leaned forward, clasping his hands before him on the desk. 'As far as I'm concerned, you can continue to do so until this war is over. But I think – no, I'm sure, that you should get away from this place and everything to do with it, at least for a time. I have a feeling this is something you've been thinking about over the past weeks. Am I right?'

'Well, yes. I'm sorry if it was obvious.'

'It wasn't. You're something of an expert at hiding your feelings.'

'I don't *want* to go. I can't imagine starting all over again with someone else. I've been very happy with you, sir.'

'I'm flattered; God knows you're the only female who ever has.'

'There has to be a first time for everything, sir.' She gave her crooked grin. 'But I can't think where else I might go…'

'You don't *have* to think; I've already done that; Naval Intelligence at Combined Ops in Oxford is screaming for a French speaking liaison officer. It should be interesting and you'd be back on your home ground there, wouldn't you?'

'Yes, sir, I'd like that if it's a real job and I don't just have to waffle around being nice to a lot of Brass and getting my bottom patted!'

He scowled.

'If your time with me hasn't cured your damned impertinence then God help anyone there you take against. But you'll take the bloody job whether you like it or not, and when you come back here I want you fit and with some meat on your bones, otherwise there'll be hell to pay. Understood?'

'Aye aye, sir.'

'That's settled then. You go next week and Miss Finch can take over now she's made up to Second.'

'Sir,' she hesitated, 'might I ask a favour?'

'Depends; what is it?'

'When I leave here I'd rather just disappear as it were, at least for a while.' She felt the colour creep up her face, 'not have my whereabouts made known to – to anyone. I think that would be best.'

He studied her in silence for a moment then nodded.

'All right, as you wish, you could be making a mistake but I'll do as you ask – but you don't disappear for good. Let me know when the ban is lifted, eh?'

'Yes, sir, thank you.'

He swivelled his chair from side to side, watching her leave with sharp, angry eyes. 'By God,' he muttered, 'but that man is every kind of a fool.'

She walked that evening along the banks of the Estuary, making her farewell to all the familiar places. She would be glad to get away now. If she stayed this close to Porthryn she knew she would continue to be drawn back again and again, in the futile hope that Mark would be there. But that chapter of her life appeared to have closed for good. He was gone. Not a word from him in all this time … and if he *should* suddenly return as angry and unforgiving as before … she shivered. No, she simply couldn't face another row like that. She must put the years they had spent together behind her and start her life over again, in a different place with a new job to fill her working day and fresh friends with whom to pass the empty hours when work was over and done.

Back to the dreaming spires. She gave a wry grin. Hopefully, there would be little time to dream…

*   *   *

Leo, my pater familiaris...

I give you my new address on the understanding that you pass it on to no one other than Monica. Please don't try to make me change my mind over this – it really is for the best. I should love to meet you in London from time to time, and if you get the opportunity to visit Oxford I promise I will do any fainting in the very best bar the city has to offer.

Thank you for finishing the work at the flat. I shall still use it when I come up to London, but think I shall sell as soon as a prospective buyer appears on the horizon. Audrey planned to move after the war and had no great sentimental feelings about the place.

I can't tell you what I am doing here but it is very demanding and leaves me satisfyingly tired by the end of each working day, but not too tired to enjoy some very good company.

Write soon. Love to my favourite, my one and only papa cher,

Jo.

*   *   *

Mark stared at the girl seated at Joanna's desk. 'Gone? What do you mean, *gone*?' his heart swooped somewhere around his knees, 'gone where?' he demanded.

Nervously Jean Finch rose to her feet, casting an anxious eye at the Commander's door. 'I don't know, sir. Really I don't!'

'When did she leave?'

He was alarmingly big and powerful and her mouth dried as the flinty grey eyes bored into hers. She wished she had Joanna's knack of dealing with these forcible, demanding men. 'Three weeks ago, sir,' she managed at last and gave a whimper of relief as Commander Naughten popped his head around the door like a small fierce Jack-in-the-box.

'You're in the wrong place – again!' he glared at Mark. 'If you've come to see the plot we don't have one here.'

Mark came to attention, ground his teeth and counted silently to ten.

'No, sir, I do *not* want to see the plot. I have come to ask where Miss Dunne has been posted.'

'I dare say you have, but you're a little late. She is...' his eyes snapped, 'incommunicado ... and that's official!'

Mark almost committed Conduct Prejudicial to Good Order and Discipline with a forcefully uttered obscenity, but controlled himself with an effort. His eyes met the Commander's with steely determination. 'Sir, I need her address.'

Alec Naughton glared. 'I daresay you do!' He crooked the well-remembered bony finger. 'My office. Now Mr Eden, if you please.'

'Sir!'

Mark followed him, fuming. *These bloody shore establishments. Making up the rules as they went along...incommunicado, my arse! Of course they all damned well know where she is, and I'll bloody choke it out of somebody here before I leave...*

'I'll be perfectly frank with you.' The Commander settled himself behind his desk, his gaze raking over the angry man before him. 'I am responsible for sending the quite irreplaceable Miss Dunne away at great inconvenience to myself because I considered that staying here, and grieving over God knows what pain *you* had inflicted on her, was doing her a great deal of harm.' He put up a hand as Mark made to interrupt. ' I don't want to hear any why's, where-fore's or excuses from you, Mr Eden, and you will not, I repeat *not*, attempt in any way to discover from anyone on this base where she is. That is an order. Do I make myself quite clear?'

'Abundantly sir.'

Mark's lips were a thin straight line and his voice icy. The Commander sucked in an exasperated breath, then continued with equal coldness: 'She will I hope, be returning here at some time in the future and I want your word now that you will keep away from this place until, and if, she is willing to hear from or see you again.'

Mark scowled, struggling for a moment or two before giving a brusque: 'You have it, sir.'

'Good, so long as we understand each other.' The eyes under the bristly brows lost some of their fierce regard. 'I have a great respect for your Service record, Captain. If you would just care to stop looming over me like that and sit down I will endeavour to 'rustle-up some cawffee' as our American friends down the corridor put it, and hear how a great nephew of mine, Simon Webb by name, is coming along. He is, I believe, one of your Midshipmen...'

Oh, *shit*! For a moment Mark's shoulders sagged, then giving the man behind the desk a half-smile he seated himself, ruefully acknowledging the well-timed master-stroke which had at once disarmed his anger and at the same time put him neatly on the spot.

'Sir,' he answered carefully, 'I have to report that Midshipman Webb is a rather *impulsive* young man.'

20

Oxford, April, 1944

'This is a most beautiful city, and it is most kind that you spare the time to walk me to it!'

The Major's English was coming along nicely, thought Joanna, feeling she could take most of the credit for that fact. Apart from interpreting for him at conferences and meetings, she had also been spending quite a lot of off-duty time with him over these past few weeks, once again in the novel position of being able to enjoy a man's company without fear of being pounced upon.

Major Charles de la Tour, ostensibly of the Free French Army but in reality attached to the French section of the British SOE appeared, despite his comparative youth, to be a member of a vanishing breed of old-fashioned gentleman. For such an extremely handsome and charming man this was pretty surprising, but made him a companion eminently suited to her present state of mind and body.

'This used to be my College.' She stopped outside the entrance to Somerville, feeling nostalgic and rather sentimental. 'I was an undergraduate here and had already taken Greats when it was apparent that war was inevitable; I decided to join up then, while I had the choice of service.'

'So … and you will come again after the war is finished?'

'I might if they have room for a Junior Lecturer in English Literature, although it will seem pretty tame after the Navy.'

'You do not look like … *pfff*!' he clicked his fingers and frowned, 'what is it you English say about the blue socks?'

She gave a gurgle of laughter, 'Blue *stockings*!'

'Ah, yes; stockings; I must remember!'

'As we are off duty we can speak French if you would rather.'

He made a comic face. 'You should not tempt me. I must have the good English before I leave to go to my next appointment, where I think I will not find such a kind and beautiful lady to come to my rescue.'

'Oh, I shouldn't think you'll have any difficulty on that score.' Her tone was dry, and he gave her an amused glance.

'No, Mademoiselle, I do not go looking … and you?'

'I also have better things to do, or so I tell myself.'

'Ah, I was right in my thoughts; the fingers, they have been burned, yes?'

'Yes.'

'*C'est dommage.*'

She gave a bleak smile.

'May we leave that subject?'

'Of course; but it is good to get such things clear between friends, *n'est-ce pas*?' He smiled. 'Now I can ask you to have dinner with me and you will not think: "This man, he is a fox."'

'*Wolf.*' She spluttered into sudden laughter and he smiled.

'Better, much better. So now, where do we go to dine?'

'The Mitre, I think. Even in wartime the chef performs miracles with rabbit.'

'*Lapin?*' he made a face, 'ah … to be in France again!'

'Thank you for a lovely meal.' Joanna smiled up at him as later they left the restaurant and stepped out into the darkened street.

'I enjoyed it also. So shall we walk a little and exercise our digestions?' He drew her arm through his. 'I must thank you for all your kindness to me these past weeks. You have made it possible for me to accept with patience this so tiresome waiting.'

'You must be anxious to get home again to France, especially now that the time is getting so close.'

He frowned. 'Perhaps. Certainly there are things I must do. But I fear there is little left of the life I once knew.'

'Starting again is always hard.'

He glanced at her suddenly unguarded and wistful expression. 'For you also?'

'For me also – but you will have friends and family. They'll be so relieved and happy to know that you are still alive.'

'No family, and I think, few friends. Most were in the Resistance with me and only two that I know of still live.'

They walked in silence for a few minutes. She glanced sideways at the impressive rows of medal ribbons, both French and British, on his uniform jacket and wondered what his life of map-making and gathering intelligence information in his own country all through the Occupation must have been like. She knew he had been hunted by the Gestapo and made his escape over the mountains into Spain, and that since then he had returned regularly to France on various missions, but he spoke little of his life before Oxford and she knew better than to ask.

If she had allowed herself she might have thought that in another time and place she would have been able to love this man; that his calmness and gentleness could have helped heal her wounds. But soon he would be going away again on a mission from which he may or may not return, and despite his denial she had a feeling that somewhere there was someone with whom he would like to spend *his* future.

So she walked the familiar streets that were old friends rediscovered, but remained lonely amid all the people and places. She missed Audrey and the warm security of a home; ached still for Mark and the strength of his arms; longed for Kit and Monica and silly jokes. She wanted Leo's kindly comfort and when she reached her desk each morning and the white-haired and charming Colonel Vincent greeted her with a courteous 'Good morning, Joanna', she missed most dreadfully not having that bristly little terrier Naughton snapping at her heels.

But she was busy, time passed quickly and she felt privileged to be working positively towards that day, growing now very close, which in their files was known as Operation Overlord and would perhaps be the first step toward the ending of this war.

*   *   *

Leo wrote:

Dear Jo, I miss you. Yesterday I bought a bunch of spring flowers from the ancient crone outside the hospital and took them to Audrey's grave. The rose bush I planted is flourishing, and in the sunshine and bird-song she felt very close and dear.

Mark only writes briefly to Mary. She is convinced that he will eventually sort out all his problems, including me! But he volunteers nothing and she won't pry. He is such a restless spirit and shies away from all help. If only he would say what he really feels but Mary says that he seems now to have shut from his life everything but his boats and his men.

I can't help being angry with him still, but try to keep that to myself. He must I suppose, find his own salvation as best he may. Perhaps one day you will both feel able to forgive the past and be brave enough to meet again…

Joanna read the letter leaning over Magdalen Bridge in the bright sunshine of a May morning. Now Major Charles de la Tour had departed for Hampshire and his own part in the final preparations for crossing that little strip of blue water she looked for no other companion for her leisure hours. He had offered a breathing space and an interval of peace: a friend to be remembered always with gratitude and affection.

She would have welcomed his presence now as she watched the water beneath her and struggled not to think of Mark, withdrawn and alone and thinking of … what? The love they had shared or the deed that had shattered it? Did he feel the pain of a still-present need or nothing but coldness, suspicion and mistrust?

She leaned over and dropped a stone into the water, watching the ripples spread, then turned and went back to the welcome oblivion of work.

* * *

The English Channel, 2100 hours, 4th June, 1944

They were running quietly under cover of darkness and close to the French coast. Only Mark's quiet orders to the helm disturbed the silence. Essential on these last days to keep the channel clear and the massing of the Allied invasion fleet secret, the enemy E-Boats and subs pinned down in their harbours and attacked without mercy at any move out into open water.

'Signal coming in from number seven, sir,' Webb was at his elbow. 'Lieutenant Matthews says something's out there moving westward and hugging the coast. They've done a couple of sweeps, but couldn't pin anything down because their radar's on the blink.'

Mark frowned, deep in thought. Matthews was new to the flotilla. A young Lieutenant inexperienced on MTBs, he'd been pulled in hastily to replace the captain wounded a week since. 'We'll take a look. Grant, get me a bearing; Mid, pass the word to keep absolute silence – and tell Stevens to keep his eyes and ears on the asdic.'

Calling up two of the nearest boats from the flotilla to join him, he gave the change of course then wedged himself tightly into his corner, gripping his night glasses in both hands, his head sunk into the neck of the thick sweater he wore beneath his duffel coat.

It was foul weather, wet and blustery with the wind rising to near gale force. Everyone was on edge, knowing that they were only waiting for it to calm before Overlord could begin. The boat rolled and pitched, the seas breaking over her bows and streaming along the deck. On the starboard side of the wheelhouse Richard Stone staggered and almost lost his hold on the rail. Mark said quietly, 'Slow engines. Steady now.'

They were coming up to St-Cast, creeping along the shoreline as close as they dared to rocks that guarded the cliffs. Their craft rolled heavily and Mark raised his glasses, straining his eyes to where the sea sent great plumes of spray over the rocks. If anything was out there why the hell wasn't it showing on the screen? And where in the name of God was Matthews?

Only the steady *ping* of the Asdic and the creak of the boat's timbers broke the silence until a sudden frantic call from his First Lieutenant split the air. 'Port side! Port side! Oh, *Jesus…*'

Mark turned a fraction of a second before the darkness was split by flame. He heard and felt the tear and crash of timber and screech of torn metal beneath his feet; then the deck tilted and he spiralled off into a great roaring darkness of confusion and pain.

Richard Stone signalled: "Am returning to base" and leaving the other boats to hunt the wolf amongst them, turned his badly damaged but still seaworthy craft to make what speed he could in the worsening weather. A calm, but white-faced Bos'n clambered up to where he stood, clinging grimly to the rail with his elbows and nursing his heavily bandaged hands.

'Sure you're all right, sir? Those hands are a bit of a mess and that gash on your head needs stitching.'

'It can wait until we get back to base and Doc Faraday can see to it. How are the others?'

'Half a dozen with cuts and bruises. Thoms and Blakely have both got leg and back injuries and will need to go to hospital, but I've patched them up and they're OK for now.' His face creased into a worried frown. 'Skipper caught the worst of it. He's unconscious, sir, and both legs bleeding heavily. I think that's splinters from the blast, but he's in one hell of a mess. I daresn't even try to get the remains of his sea boot off. It looks as if the right foot's shot to pieces.'

'Just watch the bleeding doesn't get any worse and stay with him. No, wait.' He changed his mind; he needed all the experienced help he could muster to get them back safely. 'I need you here. Leave the middy to do the honours and tell him the Skipper will have his hide if he throws up on him…and that's nothing to what I'll do if he lets him bleed to death! See he knows how to deal with the tourniquet then get back here.'

'Aye aye, sir.'

What a bloody mess, in every sense of the word. Richard mused over the vagaries of fate. The bugger must have taken refuge behind the off shore rocks, just lying in wait until they passed and could nip out and get in that one shot. Still it might have been worse; but for the pitching and rolling of their craft, the shell would most probably have found it's mark and blown them all sky-high instead of tearing alongside the bridge... Still, no use thinking about the might-have-been when the present was quite bad enough.

The depressed crew stood in a disconsolate group and watched the ambulance away, young Webb riding as escort and detailed to report back from the hospital.

He sat between Thoms and Blakely, watching his captain's unconscious face and fighting his own nausea. His knees trembled from fear and fatigue, but seeing the medical orderly's eyes on him he controlled himself with a heroic effort, squaring his shoulders and sitting as straight as the swaying of the ambulance allowed. He wasn't going to let them all down in front of some bloody shore-wallah!

* * *

'I don't like the look of that – not one little bit…'

The very young Surgeon Lieutenant peered down on the apparently unconscious casualty. 'I reckon that foot is going to have to come off, and quickly. Better get him ready for theatre pronto.'

Suddenly, as if on strings the patient's eyelids flew open and a pair of cold grey eyes glared balefully into his.

'Keep your bloody butcher's hands off me … you fucking *touch* me and I'll have your balls on toast!' snarled Mark, before lapsing again into merciful unconsciousness.

The Surgeon Lieutenant gave his awkward patient a bleak look, before raising an inquiring eyebrow at Webb. 'I shouldn't if I were you, sir.' advised that young man nervously. 'I think he means it!'

'In that case...' the doctor turned to the orderly, 'you can load him straight back on again; I know the very man to deal with this. I did my surgery under him at St James' and this is right up his street. If anyone can keep this bloke's foot and leg together, he can.' He grinned maliciously as he scribbled a swift note, pushed it in an envelope, addressed it and licked the flap. 'He'll blast the bugger's hide off if he gives *him* any lip! I'll give him a shot now then you can get that bell ringing and drive like hell.'

Lionel was in the act of unlocking his car door when his Registrar came hastening across the hospital forecourt.

'Sir Lionel, there's a casualty just come in you should see.'

'Not now.' He was firm. 'I've been looking forward to being home by teatime today. Give it to one of the juniors, or Gwyn-Jones – he's on his last one.'

'I really think you should see this chap before you go, sir, he's been rushed by the Navy all the way from Dungeness and there's a note from a Surgeon Lieutenant Ryder there to say he thinks you might have a go at the chap's foot. He was prepared to take it off but the blighter wasn't having any!'

Lionel hesitated. 'Ryder, you say? Since when did *he* start allowing his patients to dictate treatment?' he dropped his keys back into his pocket. 'Confounded nuisance; all right, I'll have a quick check on the stroppy so-and-so, but that's all.'

Five minutes later he stood looking down on the still-as-death form of his eldest son, a host of chaotic emotions rushing wildly through him, before the surgeon took over from the father and he concentrated on the bloody legs and mangled foot presented for his inspection. It took only seconds to make up his mind.

'Get him cleaned up and ready for theatre right away. I'll need X-rays and a blood match and all the plasma Haematology can spare. Call Sister Anderson and drag my anaesthetist back on duty.' He took a swift glance at the clock as the trolley was wheeled away, then went straight to his office and picked up the phone.' Get me Mr Gwyn-Jones, will you please.'

He stood frowning at the wall until a cheerful: 'I thought you had a home to go to. Make it quick…I'm scrubbed and my bloke's already on the table!' brought him to life again.

'George. I have a problem. A very messy job has just turned up from the Navy. He's lost a hell of a lot of blood so he's in shock and it's got to be quick. He's being prepped now but it will be touch and go whether or not he'll need an amputation.'

'What do you expect me to do, hold your hand?' A guffaw of laughter crackled down the line.

'It's a bit tricky in the medical ethics department, George. The patient happens to be my son.'

'Oh.' There was a silence, then a long, low whistle. 'I'm sorry, Lionel. Are you feeling up to it?'

'Of course, but…'

'Well, there's a war on, isn't there? And it doesn't sound like a job for your registrar to tackle. You'll just have to tell your theatre staff to keep their mouths shut. If there are any repercussions, which there won't be I'm sure, you have a body needing immediate surgery, I have another equally urgent who's already in the land of Nod and there's nobody else around experienced enough to take over for at least an hour. We could swap, except that this is my second go at my chap; it's also urgent and a tricky one I'd rather not hand on at this late stage… So what are you waiting for?'

'Just hedging my bets, George; just hedging my bets. I'll expect you to stand by me if I get hauled up before a disciplinary board!'

After placing the receiver carefully back on the rest, he sat for a few moments on the edge of the desk, eyes closed. 'Dear, God,' he breathed, 'Dear God…' He opened his eyes and held both hands straight out before him to contemplate his fingertips. 'Steady as a rock. Not bad for an old man.'

He walked to the door, his mind already grappling with the task ahead.

Mark was not unconscious; hadn't been for some time but Ryder's injection of morphine to help him on the long journey from Kent had been powerful enough to keep him comatose and unwilling to surface completely. Now the pain was beginning to crawl again up his legs, rousing him and making him aware of a bright light beyond his closed lids; a jumble of words and the clink of metal on metal. Then out of the confusion came a horribly familiar voice. 'Ready or not, you'll have to put him under now. I can't wait any longer.'

The voice boomed and faded, boomed again. Mark frowned then painfully and cautiously opened both eyes, gazing up through narrow slits at the figure gowned in green, with nose and mouth masked and gloved hands raised as in prayer. For a long moment grey eyes locked with blue, then Mark groaned aloud, 'Christ, pa, you haven't come after me for those fucking petrol coupons…'

Lionel cast a jaundiced eye at the startled anaesthetist. 'Don't ask,' he ordered, 'just put him right out before he makes even more of a damned nuisance of himself!'

Three hours later he stripped off his mask and cap. 'All right, he'll do!' Nodding wearily at the other figures clustered around the table he added, 'Thank you very much everyone. Before you go...' his tired eyes held a faint twinkle, 'the patient's name being the same as mine is just an amazing coincidence and one I'd rather wasn't commented on to anyone outside of this theatre.'

'I'm sure none of us even *noticed*, sir,' assured his theatre sister untruthfully as the patient was transferred to a trolley and wheeled away. 'All the same, a nice box of chocolates for the nurses on the ward might distract *them* from wondering.'

'You surprise me, Sister – and where would I find such delicacies in wartime?'

'I'll have a word with the orderlies on the private wing, sir. They are given all kinds of things by grateful patients and I've often heard it said that hard cash is even more appreciated.'

'Really?' He mused silently for a moment or two before asking hopefully: 'No chance of an orange or a banana, I suppose?'

'Sorry, sir; absolutely not,' she tucked in her lips on a smile. 'Only the best-looking medical students get those!'

Dawn was washing the room in a faint grey light when Mark began to stir into consciousness. Lionel left his seat by the window and crossed to pull back the coverlet, lifting the sinewy brown wrist to feel the pulse beating strong and steady beneath his fingers. He looked thoughtfully at the involuntary flicker of his patient's eyelids. 'You can stop playing possum,' he said dryly. 'I know you're awake.'

'No I'm not. Get out of my dream...' the voice was weak, little more than a whisper, 'it's hellish enough without *you*!'

'It's no dream. I am all too real.'

There was a very long silence before the faint voice spoke again. 'I was afraid you might be. Was it you took it off?'

'No, I left it on…most of it. It was bad, but not as bad as I at first thought.'

The eyes remained tightly closed, but a small sigh of relief passed the dry, cracked lips. 'Have you been here all the time?'

'Uh huh, more-or-less.'

He struggled to rise. 'I have to get back to my blokes. How long…?' Sweat broke on his forehead and Lionel eased his head back onto the pillow.

'You won't be going back for quite a while. Now stop talking and sleep again. Your mother will be here by mid-day and you'll frighten her even more than you already have if she finds you out for the count again.'

'You're the boss.' His son's eyes opened wide at last in a long, steady look as he took a deep, painful breath to observe: 'But then you always have been, haven't you?'

'Not for some time I haven't.' Lionel Eden's tone was grim. 'However, I'm quite happy to take up that position again as there *are* still one or two matters outstanding.'

Mark closed his eyes again. 'Yes, pa.'

'I shall see you again later when your mother has visited.'

'Yes, pa.'

'And don't keep calling me that!'

A faint grin touched his mouth, 'No, pa!'

Lionel went in search of breakfast, suddenly aware of the toll taken on his strength by the past hours, and feeling every one of his sixty-three years. He told himself firmly that it was just plain exhaustion causing his vision to blur and the breath feel tight in his throat; finding it difficult to acknowledge even now that such unusual phenomena might possibly be due to the release of a long repressed emotion.

'Coming down with a cold, Sir Lionel?' queried matron solicitously as she passed him in the corridor, only to be met by an unusually surly growl and the muttered reply that he was 'perfectly fit, thank you', and merely had a piece of grit in his eye…

Mary Eden arrived looking strained and anxious, clinging for a moment to her waiting husband as she stepped out of the taxi into his embrace.

'How is he? Is he in a lot of pain? Oh, I thought the train would never get here!'

'I've just looked in. He's fine; wide awake and waiting for you.'

His arm about her shoulders was reassuring, but she paled at the fatigue apparent on his drawn face. 'You look exhausted; you should have let George operate,' she scolded, 'if the worst had happened you might have been in the most dreadful trouble.'

'I know, but it was all a bit of a shambles. He was in such a mess and George was busy... I had to do it.' He gave her shoulder a squeeze. 'I couldn't have left him to a junior and there wasn't anyone else but me – and I am pretty good, you know!'

'Will he really be all right? He won't be scarred or crippled?'

'Well, his face looks as though he's been in a bare-knuckle prize-fight; he's minus five toes and he'll never win a beautiful legs contest – I took enough wood and metal splinters out of *them* to build a model of the Titanic!' He gave a faint smile. 'It's going to be a long job I'm afraid, but if he works hard I'm quite sure he'll make it back to near normal. He's a bit low at the moment, so come along and do what you do so well: spoil him and make him feel a hero.'

'He *is* a hero!'

He gave a non-committal grunt. 'That depends on one's particular point of view.'

'Hello, Mother – Pa stuck his head around the door a few minutes ago, glared at me as though I was a specimen in a test tube and said you were on your way,' Mark smiled uncertainly. 'He doesn't change, does he?'

She sat down beside the bed and smoothing back his hair asked, 'Have you two talked properly yet?'

'Not really, I've been sleeping most of the day. Anyway I don't think either of us is quite up to it right now.' He gave a faintly sardonic grin. 'As at present he has me at a disadvantage I suppose it's very gentlemanly of him not to have rubbed my nose in it already, but I'd hate to take a bet on how long he'll resist doing so.'

She didn't answer. He fell silent under her sharp scrutiny then pulled a face. 'I'm doing it again, aren't I?'

'Yes, and if you don't stop I shall go straight home. Your father thinks I've come here to spoil you. I haven't. I've come to make sure you are behaving yourself.'

'Mother ... *please,*' he began to laugh. 'Stop trying to look cross and tell me how glad you are that I'm still alive.' He squeezed her hand gently as her eyes filled with tears. 'I know things are different now. He pretends to me that I was in no danger of losing my foot, but if it wasn't for him it's almost certain I would have done...George told me it was touch-and-go. And I know he spent all night sitting in that chair until I came round after the op. It's just going to take us a little while to find our way back over the past ten years, that's all.'

* * *

London, June 6th 1944

'Feeling strong enough for some good news?' Lionel asked, pulling a chair up to the bed.

Mark turned his head restlessly. 'You mean like the war is over?'

'Not quite, but this morning the first troops landed in Normandy; the news is good.'

Mark lay still, staring at the ceiling. 'Trust me to miss the best part.'

Lionel looked with understanding at his embittered face. 'Stop feeling sorry for yourself. It's natural to feel depressed at this stage. Tomorrow, the world will look brighter, trust me.'

He smiled faintly. 'Sorry. I hate that I'm stuck here and it's all going on without me.'

'How's the pain?'

'OK. Bearable,' he fixed his gaze on the ceiling again. 'I need to ask you something.'

'Ask away.'

'Do you know where Joanna is?'

'Yes.'

He sighed. 'I thought so. Is she OK; you know … happy?'

'Not particularly, but she's coping in her own way.' Lionel met the eyes that were suddenly switched again to his own. 'I think you should let me tell her where *you* are now.'

'No.' Mark's mouth set in the old stubborn line. 'She's made it clear she doesn't want to see me, but I know her; even if she loathed my guts she'd think she ought to come tearing up here, and I won't have it that way.'

'It's up to you but I think you're making a mistake.'

'Well, I'm something of an expert at doing that,' he gave a dry, humourless smile, 'and before the world starts looking better tomorrow, there's something else.'

He paused then took a deep breath. 'I want to say I'm deeply sorry and ashamed for the way I've behaved towards you in the past. I should have at least had the decency and the guts to face you and explain how I felt, not just walked out on Medical School. From the perspective of my forty-one years I think I deserved pretty well everything you slung at me then. Now I'd give anything to wipe it all out. I can't do that, but I can try and be less of an awkward sod in the future.'

Lionel left the bed abruptly and walked to the window, staring down at the London traffic. After a long time he stirred and turned back to face his son with drawn brows.

'Does that apology also cover the petrol coupons?'

'Yes – and the odd bottle of whisky from your store in the cellar that I've had from time to time on the visits home I made behind your back.'

Lionel held up his hand. 'Please; I was perfectly well aware of who was spiriting that away, and you need not rush to get everything off your conscience in one fell swoop.'

'Joanna tried to make me see you to put things right, but I wouldn't. I thought you might chuck me out again.'

'I might have – then.' He gave his grim smile. 'You and I have a lot more talking to do and you'll be stuck in that bed long enough for both of us to wash *all* our dirty linen and hang it out to dry, but for now just shut up and rest.'

'Yes, pa.'

He crossed to place a hand for a moment on his forehead, 'Next thing you'll be running a temperature and making a damned nuisance of yourself again.'

‘Yes, pa.’

‘And you can stop the meek and mild act. It doesn’t suit you, does it?’

‘No, pa.’

‘Will you stop calling me that?’

Mark’s face creased in a grin. ‘I have called you worse.’

Lionel paused in the doorway. ‘You always were a quietly subversive devil. Forty-one, is it? Well, still time, and room, for improvement, I suppose.’

Mark grinned again at the closed door. ‘You too, pa, you too.’

Well, that hurdle at least had been successfully taken. If only he could get to Joanna and put things right with her, but he had given that old fox Naughten his word and must stick to it…

Lying still with closed eyes, he thought of all the things he loved about her; her laugh and her smile, her compassion and the yielding warmth of her… What were those last lines of Brooke’s poem that said it all and summed up what he was feeling in just seven short lines? He teased his weary mind, then remembered, and spoke the words softly to the empty room:

‘“I would come back, come back to you,
Find you, as a pool unstirred,
Kneel down by you, and never a word,
Lay my head, and nothing said,
In your hands, ungarlanded;
And a long watch you would keep;
And I should sleep, and I should sleep.”’

He moved his head restlessly on the pillow, almost welcoming the pain that again began to eat at his wrecked foot, stifling all other thought.

What he would give to be in Joanna’s arms again….

21

Oxford, September 1944

'What on earth are you doing here?' Joanna stopped dead outside the Ashmolean. 'Is there no escaping you? And who told you where I was?'

'No one, honestly,' Josh Milton's delight was all too apparent. 'I'm as dumbstruck as you.'

'I wish I could believe you.'

'Scout's honour!' he seized her arm, 'Come on, this calls for a celebration; thank God the pubs are open – let me drag you into one and have my way with you!'

'You are an idiot!' Laughing, she allowed herself to be hustled around the corner into St Giles and the nearest tavern, where he seated her at an empty table before plunging into the mass of tightly packed bodies around the bar. In less than a minute he reappeared bearing two glasses of beer. 'How do you *do* that?' she asked admiringly as he set them on the table.

'Do what?'

'Get a drink that fast with that crowd around the bar.'

'I'm good in a scrum – used to play rugger,' he winked, 'and barmaids find me irresistible!'

She raised her glass. 'To susceptible barmaids, wherever they may be.'

He eyed her up and down with his customary thoroughness.

'Not very fat, are you, dear?'

'Always the flatterer...I've never been what one might call buxom.' She made a mournful face. 'I'd love to really *fill* a swimsuit.'

He propped his chin on one hand and grinned. 'Now there's a thought!'

Suddenly she remembered just whom she was with and blushed. 'Josh, don't start again,' she begged. 'I'm used to a little gentle flirting with the cream of Combined Ops; not being eye-stripped by a randy Cornish Veterinarian masquerading as an Officer and Gentleman!'

His eyes mocked her. 'You haven't changed your ways then; that's a pity.'

'No, I haven't, and I'm not likely to while you're around.'

He dabbed at a drop of spilt beer with a long forefinger. 'When did you leave Falmouth? I went looking for you there and nearly got my ankles savaged by your Commander.'

She gave a gurgle of laughter. 'I bet you did and as you didn't get any information about where I'd gone from him, how *did* you know where to find me?'

'Just coincidence, honestly – I came here hunting my old mate, the sexy Squadron Officer Caro Penrose. I know she's somewhere in Oxford, but I'm buggered if I can find her.'

'I'm sure I met her once – at a party; at least I met a girl called Caro and she was the sort of girl you don't easily forget.' She wrinkled her brow. 'I *think* she came with a smashing-looking blonde Polish pilot; she certainly danced most of the night with him.'

'Sounds like her.' He looked glum. 'Perhaps the Pole is the reason she's gone to ground. However, you're here and she isn't. So, tell me about you.'

'Not much to tell; I came in January. I'll be returning to Falmouth on Wednesday week to help wind up our business there before we go back to Tollmouth.'

He gave her a sideways look. 'You've heard about old Mark of course?'

'Heard what?' her voice sharpened.

'Well, you know he caught that packet just before D Day? Now he's back home from his convalescence, hobbling on a stick and being administered to by half the Physiotherapy lovelies at the local hospital, the lucky sod –' he broke off at the sight of her stricken face. 'I say, are you all right … I'm sorry, I thought you'd have known.'

'I didn't.'

She felt faint and sick. Mark wounded all that time ago? How long had he been in hospital, and why hadn't he sent word to her? He must have known she would come…

'You've seen him?' her voice was strained, her hands tight around the glass.

'Sure. His father drove him down to Porthryn a couple of week's back to see Jim. They came over to visit me as I was on sick leave: still am. I got a bullet in the bum ...very rough, those Germans.' He grinned. 'Bugger shot me right off the top of my tank in St-Méen-le-Grand; bloody nerve.'

'Oh, Josh, I'm sorry – are you all right now?'

'Absolutely firing on all cylinders, old dear. No broken bones but it tore a muscle or two. Frightfully unromantic, though and goes down with the popsies like a dead hippo in a swamp!'

'Dear Josh; you're better than a tonic!' she laughed aloud, although tears were in her eyes. 'I haven't felt like really laughing since … Oh, I don't know when.'

'Since you last saw Mark?' he ventured, and she shook her head.

'*That* occasion was no laughing matter,' she laid her hand on his. 'Josh, tell me about him. Was he very badly hurt? And when you say he's at home, do you mean Stonehams?'

'Of course. It must have been pretty bad because they brought him all the way up from the coast to St Marks where Lionel did his op. Got his legs peppered with shrapnel and came pretty close to getting more than his tootsies chopped off. He spent almost a month lying flat on his back in hospital.'

'And Lionel drove him to Cornwall?' He nodded and she summoned up a smile. 'I'm so glad.'

'Joanna, lovely lady, I hate myself for saying this but that man still needs you. He went hunting you in Falmouth a few weeks after you'd left and according to his mother has never been the same chap since.' He took her hand in both of his. 'I think you should let him know if you are still carrying a torch – you are, aren't you?'

'Yes, but if he was feeling the same way about me he would have let me know he was wounded and in hospital, but he didn't make the effort.' She shook her head decisively. 'It's no use, Josh. He must have made quite sure his father and Monica would keep me in the dark because Monica writes regularly; I had dinner in London with Lionel only a few weeks ago and neither of them has so much as mentioned his name.'

'Well, you know old Mark. He wouldn't want anyone to soothe his fevered brow out of pity. He's the sort to think that might be looked upon as taking an unfair advantage.'

'I don't think it's that, Josh. He's much more likely not to want me around. You see, I never did explain. I should at least have tried, but the whole thing was such a mess and he was so furious...' Her voice faltered. 'At a guess I should say the only reason he went looking for me in Falmouth was to have another fight.'

'Don't tell me any details, ducky, or you may start crying on my shoulder then God alone knows what might happen! Drink up and we'll go for a nice bracing walk then have dinner. That way I shan't be tempted to play footsie with you under this table ... I'm only human, you know!'

She shook her head wordlessly and sat with hunched shoulders. Josh looked at the bent head and found himself washed suddenly by an unusual emotion; a mixture of pity and tenderness and a need to comfort and protect her. The desire that now stirred in him was deeper and much subtler than mere lust. He wanted to put gentle arms about her and stroke that curly hair, and make very tender love…

She looked up and as their gaze met his heart skipped a beat to see the pain and stark need in them. He said softly, 'Joanna, darling. Do you think it would help if we were to go to bed?

Her eyes widened. 'Together?'

'Well, yes – otherwise asking you rather misses the point!'

For a long moment she hesitated before the smile began: at first sad, then rueful then unbearably poignant. 'I should like to, *want* to and certainly need to – all the right reasons. But I doubt I should be able to face either you or myself in the morning. Thank you for asking, though. It was quite the very nicest immoral proposition I have ever had!'

'And that was quite the very nicest refusal *I* have ever had.' his big hand closed around hers, his voice unusually soft and gentle. 'Come along now and I'll walk you to wherever you wish to lay your head tonight … alone.' He gave a crooked grin. 'Something tells me we should forget that dinner and that I must take the next train out of this place and back onto safer ground.'

After he had left her outside her quarters she collected a drink from the wardroom bar then went to her own room, to sit staring out of the window as the sun went down and all the buildings fell into blue shadows around the green lawns.

Why had she let him go, when now more than ever she wanted gentle hands to touch, and arms to hold her close? Why, against all sense and reason, did she still only want those hands and arms to be Marks? Why was she still chasing a dream? And how was she to get on with living the rest of her life when she still needed and wanted him so desperately?

She shrugged the thoughts away; finished the whisky and tidied herself to go down to supper.

'What will you do?' Leo had asked all those many months ago when Mark left. Now she squared her shoulders and gave herself a mental shake.

Back with the same old problem and the same old answer: "*I might go on: naught else remained to do….*"

A clever chap, Shakespeare: a quote for every occasion.

*   *   *

Josh sat hunched in the dingy second-class carriage studying first his railway timetable then consulting his watch as the train clackety-clacked its way over the points and wound slowly into Paddington Station.

If he found a hotel for the night he could take a train to Weymouth in the morning, then a taxi to Stonehams in time for lunch, he thought. That would give him the whole afternoon and following morning in which to work on that bonehead Eden before he had to get back for his own Medical Board in Aldershot…

For a moment Joanna's face swam before his eyes and with a muttered curse he jammed his cap on his head and stood to take down his case from the rack; he must be going completely ga-ga to even *think* of doing her courting for her!

* * *

Joanna finished her packing and snapped the locks on her case, aware that the car was waiting and the Commander champing at the bit to leave for Tollmouth.

'He's beginning to foam at the mouth, ma'am,' a nervous Wren put her head around the door. ' He say's...' she gulped, ' I'm sorry, ma'am, but he says I'm to tell you that if you're not ready right now you can bloody *walk* to Tollmouth!'

'I'll bet he did.' Joanna was unperturbed, having lived through too many such crises in the past four years to be panicked by such a threat. 'Just keep out of his sight and let me take the flack. I'm used to it.'

When she was finished and descended to the street he was sitting forward in the car watching the doorway with eyes like chips of blue ice. As the driver saluted and opened the door she put her case down and gave the impatient occupant her most devastating smile.

'Good morning, sir; I'm sorry to keep you waiting but I didn't get the message that I was to travel with you until fifteen minutes ago.'

'You should have known and been ready, dammit.'

'Sir, there was a problem about that.'

'Oh, was there; such as?'

She ducked into the car to sit beside him, straight-faced and arranging her skirt over her knees.

'I don't have a crystal ball!'

There was a strangled snort from the driver. The Commander leaned forward again and slammed the glass partition shut. 'Since you arrived back from Oxford,' he observed testily, 'this has returned to seeming a very *long* war.'

She smiled again.

'I missed you too, sir,' she said.

* * *

She couldn't quite account for the lightening of her heart as they left Falmouth behind. Certainly she was glad to be returning to Tollmouth and the predictable unpredictability of the Commander, and there would be plenty to occupy her once they were back at headquarters. With her work in Oxford gradually winding down over the past weeks, she'd been made painfully aware that too little to do meant too much time to think, and the sleepless nights had begun to creep back.

For a time after Josh's visit she had felt a lift in her spirits that Mark had at last made peace with his father. But that elation was temporary and soon counterbalanced by the knowledge that despite his wounds and the pain he must have suffered, he still had not wanted to see her, which seemed proof enough that he had cut her out of his life for good.

Late sunshine broke through the clouds as they approached the comforting familiarity of a town that had for so long taken the place of home. Filled with a mixture of joy and sadness Joanna waited for her first glimpse of the harbour. Although she knew there would be memories of Mark at almost every street corner she could bear with that. Better the pain of remembrance than the exile of these past months. As the car breasted a hill and came within sight of the sea she leaned forward to view her 'little strip of blue water' lying calm and sparkling in the mid-day sun. Under her breath she chanted: '"*…and there I saw the channel glint and England in her pride...*"'

'What's that?'

She turned her head and smiled, 'Nothing, sir, just that I feel as though I'm coming home.'

'Hum,' he stared at the back of the driver's head. 'I wonder why?'

22

Tollmouth, October 1944

She was settling into the first full day's work in her old office when Commander Naughten came in and dropped an opened envelope onto her blotting-pad.

'Just have a look at that, will you? If you can't oblige the chap yourself I suppose it could go on the notice board in your wardroom. Someone else may care to take up the offer,' and he left the room very quickly, unaccompanied by the usual slamming door.

She picked up the envelope then dropped it again as though it was red hot. Her heart began to beat unevenly and she felt the blood drain from her face. She'd received enough letters written in that hand to know from whom this particular missive had come.

But addressed to the Commander? She picked it up again. What on earth…

With unsteady fingers she took out the single piece of paper, smoothing it flat on the desk before her.

To whom it may concern, interest, involve, pertain to, etc. etc.

Elderly, not very bright, unsteady on the (only partial) feet, Naval Officer, still "Sighing his soul toward the Grecian tents", wishes to meet with young, intelligent, wonderful, adorable, totally without blemish Wren Officer, still (hopefully) with "immortal longings" in her.

There was a footnote, which read:

If Commander A.C. Naughten RN, releases Lt. Commander D.L. Eden RNVR from his given word, please tick here [...] and circulate.

In the place indicated was a large, forcefully executed red tick.

'Bloody *men*!' wailed Joanna Felicity Dunne, and put her head down on her desk and wept.

* * *

She was still sniffing and studying Mark's absurd message, thinking how much she'd like to know about the Commander's part in it all when the door flew open and he stood on the threshold, whiskers positively bristling. She gazed up with drowned eyes. 'Don't look at me like that,' he snapped, 'this is a Naval HQ, not a ruddy matrimonial agency – and don't you forget it!'

'No, sir.'

'And stop snivelling.'

She wiped her eyes with the back of her hand.

'Yes, sir.'

'Damned women in the Navy,' he glared at her across the room then stomped into his office fulminating, 'bloody unnatural – I could have told the buggers it would be a friggin' disaster!'

*   *   *

'Are you sure you want this sent as written?' The postmistress peered doubtfully at the telegraph form Joanna handed her.

'Exactly as written.'

Piqued, Miss Pardoe adjusted her spectacles and peered again at the form, following each word with a forefinger and muttering the contents loud enough to be heard by those in the queue behind Joanna.

IF HENRY 2 COULD CRAWL ON KNEES TO BECKET'S TOMB STOP EXPECT TROILUS CAN DO SAME TO MY QUARTERS BY 1900 HRS SATURDAY STOP CRESSIDA

Joanna paid for the telegram and smiled brightly at the interested members of the waiting queue.

'I'd love to invite you all, but,' she laid a conspiratorial finger on her lips, 'it's very hush-hush – and walls have ears…' then exited to a cackle of laughter from one old man and an in-drawn breath of disapproval from the postmistress.

*   *   *

'Your telegram – it's arrived!' Monica's voice was hushed.

'Speak up, can't you?' Joanna plugged one ear with her forefinger against the noise coming from the wardroom and ground the receiver into the other. 'You sound as though you're in Australia at least.'

'I can't speak any louder. I'm in Lionel's study and I'm sure Josh is lurking at the door.'

'What the hell is *he* doing there? Don't tell me even the Army won't have him back.'

'He's down for a few days and not due in barracks until Monday. Listen, he's driving Mark down in the Riley on Saturday then training it back here.'

'I'll murder that unprincipled bastard when I get hold of him!' Joanna fumed. 'He's got it all tied up, hasn't he? Ready to be Mark's bloody chauffeur and so damned sure I'll be waiting all of a flutter to take over from him.'

'Now don't go flying off the handle.' Monica was soothing. 'Just remember to be your old sweet self. Mark is putting up a good front but he's got a bad case of the jitters. Lionel had to practically kick him into writing to old Naughton, so handle him with care. OK?'

'Someone's head will roll for this...' Joanna threatened then hung up, grinning idiotically and tingling with excitement.

Four more days and she would see him again – but, a steely glint showed in her eye. He needn't think he was going to have her fall into his arms and back into bed all that easily. She took a deep breath. No, she would be absolutely cool calm and collected. This time it would be his turn to make the running.

*　　*　　*

Lionel looked up enquiringly as Monica came into the kitchen, where he was arguing with Mary about Mark making the journey to Tollmouth. Mary anxious that if Joanna decided it had all been a mistake the poor boy would be stranded and left to find a hotel for the night, and Lionel growling that she should stop treating a grown man like a dim-witted schoolboy. 'He got himself into it. Let him get himself out!' being his exasperated and heartless comment, delivered with a finality that brooked no further argument.

'How is Jo?' he asked Monica, then answered his own question, 'don't tell me; nervous, stroppy and after Josh's hide!'

'Oh, don't mind me!' Josh grinned wolfishly and Monica stuck her tongue out at him.

'I should say that just about sums it up,' she sat down at the table, propping her chin on her hands. 'If her nerves stretch any tighter they'll probably go *twang* and she'll fall in half.'

'If it all works out I think she should she come here soon for a good rest,' Mary spoke quietly, 'I owe her that at least after the way I treated her the only time we met. And if it doesn't work out I shall send Mark away and she shall come just the same.'

Lionel snorted. 'The way this place has been since Major ruddy Milton here arrived, she'd be better off looking for peace and quiet on Waterloo Station in the rush hour.'

Monica gave a wistful smile. 'It's almost like having Kit here again, stirring everybody up with both hands.'

'Not this Christmas, but certainly by next, you'll see, Kit *will* come home.' Mary put an arm about her shoulders. 'I know he will. Then we shall all be together again and this house will be host to the biggest party ever.'

Before Monica could reply Ellen entered the kitchen, carrying in her arms the child who accepted without question the angular grim-visage old lady as her devoted slave. 'Here's one little girl who can't get to sleep,' Ellen wagged an admonishing finger at Lionel. '*Some-body* has been reading the wrong sort of bedtime stories.'

'Oh, Lionel,' Monica took a satisfied-looking Laura into her own arms, 'it wasn't *Strewelpeter* again, was it?'

He looked baffled, scratching his head. 'But she *likes* it!'

'Of course she does,' Monica gave a peal of laughter. 'It gives her the perfect excuse to be frightened and have Ellen bring her back over here.'

Unnoticed for a moment Mark stood in the doorway, thinking that he would give all he had in the world to one day see Joanna sitting as Monica was now, laughing and with their child in her arms…

* * *

He sat silently beside Josh as they crossed the border into Hampshire. Added to his permanently aching legs he now had a crashing headache from lack of sleep the previous night. Some lover, he thought, derisively. The fifteen years between Joanna and him yawned impenetrably. Not only was he badger-grey and his face noticeably more lined, but still limping like a crippled duck into the bargain; how could she possibly feel the same about him? They hadn't met for almost sixteen months and surely the memory of that last encounter must still be a barrier between them. And yet ... his insides twisted at the sudden recollection of the bite and lancing humour of that telegram.

But you never could tell. Joanna was capable of keeping a very tight control over even her deepest emotions when she thought it necessary. If she forgave and still loved him, he had a chance. If not, she'd be waiting with all her guns loaded and ready to fire.

He made an impatient gesture and glared at Josh's cheerful profile. 'This is bloody stupid; it will be a complete disaster.'

Josh shot him a sideways glance. 'No. It's the first sensible thing you've done in a long while. Relax, will you?'

'How can you be so sure?'

'I've *seen* her.' Josh kept his eyes on the road. 'Look, you don't need me to tell you about service life, the live-for-the-day attitude that infects everyone in wartime and you know me, Mark. You left a desperately lonely and unhappy, very lovely and loving woman alone for all these months. I'll bet I wasn't the only one to find it impossible not to want to make love to, and care for her. But you were always in the way, damn you, and I'll lay odds it was the same for anyone else who tried. There's still only one man in her life and that's you.'

'What worries me is that sixteen months is one hell of a long time to have been apart. She must have met other younger, more attractive men; she's bound to make comparisons.' Mark was still despondent. 'Even if she still cares she may change her mind once she sees me again.'

Fat chance, thought Josh, but without rancour; the eye that could so swiftly assess a woman's charms also told him that the man beside him was no less attractive than before. Above the uniform jacket and sharp white collar, the hair now well swept with silver served only to highlight a face full of strength and character. His body was still strong and muscular, his shoulders as broad and straight as ever. No woman in her right mind would turn her back, and Joanna was certainly in her right mind. Worst luck!

'Just don't mess around when you see her,' he advised sagely, 'grab her and kiss her before she gets a chance to belt you; I bet you a tenner you'll be right back where you were, you lucky, undeserving swine.'

They swept into Tollmouth on the dot of five o'clock. 'Where to first?' he queried as he reached the Town square.

'Turn right here and keep going for a couple of miles. It's called the George Inn. I've booked a room.' Mark rubbed his chin. 'I'll have another shave then we could have a quick bracer before you drive me back. If you drop me off at her quarters it's only a short drive to the station. You can leave the car on the forecourt there, if that's OK with you?'

Josh snorted. 'Fine, just so long as she doesn't catch sight of me today. I have a strange attachment to my head and I'd rather not have it blasted away by any of madam's ladylike verbals!'

* * *

'How nice to see you again, sir, after such a long time,' the dragon in reception smiled her toothy smile. 'We have reserved your old room as you asked.' She eyed Josh speculatively, 'You did say two for dinner. Will the lady not be joining you as usual?'

'There'll be hell to pay if she doesn't,' put in the irrepressible Josh with a leer then yelped as Mark's stick connected with his ankle.

'You should get something for that rheumatism of yours,' commented Mark blandly. He signed the hotel register, giving the dragon the full benefit of the Eden charm. 'Fortunately for all of us, the major here is in *the* most tremendous hurry to get home again, but with luck the lady will be here shortly and it will just be dinner for two.

* * *

'You look as sick as a parrot.' Joanna eyed her reflection in her dressing table mirror, applied another layer of Pan Stick and stood back to assess the effect. 'Not bad, Max Factor would be proud of you!' She smoothed on lipstick with a more-or-less steady hand then wiped most of it off again. 'Don't want to look more of a tart than you can help, ducky,' she murmured admonishingly. Flicking a brush through her hair she settled her hat before twisting to check if her stocking seams were straight.

She glanced at her watch. 'Right, here we go again, then…' and slinging her bag over one shoulder and tugging down her jacket she walked on shaky legs to the door murmuring aloud, 'Please, God, let it be just as it always was…'

At the top of the steps she paused to look up and down the short street. There was no one in sight so she had a few extra minutes respite. Then out of the corner of her eye she caught a movement by the laurel bush at the foot of the steps as metal walking stick with a white handkerchief attached to the tip rose slowly above the bush and began to wave to and fro.

Joanna took a deep breath. *Remember: Cool, calm and collected...* Not quite in full control of her legs, she completed her journey down the steps to where Mark waited, a set, unreadable expression on his face.

Reaching him she untied the handkerchief and tucking it into his breast pocket ran an unsteady finger along the row of campaign and medal ribbons. 'You *have* had a busy war,' she observed then added straight faced, 'and bye the way, you owe me thirteen shillings and sixpence three-farthings for the front door lock at Gordon Mansions.'

There was a long, long silence before he found his voice. 'Have you got change for a pound?'

'No.'

'Oh.' He cleared his throat and ventured. 'Would you be the

young, very intelligent, wonderful, adorable, totally without blemish Wren Officer I advertised for?'

'I don't know about all *that*, but I do have an awful amount of immortal, not to mention immoral, longings in me still!'

He propped his stick carefully against the hedge and taking her in his arms held her close, his lips against her hair. 'I've been so *scared.*'

'Me too.'

He swayed a little so that she tightened her own arms about him. 'You're not going to fall over, are you?'

'Very possibly, should you suddenly let go.'

'No danger of that.' She looked up into his face with an uncertain grin. 'I meant to be very calm and collected about this ... I'm not doing it very well, am I?'

'No, darling; quite abysmally badly, bless you.'

'We can't stay like this. If an Admiral happens along we could both end up in the brig.' She was dangerously weak about the knees again and leaned to pick up the walking stick. 'Just get back on this, Eden and lead me to where the dastardly Josh has hidden your car.'

'I see someone at Stonehams has been blabbing.'

'My spies are everywhere.' She hugged his arm. 'Are we having dinner?'

'Yes.'

'May one ask where?'

'At the George.'

'I see. And where are you sleeping tonight?'

'At the George: and you?'

'Would you be surprised if I said the same?'

'No, just delighted and humbly grateful and thankful and – '

She interrupted him with a dry, 'It doesn't suit you.'

'What doesn't?'

'Being meek and mild.'

He smiled. 'Funny. That's just what pa said.'

They had reached the car and she stopped to look searchingly at his face.

'Is everything really all right with you two?'

'Yes, everything; cross my heart.'

She put her arms about his neck. 'Have I told you that I love you?'

'Oh, darling...' He let his stick clatter to the ground; wrapping his arms around her he buried his face in her hair. 'Not for the past sixteen months, you haven't!'

*　　*　　*

After so many long and bitter months apart, the craving to be alone together evolved into something akin to waiting for a slow-burning fuse to ignite a barrel of gunpowder. Driving almost in silence to the George, they then sat in a mounting agony of need through a dinner that neither could taste, and by the time they were finally alone both were strung with an unbearable tension.

Greedy passionate and wild, their lovemaking was spoiled and rushed until the familiar joy and delight in each other took over and they could regain their own remembered joy of loving and giving. Joanna's surrender to him after her first storming, demanding passion filled Mark with a melting tenderness, so that he took her then with a depth and ardour that left them both close to tears.

'How can I ever put into words how I feel about you?' he looked up into her eyes as she smoothed the fading scars on his face with gentle fingers.

'There's no need; you've just shown me. I love you so much, and there *are* no words to tell.'

'When can you come home to Cornwall again?'

'Soon, very soon,' she stroked his hair. 'Now go to sleep.'

'If you keep watch…'

They lay close, the steady muffled beat of his heart lulling her asleep. At first light she stirred with a sleepy, 'Hello, you...' and he turned her to him again and made love with tender lips and hands and the remembered words soft on his tongue:

'"*I would come back, come back to you…*"'

23

Malaya, March–July1945

They had buried Arnie where they'd buried so many others, in the area of cleared jungle outside the perimeter of the camp, whilst Kit prayed to the God the Australian hadn't believed in and mourned a friend.

One more pointless, vicious death…

They'd been unloading the big boxes marked with the Red Cross and destined not for the prisoners for whom they were intended, but for the Jap storehouse. When one had fallen and burst open, spilling hundreds of boxes and bottles of anti-Malaria pills and Vitamin B tablets in all directions, the opportunity for Arnie had been too good to miss. 'Mill around, you bastards!' he yelled to his fellows, 'Get some racket goin'!'

The men responded magnificently and with deafening enthusiasm to his call, and amid the resultant confusion of kicks, blows from rifle butts and shouted commands, Arnie crawled between the scuffling concealing legs, shovelling everything he could lay his hands on deep under the hut.

That night he made his way back and forth, flitting like a shadow between the huts, returning each time with a knotted lion cloth full of his booty, each item snatched by eager hands and stowed in a hundred different hiding places. Then, with only a couple of trips to complete the *cache*, the bored eye of a sentry fell upon him, and Arnie made no more trips.

The screams and yells of the sentry and the thud of his boots and rifle butt brought the prisoners flooding from their huts and guards racing with fixed bayonets, while a kimono-wrapped Commandant left his bed to appear on his veranda.

Kept at bay by the ring of rifles around the sentry and his trampling, blood-spattered boots, the POW's could only look on in sick horror at the mindless violence until the Jap soldier stood back, leaving Arnie limp and unmoving under a cold, bright moon. With a low growl the prisoners moved forward *en mass,* only to halt again as the click of released rifle catches echoed around the camp.

All but one who, heedless of the threatening guns, stepped out, walking steadily to where the bundle of bloodied rags that was Arnie lay.

'Leave him!' Yoshido raised his hand to the guards, his black impassive eyes focused on the lone rescuer. Unwavering, with firm, unhurried step the tall figure brushed past the Jap guards and they, obedient to Yoshido's command and uncertain for once in the uncanny, charged silence of the hundreds of watching men, fell back and let him through.

Still without speaking he knelt and gathered what was left of a man into his arms and with strength from somewhere beyond the ability of his own emaciated body, lifted him and stood looking for long moments directly into the Commandant's unwinking eyes. Then he bowed; the figure in his arms groaned and the head lolled. He bowed again then turning about walked back through the circle of guards and into his hut.

The watching men held one huge collective breath, their eyes on the stocky figure standing impassive on the veranda.

Not one muscle in Yoshido's face moved, he might have been carved out of stone. Then he gave a single dismissive gesture and word of command. The guards trotted back to their quarters, the sentries resumed their posts and in an eerie unbroken silence the prisoners melted away into the huts.

Kit knelt on the floor, surrounded by silent men and cradled Arnie's head in his arms, rocking slowly and saying the familiar words he had said uncounted times in this place:

'Out of the depths have I called unto Thee, O Lord, Lord, hear my voice...'

Arnie's swollen eyes opened a fraction. 'Nice try, mate, but I still don't believe a word of it!' then his bloodied lips parted in a grin and he was dead.

* * *

In some strange way the Australian's death seemed a turning point. There was no attempt to search their huts for the drugs. No reference ever made by their captors to the incident. Captain Yoshido remained his own impassive self and Kit was left puzzling anew over the Japanese psyche that could combine cruelty beyond belief with a strange, almost medieval chivalry, even towards a despised prisoner of war. It was a repetition of the day Yoshido had beaten Kano for his attack on Kit himself, an equally incomprehensible act. One might learn their language, he thought, but never even glimpse what might be going on in their minds. He went cold every time he thought of his automatic unthinking walk to fetch Arnie's body. What the hell had he thought he was doing? Yoshido could have easily ordered the guards to mow down the whole lot of them.

A few days after this incident some shreds identifiable as vegetable matter appeared in the rice and a month later Red Cross parcels were handed out; the first they had ever received, followed in a week or two by a steady trickle of basic medical supplies.

When Kit paid his weekly visit to the women's camp the day after the first large square box of quinine tablets had been placed in his arms, no guard accompanied him.

'Something's up,' he said, when he'd tracked Vivienne to the infirmary hut, 'I do believe our blokes may be making a nuisance of themselves after all these years... We heard a plane, heavier than a Nip fighter but too light for a bomber, going over late yesterday.'

She straightened from where she was tying cloth around a small boy's arm, infected and swollen from mosquito bites, and brushed a hand across her face.

'Theirs or ours, do you think?'

'Ours, I reckon; it could have been on reconnaissance.' He looked at the boy, whose face was beginning to screw with pain. Squatting down on the floor Kit made his hands into fists, pretending to pull off the first joint of his own thumb, then showed him how to copy him. The boy squealed with delight and when the dressing was finished, Kit lifted him from the bed, smacked him lightly on the backside and sent him off to demonstrate to his peers.

Vivienne laughed. 'And I thought we'd all grown up at last.'

He gave her an affectionate grin. 'I've grown older, if that's anything to go by, but I sometimes find myself waiting for a voice to say: 'Maturity has arrived, Kit Eden, go forth and demonstrate.'

'I don't know about that but you can go forth with a few boxes of vitamin tablets if you like. We have quite a store at the moment.'

'Thanks. I'll take some … and that's another thing...' he told her about the continuing increase in the rice content and the morning release of quinine. 'Now why should they be doing that? They've even stopped beating the working parties on the way back in the evenings; just let them move at their own pace.'

'Perhaps the end is in sight.' She caught her breath, 'Do you suppose Dougie is still alive somewhere? I couldn't bear it if he was dead after all. I really was horrible to him sometimes, but I did love him, well, in a way, and he loved me, even if I was a spoilt bitch. It would be too awful if I never see him again to say I'm sorry.'

She turned away then, busying herself smoothing and folding the pieces of cloth and Kit watched her in silence, wondering how she had managed not only to adapt to the conditions of internment, but even rise above them while still remaining essentially the same old Vivienne.

No one could doubt her remorse and sorrow over poor old Dougie, that was genuine; but more than enough of the arrogant, spoilt little rich girl still remained. Perhaps, he thought, with sudden insight, it was what had made her survive all the horrors and deprivations; to assume the responsibility for the camp, fight with the Commandant for medicines and get away with treating the guards as the uneducated peasants they undoubtedly were. Others had made the effort to learn at least basic Japanese, but not Vivienne.

In her way she was as bloody-minded and difficult as Arnie. If the Nips couldn't make their orders in English, she declared, she couldn't carry them out, and such was her belief in herself that it seemed even the average Jap soldier wasn't prepared to challenge her. Of course it had helped having an educated and unusually humanitarian Camp Commandant, but all the same…

She looked up and caught the contemplative expression in his eyes.

'What's the matter with you, Kit Eden? Not lusting after my body, are you?'

'Hardly that; after more than three years on a diet of rice I've forgotten what lust ever felt like; you could lock me in a small room with a half-dozen nautch girls and I still wouldn't know if it up and bit me!'

'Not really into the business of making a girl feel good, are you? Well, I hope for your wife's sake it will all come back to you.'

'That's very civil of you, Vivienne.'

'I have my moments.'

She sat down, holding the folded cloths in her arms, staring out through the open doorway over the dusty compound. 'I wonder if Mark is still having a good time with his piece,' she mused. 'I've made up my mind that the first thing I do when we get out of this bloody awful dump will be to sort out the divorce. Living apart all these years should do the trick, don't you think, especially as I did the leaving.'

'Undoubtedly; a pity you didn't untangle the mess earlier though, isn't it? I can't help feeling you might have had fewer regrets.'

'Don't start trying to get me joining the goodness-and-light brigade.'

He looked at the threads of grey in the dark hair, the eyes challenging in the painfully thin face and smiled. 'I rather think you joined that some time ago.'

'I shouldn't begin counting me amongst your saved souls just yet.' She stood up. 'Now shove off, Kit, or you'll be late for your portion of rare roast beef and Yorkshire.'

He gave his slow smile.

'God keep you, Vivienne, as Mark would say.'

*   *   *

He began to hold his Communion Services in the middle of the compound, watched by the silent, subdued Japanese, the knowledge of their impending defeat showing clearly in their sullen expressions and drooping shoulders. Faintly, from the mountains and jungle could be heard the first rumble of guns. Further away still, and known to only a few, the politicians and the five-star generals were clustered around conference tables and over maps in War Rooms, deciding on which Japanese city to drop the bomb which would change the world forever.

*   *   *

London, May 1945.

Joanna saw the new owners of the flat out of the door then threw her hat into the air and executed an undignified jig in the hall. 'All done, Audrey; you always said you'd sell when the war finished. Well, it is, almost, and I've done it for you.'

For the last time she wandered from room to room of the empty flat, recalling the times spent there on leave, the laughter and confidences shared; realising that here she had known her mother better then than in all the pre-war years of school and university. She stood for a while at the window of the sitting room, thinking of the times Audrey must have waved to Leo as he left after an evening together and wondered fleetingly if she had enjoyed going to bed with him as much as her daughter still did with his son. She hoped so.

She glanced at her watch. Almost time to leave for Portsmouth, where Mark would be waiting for her in the Bedford's bar to properly start their leave. After all the months behind a desk, the *Dawlish Star*, his first command since his injuries, had docked yesterday after a month steaming to and from Italy bringing troops home. The planned flying visit they were due to make to Dorset before heading down to Porthryn was an ordeal she preferred not to think about too closely

She crossed the bare echoing hall to the kitchen and took the sheaf of flowers from the sink. She would go to Highgate now then drive straight down to Portsmouth; only six days of her leave left and then it would be time to part again for the same old round of watching and waiting.

She coaxed the Riley into life. Mark had said that like him it was getting on in years and would soon be headed for the scrap-yard. This leave over she thought she would find time to get herself a small car. It would be an extravagance, but she'd hardly touched any of Audrey's money and needed to have her own transport at hand: it would be easier then to slip down to Porthryn whilst Mark was at sea.

'Well, Audrey.' She squatted back on her heels, laying half her flowers then reaching to pat the earth around Leo's rose bush. 'It's all finished and I've said my farewells to Gordon Mansions. Leo will look after you while I'm away, and you do have Archie for company.'

Taking the remaining flowers, she placed them on the adjacent grave then standing for a few moments read again the weathered headstone.

Lieutenant Colonel A.G. Dunne
The Duke of Ruthven's Own Rifle Brigade
1874–1923

'I wish I could really remember you, but I can't – only as a tall man who used to swing me up in the air and ask: "How's my Jo today?" but in all the years without you, *she* never forgot.'

She saluted the graves, then turned and walked away, melancholy at having to leave them both in this quiet place beneath the trees, with just the birdsong and the muted hum of traffic on Highgate Hill for company.

* * *

'Darling,' Mark took her hand, 'was it very sad to say goodbye? I should have left Dicky to deal with all the guff on board and come with you.'

'I'm all right now.' She smiled, studying his face as she always did when they met, even if they had only been a few hours apart. 'I know Leo will look after them both.'

'Did Monica tell you Pa is retiring at the end of the year?'

'Yes, she said your mother finally put her foot down.' She grinned. 'Won't he just be absolute hell at first?'

'She's already thought of that. He's being dragged off on an extended tour of the Highlands in the New Year. That should give him something to think about if he has to dig the car out of snowdrifts every morning.'

She laughed. 'I'll bet you he finds some excuse for not going. But come on, drink up or we shall be late for tea at Stonehams; as it is we shan't make it to Porthryn until midnight.'

They began to walk to where she had left the car. Mark stepping out with the slightly rolling gait he had perfected to balance his shortened foot. It couldn't be easy, she reflected, to keep his feet on deck in a gale, but he doubtless managed that as he did everything else these days: competently and without complaint.

'You don't have to slow down for me,' he observed now, with a sideways glance and she made a face at him.

'Don't flatter yourself. We had full Divisions last Sunday then marched half around flaming Tollmouth; I got a piece of grit in my shoe and couldn't stop to do anything about it. You should just see the blisters.'

'I'll kiss them better. You know I've developed a foot fetish since this one of mine lost its beauty.'

'I can't say I'll find that a very erotic experience; it's where you get to *after* my blisters that makes my day.'

'Later, darling, later...we don't want to do anything in the street that might frighten the horses, now do we?'

'That rather depends,' she answered, 'on how easily they frighten, doesn't it?'

* * *

'How is he?'

She smiled and took Lionel's arm as they strolled together in the garden while Mark walked to the village with Monica and Laura. 'Fine; rather quieter than he used to be."

'No problems now between the two of you?'

'No, although it took a while for us to really shake down again together.' She hunched her shoulders, 'mind you, he can still be a bloody-minded so-and-so when he chooses.'

He laughed, giving a pat to the arm linked in his. 'That makes two of you.'

'Yes, well, a girl has to have her own way at least half the time.'

They walked in silence for a few minutes until they reached the far hedge and stepped through onto the headland. 'You know,' she looked out over the water, 'just lately I have the feeling that I've grown up at last, which is odd. I was so sure at twenty-two that I already had, that it comes as a bit of a shock to realise the difference almost five years of war – and Mark – has made.'

He grunted. 'He'd age anyone. Put years on me.'

'Don't put on an act, Leo. You know you're proud of him now.'

'I always was, well, almost always.' He grinned broadly, 'It's an old man's right to be cussed and I'm beginning to enjoy being an old man. It has its compensations.'

'Such as?'

'You and Monica for a start, he patted her arm again. 'Come along and see if tea is ready before I get really maudlin and start sounding like something out of a very bad production of Little Nell.'

Impulsively, she turned to kiss his cheek. He gave her a quizzical smile. 'What brought that on?'

'Oh, things… I went to Highgate to leave flowers and say goodbye. I started thinking about my father and how little he means to me.' She sighed. 'Awful, but all I could remember clearly was that he called me Jo. Perhaps I was doing a spot of unconscious regressing when I let you call me that the first time we met.'

He transferred his arm to around her shoulders. 'That has to be one of the very nicest things anyone has ever said to me.'

Her eyes glinted with laughter. 'You must have led a somewhat deprived life.'

'Perhaps, but once you are out of uniform for good I shall expect you to be very dutiful and regularly visit an old man in his dotage to make sure that he is kept feeling reasonably young and frisky.'

She gave a gurgle of laughter. 'Are you flirting with me, Leo?'

'Yes,' he grinned, 'but then I always have, and you with me, you shameless hussy. Nice, isn't it?'

'Lovely,' Joanna squeezed his arm as they turned to leave, 'but then it's allowed for a girl to flirt with her paterfamilias, isn't it?'

Porthryn, Cornwall, May 1945

'How was he?' asked Mark, as they left Stonehams behind and she smiled.

'Fine.'

He gave her a suspicious sideways glance. 'What are you grinning about?'

'Nothing, only that he asked the same question about you.'

'And what was your answer?'

'I was very truthful and told him you were as bloody-minded as ever.'

'Confounded cheek,' he pulled onto the side of the road, stopped the engine and turned to take her face in both hands and thoroughly kiss her laughing mouth. 'I suppose I shouldn't be doing this with you now that you have so much more shiny braid on your own sleeve!'

'You can take my jacket off if that worries you.'

'All in good time,' he tangled his fingers in her hair and kissed her again, long and slow then asked breathlessly, 'Do you still love me, in spite of my great age?'

'I do.'

'And will you still marry me at the first possible moment?'

'I will.'

'I can live with that, but for now…' he kissed her again. 'Seven days – no newspapers, no radio with Alvar Lidell telling us about the war, or a load of brass hats guessing when it might end … Just you and me and Oscar.'

Six days alone together … Joanna drew a deep breath and settled back into her seat as they headed for Porthryn and home. Dorset hadn't been such an ordeal after all, she reflected. Mary Eden had put herself out to be pleasant and welcoming, and although Joanna doubted they would ever become bosom friends, it seemed a state of war no longer existed between them, which was just as well. With the stumbling block of the absent Vivienne still plonked firmly in the way of their marriage she could do without a hostile mother-in-law to add to her problems…

* * *

'What the hell?' Frying pan arrested in mid-air, Mark turned his head to look at the wall clock. 'That's a confoundedly odd time to be ringing church bells – at twenty past eleven for heavens sake; don't tell me the vicar overslept.'

Joanna cocked an ear.

'That's not just one set of bells. I can hear them from all directions … Mark,' she looked at him with dawning comprehension, 'you don't think…?'

They both leaped for the radio they hadn't listened to for the past four days.

'Bugger them licensing laws! We'em goin' tu keep this up all day an' all night too!'

In the Wreckers, George Tregorran pulled beer and cider into waiting tankards and glasses. ‘First rowns on the ’owerse, m’dears, then you’m can all buy one fur I!’

‘To the first hour of the first day of peace,’ Mark touched his glass to Joanna’s as she smiled through the tears that kept welling in her eyes.

‘All we need now is Kit’s war to end and for him come back.’

He smiled and offered his handkerchief. ‘Give ma and pa and Monica a little time to recover then we’ll telephone and all have a good howl together.’

‘Now, me old sailor, you’m c’n get back to the cows an’ ’osses.’ A weather-beaten farmer slapped Mark on the back, jogging his brimming glass. ‘I sez to my missus, says I, now poor ol’ Jim c’n pu’ his feet up a’ last!’

‘I’ve a few more trips to make yet, Mick; there are an awful lot of our blokes to bring home, and the Nips to sort out before they beach me.’

‘An’ you’m, m’dear.’ Mick planted a kiss on Joanna’s cheek. ‘When do we al’ see you tucked up along o’ his self in that ’ouse up there?’ He gave a leery wink. ‘But never you be minding if he en’t wi’ you … just you call for I if you be needin’ company.’

‘You’d better watch out for the minefield, Mick.’ She laughed up at Mark. ‘I reckon the boss here will be laying that for Josh, if no-one else!’

* * *

As Lionel switched off the radio Monica ran from the house; Mary half rose from her chair and he put a restraining hand on her arm. ‘Let her go. It’s not all over yet and she’ll have some mixed feelings to sort out until Kit is safe home.’

‘Will she be all right, do you think?’

‘I’m sure she will. She’s headed for the old summerhouse.’

They smiled in mutual understanding for a moment, then the tears she had held back for so long spilled down her cheeks. He put his arms about her, rocking her gently and stroking her hair. ‘It’s all right. Mark has come through it all and so will Kit, you must believe that. We just have to wait a little longer for him.’

In the kitchen Ellen sang ‘Jerusalem’ off key, but with great enthusiasm to a delighted if uncomprehending Laura. In the summerhouse Monica curled up in the wicker chair and held the flowered cushions to her breast.

‘You next, my darling, darling Kit, and we shall have that party

Mary promised; you'll see…we'll have it this year,' and she smiled and cried and laughed in turn as the warm sunshine flooded through the open doorway and the gulls swooped and called high above in the sweet spring air.

24

Tollmouth, July 1945

Joanna finished checking the last batch of documents, tidied them into folders and gave a sigh of relief.

Peace had hardly made her job any easier or less busy, added to which the day had been blazing hot and she was longing to have a cool shower and change her shirt, which stuck determinedly to her back each time she relaxed into her chair. She looked at the clock. Just time to nip along to the plot room before they broke for lunch and see how close Mark was to home…

'The *Dawlish Star*? She's due into Portsmouth on the twenty-fourth; only four days now ma'am.'

'Umm, Tuesday, thanks, Taff.'

There were few who didn't know of her interest in the *Star's* Captain and as several broad smiles were cast in her direction she grinned back amiably, 'All right, you lot – keep your minds on your work!'

Still smiling she returned to her office to find the Commander had arrived back from his meeting and was making himself at home in her one comfortable chair. 'I've come to collect the reports and a cup of coffee wouldn't go amiss…' he broke off to scowl as her 'phone began to ring. 'Better answer that blasted thing first.'

She answered it standing, watching him flicking through the completed files.

'First Officer Dunne…'

'I have a personal call for you, ma'am.'

She was curt. 'You don't put personal calls through to me in this office.' She watched his head come up and stared back unblinking into his sharp eyes. Hell's teeth, she thought, what idiot could be calling her when she was on duty? If it were Josh she'd really do him a mischief. She said briskly, 'Tell who ever it is to call my quarters later.'

'Sorry ma'am, but I've a lady on the line … she is very upset and says she must speak to you now.'

'A *lady,* wait,' she put her hand over the mouthpiece, 'I'm sorry, sir; the switchboard seem to think it's urgent…'

'Take it.'

'Yes, sir; all right you can put her through now.'

'Miss Joanna?' For a moment she couldn't place the voice, 'I'm sorry to call you, but there isn't anyone else and I don't know what to do.'

'Mrs Bodley,' she realised the voice belonged to Mark's housekeeper and was immediately alert. 'Where are you? What's happened?'

'I'm at Mr Mark's – Oh, dear! I don't know how to tell you...' she began to sob uncontrollably. Joanna gripped the 'phone hard as a sudden vision of the house burning down presented itself. But no, that was silly, the distraught woman was there and using Mark's 'phone.

'Mrs Bodley, please don't cry. Try to tell me what's happened. Has there been an accident?'

'It's Mr James.' She wept uncontrollably, then as Joanna continued to sooth her eventually managed to gasp between diminishing sobs: 'He's dead, Miss Joanna! Poor Mr James … he was just lying there and now they've taken him away and I don't know what to do first.'

It took several more minutes for Joanna to discover that Jim had died in his sleep; a sudden heart attack, the doctor had said. Mrs Bodley had found Oscar howling outside his door when she'd arrived and discovered Jim lying peacefully in bed as though he was just sleeping. 'I'm taking Oscar home with me, Miss Joanna,' she finished, 'please can you or Mr Mark come soon? I don't know what to do about his lists and all the arrangements; the 'phone's been ringing non-stop this past hour with everyone wanting to know why he hadn't made his visits.'

Acutely aware that Commander Naughton was listening to every word, Joanna eventually rang off with the promise to call her at home later. She put down the 'phone, ran a hand through her hair and raised apologetic eyes to his face.

'I'm awfully sorry, sir, but that was the housekeeper at Porthryn; Captain Eden's partner has died suddenly and she's in a terrible state.'

'Of course she is; better get your kit together then go down there and sort it all out.'

'Thank you, sir.'

'Anything I can do?'

'A message to the *Dawlish Star* would help. She's due into Portsmouth on Tuesday. If he knows ahead of time her captain can make arrangements to leave ship as soon as she docks.'

'I'll deal with that. Now clear off … your Miss Finch can hold the fort again for a few days.'

She felt like kissing the irascible soft-hearted old termagant, but contented herself with the sort of smile that still made his ears pink a little at the tips.

Skimming over to her quarters she threw a few clothes into her bag and sped to the car park behind the base, thankful beyond words for the second hand Austin Ten, kept ready and topped-up with petrol by a grizzled old CPO from Supplies.

She drove fast, fending off her tears and thinking of Jim as she'd last seen him; off for a day's river fishing, turning to wave a jaunty goodbye from the gate and smiling his crinkled smile. She hoped Mark wouldn't feel guilty at the amount of work his absence had put on the old man and start laying the blame on his own shoulders, but Jim had been stubborn, always refusing to countenance a locum.

She pulled her thoughts together. Well, there'd have to be one now, but how in hell did she start looking for a locum veterinary surgeon in the wilds of Cornwall?

Once arrived at the cottage common sense took over. With luck, Mark would be with her shortly, by then she would have had time to contact relatives to make the funeral arrangements…'Oh, *hell*' she groaned and leaned against the window to cool her forehead as she remembered that Jim had been a widower, his only daughter married and living in Canada, so there was no help to be found there. Surely there was some other relative rather nearer at hand? She had better brave the tearful Mrs Bodley, fetch Oscar and worry about everything else tomorrow.

*   *   *

By the time Mark had telephoned from Portsmouth that he was on his way, she had tracked down a sister in Cardiff and a niece in Kidderminster, made the funeral arrangements and engaged a locum, a lanky, blonde-haired, thirty-five year old Scot with a soft incomprehensible Highland accent. She could hardly understand a word he said but he had an impressive array of references and was willing to help out until the spring, when he was due to join a practice in New Zealand.

Let the Cornish farmers and Callum Maclean sort out the language problem amongst themselves, she thought wearily as she waited for Mark. A wild Highlander speaking what appeared to be a foreign tongue would give the locals a new topic for discussion in the pub every night.

*　　　*　　　*

'Poor old Jim; this place was his life, you know.' Later that same evening Mark walked around the surgery, fingering jars and bottles. 'He was a real old bugger – fought all my 'new-fangled ideas' as he called them, tooth and nail when I first came. But it's been fifteen years. I shall miss him like hell.'

'I hope our friend Callum won't lose you any patients.' She made a rueful face. 'I have nightmares that no one's going to be able to understand a word he says.'

'The farmers will manage, and the cows won't care!' he put his arms about her. 'Darling, you've been brilliant … I expected to come back to chaos and instead all is beautifully sorted out. I should have known better.'

She grinned, 'Yes, you should. Come along now, we must go up and see if friend Callum has settled in, then take him to the Wreckers and frighten the locals.'

They had to admire his efficiency. He had already unpacked and the little flat above the surgery was neat and bright, with a few watercolour landscapes on the walls and a beautifully worked patchwork quilt on the bed.

'My grannie gave it me to keep warm!' he explained, with a wide smile on his long, monkish face as Joanna fingered this beautiful object, 'I think she believes I've come to the ends of the earth down here.'

'You have.' She looked at him with narrowed eyes. 'What happened to your accent?' she asked suspiciously, 'when we talked yesterday I didn't understand more than one word in ten.'

'Sorry … just having a wee bit of fun.'

She appraised his guileless expression for a moment. 'Cornwall is full of people like you, so you should soon feel at home.'

Mark was examining the pictures. 'These are very good.' he bent to read the signature, 'Maclean ... any relative?'

'They're mine. I like to keep busy once the day's work is finished, an' as ma grannie says, it keeps me off the streets!'

That's all we need thought Joanna, an artistic vet with a nice line in modest understatement. At least he's not likely to neglect his work in order to play rugger or chase the local girls.

'He's a gem,' said Mark later as they sat in a corner of the bar, 'just look at him charming the socks off everyone. You are a clever girl, J.F. Dunne. It's a pity he's set on going to New Zealand; I'd quite like to have asked him to stay on when I return for good.'

'When will that be now? Jim's death will make a difference, won't it?'

He grimaced. 'Yes. I shall be out before long, I imagine. There's no doubt but that the Navy will release me very soon on compassionate grounds. I should have liked to see it through to the end, but there are lots of younger blokes coming along now. I daresay they'll be glad to see the back of a beaten-up old fogy like me.'

'Well you'll have to wait a bit longer for *me* to come home and warm your slippers; I'll be damned lucky if I'm out before *next* Christmas!' She stared gloomily into her glass. 'I feel as if I've been saying 'Yes, sir' to old Naughton for ever.'

'But you'll miss the old blighter when it's all over, won't you?'

She sighed. 'Yes, I suppose I shall … no one to outwit and score off from time to time. Even since I was made up to First and kicked upstairs he spends half his time popping in and out of my office and harassing me!'

'Never mind, darling,' Mark raised his glass and eyed her sardonically over the rim. 'Once you've exchanged old Naughton and Tollmouth for Porthryn and me, I daresay you'll manage to reverse the trend and do some of the harassing yourself.'

She murmured, 'Come home now and I'll show you how – sir!'

He finished his beer and stood up. 'Last one in bed turns the light out!'

23

Malaya, August 1945

An uneasy silence hung over the camp. Major Buckley awakened slowly, aware that no *Serits* had been called; no orders made to bow and pay homage to the Emperor. For the past week 'planes had passed overhead daily while the sound of heavy gunfire seemed nearer each hour and nervous guards had returned to the old regime of bullying and brutality, the whole camp suffering days of threats and beatings. Even more sinister was a persistent rumour that if the guns grew much closer they would be force-marched through the jungle ahead of the invading forces.

The Major padded across the floor and peered cautiously across the silent deserted square. His heart began to thump painfully and his mouth dried. Kneeling beside Kit's sleeping form he shook his shoulder urgently. 'Padre, wake up!'

Kit woke instantly at the hoarse whisper. 'What is it?'

'There's nobody here, old boy; not a Nip in sight – I think they've all buggered off.'

'Are you sure?' Kit rolled off his cot. All around him men were waking, asking what was up. The air began to buzz with excited whispers, almost as though every man feared to voice his hopes out loud. Hesitantly at first, a few stepped out into the deserted compound then with a rush and a roar the rest erupted and raced across the square. Within minutes, hundreds of scarecrows were laughing, weeping, dancing, hugging; some still in tatters of old uniforms, some in the loincloths that was their only clothing, some stark naked as they had jumped from their cots. Someone yelled 'The stores!' and there was an immediate rush to batter down the doors. Red Cross boxes were broken open: tins, packets and bottles flew through the air as they looted the food denied them for so long.

Kit leaned against a tree cramming tinned peaches into his mouth from a jagged tin unceremoniously smashed open against a sharp stone. He licked his fingers as the juice ran over them, knowing he would almost certainly be sick, that it was madness to eat so after the years of starvation. But he was helpless to prevent either himself or anyone else from this first wild, delirious indulgence in anything edible that came to hand.

Eventually he staggered over to Toshido's bungalow and with a glorious feeling of defiance and power, climbed the steps and flung open the door.

He had a moment of pure, bone-melting terror.

Toshido sat at the table, leaning back in his chair and staring straight at him with his black shark's eyes. For a long minute Kit clung to the door, the strength draining from his legs until he realised the hypnotic eyes were lifeless. In the centre of the commandant's forehead was a neat hole, the edges rimmed with dried blood; behind him on the wall already a-swarm with flies was the contents of his skull. Recovering himself he approached the desk, circling it cautiously until he could see where Toshido's right hand hung down over the chair arm, his rigid fingers appearing to point at the revolver on the floor by his side.

Kit turned and staggered out again to stand shaking and delivering his hastily swallowed peaches on the steps Toshido had so many times tyrannically bestrode in those highly polished boots.

A very merry young naval lieutenant was clinging to the veranda support with one hand, clasping a bottle of the late Commandant's saki in the other. 'What's up, Padre?' he asked and gave an alcoholic giggle. 'Seen something nasty in the wood-shed have you?'

'You could say that.' Kit bent over the veranda rail and retched again, then straightened, wiping his mouth on the back of his hand. 'If you're not too pissed, Tom, I think you'd better help me dig a hole somewhere ... and leave some of that booze for me!'

An hour later, still queasy and staggering slightly from the effects of wielding a spade on a stomach empty of all but a generous measure of saki, he made his way down the jungle path to the women's camp; discovering there a more restrained but no less joyous outpouring of excitement. He sought out Vivienne, finding her with a half-dozen of the older women presiding over a much more orderly and sensible distribution of food. Pushing through the crowd surrounding her he pulled her into his arms. 'We've made it! We beat them! We're still alive!'

Overwhelmed they clung together, Kit repeating over and over again. 'We beat them, we beat them … we're still alive!'

Later, only slightly less euphoric and the saki still making inroads on his uncertain stomach, they sat on the steps of one of the huts, munching their way very slowly through a packet of Garibaldi biscuits and making absurd, impossible plans for getting home.

Vivienne said, 'Back to Singapore first, I have to find Dougie ...

come with me, Kit.'

'Of course, but how do we get there … walk?'

'Too far, and I'd never make it in my three-inch heels and satin evening gown.'

'We could commandeer a bullock from the Thais; we could *both* get on a bullock.'

She gave a solemn shake of the head. 'They'll have eaten them all by now – and when I roll up in front of the Raffles, Kit Eden, it won't be on any bloody bullock; I want a Daimler, with red ribbons and a loudspeaker playing The Entry of the Queen of Sheba.'

Kit hiccupped with tipsy laughter, 'More likely to be *She'll be Coming Round the Mountain*!' he fell back to gaze dreamily at the straw roof above him. 'I love this place. I love everyone in it…' he twisted around to put his arms about her waist and pull her down beside him, 'but most of all, I love *you*, Vivienne!'

She laughed and pushed the last Garibaldi into his mouth. 'In a pig's ear you do, Vicar. If only the Archbishop of Canterbury could see you now – drunk as a skunk and trying to get your leg over your sister-in-law!'

* * *

A further two days were to pass before the first troops of the 14th Army entered the camp. A mix of British and Australians, tough men who stared in open disbelief as they were surrounded by euphoric tattered men and women; small children clasping the newcomer's hands with a kind of confused desperation, as though they thought their rescuers may at any moment melt away back into the jungle.

'When do we get out? When do we get home?'

The new arrivals were bombarded on all sides as they made their way through the camp. 'Blimey, how long since you all had some decent tucker?' one bush-hatted rescuer looked around him, bemused and stunned. He turned to Kit. 'Holy smoke – you got Sheilas an' kids here too? Bleedin' cosy, innit?'

'Only a recent delight,' Kit assured him, 'they were in another camp about a mile along, but moved up here when the Nips went. It's better for them here; less mosquitoes.'

'You don't say. It must have been quite somethin', then.'

A tall officer shouldered his way forward. 'Chaps say you're the padre; are you the senior officer?'

Kit grinned at the clipped English voice and shook his head; he wasn't getting caught on that one with all its resultant headaches. 'No, sir,' he replied with a certain amount of malice, 'that's the Major over there.'

'OK. See you later, Padre.'

'He's going to love all this...' Vivienne indicated Buckley on the steps of Toshido's hut and nudged Kit in the ribs with a painfully sharp elbow. 'Just look at the old fart puffing out his chest. You'd think him a Brigadier at least.'

'He probably will be when he gets back, but he's not so bad.' Kit was feeling charitable. 'Even he's learned a thing or two in this holiday camp and he's welcome to the job of sorting this lot out.'

* * *

They filled in their official postcards to be sent home to say they were still alive, then waited to leave the camp, but it was a further ten days before they were moved out. Kit, by then in the remorseless grip of yet another bout of malaria with the added misery of dysentery, found himself to his chagrin parted from Vivienne and bundled onto a transport bound for the hospital in Johore.

Discovering that the Raffles Hotel had been taken over to house civilians until they could be shipped home, Vivienne refused point blank to enter any other temporary accommodation whatsoever, saying she would find a bed in the hotel if her own house was uninhabitable. Not being subject to military discipline, she got her own way as usual.

'Just see they let you go PDQ,' she ordered Kit as he was helped onto the crowded lorry for the first leg of his long journey, 'and contact me through the Raffles. I'm going to find Dougie first then see if our house is still in one piece. If it is you're to stay there until we all get shipped home.'

'Yes, ma'am,' he saluted her shakily. 'You remind me of my mama!' he called as they began to move.

She grinned. 'God forbid!'

He hung over the tailboard as the truck gathered speed and the tall, indomitable figure in the tattered washed-out blue sarong stood waving them on their way until a bend in the track took them out of sight.

'That's some Sheila, mate.'

Kit looked at the small Aussie private who had made this observation, then collapsed back into the truck. 'Damn' right, mate,' he agreed. 'In fact, that's one *hell* of a Sheila, and what's more, I've got a date with her in Singapore.'

'Bleedin' Pommy Jesus freak,' The man spat over the tailboard and Kit was reminded irresistibly of Arnie. 'Trust one of the God-Squad to line hisself up a bit of skirt when he c'n hardly stand up straight ... you should be bloody ashamed of yourself, Padre!'

'Oh, I am, I am,' Kit laughed then suddenly doubled up as his bowels were gripped by a familiar agonising spasm. He gasped, 'Stop this bloody lorry before I do something else to be ashamed of.'

The private looked at him in disgust. 'Ke-*rist!* We've only managed 'arf a mile – 'ave we got to put up with this all the bleedin' way to the airstrip?' He banged on the side of the lorry bawling, ''ang on the brakes corp, the padre's got the squits!'

Kit scrambled over the tailboard and staggered into the undergrowth to the accompaniment of a solemn off key rendering by his companions of *Nearer my God to Thee,* returning a few minutes later to a rousing cheer while a dozen willing hands hauled him back on board. 'Come on up, Padre,' a young pilot wearing only a loincloth and his tattered cap put an arm about his shoulders. 'As you've been holding us lot up for all this time I reckon it's our turn to do the same for you. You've got to keep going now; it's only a few thousand miles to home.'

The Aussie banged on the truck side again, eyeing the half-naked skeletons as they lurched on their way to a rousing Hallelujah Chorus sung with more gusto than accuracy. He shook his head. 'You're all bleedin' barmy; the whole bleedin' lot of you.'

Kit managed a shaky grin in return. 'Ah,' he said, 'what it is to hear the glorious language of Shakespeare once again … and spoken by a master!'

* * *

'You can go on to Singapore tomorrow, Captain, and then very soon you will be home again.' The young Eurasian doctor smiled down on Kit as he sat restless and bored on the hospital bed. 'But you must take care. It will take a long time to build up your strength. Just do not try to run before you can walk.'

'I feel I may never run again,' Kit smiled back, but his eyes were bleak and the doctor looked at him keenly.

'There is something troubling you?'

'No,' he hesitated. 'You're sure it's OK to go home now? I shouldn't want to get half way and come down again with another bout of malaria.'

The doctor seated himself on the edge of the bed. 'You may

always get a recurrence, but if you have the right medication it will not be as bad as the attack you have just had. You were very weak with the dysentery and it was unfortunate you had the long journey here in such rough conditions. If you are worried now about going to your friends, I could arrange for you to stay in hospital in Singapore until your passage home is ready.'

'No. Thanks, I'll be fine.' He swung his feet to the floor and bent to put on his shoes. 'Might as well get the old legs moving properly again.'

I'm weak as a bloody kitten, he thought, walking slowly across the green lawn of the hospital. That's what's causing my problem: that and years of lousy Nip rice. He made for an empty bench, and sat watching other skeletal figures shuffling around in dressing gowns, their jungle ulcers still wrapped in bandages.

There's always someone worse off than you are, you ruddy misery, he chided himself. All the same, he hoped the transport home wasn't imminent. He wasn't ready for that. He just couldn't face Monica as he was now.

In an effort to rid his mind of the nagging worry about the future awaiting him, he took Vivienne's letter from his pocket and smoothing it on his knee, re-read it for the *nth* time. Reading between the lines, he could sense her own uncertainty about the future.

Kit dear,

I hope you can come soon. It is very lonely here and the house seems so huge and empty without Dougie. I suppose that in a way I should feel grateful that he didn't suffer longer in the horror that Changi became; I just wish he had died peacefully and not in such a brutal fashion. It seems you were right about him using Hanif as messenger; Allan Makepeace – he was Dougie's partner and with him until the end – told me that Dougie had been smuggling out letters for himself and a few others. When the Japs found out and Dougie wouldn't say who had taken them, he was just taken straight out and beheaded. I feel so dreadfully sad that all this time I've been waiting to get back to him to try and make up for past sins, he was already dead.

Don't laugh, Kit, but I actually went to church on Sunday. No sudden flash of light or voices from above, I'm afraid. But it was rather nice and peaceful, apart, that is from the choir, which appeared to be composed of twenty or so urchins who hadn't quite got the hang of keeping in either tune or time and gave a whole new slant on counterpoint!

I've managed to acquire a car, former property of another friend who didn't make it – there seem to be a great many of those. Some half-witted Nip has nearly wrecked the gearbox; it goes down hill all right but can be rather uncertain about getting up the other side.

How could you collapse after keeping on your feet for so long? When you have got rid of all your malarial bugs come to my house on the hill and we can watch together as the lights blaze out over the harbour at night the way they used to do.

I wonder if the lights of London will seem any brighter to this returning exile.

Love from your Sis-in-Law,

Viv.'

He smiled, folding the letter again and returning it to his pocket. Perhaps if he went in and had a go at charming the severe maiden lady on the hospital switchboard, she would let him put through a message to the Raffles. Lending Vivienne an ear and a shoulder for her troubles was the very least he could do, and it would help keep his mind off his own.

*　　　*　　　*

The house on the hill had been commandeered by a Japanese Admiral throughout the occupation, and consequently was in immaculate condition.

On his first morning there Kit lounged on the long veranda in a steamer chair, watching the sunrise and feeling that at long last life was beginning to pick up again. As Vivienne appeared bearing an early breakfast tray he jumped up, hastening to pull a table between their chairs.

'There is something terribly decadent and Somerset Maugham-ish about sitting around in this setting, wearing pyjamas and dressing gown and having one's breakfast served,' he commented, and she gave him her teasing smile as she laid down the tray.

'I may be serving, but Toomi prepared it. You can't imagine how quickly I've slipped back into my bad old ways.'

Kit noted with compassion that her eyes were a little puffy, her face still strained. They had talked long into the night about the camps and Dougie and her feelings of guilt, of having let him down.

'If I'd taken notice of you when you came that Christmas, I could have persuaded him to leave,' she'd said, 'but I was enjoying myself too much. I didn't want to go back to England and face all the problems of Mark and the divorce. And I was such a bitch to you…'

'Don't take it all on yourself. I wasn't exactly on my best

behaviour that day either, and I could have taken time to be more persuasive.'

Now she looked up from pouring coffee and gave him another smile.

'Thank you for last evening – you make a very easy and comfortable confessor. You'll be an absolute wow with all the old ladies when you go home. I can just see you at the church porch with them twittering all around you!'

He shook his head. 'I hate to disillusion you but I could never be a parish priest … not after these last few years. What do I know now of Parish work and what could I possibly bring to it?'

'Then what on earth will you do?'

He shrugged. 'At one time I thought I might like to stay in the army, but not now. I don't want church parades with a captive audience composed mainly of unbelievers. Not that I mind the unbelievers, just the fact that most are only there because they've been ordered.'

'So, no parish and no army; not thinking of being a missionary in some far-flung place are you?'

'I think I've had my fill of far-flung places, and I do have a family to consider now.' he buttered his toast thoughtfully. 'Actually I've been wondering...' he hesitated then grinned, 'no. I don't think I'd better tell you, you might just drag me to a head doctor.'

'Oh, come *on*, Kit; buddy to buddy, you can tell me. After all, I bared my soul to you last night. Fair's fair.'

'OK. But you laugh and I shall go off in a huff.'

He leaned forward, elbows on his knees, looking down at his clasped hands. 'I think I'd do rather better as a prison Chaplain. You see I know how it feels to be confined: to be constantly watched and ordered about. I understand about the black days and what it's like to be apart from your family; how easy it is to become brutalised and without hope.' He gave a lopsided grin. 'At least nobody there would be forced into my company, you never know, I may even be able to help just one or two. I'd like to feel I could give something back for being lucky enough to survive the camp and come out of it more or less sane; a sort of gift from all those who weren't so fortunate. Or does that sound too pious and pretentious?'

'No,' she said softly, 'I think it's a brilliant idea and I hope your Monica realises just what a very nice man she married. The sooner you get back to her the better; it's time you had someone to properly love and care for you again.'

For a fleeting moment a spasm of pain crossed his face and she saw his clasped hands tighten before he looked up to say quietly:

'Oh, no, *I'm* the lucky one. I only hope she'll not be disappointed by what she's getting back.'

She studied him shrewdly and he turned away from her look and stared out across the bay as a silence fell between them. 'Kit,' she said eventually, 'is there anything that *you* might want to tell *me*?'

'Not really.' He spoke without turning his head then returned to his neglected breakfast, pointedly changing the subject. 'How do you manage to get such good coffee? Or shouldn't I ask?'

'I know a little man...'

'I'll bet you do!'

She laughed, but continued to study him covertly, sure there was something on his mind that he wouldn't, or couldn't tell. She remembered one of Dougie's favourite sayings: "Softly, softly, catchee monkey". She would watch and wait for a crack in his quiet reserve which might let her in to what was troubling him. She thought sadly that the old, hare-brained, live-wire Kit had been left far behind in the camp; now he was quieter with a certain *gravitas* about him that was uncannily like that other young Eden whom she had wanted, then spoiled; grown tired of and made old before his time.

Now that it was too late she was feeling a sad regret for her failed marriage and all the wasted years. She wanted to settle down, love and be loved. On the long march and in those mosquito-ridden camps Singapore, high-life, Bond Street and London nightclubs had somehow lost their charm. It had taken the years of internment and suffering to bring her to acknowledge that the life with Mark she had so carelessly and selfishly thrown away might, given a chance, have been a good one.

In two weeks I shall be thirty-six years old, she thought, but today I feel about a hundred, and a pretty old hundred at that.

25

Porthryn, October 1945.

Monica wiped her daughter's mouth with her bib before lifting her from her highchair to the floor. 'I can't help being just a bit appreh-ensive.' She watched as Laura trotted off into the garden. 'Over three and a half years apart when we've only actually lived together for such a short time. It will be like starting all over again.' She looked at Joanna with worried eyes. 'Kit must have changed, mustn't he?'

'Probably, but then so have you. It's called growing-up, ducky.'

'I suppose that's it,' she sighed. 'I just hope he still fancies me.'

'Does he say in his letters that there's something wrong with his eyesight?'

'No.'

'Or that he's fallen in love with an Oriental bird with size two feet and a rich father?'

'Well … no.'

'Then you've nothing to worry about.' Joanna flipped her with the tea towel. 'Stop mooning around and start drying. I have to leave in an hour and I don't want Mark complaining about being left to wash-up – again.'

Monica was silent for a minute, looking out of the window to where her brother-in-law was deadheading of the last of the roses and dropping the papery petals into Laura's outstretched hands.

'What was it like,' she ventured at last, 'you know, when he came back after so long, and wounded like that…' she hesitated, 'he must have been, well, different. I've been dying to ask; you know, sex and all that. Was it difficult and awkward to be together again?'

'The first hour or so was a bit hairy but by the time we got to the bedroom neither of us could think of anything but getting each others clothes off in the shortest possible time; I was utterly shameless and he was even worse.' Joanna felt herself blush at the memory of just how utterly shameless they both had been. 'I wonder the people in the room below us didn't complain to the management and demand a refund; they couldn't have got any more sleep than we did.'

'Didn't you worry about his foot – what it would look like; even if you might not want to get too close to it?

'Not really.' Joanna gave a gurgle of laughter. 'I hadn't even noticed his legs, or remembered that he'd lost bits of his foot until he got out of bed next morning and did a sort of lame chicken hop into the bathroom. But as he'd already spent the night proving all his vital parts were still in perfect working order, who was I to complain?'

They both started to laugh and Mark, recognising the bawdy nature of their laughter and guessing its cause, grinned at his small companion. 'As you will in time discover, nothing is sacred when women get down to digging the dirt,' he informed her, 'and those two shouldn't even be allowed in the same county together, let alone the same kitchen!'

Still hiccupping with laughter Monica wiped her eyes on the tea towel. ''Did you know Vivienne is coming back with Kit? I wonder if she'll want to see Mark.'

'Bound to, the dismal old bitch, Mark wants the divorce dealt with as soon as she's settled her own affairs; after all this time Arthur Hallam says he should be able to get one on her desertion,' Joanna hitched onto the table and sat swinging her legs, 'but with all those years spent in internment he's not yet sure quite how the law stands; if she's still bloody-minded and ready to fight it could drag on forever.'

'Don't you mind her seeing Mark again?'

'Why should I?' She shrugged. 'I used to hate her guts but that's all in the past now; after all this time I don't really give a damn whether the divorce happens or not. No little piece of paper is going to change how I feel about him and it's unlikely to give us leave to do any more than we've been doing since nineteen-forty.'

'But Kit and I had hardly got started!'

'Don't worry; he'll soon make up for lost time.' Joanna said dryly, 'I can't imagine any of the Eden men would have much difficulty doing that.'

* * *

'Goodbye, darling,' Mark held her close. 'I'll come up to Tollmouth the first weekend that I can. Callum will hold the fort.'

'I wish for your sake he'd stay here and not want to go haring off to annoy the animal population in New Zealand.'

'Well, he's promised to see me through until you come home and take over the paperwork. That's what bogs me down.' He grinned at the sarcastic sideways look she gave him, and kissed her neck, murmuring, 'I'm going to enjoy taking old Naughton's place.'

'I can't get used to going back and leaving you here.' She

fingered the sleeve of his tweed jacket. 'I do like the feel of you out of uniform. All those brass buttons were hell on a girl's tender parts.'

'I like the feel of it, too. Now all I need to make things perfect is to have you here with me all the time.'

'All the lucky little ratings are throwing their caps in the air and going home, but the higher up one is, the slower one falls and it will take time to tie up all the loose ends in *my* section.' She slid into her seat as he held the car door open. 'Look after Laura and Monica. See she doesn't have too much time to mope about having to wait for Kit to come home.'

'I will, and I'll take them back to Stonehams when they've had their fill of Porthryn in winter. Drive carefully, and don't speak to any strange men.' He closed the car door then opened it again to ask, 'Did I tell you I love you?'

'Not for at least ten minutes.'

'I must be slipping.' He bent to kiss her before shutting the door firmly. 'Now clear off, before I drag you back into the house and have my way with you, ma'am.'

She chuckled and blew him a kiss before making her customary swift getaway. He stood at the gate, smiling and lifting his hand in farewell as she turned the corner and was lost to sight. He stepped back to the house, longing for the day when for the first time in five long years there would be an end to all farewells between them.

*   *   *

Singapore, October 1945

Vivienne was instantly awake at the pad of bare feet on the veranda outside her door. Always a light sleeper, she needed only the slightest sound to bring her fully conscious and alert. Silently, she slid open the drawer of her bedside cabinet and taking out a small ivory handled pistol eased off the safety catch. Keeping her fingers curled around the butt she slipped it into the pocket of her robe and crossed the room.

Now the footsteps were moving around the side of the building. Easing open the long French windows of her bedroom she trod silently after the shadowy figure just discernable in the dusky night, quickly narrowing the space between them before stopping a mere three yards away to demand crisply in Malay: 'Stay where you are, or I'll shoot your feet off!'

'Jesus Mary and Joseph...' Kit spun around to look straight down the barrel of the wicked little automatic. 'Put that bloody thing away, Vivienne. I don't know what you've just threatened me with but it sounded pretty unpleasant!'

'It was,' she slipped the safety catch on and dropped the gun back into her pocket. 'I thought you were one of the local looters working a night shift. What in hell are you doing paddling around out here at three in the morning?'

'I couldn't sleep.' He was still staring at her incredulously. 'Make me feel better and tell me you wouldn't have used that thing.'

'I most certainly would. You don't know this country as I do. One doesn't stop to have a reasoned argument with a burglar. If some nasty-minded Malay baddie came at *you* with his panga I bet you'd do the same.'

'I wouldn't be too sure about that – and where on earth did you ever get such a thing?

'If one knows the right people one can buy anything here, from a pistol to a pagoda. Now get back inside. You should know better than to wander around in this country without shoes. Come along, I'll get us both a drink.'

She led the way back to her room and he followed, locking the doors securely behind them as she crossed the bedroom and went down to the comfortably furnished sitting room, with its light cushioned chairs and thick sheepskin rugs on the polished wood floor.

'Whisky?' she looked at him enquiringly, a bottle in either hand and when he nodded, waved them both invitingly, 'Irish or Scotch, Vicar?'

He grinned. 'Irish, please.'

'Very sensible … beats Communion wine any day of the week.' She poured both drinks then settled herself comfortably into a chair. 'Now then Kit, it's time you came clean. For the past three weeks you've been coiling tighter and tighter as though someone were winding you up and your spring was about to break. Five days from now we take ship for home. So why, I ask myself, are you in such a state?'

'Rubbish!'

'No,' she shook her head, 'that won't wash. It's time you returned to being Honest Kit; the man we can all rely on.'

'You won't let it go, will you?' he looked down into his glass.

'No. So come along. It's confession time for you now.'

He sighed. 'OK, but before I start let me ask you a question. Use your considerable imagination, Viv and tell me: how would *you* feel if you were me, returning to your wife after almost four years apart, with a sex-drive several degrees less than that of a castrated sloth?'

'Abso-bloody-lutely terrified, I should think!' She stared. 'Is that true?'

'Unfortunately, yes.'

'You poor sod.' The violet eyes were fixed on his face. 'Since when?'

'Oh, I don't really know … years. Remember when I said that I'd forgotten what lust felt like?' She nodded. 'Well, long before then I'd given up on even thinking about it. It actually wasn't all that difficult, I'd done it before,' he gave an embarrassed grin, 'I was a bit of a randy so-and-so in my salad days; I even left Mark standing, but when I went for ordination it had to stop. The Church tends to frown on its anointed priests chasing every skirt in sight.' He took a long pull at his drink, 'so I became celibate until I married Monica, when I became *un*-celibate very quickly and with no trouble at all!'

She frowned, 'so why the problem now?'

'I wish I knew. For the first few months in Changi I used to daydream myself into bed with Monica until it became an obsession. I think it was then that I set out to deliberately block out that part of my life. You could say that in order to save my sanity I was forced back into celibacy. That's very different from choosing it of one's own free will, as I'm now finding out to my cost.'

'Give yourself a chance, Kit. After all, how many women have you got near enough to find out since you've had your freedom?'

He gave a wry smile. 'I spent a month in hospital with a bunch of exceedingly attractive nurses doing all kind of intimate things to my relevant parts. As not one of them managed to produce so much as a flutter the likelihood of my libido being miraculously awakened in the nuptial bed is frankly nil; now I'm so bloody terrified of failure that I can't face having to even try.'

'Well, What a thing!'

He burst into sudden laughter. 'That's one of Joanna's expressions – and I don't mind telling you now that if thinking about her legs and the body at the end of them doesn't produce a reaction, nothing ever will ... you simply can't imagine the difficulty that woman caused me.'

'Kit, you're actually laughing…that has to be a good sign.' Vivienne patted the rug beside her chair. 'Come here and let me uncoil that spring. I'm a dab hand at massage, you know,' she added modestly, 'Shun Mung Quong at the Club taught me, and he's a master.'

'Don't expect me to pay you his sort of fee,' he warned, settling at her feet. 'I'm stony-broke after having to cough for your little Chinese tailor to make a new uniform – and I bet I'll not see that cash back from the army. They'll probably bill me for loss of uniform and accoutrements.'

'Sit still, and don't move or I may cut myself on your shoulder blades!' she drew his dressing gown down to his waist and began to slide her long fingers over his neck and shoulders, gently probing and massaging. After a while the effect of the whisky and the hypnotic feel of her hands made him drowsy, his head began to nod and within a few minutes he was fast asleep.

As a faint snore sounded Vivienne looked down at his bent head and gave a crow of laughter 'Well I'm damned, I must be better than I thought…' very gently, she lowered him to lay full-length on the soft rug. Putting a cushion under his head and fetching a silk shawl to spread over him, she yawned and snuggling down into the chair cushions, closed her eyes and slipped into a light doze.

'How did all that start?'

Kit whispered the words against her mouth, his heart thundering in his ears, sweat still welding their bodies together. He felt her breasts move against his chest as she shook with silent laughter. 'Well, initially I was asleep until you pulled me down like a hungry tiger…it's a very long time since anyone took me quite so much by surprise!'

'Oh, my *God*,' He gave a despairing groan. 'I actually *jumped* you, didn't I – like a bloody rabbit?'

'Something like that although you may recall that I didn't exactly fight to retain my virtue.'

'Oh, *shit*!' He was stunned by the enormity of what he'd done and shocked by the fact that he was still lying sunk between her warm moist thighs, apparently powerless to move. 'Why the hell didn't you just clock me one?'

'Well, as it was so long since I was fucked in quite so determined a manner, I thought I might as well enjoy myself and ensure that a good time was had by all.' She gave him a sudden exasperated pinch on his buttock. 'You really are an idiot. Celibacy indeed – did no one ever tell you that you just can't lock away every sexual instinct for years without making all kinds of trouble for yourself?'

'Oh, shit,' he repeated, 'how am I ever going to explain this to Monica?'

'You dare to do anything of the kind and I'll brain you.'

He raised his head to meet the cool, violet eyes, his face flaming in an agony of embarrassment and shame. 'Vivienne, I must.'

'Just stop panicking, will you, and *listen*.'

'Sorry. I'm sorry.' Suddenly galvanised into action he left her body and sat up, pulling his dressing gown over his nakedness, a portion of which was already giving notice of an embarrassing resurgence of strength. He shivered in the chill of early morning. 'You're absolutely right. I couldn't possibly drop you in it like that.'

'I don't matter that much, being *persona non grata* as it were with the Eden family in general, but Monica and your little daughter do matter. What happened tonight we keep just between us; it is over and done with and has no bearing on, or place in, your marriage.'

She stood, shrugging herself into her gown and he almost groaned aloud at the involuntary reaction of his treacherous body to her nakedness. She drew the gown about her, knotting the sash slowly and giving him a knowing grin. 'There's absolutely nothing wrong with your mechanics, Kit Eden, so stop blaming yourself for behaving as nature intended. Why do you think God gave you all those pleasurable parts if He didn't mean you to use them? What you should have done was make the most of what you had. You wouldn't then have landed yourself in such a mess.'

'I suppose not, but, Vivienne, I'm most desperately sorry. I've never in my life grabbed at a woman like that. Did I hurt you? I hope I haven't…'

She gave him a very level look.

'Rendered me somewhat bruised and battered? No more than you I imagine; that was a lot of passion you unleashed there, but as *I* never vowed myself to celibacy I'm not complaining.' She began to grin at his appalled expression.

'Hell, Vivienne, you aren't likely to, to…' he floundered, suddenly horrified by the thought of possible consequences.

'Make you a daddy again? Have a heart, Kit, near starvation plays hell with a girl's natural functions.'

He paled. 'Please, don't tell me any more right now. I feel guilty and ashamed beyond words.'

She gave him a comradely nudge with her foot. 'Get up, get yourself decent and we'll make an early breakfast.'

Later that day while Vivienne took her siesta, he walked down the hill to the Anglican Church. It was all very fine for her to dismiss his lapse so lightly, but he knew himself well enough to know he couldn't ignore what he had done and put the whole thing from his mind as though it had never been, especially that despite his genuine shame and remorse he had to admit it would be all too easy to do it all over again.

In the dimness of the little vestry and on his knees, he unburdened himself to the elderly priest, his face flaming again as he recounted the events of the past night. How he had half-wakened, pulling her warm, sleepy body onto him and begging: 'Help me, Viv … Help me!' His frenzied response to her hands and lips as they caressed and coaxed and lifted him up and out of the dark pit and back into life … and the swift return of desire when she had stood to pull on her robe.

'Few of us ever live up to our expectations of ourselves,' said the old man gently, when he had heard him out. 'The priesthood does not make saints of any of us; we are but ordinary men with ordinary weaknesses and desires. I do not think God will condemn such an act after the things you have suffered – but to repeat it might cause Him some pain. Also, while it may ease your conscience to tell all this to your wife you must not make her suffer for *your* transgressions.'

Kit went back to the house on the hill and later that evening, with a certain degree of rueful regret and conscious of metaphorically well and truly locking the stable door after the horse had bolted, once more put on the armour of his clerical collar and took Vivienne out to dinner.

And she watched him, her heart aching a little, aware that the night just passed would live in her memory long after they had parted and gone their separate ways. Ironic that it should be Kit who had wakened fires in her she had thought long dead. For all that it had palled so quickly, Mark's lovemaking had roused her body to heights never attained with Dougie, or any other man until last night. How fortunate, she thought wryly, that the last few years had at least taught her to think of others before herself because, Kit's conscience notwithstanding, had she put her mind to it they would have been unlikely to stop at just that one night.

Starved of a normal sexual outlet for so long, she had given herself willingly and passionately to his demanding need. Now the need was hers, but she must hide it well and send him back to his wife and daughter with just the one sin on his soul; unlike herself who had so many.

26

Tollmouth, November 1945

'Just as well you are taking a forty-eight this weekend. There's damn' all happening here right now and it doesn't need you cluttering up office space and twiddling your thumbs.'

The Commander was grumpy, staring out of Joanna's window and jingling the coins in his pocket. He turned his head to look at her for a moment, adding abruptly: 'I'll be going soon after you, y'know. I'm being retired in March next year.'

'You'll miss the Navy, sir.'

'I dare say.' he cleared his throat, 'been in since I was a fourteen-year-old Snotty, y'know. Shall miss you too, Dunne … no, dammit! I shall miss you, Joanna.'

'Steady, sir, I'm not used to such a rush of humanity from you!'

His chuckle sounded like a very rusty hinge. Lord, she thought, but I *am* going to miss you, you old fraud.

* * *

'I was waiting until this evening to ring you,' Joanna thought Mark sounded suspiciously velvety-voiced when she called to tell him she would be at Porthryn the following evening, 'I've had a letter from Kit … I can't see why he couldn't phone like any normal person but I suppose he didn't want old Ellen listening in and clicking her dentures … hang on, will you, I'll just get it…'

'Oh, darling, hurry up. This is my lunch break and you know how fast the food disappears in this place.'

He was back within seconds. 'It isn't too long, here we go:

Vivienne is spending the next few days in Dorchester in order to see Arthur Hallam and sign some papers about the divorce. I don't care to think of her alone. She's OK for cash as the Bank are sorting Dougie's will and have already released everything her father left her, but that's little comfort at present. I tried to bring her to Stonehams, but she dug her heels in at that. She won't admit it but I think the thought of meeting Pa terrifies her, if so, it's about the only thing that does.

I could not possibly begin to tell you all that I owe her, both while we were in the camps and since our release. She took me from the hospital and fed me, cared for me, put me back on my feet ... the fact that I am home and functioning as a normal human being is due almost entirely to her. It is a debt I shall never be able to repay.

So please, Mark, go and see her and help all you can. She won't get in touch with you herself ... says you need to get on with your life without any further disruption from her.

My love to Joanna and tell her that her legs are still an inspiration. She'll tell you what you should do about Vivienne, without a doubt ... Kit.

He finished and there was a pregnant silence. She could hear him putting the letter back in the envelope.

'I'd planned to shop in Dorchester on my way down tomorrow; if I don't get home, it'll be because Vivienne's spotted me and shoved me under a Corporation bus,' she said and heard him laugh. For a few moments she stood chewing the tip of her little finger then said abruptly, 'Look, I hope you are not going to leave her wandering the place by herself after all she's been through? Why don't you come to Dorchester by train and see her at Arthur's office, then I could meet you afterwards and we could travel home together?'

'Sweetheart, I can't do a thing until we finish tomorrow *evening*, and that's only if Callum's through his rounds and able to do the evening surgery for me. This is a bad time of the year and we're up to our ears in it right now,' his voice deepened. 'Joanna...darling...?

She sighed gustily. 'You *bastard;* you want *me* to see her, don't you?'

'Did I tell you that I love you?'

'You may never get another chance – and it's no laughing matter!' Reluctantly she began to grin. 'All right if I *must*, I'll meet her, but don't expect me to fall on her neck and say all is forgiven and let's be friends. Do you know where the wicked witch of the west is staying?'

'Yes, there's a postscript: The Antelope.'

'OK. I'll leave here first thing tomorrow, see her then do my shopping ... be with you by the evening, I hope. Seriously, though,' she furrowed her brow. 'I may be quite the last person she wants to see.'

'Just try, darling, for Kit's sake; see if there's anything she needs and when and where she wants to meet with me before she returns to London. Presumably she has something planned for the future. I'd like to help if she'll let me. Tell her that, will you?'

She said dryly, 'Oh sure I'll tell her – if she doesn't knife me first!'

*　　*　　*

Vivienne had never felt so cold. Despite the warm skirt and fur-lined boots, thick jersey and long wool coat, she was shivering as she entered the hotel foyer. This goddamned country – how in hell had she ever survived it for so long?

At the reception desk she noticed a tall girl in Wren uniform. With a twinge of envy she registered in passing the confident, youthful tilt of the head. Nice, she thought, to have been able to do something positive in the war other than sitting in a Nip camp picking maggots out of fellow internee's jungle ulcers.

'Mrs Eden!'

She stopped at the desk clerk's call. 'Yes?'

'This young lady has been waiting for you.'

The girl turned to face her. No, Vivienne amended silently, not a girl, a woman, and a damned attractive one at that.

'Vivienne Eden?' She came forward, only slightly hesitant. 'I'm Joanna Dunne. I hope you don't mind, but Mark asked me to come and see you.'

'*Did* he?'

For a moment they both stood in the centre of the foyer, like actors who had temporarily forgotten their lines. Then the girl gave a polite smile. 'If you like and if the right chap's on duty in the bar I might be able to get us a couple of decent gins.'

Vivienne was cautious, unsure of how to respond to this woman of Mark's, who had with easy authority annexed a table nearest to the fire before ordering their drinks. That Mark should have replaced her with someone with quite so much poised and youthful beauty filled her with a smouldering resentment.

Joanna in turn had been grudgingly intrigued at her first sight of the present Mrs Eden. Studying her covertly as she waited for their order she rapidly revised her previous conception of a ravaged harridan with a rattrap jaw and possible homicidal intentions towards herself. That she was painfully thin beneath the bulky clothing did little to detract from the fact that Mark's wife was still an attractive woman.

I wonder if she will still stir him up, even just a little, she thought, and smiled grimly to herself. Well, she'd faced, and in her own way fought Lionel, Mary and Mark himself and won; she wasn't going to sit back and wait for Vivienne Eden to chuck a spanner in the works.

'I used to have nightmares about you,' she observed as the barman left after placing two glasses on the table between them, adding with disarming but deadly candour, 'you can't imagine how many times I've killed you off over the past five years!'

'And I called you 'Mark's piece' to Kit and watch him go hot around the collar.' Vivienne raised one satirical eyebrow. 'God, but little brother fancied you, didn't he?'

Joanna said with swift loyalty. 'He has been a better friend than you will ever know, and I love him for that.'

The older woman smiled thinly. 'A good job Mark has always trusted him or the sparks might have flown.'

'Our life isn't without its difficulties but Kit isn't one of them.'

'No?' Her tone was dry. 'However, Mark out of uniform has doubtless reverted to type; hence the difficulties. But I'm sure that service life has toughened *you* sufficiently to meet the challenge.'

Joanna propped her chin on one hand and met the stunning violet eyes, *I've hated you for years and can easily go on hating you, Mrs snooty bloody Eden,* she mused rancorously, *but as I want to marry your husband and Kit clearly thinks the sun shines out of your derriere, I'll try to refrain from slitting your throat, however much I'd enjoy doing so...* She fingered her glass, answering without a change of expression. 'I think I can deal with any breakers that may be ahead.'

She itched to make this coolly sarcastic and remote woman come down off her high horse and stop acting as though she found this meeting a matter of complete indifference, and Joanna herself nothing more than a passing irritation. Absently she stirred her gin with a forefinger. 'May I ask you something?'

'Ask away...' Vivienne waved a disinterested hand.

Joanna thought, *bitch!* But only smiled with saccharine sweetness and enquired, 'Why on earth are you hanging around here on your own when you could have gone to Stonehams with Kit?'

She shrugged. 'Is that really any of your business?'

'Yes, because if you had I wouldn't be wasting a bloody great chunk of my forty-eight with you when I could be spending it with Mark.'

For a long moment Vivienne stared at her then uttered a sudden and unexpected bark of laughter. 'Good God, you sound just like me – poor old Mark – he does pick 'em, doesn't he?'

She thought, did I really say that – it must be the gin ... what *was* it about Mark's woman that made it hard to keep her at a distance? But better not let her get too close – and discussing Mark was not one of her favourite pastimes. She took a firm hold on herself and changed the subject, asking with faint, but deliberate condescension, 'What do you do in that uniform?'

'Keep tabs on what the Navy is up to, at least, the part that's based in Hampshire.' Joanna wasn't thrown by the sudden return to a thinly veiled hostility, 'but only until February, when it's off with the uniform, on with the civvies and down to Porthryn and Mark and sanity.'

'Yes. I imagine you would enjoy the life there.' Vivienne grimaced. 'Frankly I loathed it; I was utterly, hopelessly bored with the place, the people and eventually, Mark himself.'

Joanna had to remind herself that she was doing this for Kit and took a deep breath. The bloody woman really was insufferable. She forced herself to remain distantly polite. 'Mark really is very concerned about you and what your plans are for the future. He wants to help. That's why he asked me to meet you today.'

Vivienne shrugged. 'Well you can tell him I have no plans; I don't even know if I have a future. I didn't want to stay in Singapore alone, not after all that had happened. I've left the house with an agent to sell as soon as possible. I have enough money of my own to live on without penny-pinching; *where* to live is the problem.' To Joanna's amazement Vivienne's voice shook and all at once she looked lost and vulnerable as she pulled her coat around her in a sudden defensive gesture, 'God, but I'm so *cold.* How the hell can I stay in this country? I'd forgotten what it was like here in winter.'

The gesture and the unmistakable note of despair in her voice caught at Joanna's susceptible heart; impulsively, she said, 'Why don't you come back with me today – to Porthryn?' To her horror she could hear herself begin to babble enthusiastically. 'You can sit before a roaring fire and have all the time in the world to sort things out with Mark.' *I must be insane*, she thought, *and what will Mark say if I turn up with her on tow?*

Vivienne answered her with a dry, 'He is hardly likely to be very keen on that idea.'

'Honestly, he won't mind at all.' Joanna lied, hoping she sounded more confident than she felt. Now she'd painted herself into a corner, she might as well put a brave face on it.

'Are we speaking about the same man?' Vivienne raised her brows in disbelief. 'If so then your Mark and the one I remember are two very different creatures. I really think you should consult him first before you think of dumping me on his doorstep.'

'If you insist...' relieved, Joanna stood and crossed to the bar, her smile bringing the barman falling over himself in his haste to reach her.

'Madam?'

She was urgently conspiratorial, 'Might I use your phone – it could be a matter of life or death!'

'In that case … he winked and slid the instrument towards her. Taking a deep breath Joanna began to dial.

'You just caught me going out of the door.' Mark gave a theatrically sinister laugh. 'I gather you are not under a Corporation bus?'

'Quite right, darling – I'm in a bar as a matter of fact. No comments, please. Look, Vivienne is coming down with me to the cottage. I've got my Christmas shopping to do first but we should be with you for the evening meal: that's if you can delay it a bit, say until eight-thirty.'

'Oh why not?' he was sarcastically laconic, his voice betraying no hint of the shock her words had given him. 'I'll ask Mrs Bodley to stretch it to four as Callum will be with us.'

'I think you might at least *sound* surprised,' she grumbled.

'You should know me better.'

'I could write a book,' she answered cryptically, 'but for now could you just buzz off and kill the fatted calf.'

'What do I get as a reward if I do?'

She lowered her voice, 'You get to sleep with a naval officer. What more do you want?'

Grinning at his answer she returned to Vivienne. 'That's settled then. Can you be ready by about two? I've loads of shopping to do – my last chance before Christmas.' She squinted down into her glass and pulled a face. 'Perhaps a drink this size on a relatively empty stomach wasn't such a good idea. Choosing Christmas presents when half-pissed could result in total disaster!'

Vivienne watched Joanna's smooth, unselfconsciously sexy walk away from her across the foyer draw every male eye in the place like a magnet. But that outward air of innocent serenity was deceptive, she thought wryly, and barely covered the steel beneath. She had no doubt that this calm and composed woman knew exactly how to handle the difficult and obstinate Mark, not to mention his hellish old father.

Finishing her own drink she went slowly up to her room, wondering what on earth Mark's oh, so polite but inflexible mother made of Joanna Dunne; not a lot, she imagined, but would take a bet that Joanna could cope with whatever Lay Eden cared to dish out, and probably had the frankly terrifying old Lionel eating right out of her hand!

27

Porthryn, Cornwall, November, 1946.

Mark carried in an armful of logs and stacked them by the hearth. The evening was clear without a hint of foul weather and he was pleasantly tired after a day spent mostly in the open air visiting farms along the coast. The evening surgery had been light, giving him a welcome hour in which to wash and change before the arrival of his lover and his wife.

Trust Joanna to throw out her news in that off-hand manner, as though it was the most natural thing in the world for him to be entertaining both wife and mistress for the evening; if she imagined she was getting away unscathed with dropping him in it like that, he thought, then she had another think coming…

For all his outward calm he couldn't help but be apprehensive about seeing Vivienne again after so long. Dealing with the meeting in a solicitor's office would have been uncomfortable enough, but here, in the home they had shared? Kit said she had changed; he certainly hoped so, otherwise this meeting could well be a disaster, with both of them treading around each other like feral cats, looking for an opportunity to strike and wound.

Oscar lifted a greying muzzle and gave his low growl at the sound of tyres on gravel. Bracing himself Mark crossed to open the door.

'We are hungry and Vivienne is freezing,' Joanna said brightly, avoiding his eyes. She kissed his cheek. 'Umm, lovely; you smell of wood smoke and…' she sniffed hard, 'and whisky, you low-lifer.'

'It's a fair cop, Sherlock.'

Momentarily he tightened his arm about her shoulders. She flashed a quick glance at his face then turned to draw her companion into the warmth of the house.

'Let me take your coat, Vivienne – I should sit on top of the fire if I were you. Mark will fix a drink. I'm going up to change out of this uniform…'

Vivienne watched her cross the room, with a caress for Oscar's ears in passing. She turned inquiring eyes on the man who was still technically her husband.

He shrugged. 'Don't ask how it's done, it's a gift she has. Her own personal radar,' he explained, at her lifted brows, 'knowing when to disappear and leave others to say what they have to.'

'Very astute.' she said dryly.

He hesitated, then taking step forward took both her hands in his, 'Well, Vivienne?'

'Well, Mark!'

'You heard the lady. Sit down and I'll get you a drink.'

She sank onto the long couch saying, 'She is everything Kit said, and he said a lot … where did you find her?'

'On board, at a party, she was very rude to me; put me in my place the first time she opened her mouth,' he smiled over his shoulder, his hands busy with bottle and glasses, 'apart from being intelligent and astute and not suffering fools gladly, she also has a capacity for loving that is almost an art form in itself.'

'Lucky you,' she said without bitterness, 'God knows you deserve it after the time I gave you.' She let her eyes travel over him as he stood before her offering a glass. 'Was I responsible for all those silver threads?'

'Only a few, I can thank the war and Joanna for the remainder. Our path has not always been smooth.'

'And the limp?'

'That wasn't Joanna, just a German Gun Boat.'

He sat comfortably beside her and raised his glass. 'Well, here's to all of us … the good, the bad, and the middling…'

Joanna paused in the act of dragging a jersey over her head. They were laughing, thank God! She gave a huge sigh of relief. *Really*, she admonished her reflection, as she pulled a comb through her short curls, *what did you expect him to do, tear her limb from limb? Mind you,* she continued the silent conversation with her image, *what's the betting he'll have quite a lot to say to you later on? You surely don't imagine he'll let you get away that easily with putting him on the spot.*

It hadn't been a bad journey down, she mused; although Vivienne hadn't been exactly chatty, after a while she had dropped her air of bored superiority and their consequent conversation had been amicable and between equals. 'I could quite get to like her,' Joanna murmured aloud and was surprised at the thought. All things were possible, she supposed, but actually getting pally with the detested Vivienne seemed a little far-fetched, however congenial she might seem at the moment.

*   *   *

'It's bloody freezing out there tonight!' Callum reached to hang his coat on the hook by the door, caught sight of Vivienne, missed, and let the garment fall unheeded to the floor. His pleasant Scots face sparked into sudden life. 'Ah, you have company, Mark.'

Mark, turning to pour another drink gave vent to a resigned sigh. 'Let me introduce you, you uncivilised Celt,' He waved an introductory hand, 'Callum, Vivienne. Vivienne, Callum – you can both take it from there....'

I really can't imagine what I was worried about, Mark mused silently as they sat at dinner, *even if this meal does have a passing resemblance to the Mad Hatter's Tea Party.*

Joanna, he saw was at her most poised and relaxed, looking coolly and infuriatingly innocent, when he knew quite well that beneath the veneer she was like a schoolgirl waiting to be asked for homework she hadn't done. Vivienne, who was capable of freezing water with a look couldn't possibly have been more pleasant, although he realised with a sudden stir of disquiet that there was quite a *frisson* between herself and Callum, although he couldn't imagine she would go for another country vet. He certainly hoped not, that was one complication he could do without; good vets were in short supply and hard to find. He could only hope Kit was right when he said she was a different woman from the old Vivienne. He stifled a sigh, ah well, time would no doubt tell. Meanwhile, there was another little matter needing his attention...

'Joanna?'

She looked up from clearing coffee cups from the table as he cocked his head toward the door, 'What?' she enquired innocently. He didn't answer, just took the tray from her hands and carried it into the kitchen. She followed and stood eyeing him warily, her back to the door. 'What may I do for you, Mr Eden?'

He put down his burden and crooked a finger.

'Come here.'

'Not until I know what you want.'

He reached her in two swift strides, pinioning her arms. 'You called me a bastard on the 'phone yesterday.'

'Well you were – but I smiled when I said it. Honestly I did.'

'And you took one hell of a chance that I'd back you up over bringing Vivienne here.'

'Did you just get me out here to tick me off, or is there something else you want?'

'You bet your life there is…one night isn't enough to do all I want to do to you for putting my back against the wall over Vivienne.' He gripped her arms tighter and ground his mouth down on hers.

'Rough, but not bad,' she said primly when he had finished, 'but, begging your pardon, sir, there's one hell of a lot more evening to be got through yet before you can haul me into bed.'

He slid his hands down under the band of her skirt. 'They can go for a moonlight walk.' He sat on the table edge, pulling her between his knees, 'and we can sort things out right here.'

She simpered and fluttered her lashes. 'Oh, la sir, not on the kitchen table again!'

There was a discreet tap on the door and Callum's head appeared around the edge.

'Mark?'

'Go away!'

'I'm going, Mark, I'm going. I'm taking Vivienne to the flat – she wants to see my paintings.'

'Good. Take your time.'

They looked at each other as the front door closed, listening for his car to crunch over the gravel and out of the gate. 'Do you suppose,' Joanna's voice shook, 'that he actually has some *etchings* to show her?'

'Did you put him up to it?' she asked, as Mark hung the last item of her clothing on the fire irons.

'Certainly not,' he ran his fingers up her thigh.

'Don't lie to me.'

'Well, maybe I gave just a small hint.'

She gave her husky laugh. 'How long, do you think, before they come back?'

'Long enough for what I have in mind…I don't know why I love you so much, you infuriating, exasperating woman, but I can't live without you now, that's for sure.'

Joanna wriggled further into the thick rug, watching the flames reflected from the fire dance over his bare muscular back. She asked slyly, 'Didn't you get even just the tiniest little blip for Vivienne when you saw her again?'

'Would it make you jealous if I said yes?'

'No, but I think I might kill her, that's all.'

'Well I didn't; I have enough trouble as it is just coping with you.' He nipped with his teeth and she gasped, catching his head between her hands, her body suddenly urgent and aroused. Fiercely she tightened her hands and dragging his mouth up to hers whispered, 'Prove it then, and quickly, before Callum runs out of etchings!'

27

Porthryn, November 1946

'Vivienne has agreed to stay on here for a few days.' Mark said as he sat on the end of their bed, watching her pack. 'It will give us a chance to get the business of the divorce finally straightened out before we go to see Arthur together. You don't mind, do you, darling?'

She shook her head, 'Not at all … give me a chance to have a fling with Josh if you're otherwise occupied with your wife.'

He pulled threatening brows together.

'By God, but there are times when I'd really like to give you a slap; just behave yourself, will you? I don't need you stirring up trouble with your bloody great spoon.'

'Only keeping my spirits up,' she swung her bag onto her shoulder and as he stood, slid her arms around his waist beneath his jacket. 'I love it when you pretend to get all cross and masterful.' She kissed him lightly. 'I do love you.'

'I know.' He smiled. 'Ring me tonight before I go to my lonely bed.'

'I don't want to leave you.'

'I know that too.'

They walked downstairs together and out to the car.

Watching from her bedroom window, Vivienne saw Joanna reach up to touch Mark's cheek as his arms went around her. 'God keep you,' she heard him say and turned away, sudden tears stinging her eyes.

Lucky Mark; lucky girl.

She waited until the car engine faded then went downstairs, relieved that he had invited Callum to supper again that evening. This new Mark was a stranger to her and she wasn't quite sure yet how she might pass time alone with him without Joanna to stand as a buffer between them.

Later that night Callum left the cottage reluctantly and turned his car towards Porthcurnow. He wished Vivienne and not Mark had come to the door to see him away. Not that he would have kissed her this time, but tomorrow he would see her again and perhaps then … Well, he smiled to himself, sometime soon anyway.

A man may rush such things at twenty, but in his thirties a man should know when to take his time.

Back in his flat over the surgery he made a coffee, lit his pipe and thought how Fate sometimes threw something unexpected and precious on the path of life. She was certainly unexpected and he would like her to become precious to him, but all his senses told him to move slowly, just one step at a time. Beneath that air of rather remote and studied calm he felt there was much pain and heartache and memories of which he as yet knew nothing.

Finishing his pipe he wandered into the bedroom; pulling off the heavy Guernsey and unbuttoning his shirt he went to the basin to wash before making a frank appraisal of his unremarkable features in the mirror. *You're no raving beauty, Callum Maclean,* he acknowledged honestly, smoothing the thick straw coloured hair from his forehead, *and the pair of you are past the foolishness of youth, or should be, but I think she likes ye, man … I think she likes ye!*

He finished undressing and rolled into bed, patting the patchwork quilt and murmuring aloud, 'Aye, grannie, and I'm thinking this to be a fine piece of working to cover that nut brown maid…'

Mark closed the door behind their guest then returned to stretch out in his chair, contemplating the dying fire for a moment before turning serious eyes on his wife. 'He fancies you, you know…'

'That's nice, because I rather fancy him.'

'Don't lead him on Vivienne. He's no innocent, but neither is he a sophisticate. I'd hate to see him get hurt.'

'Strange though it may seem, Mark, so would I.'

'Well, then, what are you up to? You certainly set out to charm.'

'I can't help that. Like you, it's second nature,' she gave him a challenging look, 'but I wasn't just flirting. I really do like him.'

'Bit sudden isn't it – but if I remember correctly you never did let the grass grow under your feet.'

'Are you being censorious, Mark?'

'Possibly,' he gave a grim smile, 'let's just say I have a long memory.'

'Then it's time you shortened it,' she was caustic. 'After all the bored grass widows you've managed to console, I could as easily have asked what you are doing with a young woman fifteen years your junior. How old was she when you first met – twenty-one – twenty-two? And how long before you added her to the list of your bed-mates?'

Momentarily his eyes fell before her angry and accusing gaze. 'I'm sorry. That was out of order,' his mouth twitched slightly at the corners, 'although in answer to your last question it was quite some time.'

'We can't help ourselves, can we?' she shrugged ruefully, her sudden anger evaporating, 'however much we might try to lay the ghosts of the past, they will probably always pop up and set us against each other.'

There was silence between them for a few minutes. Mark half lay in his chair, eyes studying the ceiling, his long legs stretched out across the hearth. Hunching forward Vivienne threw wood onto the fire. Taking up the poker she prodded the logs into life before holding out her hands to the flames.

She was the first to break the silence. 'I'm sorry I hurt you so much all those years ago, Mark.'

His eyes shifted from his contemplation of the ceiling to her face. 'And I am deeply and sincerely sorry for being such a bastard. It wouldn't have hurt me all that much to accept your father's offer, or at least to have given it a trial. Things might have been very different if I hadn't insisted on dragging you down here.'

She considered him for a long moment before breaking into an irresistibly infectious smile.

'You know, I think perhaps we have both changed for the better ... and Mark, I really do like Callum rather more than just a little, so please don't get ratty and awkward if I don't exactly discourage him.'

'Does that mean you're likely to want to stay around Porthryn for a while then?'

'If you'll let me and if your Joanna won't mind.'

'My Joanna,' he said grimly, 'is the reason you and I are sitting here tonight having this conversation. Right now she is doubtless congratulating herself on her coup. That young woman has a great deal to answer for.'

'Yes, she has, hasn't she,' Vivienne laughed outright, admitting, 'I gave her a few hard jabs when we met and she came right back at me without batting an eyelid.'

'I'm told she did the same when my mother was rash enough to cross swords with her.' He looked at the dark circles beneath those violet eyes, at the too-sharp cheekbones and thin hands and wrists and felt a sudden painful wrench of compassion and pity for all that she had suffered and endured. He sat forward and taking one of her hands in his said, 'Stay as long as you wish, flirt as much as you like.

Callum's a big boy and can take care of himself – and if the two of you stay the course, it is I believe always pleasantly warm in New Zealand!'

*   *   *

'Must you go back to London so soon?' Callum took her hand, tucking it into his overcoat pocket as they left the cottage, 'You've scarcely been here above a week. If you're getting fed-up with being at the cottage you could always stay at the pub in the next village; it's no more than a mile from here.'

'It's not that,' she lifted her face to the bright winter sun. 'We're getting on surprisingly well, but I do need to start putting my house in order and make at least some short-term plans for the future. Also I have to go back and sign more papers before all of my affairs are settled.'

He was silent, pacing steadily along the headland, his hair flopping over his forehead, his keen, far-seeing slate-blue eyes screwed up against the sunshine. 'I shall miss you,' he said eventually and gave her hand a squeeze, 'it's been good to wake up each morning and know that I have someone special to think about during the day.'

'Surely that can't be such a novelty.'

'It is these days.' He gave a wry grin. 'There used to be someone: we were together through the war until I picked up a viral pneumonia – in Italy, would you believe, and ended up being invalided out of the army with a damaged lung. I think she imagined I was going to be a burden for life and just took off.'

'Better that way if she wasn't a stayer. Trust me, I know all about bolting, I've done it; but you seem well recovered now.'

'I'm pretty fit, much better than a year ago; the reason I'm off to New Zealand soon is because the medics tell me the climate there will help keep me that way. Mind you, it's done me a power of good living in Cornwall, even in winter it's a hell of a lot warmer here than Scotland.'

'After Malaya, it doesn't feel very warm to me.' She shivered, and pulled up her coat collar. 'I can't get used to it. I was born in India and only came to England when it was time for school. I hated every winter with a fearful hatred.'

He looked at her curiously. 'Tell me if I'm being nosy, but why aren't you staying with your family?'

'None left, apart from an old Aunt in Wales. Mother took off when I was about seven with a very dashing Cavalry Officer from the Regiment. Shortly after that I was sent back here to school. My father died just before the war.'

'That's terrible!' He was shocked. 'We're a very big family. I've two brothers and three sisters, *both* parents and a granny, who according to my father is a witch and has the second sight.'

'Sounds lovely; I always kept hoping for a sister, but nobody obliged.'

They began to climb the path to the Wreckers, Callum pulling her up the last few steps then pushing open the Inn door to a welcome rush of warm air.

George Tregorran greeted them, giving Callum a prodigious wink. 'How about I make ye a hot toddy, m'dears?' he asked, 'Make a proper job o' warming up the lady that will … if you haven't managed that already!'

'Yev a dairty auld Sassenach mind, Georgie man!' Callum reverted to broad Scots and George slapped his great hands on the counter, bellowing with laughter and calling for his wife to, 'make a decent Cornish toddy for this heathen Scot and his Queen.'

Later, fortified by the toddy and the roaring fire they made their way back to the cottage where Vivienne stood at the gate waiting for him to unlock his car. 'Don't go away without telling me, will you?' he asked, and she shook her head and smiled.

'No. I promise, and it won't be for a day or two yet.'

'You know Mark and Joanna are away to Dorset for Christmas, do you?'

'Yes.'

'Where will you be?'

'Oh, somewhere ... I hadn't thought much…'

'Come back.' He turned from opening the car door and caught her hands in both of his. 'Come and spend Christmas with me. Two exiles together, eh?' He hurried on, 'then when Mark comes back and if you think you could bear it, come with me and spend Hogmanay in the Highlands.' He held her hands tighter, his eyes suddenly shy, saying softly, 'My granny will tell your future, my father will make you hot toddies for breakfast, dinner and tea if you wish, my brother Sandy will play the pipes and I'll wear my kilt for you an' teach you to dance a reel, my bonnie lass…'

Her eyes were bright with the sheen of tears and he drew her closer, 'Come with me, for I'd be so proud, and if it blows and snows I'll keep you warm against my heart.' He put his long arms right around her, and his cheek against hers.

She leaned against him, breathing in the warmth of him: the tweed and the pipe smoke and the clean, smooth skin. 'How can you say that after just eight days? You scarcely know me.'

'Oh, I could have said it after one day … No, less than that. I had you marked for me from the first moment – and I know you very well.' He dropped his voice to a mysterious whisper: 'Like my Granny, I have the second sight!'

28

Stonehams, Dorset, Christmas 1946

Mark slowed the car to a stop and grinned wryly at Joanna. 'Brace yourself,' he pulled on the hand brake and silenced the engine, 'if you think you've had a hard war, see how you feel after this lot.'

'I'll live!' She leaned across to kiss him. 'It's worth suffering Christmas at the ancestral pile just to know that at long last you and Kit have both made it safely home.'

He raised a warning finger, 'No fighting with my ma, now; she's coming around slowly; Kit says she's even allowing us to sleep in the same bed.'

'There's progress now … you won't even have to pad around in the dead of night to find me.'

*   *   *

'You're already half asleep.' Lionel put his arm around Joanna's shoulders as they left the church after the midnight service.

'Too much to eat and drink,' she answered. 'And turkey tomorrow with all the trimmings … I don't dare think from where Mary got *that* monstrous beast!'

Lionel glanced back to where his wife walked behind them, her hand clasping Mark's arm. 'I'm afraid Mary is making up for lost time,' he observed dryly ... a mother celebrating the return of the prodigal son and all that…'

They walked in silence for a while before he said quietly: 'Audrey is still very much in my heart, Jo.'

'She's in mine too … she loved Christmas. I've been thinking about her all day.' She swallowed hard. 'I shall cry in a minute and disgrace myself.'

'Not you; like me, you'll only do that when you are alone.'

Joanna blinked away the threatened tears and concentrated on Kit and Monica, who walked ahead of them, arms about each other, heads close together. She asked, 'Is Kit really going to be all right?'

He sighed, 'Yes, although it will take time; I thought Mary was going to faint when he first walked through the door, but Monica was absolutely marvellous and never turned a hair.'

'You can't beat a Cheltenham girl,' Joanna grinned, 'they don't come much tougher, all that hockey and lacrosse builds high moral fibre, you know.'

'By all accounts she isn't the only one. What's all this I hear about Vivienne?'

'What do you hear?'

'According to Kit, she's a cross between St Theresa and Joan of Arc.'

'Umm … a bit over the top, but he has a point,' she added straight-faced, 'You'll be thrilled to know *you* scare her to hell.'

'Nonsense, we've only met once and that was years ago.'

'Well you obviously made an impression because she's not looking for a second meeting. I should have told her what a fraud you are.'

'Don't forget that *you* once had me down as a rotten old sod.'

'Yes, well...but honestly, Leo, Vivienne is quite something and you can't help but admire her.'

He gave a cynical snort. 'Suppose we just leave it at that and say I'll take your word for it.'

'You really are an Eden, aren't you? If I didn't know better I'd have you down as an absolute rotter.'

'Ah, but you do know better,' he tucked her arm more firmly in his, 'so you must just accept that so far as Vivienne and I are concerned, even you can't win them all!'

'What were you and pa talking about?' Mark watched from the bed as she sat brushing her hair before the mirror.

She smiled at his reflection. 'Not you: Vivienne, as a matter of fact.'

'Oh,' he chuckled, 'you'll never get him to join that fan club!'

'She'll not give him the chance.' Joanna put down her brush, stifling a yawn, 'do you really think she and Callum will make a go of things?'

'Shouldn't be surprised; hurry up, darling, I'm dead beat and that child is bound to be up and visiting at some ungodly hour in the morning.'

She slid in to the bed, snuggling against him. 'It is the morning but my brain doesn't know it yet.'

He kissed the top of her head.

'Sweetheart, do shut-up and go to sleep.'

'I'll try ... Goodnight, Troilus.'

‘’Night, Cressida.’

The old house settled slowly, the smell of rich food and wine lingering in the rooms and passages. In the kitchen Oscar lay stretched on the rag rug before the range, grumbling at Lionel’s marmalade cat as from time to time it tried unsuccessfully to reclaim its own territory. In the bedroom over the old coach house Kit and Monica lay entwined in each other’s arms, while in her own small room Laura slept, oblivious of the bulging stocking that nestled at her feet.

Lionel snored faintly, and Mary prodded him gently onto his side, putting an arm around him, tucking her body along his back and smiling at his muttered: ‘That’s nice!’

Ellen slept flat on her back, blankets pulled up to her chin, nose and feet pointed at the ceiling as several unaccustomed glasses of wine floated her on a gently swelling sea.

Down in Porthcurnow, with the wide sky swept clear of all but the moon and stars, Callum Maclean pulled his granny’s quilt snugly around Vivienne’s sleeping form and took a last look at her quiet face. He touched his lips to her brow and as she stirred in her sleep and smiled, lay down with his head against hers, breathing softly, ‘Sleep well, my nut brown maiden, for you’re the one for me…’

Only Joanna lay wakeful beside a sleeping Mark.

She heard the old long case clock in the hall below whirr, wheeze and strike two. Creeping from his side she went to kneel on the window seat and look out across the frosty landscape. Tired in body, but with her mind wide-awake, the day spun a kaleidoscope of movement and laughter and colour before her eyes.

Gosh, Audrey, but you would have enjoyed today, she looked up at the sky as the first flakes of snow began to fall, *and tonight you felt so very close ... Leo felt it too, I know he did.*

Mark woke and slipped out of bed, crossing the room silently to wrap sleep-warm arms about her whispering, ‘Not tired yet?’

‘Getting that way…’

He kissed the back of her neck. ‘Are you happy?’

‘More than I could ever say.’

‘Come back to bed now.’

This is what happiness is, she thought drowsily as she settled against him; a war ended, a future grown bright, and this man’s arms about me…

‘Have I told you that I love you?’ his lips were gentle on her cheek.

‘You might have, from time to time.’

‘I shall go on telling you, always and forever…’

She stirred in his arms, settled closer. ‘Sounds good to me,’ she said.

POST SCRIPT

France, July 1948

Mark stood at the top of the harbour wall, watching Joanna leave the *boulangerie* and begin walking towards him with that beautiful smooth stride, her limbs showing golden brown against the blue shorts and yellow linen shirt. Under one arm she carried a long baton of bread, a green melon tucked under the other. After all these years, he thought, I still feel the same surge of pleasure and excitement at seeing this person walk towards me…

An old man cycled slowly along the cobbled street with a small trailer full of apples, and she stopped as he neared her. For a few moments they stood talking before she handed him the melon to hold and fished in her pocket for money. Reclaiming the melon she folded her arms to receive the apples he scooped from the trailer.

As she reached the *Camelot* Mark relieved her of the bread and apples, saying: 'Goose … we already have a bowl of these.'

'I know, but these looked so good and he was old and tired; it's more than three kilometres to Lanceaux and the nearest market so I thought that even a few apples would lighten his load.'

'Very generous hearted of you, darling. Was there mail waiting at the post office?' he asked as she followed him down onto the deck of the *Camelot.*

'Yes, two … in my back pocket; one from your mother, the other from Josh.'

He took them both then handed one back with a grin. 'You can have Josh's.'

'Thank you kindly.' Joanna put the melon down and perching on the hatch took out the single sheet and began to read.

'He's chasing yet another bit of skirt to judge by all the exclamation marks,' she gave a crow of laughter, 'I wonder if he ever caught up with his Caroline, he was trying hard enough. Each time I saw him he was looking for her, but she always managed to be one jump ahead.'

Mark glanced up from his letter. 'He's been chasing Caro Penrose, and she's been dodging him, since she was in school.'

'I wonder what happened to the sexy-looking Pole she was seeing in Oxford,' Joanna mused, 'maybe he went back to Poland. She looked a pretty strong-minded girl – just the sort to keep a chap like Josh in his place.'

'Then you would have quite a lot in common should you ever meet again.' Mark gave an amused grunt and continued placidly perusing his own letter.

She looked over at his bent head, at the way his hair peaked into a twist in the hollow of his neck, and his square brown face and the strong, capable hands … he glanced up and saw her watching and said warily, 'If you're thinking what I think you are thinking, you can pack it in; I want to be well into Spanish waters by tonight and if we miss this morning's tide we'll never make it.'

She reached for an apple and gestured at the fruit and bread. 'Better eat your breakfast then, if you're in such a hurry.'

'Is that it? Where's the bacon and mushrooms?'

She sniffed. 'This is my honeymoon, not a Cordon Bleu cookery course.'

'I had noticed,' he waved his own letter, 'Don't you want to know the news from home?'

'Of course.'

'Well, the potted version is that Vivienne and Callum have bought a practice just outside Dunedin; mother wants to know if we are enjoying ourselves and father asks if I'm a half-way decent husband. What shall I tell them that isn't classified information?'

'You can tell them I look forward to a holiday in New Zealand at some future date; I'm having a very nice time, thank you very much; you are doing very well as a husband … so far,' she smiled and bent to tousle his hair, 'and I'm very happy we have a whole six weeks before we have to rejoin the real world again.'

'So am I.' he stood, pulling her down from the hatch, 'now are you ready to cast off and make sail for the Spanish coast?'

'Ready to sail anywhere,' she said.

The tide was on the turn. Joanna loosed the mooring ropes, jumping back on deck and coiling them neatly as the engine sprang into life and the *Camelot* began to move slowly toward the harbour mouth.

She linked her arm with Mark's as he stood at the helm and leaned her head against his shoulder. She thought about Kit and Monica, Leo and Mary, Callum and Vivienne and dear Josh. It's been one hell of a long time, she thought, but we've all made it at last…

'A penny for them,' Mark said.

She said, 'I was just thinking it is seven years since I first seduced you.'

He gave a ferocious smile. 'I remember it well … now keep your mind on your work and get ready to hoist those sails, wench.'

'Aye, Aye, sir.' She bit his neck. 'Ain't that just like a man,' she said.

By the same author

A Year Out of Time

A Year Out of Time is the story of one twelve year old girl from a "nice" middle-class background and a "nice" private school (where her mother hoped she might learn to be a lady) who, in the Autumn of 1940, finds herself pitched into the totally foreign environment of a small Worcestershire hamlet.

For the space of one year her life revolves around the village school and its manic headmaster; the friends she makes, notably Georgie Little the "bad influence"; the twee but useful fellow evacuees, Mavis and Mickey Harper, whose possession of an old pigsty proves the springboard to some surprising and sometimes hilarious happenings; and Mrs 'Arris, the vast and formidable landlady of The Green Dragon Inn.

In the company of Georgie Little she awakens to the joys of a new and exhilarating world: a secret world which excludes most adults and frequently verges on the lawless.

The year comes to an explosive end and she returns unwillingly to her former life – but the joyous, anarchic influence of the Forest and Georgie remains, and sixty years on is remembered with gratitude and love.

ISBN 978-0-9555778-0-2

Available from Sagittarius Publications
62 Jacklyns Lane, Alresford, Hampshire SO24 9LH

By the same author

And All Shall Be Well

And All Shall Be Well begins Francis Lindsey's journey through childhood to middle age; from a suddenly orphaned ten year old to a carefree adolescent; through the harsh expectations of becoming a man in a world caught in war.

Set mainly against the dramatic background of the Cornish Coast, it is a story about friendships and relationships, courage and weakness, guilt and reparation. — *The first book in a Cornish trilogy.*

ISBN 978-0-9555778-1-9

Chosen as the runner-up
to the Society of Authors 2003 Sagittarius Prize

"The author has succeeded to an extraordinary degree in bringing Francis to full masculine life. The storyline is always interesting and keeps the reader turning the pages. All in all it is a good novel that can be warmly recommended to anyone who enjoys a good read."
– Michael Legat

"Seldom do I get a book that simply cannot be put down. The settings and characters are so believable, the shy falling in love for the first time and the passion of forbidden liaisons written with feeling. Many of the sequences left me with a smile on my face, others to wipe a tear from my eye." – Jenny Davidson, The Society of Women Writers and Journalists Book Review

"A beautifully written novel. Eve Phillips' writing is a pure joy to read and her wonderfully graphic descriptions of the Penzance area of the Cornish Coast made me yearn to be there."
– Erica James, Author

By the same author

Matthew's Daughter

Matthew's Daughter is the second book in a Cornish Trilogy and follows Caroline Penrose, as she returns from her wartime service in the WAAF to her father's flower farm in Cornwall. But once home she finds a number of obstacles and family conspiracies impeding her path to peace…

ISBN 978-0-9555778-2-6

Available from Sagittarius Publications
62 Jacklyns Lane, Alresford, Hampshire SO24 9LH